SLAVEGIRL OF NOOMAS

SF & FANTASY BY CHARLES NUETZEL
Published by The Borgo Press Imprint of Wildside Press

ADAPT OR DIE
*CONQUEST OF NOOMAS (with Heidi Garrett; Noomas #3)
DIMENSIONS
THE EPIC DIALOGS OF MHYO
THE ERSATZ; &, THE TALISMAN
JUNGLE GODDESS
LOST CITY OF THE DAMNED
SLAVEGIRL OF NOOMAS (with Heidi Garrett; Noomas #2)
SLAVES OF LOMOORO
SWORDMEN OF VISTAR
TORLO HANNIS OF NOOMAS (Noomas #1)
TROPIC OF PASSION; &, AMAZON GOLD FEVER

AUTOBIOGRAPHY

POCKETBOOK WRITER: CONFESSIONS OF A
 COMMERCIAL HACK

*=Forthcoming

SLAVEGIRL OF NOOMAS

THE NOOMAS CHRONICLES, VOLUME II

by

CHARLES NUETZEL

AND

HEIDI GARRETT

The Borgo Press
An Imprint of Wildside Press

MMVII

Special thanks to Fred Blonder, photographer and Val Litt, model, for their work on creating our slave girl, Sarleni.

FIRST EDITION

CONTENTS

To

ROBERT REGINALD,

Who Brought Us All Together

—On Noomas!

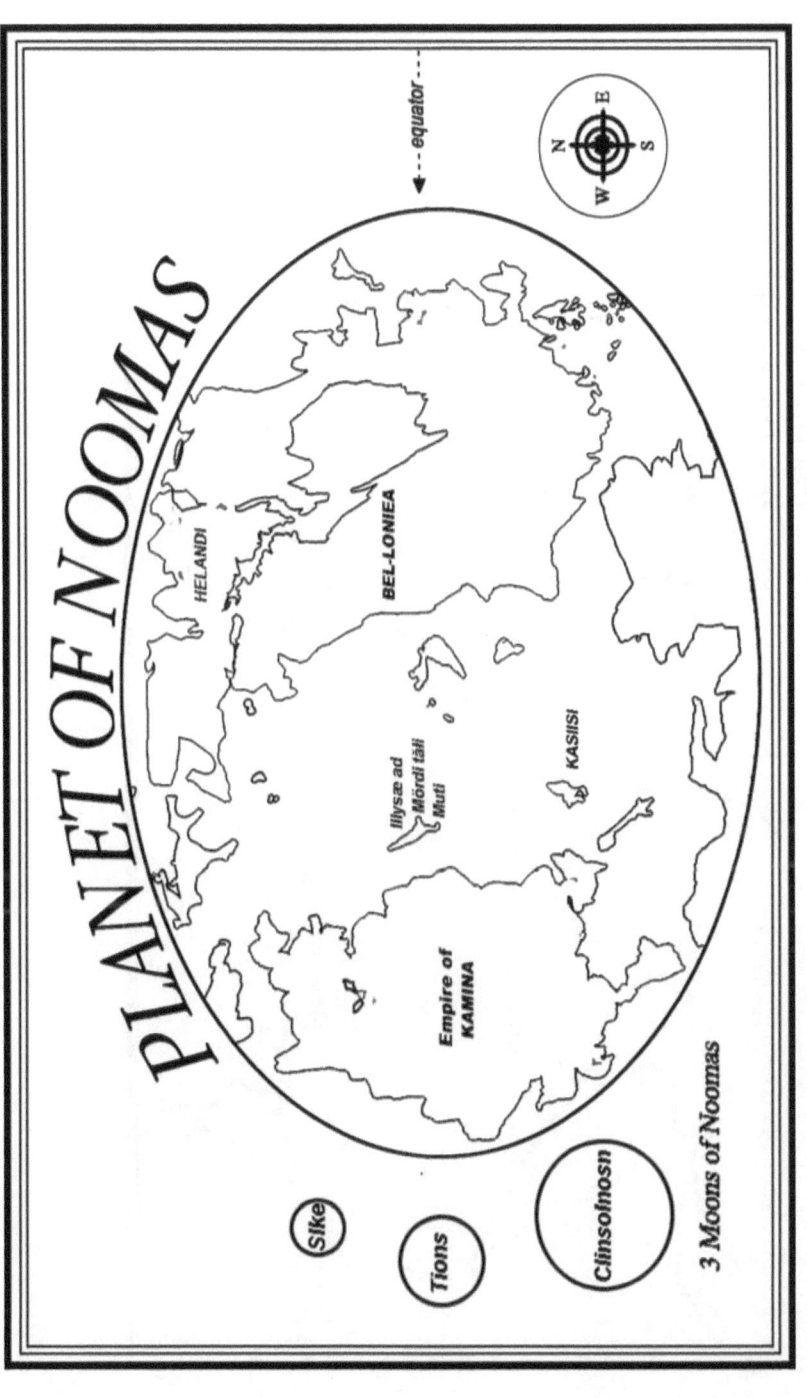

PLANET OF NOOMAS

HELANDI

BEL-LONIEA

Illysæ ad
Mördi täli
Muti

KASIISI

Empire of
KAMINA

equator

Sike

Tions

Clinsoinosn

3 Moons of Noomas

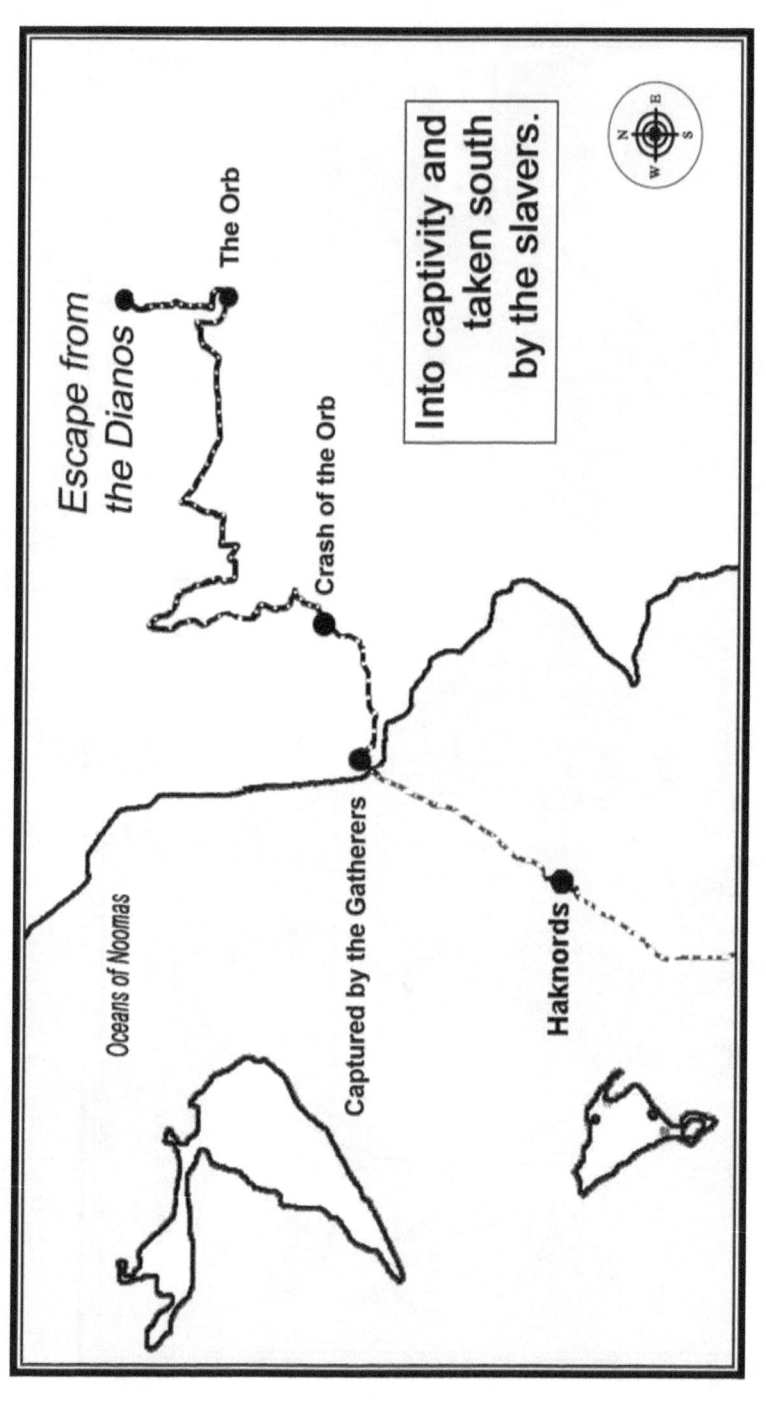

Escape from the Dianos

The Orb

Crash of the Orb

Oceans of Noomas

Captured by the Gatherers

Haknords

Into captivity and taken south by the slavers.

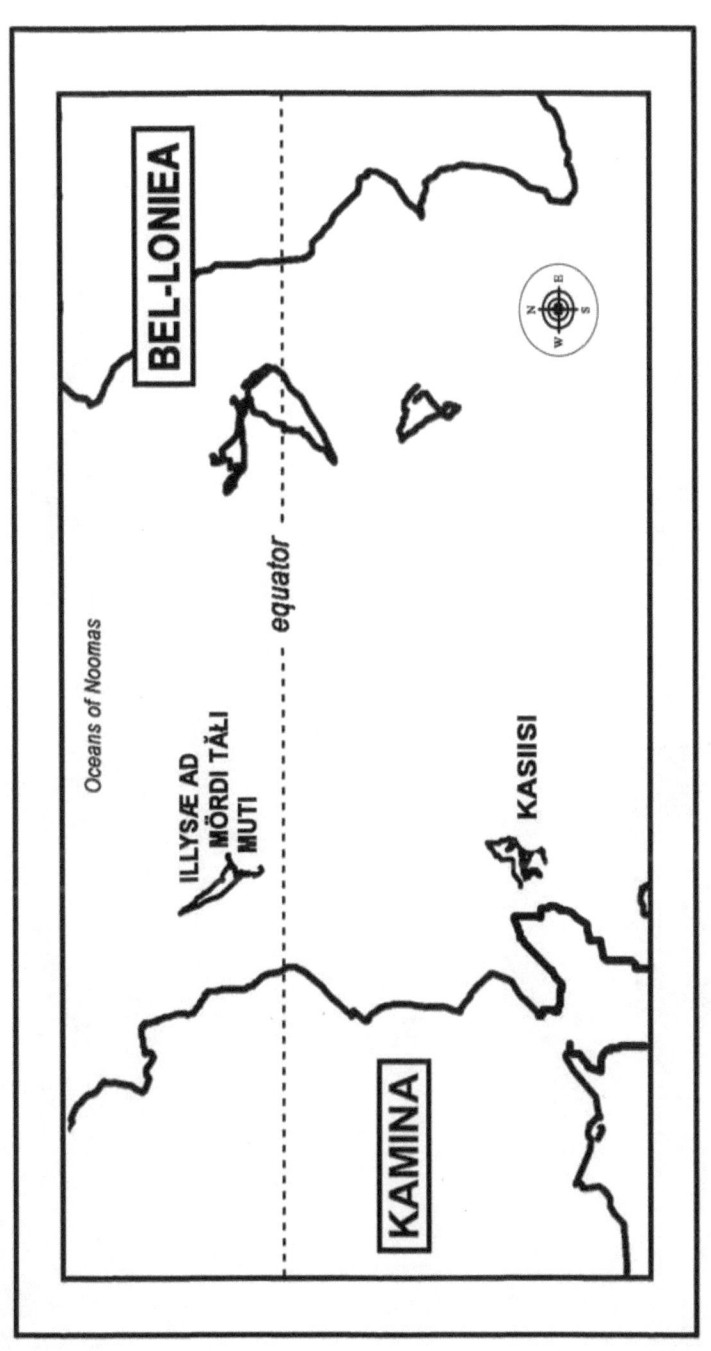

INTRODUCTION

It was through Dr. Spencer and Dr. Donaldson that I first became aware of Torlo Hannis. The present book is the long awaited sequel to the Noomas adventures published some decades ago and now released by the Borgo Press imprint of Wildside Press as *Torlo Hannis of Noomas*.

Paul Spencer had been doing extensive research in telepathy, based on the principle that if telepathy did exist, there must be a logical scientific explanation as to why so few had the ability. His research identified certain specific electrical impulses emitting from each person's thinking brain that were resonating at slightly different frequencies, therefore isolating one mental world from another. "It would be very awkward any other way," Paul once pointed out. "You might say it's Nature's way of protecting us all from the mass, collective thoughts of everybody around us." John Donaldson, who was telepathically sensitive, had served as his subject in the practical application of the theory. The last communication between Torlo Hannis and the doctors was the following:

> Romos, Proctor of Bel-loniea (Youi Janis' grandfather), has just called me for an emergency meeting. As I told you, Adt Dorta returned last night and now has gone into private conference with Romos. A lot of speculation has rumored its way throughout the city, suggesting that he had something of vital importance to report to our Proctor. I'll be in communications with you tomorrow.

That never happened.

After over a year of silence they shut things down. We all lost contact with one another after the publication of the original editions of *Warrior of Noomas* and *Raiders of Noomas*.

Then some years later I got a letter from Paul Spencer's daughter, which said, in part:

> I remember how pleased Dad was with the pub-
> lications of the story of Torlo Hannis. I have sad
> news to relate concerning the two doctors. Dr.
> Donaldson died in 1981. Natural causes. And left the
> documents with Dad, who just passed away not long
> ago. I still have some of their papers. Dad gave me
> your name, suggesting you might be interested in his
> research.

There were a few more comments about the two friends and mem-
oirs and such. I declined the offer, advising she keep the archives.

That was almost twenty years ago. It was all brought back into
focus as a result of a long email communication with Heidi Garrett,
whom I've now known for almost a decade. She came across the
Noomas books recently. Finding them an interesting study she decided to loan her copies to a friend and sci-fi addict who promptly
challenged some of the scientific data in the books. He's somewhat
of a techie with a brilliant mind. Of course, from his point of view
this was all sci-fi stuff. He detailed some critical points. She sent
some of those comments back to me, mostly off the cuff with more
than a hint of remarkable disbelief in the reality of the doctors' existence. I instantly emailed her that they were real people, and sent her
a copy of the letter from Paul's daughter.

Fred came back with significant scientific arguments and once
I'd checked out his background, I discovered he was exactly as he
claimed to be, a well-established expert in specialized communications assigned to NASA and planetary research, no less. I read several articles about his work on the transmission of signals involving
a group of planets in a distant solar system.

I encouraged Heidi to contact Dr. Spencer's daughter. And she
did. She obtained permission to gain full access to all of the remaining documents with express instructions to keep the media out of the
picture.

Heidi emailed me the following:

> Fred works very quickly and is quite amazingly
> astute. He has quite a collection of old wiring equip-
> ment long outdated, transistors and switchboards.
> Very interesting to watch him work, recreating some
> of the old circuitry from the sketches and making ad-
> justments to his own lab equipment. In the weeks

since we'd made our visit to the doctor's daughter, he'd put together a makeshift computer program and a tuner based on Spencer's diagrams. I wanted to share the results with you.

The following is a part of the message she sent me, which had come from Torlo Hannis himself!

...and it was obvious that if something isn't done immediately, all the nations of Noomas will be in great trouble. Adt Dorta's report was undeniably conclusive. He brought information that is still being examined. On the other side of the planet is an expanding empire that is threatening international dominance, and must be stopped...assuming it isn't already too late.

But it is best to simply let you hear Adt Dorta's story in his own words.

That's when my intense correspondence began directly with the Professor Fred Baxter who had no time for small talk. He wanted the details and pure facts. He was fascinated and dryly amused by the doctor's methods. "Apparently their convoluted ideas must have worked." He quipped in his very politely calculated style. He surmised a number of variables, relating them with time warp theories. He talked at length about string theory, block time, parallel dimensional space, black holes, and so on, to explain the inner-connection between Torlo's world and ours. "An alternate universe would be a simplistic term."

Heidi had written:

Fred seems to have found a link to your Torlo Hannis after all these years. Torlo is dictating details as he had done before, but this time it is all about Adt Dorta. Or more concisely comes as if Adt Dorta is dictating through Torlo.

Charles, I think this could be a fascinating story to tell. So many readers have awaited a sequel to the Noomas adventure and this is as close as I think we'll ever get. What do you think? Want to try putting something together?

She had already organized the first parts of Adt Dorta's story,

13

sifted out of the mass of exchanges they had received. Sending me the beginnings of her work, she said that she was willing to continue if I thought the project was worth the effort. Needless to say, I accepted her offer. I was quite excited and the end result gave us great satisfaction in revealing what had happened on Noomas and the peoples of that planet. She said that some of the connections were weak and sometimes unintelligible, as if they'd switched to a different language, but somehow even those parts seem highly charged and valuable. She's done an amazing job!

The present book tells the story of Adt Dorta and the slavegirl's adventures, which sent them to the other side of Noomas.

Adt had been taken a prisoner almost immediately in a battle between the Diano and Bel-loniean troops. He was held for a long period of time until Torlo Hannis released him previous to rescuing Youi, the Proctoress of Bel-loniea. Much of their relationship was revealed in *Torlo Hannis of Noomas*. The storm that sent Torlo and Youi into the vast deserts of Noomas was to also have its disastrous effect on Adt Dorta's life. What follows now is his story of survival with the slavegirl.

First, though, you will find a Prologue in which we've compiled, in his own words, a brief summary of his life previous to meeting Sarleni.

CHARLES NUETZEL & HEIDI GARRETT
2006

PROLOGUE

Everything I had ever done throughout my life had prepared me to do battle in the name of our nation and kill the enemy without mercy.

My earliest memories go back to my father, Kigor Dorta, holding a sword. I have no memories of a mother; she was gone shortly after my birth and was seldom mentioned. Dad raised me, along with the guidance of the Mutis. He was famous for his skills as a master swordsman and taught me everything he knew. To him the weapon became, through the fusion of body and mind, an extension of his nerves and consciousness. "They are one and the same," he would continually lecture. "Think and it is so. Your thought will direct the blade to your desired target."

A series of endless lessons dedicated to mastering the art of defense and killing tailored my daily life from the time I woke to the time I rested. I practiced endlessly at nothing else, in the beginning years. Later came the duels. But the art was my absolute discipline, dedication and fanatic focus while maturing to manhood. All my skills were methodically calculated formulas that came with a firm grounding in science, with little devotion to any of the many spiritual practices or religions catering to the various Gods of Noomas. I've always had a firm conviction that hard evidence be required before accepting any fact as real. Life and death in a duel could depend on recognizing that critical reality. A feint must be defined and divided from any real assault. Natural and supernatural needed to be clear and one ignored in favor of the other. This followed in all things.

So the gods and belief systems of Noomas had failed to impress me. And yet the Mutis had been a significant influence over my life. These were the mystical beings highly respected unquestionably by all people, even worshipped by many sects. They rule over our courts and high councils. They rarely spoke, never socialized, traveled in nomadic clans, and yet they were a dominant and directing force: a fact never explained. My father's personal pundit Muti had claimed I was special and must be trained with all his skills. The suggestion was more command than advice.

My father's allegiance to them, and his dedication to following their continual advice, especially when training me in matters of swordsmanship, puzzled me. His solemn loyalty compelled him to make me outclass his skills with the sword. And his legendary reputation throughout the country was well earned. I witnessed the training of the greatest swordsmen from many regions far and wide. The very best came to study the art with him. Even as a young student, I was permitted to spar with the elite members of the royal legions. I was driven with an enthusiastic ambition to learn everything he knew, and then even more.

My father's zeal to feed my hunger for learning seemed to grow equally as fast as my passion for knowledge grew. In fact, more than once he would hammer at me: "Always experiment in life and with the blade. Never stand still in your honing of new and inventive ways to make new combinations; for it is in creative flexibility that you'll master your life and your body and mind to adapt to any variable, no matter how complex it might appear. Experiment, invent, be open to all things unknown and watch for the unexpected." The unexpected. Those words would echo deep with foreboding. He would often remind me of the unexpected when during our drills a parry and thrust touched his sword's point to my body.

I knew I was special, but I attributed it to being the son of the great master that gave me unique privileges. And I guessed that I must have inherited my extraordinary gifts from him.

At times he would bring in musicians to play repetitive, rhythmic passages to which I was taught to flow in my attack and counter-attack, running through endless series of interplays, extended patterns that blended one into another.

"Swords can ring like music. They must be permitted the freedom to fly like a conductor's wand; to flow majestically from beat to beat, linking all the moves and accents to a rhythmic ride that dances through your whole being," he would tell me, sending forth a rapid series of thrusting attacks, whipping one into another, as a perfected requiem. "Yet make your moves no larger than necessary. And never let the other man take control; always be prepared to be one beat ahead of him, and slip in between those half-tones, those mini-beats, when his heart is caught between contractions."

Then he'd offer another line, and his sword would advance like a whip to tease its point on my chest, without drawing blood. I would be required to learn such moves and counter-moves until they were automatic thoughts that my whole body could set into motion without even thinking about it.

My life was forged on these skills, discovering how many dancing moves could be invented at any given time. Musicians improvised their sounds in unexpected ways, designed to drive our blades into different patterns that followed this newly designed music. "But fine-tune. Make your moves tiny events linked tightly together. Variation and creation is all a part of the endless magic! Use it not only to attack but to defend," was his continual advice. We trained until we accomplished a draw in nearly all our mock-duels. In the beginning my wins were elusive games he played with me; in the end it was obvious that I'd become a master artist with the blade.

By then I had also mastered the skill of standing firmly grounded without moving more than my fingers or wrist. Conserving energy was the key to survival in a duel.

I was still untested in actual battle though had plenty of experience in fighting and killing.

I had faced a number of swordsmen during one to one combat in matters of honor. Duels are a fact of life. No sane warrior delights in the act of killing. The first time I killed a nobleman was a wrenching experience.

I'll never forget the man's name: Kramin Lavalki. He was one of the notorious Raiders from the western dessert lands and a nasty, humorless man. My father was reluctant to accept him under his tutelage, and warned me: "Be vigilant, when you spar with my trainees, son. Some could be quite dangerous."

Lavalki was an easily provoked moody man. He gained a quick reputation of entering into death-duels, and delighted in killing. For a reason I don't even remember, he baited me into a fight which I was unable to avoid. We crossed swords one morning in the Norina Gardens, not far from where my father's classes were held. I was just barely the legal age for such death fights. He was twice my age, a mass of lean rippling muscles: a trained killing machine. He didn't even wait beyond the first touching of blades to attack. His fury and determination to kill was near madness. I simply rolled the tip of my sword around his and thrust. That quick and it was over.

The blade slipped in effortlessly right under Kramin's guard and then pulled out as if withdrawing from empty air, dripping in blood. It happened so easily.

The man's eyes drained in shock as he fell on the ground before me, a mere pile of lifeless bones and flesh.

I had sheathed my weapon in silence, looked at those around me and found it almost impossible to avoid a sudden rush of sickness to empty my stomach right there for all to see. After holding my breath for a long moment, I sucked in air, loving the feel of its fresh coolness filling my lungs. I was suddenly aware of the fact that I lived, even if the other man was now gone.

Still, that day had made an impression on me that stayed and lasted. Life is precious and should not be violated at a whim.

Then I entered officer training. That's when I met Torlo Hannis, who became my closest of friends. He knew very little about the sword, but was anxious to learn. I sensed an incredible power in this man. He had the gift of agile command I had not seen in any nobleman or master swordsman ever before, yet he was a stranger to me. I instantly liked him and taught him things few knew beyond my father and myself.

The long period of our cadet training was demanding and included Korda hunting during which time Torlo proved his amazing ability in battle by personally killing the huge beast. We had become great friends throughout those long days, and then the war escalated when the Diano violated our borderlands and moral ethics by the unexpected abduction of Youi, the Proctoress of Bel-loniea. And our nation rallied to avenge that insult with a demand for restitution.

CHAPTER ONE

"A MAN OF HONOR NEVER DIES..."

The warrior trains for battle, and is conditioned to be a brutal killing machine.

We were ready to take on our first command and all members of our class were quickly promoted from warrior-cadet in-training to officer in charge of a ten-man unit.

We were commissioned and assigned to the squadron chiefs commanding our nation's armed forces. We would live, fight or perhaps die for the protection of our Proctor.

I was quick to assert my authority.

"Come!" I glared at the ten, young, almost boyish faces that looked up at me as if I knew what I was doing. "We have a duty ahead of us to fight for honor, to fight for our Proctor, to fight for the future of our nation. This is our sworn promise to the Royal family, and our own personal pathway to glory! In the name of all the Noomasian Gods, draw your swords and follow me into battle!"

My hand was on the hilt of my blade, but my eyes already found those of the only mature face in the lot. He was our experienced under-officer, my first in charge.

He nodded, taking the unspoken cue, raised his sword and said in a loud voice: "To courage and to strength. All those who die will soon discover peace in your final reward, be that of great universal joy or endless regret!"

This motto was etched in our brains in childhood. It lit the faces of the men before me.

There was no way to lose under such conditioning. We were armed and ready to die. And True Believers embraced the promise that death in battle brought immortality in the arms of unnamed gods and goddesses. Those like myself accepted death as an ending. I had no illusions about this; nor conclusions. I didn't concern myself with anything other than surviving.

And my mind was focused drunkenly on only one mad thought: *Glory in Battle!* I thrilled to the coming engagement of a real enemy of the nation, one where killing was expected on a mass scale. My blade would savor the blood of every Diano warrior that came within its reach. It was a thirsty, gleaming length of tempered metal fashioned by the finest artisans to be found. And I was hungry, after a lifetime of ultra training, to prove my skills against real enemies truly deserving a swift trip to the lands beyond the living. Youthful rage to kill surfaced like blazing fire within me.

We had just lifted up off the ground when a collision with a Diano grav-disk shattered all our thoughts of glory and splattered them downwards toward the ground.

After the crash of our grav-disk came the swift capture. We were gathered up before we could even disengage from the tangled wreckage. Defeat without battle. One moment of dim awareness flickered as hands roughly yanked me upright. My brain went dizzy in a struggle to take control of what was happening. I tried to find my sword, but my hand was empty. Then the world seemed to tumble into a stage of raw confusion that faded.

A black void lingered over my consciousness.

Then a strange vision emerged from the darkness. A man was floating in front of me, positioned cross-legged, hands on his knees. There was a very mild expression in his intensely intelligent eyes, as he said: *"You are being prepared!"*

"For what?" I wondered, more puzzled than anything else.

"You aren't ready...yet you must prepare yourself. Friends will come. You will be guided and soon...."

The vision flickered, faded.

After that, the fog came and I tried to focus. Which was like cutting through sand with a dull knife.

I realized that the darkness pressing in around me was quite real. Not illusion. It was night. It was very dark. And the ground under my back was cold and hard.

That was my first conscious awareness; later came realization of being latched to a thick chain to which were attached a long line of fellow prisoners.

It was as simple as that. And there was no obvious escape.

We were kept in the middle of their camp at night and during the day dragged along by foot like beasts. At times we were mocked and spat at by the Diano warriors. It was a state and status completely demoralizing to any warrior and for me especially so. Right in the midst of our first moment of glory we had been swiftly squashed. Horrendous rumors circulated that our beloved Proctoress was in camp, captive to the despicable Aoiji, commander of the Dianos.

Time jumbled into a terrible game of waiting for any chance to escape. And it seemed unlikely to happen. I have retained vague snatches of that horrid captivity; I lurked, silently existing like a caged animal inside a dark well within my mind.

When sleep came it would be interrupted by a Diano guard cursing me: "Wake. Eat!"

A bowl was then shoved into my face and I grabbed it.

Captivity was like flipping through ugly pictures, leaping forward in time. Just impressions. It was difficult to connect the images, but they kept flashing through my mind on their own, incomplete.

I disciplined my body every chance I got, tensing up muscles when nobody was looking, again and again. Keeping the body toned and the nerves alive and everything at full alert was the basic training that I'd learned from my father.

My crew was nowhere near; we must have been separated intentionally, or worse, they may have been killed. The men chained with me now were common warriors of our nation who knew the name of Dorta and my father's fame. They were impressed to discover my kinship with him. One had said; "We will follow you if ever given a chance."

And I suggested that word be spread to not surrender to defeat, and be prepared for possible escape or battle. The message proclaimed that I was there to lead them. One man asked: "Do you know something we don't?"

And I'd instinctively replied: "Only that a man of honor never dies until the life is ripped out of his body—you prepare and you surrender only to the idea of making escape possible."

But that felt like an empty statement for we were quite helpless, chained and even while loosely guarded had no way to make an organized escape.

Still, I would not give up to defeat.

Then out of the dark, shortly after the sun had set, I heard a voice, very near me. I knew that voice, and felt swift depressive resignation. Surely he couldn't have been captured, too.

"Torlo Hannis!" I cried softly so as not to alert the guards, "What are you doing here?"

"Freeing you."

"But…." I was stunned.

He was in the process of unlocking the chains while hurriedly telling me his plans to find Youi, the Proctoress of Bel-loniea. He

21

was determined to rescue her from the Dianos.

The guards in charge of us were, I soon discovered, very quiet in death.

Torlo instructed: "Make as much chaos as possible. Attack, kill, and try to escape. I'll need time and your men will buy it for Youi Janis!"

I followed his gaze toward the silent grouping of warriors who had been my fellow prisoners. "You're in charge, my friend. Do what you can to help. This is our only hope."

And he was gone.

I couldn't imagine what he planned on doing. How he expected to find the Proctoress, nor how he could possibly expect to free her. But he was a man of amazing talents and all I could do was at least attempt to back his play. He deserved that much. Plus, I had nothing to lose by attempting to escape.

There was no time to plan; just react. I alerted those nearest to me, and soon they were freed of the chains. My thoughts came in fast bolts, like lightning.

I took inventory of my fellow warriors, all awaiting my command. No words needed, I moved swiftly to the dead Diano guards to collect weapons. They followed my lead. They were more than willing to have their chance to escape captivity and avoid either life-long slavery or death at the hands of some unknown menace.

Thus armed, we moved into action. We made no attempt to be silent. Raising my head high, I let out a war cry that rang loud and strong through the camp. Voices from all sides climbed high to greet mine. I estimated our numbers were many, although none could tell which were echoes and which were not. The chaos had begun. Shots and Kay- bombs rang out from all directions and immediately we were savagely, rushing towards the outer areas of the encampment. I had instantly decided to make it to the forest next to which the Diano forces had camped. It promised cover. Our loud screams must have roused half alert men to our running charge. Some had been sleeping, but most were already waking and leaped to their feet to thwart our escape. They swarmed frantically all around us.

My fellow prisoners had immediately followed me into battle.

I was suddenly facing daggers, spears, sword points, and slashing blades. I cut my way through a mass of screaming warriors. I utterly hated this enemy. My sword was an extension of my mind, fully determined to deal out death to any of these Diano freaks. The days of captivity had crushed any sense of humanity I might have had towards these men.

The Diano fell back, wounded or dead. The numbers were in

their favor; but we had passion and raw determination on our side. Surrender was not possible. Death was better than endless captivity. That made the difference.

Blood spewed in all directions from human bodies paying the fatal price tag for hindering me. I simply hacked away at them as if they were vegetation in a tangled jungle. It wasn't even personal. My actions were pure reflex, sending the sword at unguarded targets. All the years of training now erupted with this fury of killing.

I slipped my sword through the throat of one luckless warrior and then thrust it into the heart of another as my eyes found the next target. And during this wild barrage of slaughter came the shrill scream for help that violently detonated deep into my very mind. to It abruptly changed everything.

Adt. Help me!

My name was being called. At first I thought one of my fellow prisoners was trying to get my attention. But the sound was in my brain, not my ears. It was a strange illusion. And it was clearly not a man's voice.

Help me!

No time to ponder its origin or even think. All that mattered was somebody needed help.

My eyes took in everything and saw nothing to support that cry for help.

I felt it again.

Adt...come, fast!

In the heat of this slicing and dicing of human flesh, the scream pelted the skull within my head.

Adt...come, fast!

I was catapulting from one moment in time to the next. Nothing made sense. It just was.

Adt... into the forest. Before it's too late!

Without even realizing it I had covered the distance to the nearest trees, mechanically hewing through any warrior foolish enough to get in my way.

As I neared the forest I saw the woman beyond a number of Diano warriors and picked up fervor to make clear a pathway towards her.

Come...! Quick! Hurry!

Dodging several assaults directed my way, parrying sword points, cutting at different men-at-arms, I reached the woods, and suddenly found myself among a number of enemy warriors who were battling with someone I couldn't see. Swords were flashing, clattering loudly; the noise of battle came in muffled thugs without

23

any screams or verbal sounds.

Again it seemed as if I heard my name called out.

Adt...fast!

Without so much as a warning bellow I was among them, sword finding swift targets, without hesitation, chest, throat, head.

I fought my way towards the woman. As I engaged the last Diano, brushing his dying body aside with the bloody point of my sword, I glanced down at the man who had been defending her. He was savagely wounded and exhausted, near death.

Then I noted among the dead Diano warriors another man like the dying stranger, on the ground, dressed in a simple harness and tunic. I didn't recognize any identifying national colors or emblems.

The woman seemed to guess my puzzlement, and explained: "These men were friends—you saved my life. We have to get out of here."

I wiped the blood from my sword on a dead man's garments, then took a moment to pass my hand over the dead warrior's eyelids, closing them to a world to which he no longer belonged.

I sheathed the sword and as I turned, black folded in on me, followed by a haunting dream-like vision. I relived the dream I had of that strange man floating cross-legged in front of me. His words this time were only:

"Prepare yourself. You will now be guided...."

The vision flickered, faded.

Sometimes it is difficult to tell where dreams end and reality starts. For me, what followed seemed illusional.

"Warrior. Come out of it. Now!" the voice insisted. And I felt a hand slap across my face. A stinging blow.

With a startled yelp I sat up, eyes wide open. Sitting there on the ground next to me was a very beautiful female. Her clothing was that of a common slavegirl: layers of various discarded wraps put together with such an artistic flair as to appear quite modestly sensual. That was *not* common for slavegirls. Her head was framed in jet-black hair that fell freely and long over her shoulders. She looked soft and frail, yet at the same time, her stance displayed a rigid strength.

Those eyes, when they gazed into mine, were bright and deeply penetrating, determined and even demanding. She continued to stare at me so intensely that I felt stripped.

Well, that was my first impression. Soft, yielding, like a lovely mountain that could not easily be moved nor conquered. I think I must have fallen in love with her at that very moment—but it was a standard reaction to a lovely female.

24

"Warrior!" she stated, firmly. "We don't have time to waste. We need to get out of here, *fast!*"

Images literally slammed in on my mind, the darkness, the dead bodies, the surrounding forest of trees, a stream just to our left. My body hurt from cuts, and I saw the seeping blood oozing from them. Sharp evidence of having survived a nasty battle, and vague memory of it flashed before my mind—then faded as she spoke.

"Are you okay?" was her simple question. The look in her eyes was guarded. Her lips compressed, as if in deep thought. Then suddenly those eyes lowered, almost reluctantly submissive.

Strange. The sudden change.

This woman was acting like a member of royalty, actually commanding a lowly commoner.

A slavegirl? Hitting a warrior?

The whole scene was cock-eyed.

"Come!" she commanded, standing. "Follow me!"

I stood, somewhat shaky. At first everything seemed vague, confused. Then I started running, gaining strength with every step.

She was pushing through the brush without hesitation, past dark, looming trees. She never seemed to hesitate, never seemed to tire, and, in fact, was a demon of energy. Now and then she'd turn to make sure I was following.

Her image would momentarily disappear as brush and giant leaves or trees came between us.

Distant rumbling was the first alert of a storm; cold chilly air, the second warning. Then came thunder and a flash of light. Horrid ripping crackles snapped across my ears. And darkness closed in, only to be broken by sound and lightning, growing ever closer. The first sprays of rain flushed through the air. In less than a breath it was crashing in on us in torrents.

I felt a sense of very raw terror. No matter how brave and powerful a person might be, they are utterly helpless against the natural elements of Noomas. You can't escape what some call the Storm Gods! If you believed in such mythologies, then you might think that an evil demon could pick you for instant destruction. After all, gods were supposed to be the ultimate power. They could snatch life away for no logical reason at all, other than a personal whim of their own invention.

While I didn't subscribe to such illusions I still felt the sense that we were helpless to survive any real, serious storm. Certainly on foot, running through a forest without any possible shelter, we could be instantly overwhelmed. Seldom are there such deadly weather monsters, but this one felt as if it would rage with such force that

25

nothing could avoid being crushed under its killing power. I was not at all friendly with the idea of dying without a fair fight. And this was a fully unbalanced match!

An alien thought surged through me.

We're almost there.... I sensed those words more than heard them. *We can beat this thing!*

A strange illusion that felt starkly real!

Beat what? Was my impulsive response.

The storm. It will be terrible! And I realized it was this woman again. What was her voice doing in my head?

It was a thought, just like a Muti telepathic message.

I didn't have time to reason that out. I shrugged it off as part of a very odd experience. In fact, nothing seemed real.

I kept rushing through the underbrush of the now thinning forest, almost entirely hidden by the drowning rain pouring down on the world. The storm was a fury of water, stunning in its force.

Suddenly, I was startled by a bright, almost ghostly glow in the darkness ahead of us. It was a huge pulsing orb-shaped object, the outer edges distorted by some kind of energy blanket. The woman was now standing in front of it, as an entrance seemed to melt into place. She merely nodded as if to say "follow me" and disappeared into this strange place that floated above the ground.

I ran forward and was swiftly swallowed up inside the Orb's depths. It felt as if I'd been gulped by some giant monster.

Illusions are like that; magical horrors where anything can happen.

The wounds I'd sustained in the battle were now painfully noticeable. Standing there, unmoving, I felt dazed, unsteady, and about to fall.

Not a very warrior-like condition, my mind scolded.

"Hold on, you'll be fine!" Her voice came out of the dark. Gentle hands touched my arms and suddenly I felt engulfed in an energy that made an amazing difference.

We were in a strange place, a room, or craft of some kind, bathed in a glowing blue light.

Steady. That word was in my mind!

"We can stay here. I'll try to get us out of the storm...safe. Just sit down. Lean back."

I was aware of sitting on the floor.

She was standing in front of a panel. Her hands raced over objects that seemed flat and more imaginary than real.

I felt the floor lift. Forward movement gently pressed the wall behind my back. We were in a strange carrier; perhaps a grav-craft

26

of sorts. I was not familiar with this design.

And she was in control. I hoped.

The world shifted, jerked, moved violently.

I was jolted up against the wall as if some invisible hand had smashed through the air in an attempt to hammer at my body. An instant later I felt the floor race up under me.

The woman was almost knocked off balance, but managed to grab hold of the panel's sides. Her hands moved fast, then her body was blocking my view and I couldn't see what she was doing.

We were abruptly lifted and it happened so fast that things blurred. Black obscured my vision.

"Swallow this!" Gentle fingers pushed a rather large packet against my lips. "It'll all dissolve. Do it!"

I let her push it into my mouth. "Energy food and meds! Not much, but it's all we have. It'll help."

I swallowed.

"You'll be fine," she assured me. "I just took care of your most critical battle cuts. You've lost some blood. I used herbal meds and compounds that seem to have helped. You'll feel better after your body has absorbed the energy packet."

She stood over me, a huge giant shadow dominating the whole universe.

What had she said? Lost blood? I had to take it easy. I needed rest.

Then once again everything blacked out, and folded back to reality. Sound came before images.

The woman was saying: "We're above the forest. I'm not very good at this. I tried to direct the Orb towards home. I can't get above the storm! Can't battle the powerful winds controlling our flight. Even if we are safe in here."

The voice faded and the sound of wind hammered louder. I felt jostling movement. My body slid to one side, then back.

"Cursed Kordas!" she cried.

Again, I was hammered against the wall. I wanted to grab something to hold on to but there wasn't anything within reach. The world was beginning to twist, and then righted itself.

"Got it!" But almost instantly there was a sudden spinning sensation and then an invisible force stopped our movement cold! Something had grabbed hold of the craft and smashed it downwards like a wounded bird in flight. We were crashing.

27

CHAPTER TWO

LOST ON NOOMAS

Consciousness slipped in and out of my awareness, twisting and fading and then folded in on itself.

I was aware of gentle hands touching me, and then slipping away.

"Eat this."

I swallowed.

Sensation numbed again.

I heard distant thunder, felt pressure move me. Then a voice said: "I think we'll live!"

It felt like a very long time before I heard that voice again, this time saying: "Come. Time to leave!"

I struggled to open my eyes, but even when they did, there was only murky gloom surrounding me. No sound, no sensation. Just dim awareness.

"Come!" she said, dragging me; her soft fingers, almost caressing mine, and then gripping hard.

We were in the forest.

"Follow me," was her next remark, as her hand lowered away from mine. She moved swiftly away, ahead of me.

Reality had finally returned. I was keenly fixed on the slavegirl thrashing through the brush ahead of me. For that I was thankful.

Apparently I'd been hallucinating.

How long had we be been running from the Diano camp?

It was dark for a very long time. It was quiet, too. Even the normal creature sounds of the night were silent now. It felt eerie not to hear the insects, and distant birds and the moans of night.

Luckily we weren't being picked up as a feast for hungry monsters to snack upon. No Tattiliexs with their crooked sharp teeth to rip flesh off bones in one bite or Finissine who simply crush their victims within wickedly thick muscular coils, then swallow them whole to digest alive in their tunnel-like bodies. These were only two of endless threats that could slither down upon us in the dark. Or a Knoiaot. That hunting shaggy lump of hard-shelled skin and slurping yellowed lips that could curl around a body to suck it dry like a juicy fruit and then spit out the remaining shriveled skin and powdered bones like the undesired hard seed.

Those were only a few of the primal hunters of the night seeking meals after having made their brutal kills.

This must surely be that awful lull after a terrible storm—where the world stops while trying to find its balance once again.

It was then that I realized the storm had passed. Or had it even existed? Was that illusional or memory? Now I was confused and pushed those thoughts away. We had been running from the Diano camp. Strangely, it didn't occur to me that we were perfectly safe from pursuit; for the Dianos would hardly be interested in two escaped prisoners.

Her commanding voice brought me back to the present moment: "We can stop here!"

It was almost as if I'd been hypnotized. The deep, rich dark of night had waned and now there was a glow in the sky where light peeked through the interlacing branches of the thinning forest. Up until now the steady rhythm of the woman's running feet had held my attention, with only an occasional glimpse of her just a short distance ahead.

She was standing at the edge of a clearing, facing high cliffs that reached into the sky like a ragged, wrinkled wall of stone. To the right was an open grassy plain, and very distantly I could see a watery horizon; it was an even, unbroken line, shadowed by the clouded sky. But, without question, a vast ocean.

And for a moment, I found myself studying her fine features; the straight nose, the soft high cheeks and full lips. Then she said: "We can make camp here. This is where we must begin making plans."

"Plans?" was my offhanded response. I was still a little too dazed by what had just happened. But it was obvious that I must return to Bel-loniea. My mind was quickly clearing, sharpening in its alert awareness of our surroundings. Events were gathering together into a logical pattern. We'd somehow escaped the Dianos and the storm and now were somewhere near the ocean.

"Yes. We have a lot to decide." She sounded like a Proctor dictating to her followers. "But first, let's gather something to eat."

She simply pointed to the trees behind us. Immediately I saw the reasonableness of that idea. We did need food and water.

My eyes shifted and then I was back in the outer trees, collecting ripe fruit the size of my hand. There were wide, flat, waxy leaves that embraced the plump, soft fruit. Neither of us spoke as I handed some of them over to her. We were famished and my need for water was quickly satisfied the instant I bit into the fruit. It was amazingly juicy and fresh. We settled down in an open area to enjoy our meal.

I was still somewhat weakened and needing time to heal from the battle wounds.

It all had a dreamlike quality, even if now becoming more real; more like actual events.

I didn't even know her name.

"You can call me Sarleni. We have been so busy surviving and escaping we have not been formally introduced."

I studied her for a long moment. Strange that she answered my unspoken question about her identity. We were thinking the same thing, I decided. It was natural. After all, we'd been running for our lives all night, barely escaping sword and storm. She just beat me to the question. That's all.

"Adt Dorta." I replied.

"Yes," she murmured very softly. In fact, so softly that it was almost a thought. "Adt Dorta. The Magnificent Swordsman!"

I wondered what she meant by that. There was no irony in those three words, no sarcasm, but simply a statement of fact.

"Tell me something about yourself," I suggested.

"Oh, we don't have time for that." She brushed my request aside with a slight wave of her hand, dismissing it quite completely. Then, as an afterthought, offered: "I come from the north. That's enough for you to consider for the moment."

"What's there to consider?" It was a strange retort to her words, but this was a strange situation. And she was a strange slavegirl.

"Well, all in good time…Adt." She stopped and looked hard at me for a moment. I noticed her body relax slightly.

There was just the hint of soft arrogance to this woman. She spoke to me as one would to a subordinate.

That was a bit annoying.

Then she smiled slightly, and when she spoke there was a new softness to her voice. "I come from the northern lands. Which we call Helandi."

"Where primitives live?" I managed, my mind beginning to function more fully.

"Yes. I supposed you'd call them that."

I remembered the tales I'd heard about the northern territories being covered in sheets of heavy ice, where there existed very primitive tribes. Some trading was done between them and Bel-loniean explorers, but contact had always been quite limited. "You certainly aren't one of those…primitives!"

Her smile had vanished now as she stood and retreated a few paces as if distancing herself from the whole conversation.

Her eyes shifted, narrowing slightly, then closing and popping open. "How much better I feel. The fruits are refreshing. Filling. And they have quenched my thirst. How lovely a morning."

She took in a deep breath, her arms outstretched widely sweeping our surroundings and then she was quiet for some time.

She was avoiding any answer to my last statement. Strange. I decided not to push the matter.

I was, like her, taking in the terrain. The cliffs at one side, the forest on the other, and the ocean stretched out to the distant horizon.

We were both quiet for a while, trapped in our own thoughts. I kept wondering about her words, her avoidance in telling details about herself, and most mysteriously the statement about the primitives and apparently her own people.

What she called Helandi, the northern territories, were known as being cold, desolate and containing very little of importance or interest. She certainly couldn't be one of the primitives. Then where were her people? There was no known indication of a civilized world up there in the chilled north. I decided to push the issue.

"Tell me more," I coaxed, "about your people."

"Oh, that. Well, really, we're just like everybody else, with, perhaps a difference." She didn't sound like she was going to say anything more.

The silence lingered. So I pushed the silence away with: "Well, in what way…a difference?"

"Never mind. I can…answer your…unstated question: we are civilized and we are a people with a great respect for other cultures and we live…well, we're up there!" She made an almost angry wave of her hand.

She was being secretive. Avoiding any real answer.

"Oh, Adt, do we have to waste time on all this?" She frowned, and then shrugged. She was conscious of me staring at her and turned away. But only for a moment. She spun around, took a deep breath, sighed and said softly: "If you must…I suppose…."

Her eyes lowered, then suddenly snapped up, as if she'd made a decision. "Oh, we're up there in our cozy homes and isn't it just enough to know we're there?"

31

It was an empty statement, devoid of any information. It was almost as if she wanted to tell me something, but felt she couldn't. For a moment something inside me reached out and wanted to comfort her.

I made a quick decision. "Fine. We'll leave it at that."

That was surely a proud, decisive statement for a warrior of vast experience and determined power. I'd come to terms with the issue. I decided to drop it all. For now.

"So you give up that easily?" she inquired in a strangely amused and relieved tone. "I was…well…Korda kill! You can be so annoying!" Sarleni sounded more like the Proctoress than the slavegirl. "Are all men of Bel-loniea so…difficult?"

For some reason I felt that rang false. "Are all slavegirls where you come from, all like—?"

"Slavegirls?" she almost snarled, and then backed off, laughed. "Of course. We're all that way, I suppose!"

A long silence fell over us. I was wondering why no explorer had ever come across any hint of her so-called country.

Finally she broke the quiet. "We live in places that aren't so easily detected. That's why, your explorers have not…well, noticed."

Suddenly I felt defensive.

"I'm sorry, Adt. I don't mean to be evasive. Just that our people are…private. Does that make sense?"

Not really, I mentally groused.

"We have a wonderful life there and it is so lovely. I know you'll like it!" She tossed this out as if this was our ultimate destination.

I decided to drop the whole topic with a quick smile and shrug, returning my attention to our rather primitive but delicious meal.

And as I finished the last of the fruits, tossing aside the tiny hard seed, my eyes seemed to hover back to Sarleni, where she sat on the ground, cross-legged.

"What about you?" she asked.

My first reaction was to avoid going back into a question and answer mode. But then I realized, how silly. It was time to be open with this mysteriously obstinate woman. I was feeling a little less confused and I truly wanted to make sense out of our predicament. So I decided to explain to her about the Diano siege of Bel-loniea.

Only then did I directly meet her gaze, determined to break down any resistance.

"Sarleni, you seem to know my name, occupation, but what else?"

"I don't really know, only that we have so little time and I must get through to you. But how?"

That caught my attention. She sounded almost innocent. And desperate. Perhaps she didn't know any more than I did about what was going on.

"Sarleni, I need to get back home to Bel-loniea as soon as possible. My people are depending on men like me. Many lives are at stake. We're all in grave danger."

And so I began to tell her more about the Diano attack and the terrible captivity of our beloved Proctoress, Youi Janis.

"We must make our plans," Sarleni announced once I had brought her up to the point where we had met. "We had a problem back there. After I got you into the Orb and—"

That stunned me.

"Yes it was real. We crashed. I really don't know how to run those things. The Orbs, I mean. That isn't my job. I was never trained in flying them. I made a lot of frantic guesses. Of course I'd seen them flown by pilots. Generally they are not that complicated. Luckily so. I did what I could. But the storm was impossible! My two companions, who died, knew how to control the Orb."

I started to say something but she cut me short with a jerk of her hand. "I just want you to know…we aren't where we were supposed to be. The storm changed everything. We're lost."

Lost? That didn't seem possible. I'd be able to get our location once I saw the stars at night.

She was saying: "That storm took us…only the Gods would know. I have no idea where we are. Other than somewhere very much south of where we started out."

With that, Sarleni stopped speaking, and just sat there gazing off into space. It was as if she were giving me time to digest what she'd just said.

If we were south of the planetorial median plane, then it might be impossible to locate our position on Noomas. I knew very little about the sky that much south of Bel-loniea.

Sarleni shook her head; it was a gentle, yet thoughtful action. Her eyes widened as they gazed deeply into mine.

I became self-consciously aware of staring and tried to look away, but couldn't.

"That's all right. I don't mind you staring at me. In fact, I think it is very nice." Those words were flat, strangely focused, and seemed to clearly reach out like slender fingers cradling the back of my skull—not physically, but mentally soothing, yet alarming and powerful.

Yes, just continue looking at me. Just like that. Relax. Open up, inside, just rest, be calm and open up, don't resist it all. I don't want you to resist. I don't want you to ever fear this connection. It must be alive and developed fully...let it just happen. It is the most natural of all things between us.

I was aware that her lips were barely moving, if at all. Yet those words were solidly centered within my mind. As they continued to wind into my consciousness, I found myself feeling a sense of well-being. Her eyes appeared to grow larger, drawing me in to them.

I *wanted* to be closer to her. I was locked to her gaze and the melodic beauty of her soft voice seemed more in my mind than in my hearing. I wanted to sense, and absorb, those feelings. And nothing more.

The face became softly, transparent. My vision faded. I was floating in an opaque nothingness spreading through me, as if some invisible hand had soothed around all consciousness. Then things changed.

My mind seemed to narrow down and shift to the present, my eyes were focusing on Sarleni. Her face was drawn, serious for a moment, and then she relaxed, even smiled.

I found myself wanting to ask endless questions. I felt refreshed; not so dazed or tired. I blurted out: "What'd you just do to me?"

"Nothing mysterious. Just mental tension release, to be truthful."

"What?"

"Okay, if you must," she was now conversing openly, apparently having made a decision. "I'm a Hanjahnain student. On your part of Noomas very little is known of our teachings. I suppose you're unaware of the Mind Powers."

"The *what* powers?"

"Oh, forget that. Later. We have other matters to deal with," she advised, impudently. "We should make camp here, for the night."

Her commanding style annoyed me, and I don't know why that made me so angry. But there it was.

And, of course she was right.

There were a lot of things needing to be done. One was to hunt for food. We needed meat. Berries and nuts could only go so far. And we needed a means to carry water.

Without further conversation we both leapt into action.

I hurried away to find some helpless animal to kill. More importantly, I needed to be alone to reorder my mind around what had happened since escaping from the Dianos.

Hunting can be a simple affair. You go where the desired target is, wait and with whatever weapons you have, you kill. No fuss. Hunting was a man's business; and it granted momentary peace.

I walked across the open clearing towards the thinned forest to our left, near where the cliffs began to lift up out of the valley. Instinct drove me in that direction more than anything else.

Now I was creeping softly through the grass to the forest edge, taking in the delicate scents of flowers and hearing the soft buzz of flying insects.

A game trail cut through a tangle of underbrush, then in a very short time came to another clearing containing a small stream running along the cliff and making its way towards the distant ocean.

There I saw a number of creatures making their way to the fresh water. This was a natural gathering place for herding animals. But at the moment there wasn't anything that immediately appealed to me. Some rodents crawled out of dim shadows, scampering near the water's edge. They are made of ugly tough meat. Then I saw a pack of short-eared Noaruls splash nearby. They are usually very bland and undesirable. I had passed a few nasty looking Tian snakes hanging from trees or sliding like dark worms along the ground. Certainly not my kind of morning meal. I wanted a bit more meatier fair.

Even as my eyes remained alert to the immediate surroundings, thoughts of Sarleni kept bouncing back through it. I kept trying to organize my reaction to her; to tame the annoyance, to understand my anger.

She was one lovely lady packaged up as an alluring slavegirl, with an infuriatingly bossy manner and a bothersome ability to exchange thoughts with me. This kind of intrusion was unexpected. It felt dangerously like the Muti connections.

I wasn't such an unsophisticated Korda clown!

She was able to read my surface thoughts. What else could she read?

I forced my mind away from thinking about her and back to the hunt.

I looked at the field stretching out in front of me. The forest trees were bright blue and purple and darkly shadowed where they gathered together against the sun. They were a good cover for the herds that make these meadows their natural home.

All I had to do was wait.

A massive cloud of birds flew overhead. Hundreds of them speeding together. They could be a danger when on a hunting spree, but today they just shot past, creating a momentary shadow to mark their way across the gold grasses.

A warm flush of air raced across my body and I felt a mixed sensation of comfort. For a few moments I attentively watched the herds, trying to decide if they were moving in my direction. I only needed one kill. And my blade was swift enough to snap a rapid bird out of the sky if it flew within reach.

The herd closest to me was still too far to be reachable without their seeing my arrival. They would not wait to discover if I was friend or fiend.

I was suddenly at instant alert when I saw something out of the corner of my eye dart towards the herd. Swift. Long hair was flying in the wind.

Directly focused now, I watched more intently.

The figure vaulted right into a gathering of sleek, thin-legged Zionahs. Not one of them even stirred, apparently oblivious of what had invaded their space. Normally they would have bolted when approached in such a manner. They are a difficult kill but well worth the challenge and a highly desirable game to hunt. Their meat was deliciously tender and juicy when roasted over a roaring fire.

But my attention concentrated on the thing that had moved in close to the herd. It looked strangely female. My first thought was to wonder what Sarleni was doing there. But it couldn't be her. And it wasn't.

Long, flowing red hair streamed behind this shadowy figure and I thought I heard a screech on the wind. Did it come from her throat? For an instant, when the sun flashed bright, her gown flailed wildly, lingering gracefully in the air behind her and blending with the limey bluish greens of the fronds that laced the meadow.

The Zionahs bolted.

The herd scattered wildly in several directions as the female flashed out of sight.

Flying brown legs, like thin-stripped poles, galloped the fat yellowish bodies in my direction. The long, flopping dark ears were waving behind them and I suddenly realized that whatever I thought I'd seen must have been a trick of lighting.

The Zionahs stood just at shoulder height, each the length of a man's body stretched out. They were helpless in battle, yet lightning fast. Speed and good hearing were their basic survival weapons. But the herd, in mass, could be a real problem.

And here it was, coming at me. A scattered collection of pounding hoofs.

If I avoided being trampled to death, success would deliver a delicious meal. Which one I would pick I didn't know. All I could do was crouch, sword in hand.

I was downwind of them, so they hadn't sensed my presence.

Then I was surrounded, but ignored and my sword flicked out like a finger pointing, the tip targeting one of the nearest bodies rushing past me in its flight. Blood splattered almost purple red. My sword took on a new glow as it raced deep, then out, now bloodied as the dead body fell to the ground.

I leapt forward, as if to defend my kill. But that wasn't necessary. Its companions had scattered and disappeared.

I didn't waste any time at all. My wrist proficiently flicked the blade and its point slid deep into the animal, making a rapid cut, up and down on the exposed flesh. In moments I'd cut off a thick portion of meat, which I lifted with my left hand and in a few easy movements managed to trim off the outer skin.

So much for the hunt.

Then I saw in the distance the flash of a figure that didn't look animal. It seemed to be staring my way, then pulled back behind a bush, hiding. I must be seeing things.

Moments later something move behind a huge leaf hanging from one of the giant trees. Then I saw a head, a flash of fur or hair.

I froze, uncertain.

The image disappeared, and then reappeared, as if as interested in me as I was interested in it. It now stood there, brazenly staring at me.

Neither of us moved.

For a moment, confusion touched my thoughts. I felt a Muti-like probe suddenly reach in deep, then slip away. Imagination. There were no Mutis around—none that I had sensed.

I focused on mentally shutting down whatever was trying to read me.

Instantly it all vanished, including the image of the woman standing there so far away that it might have been nothing more than a trick of lighting.

I decided that it was all illusion. Who knew what might have startled the herd?

Whatever it was had made the kill easy for me; probably some animal watching, ready to scavenge the remains of the carcass.

I was almost happily content, as I started back to the cliffs barely visible through the thick grove of trees. Surprisingly it was actually a very short distance.

CHAPTER THREE

THE SLAVEGIRL SPEAKS

Sarleni had gathered wood, prepared a fire and collected a mound of nuts and fruits.

She waved when she saw me.

I felt suddenly guilty for having abandoned her like that.

I had to laugh at myself, as I approached the makeshift camp.

"You succeeded," she greeted, happily.

"What else?"

"Of course, the mighty swordsman and expert hunter!" There really wasn't any mockery in her voice, nor in her eyes. It was simply a friendly salute.

She had pieced together a couple of small, easy to carry water bags that we could swing over our shoulders.

I gave her the meat to roast.

"Here. This will give us some real satisfaction." I almost boasted. Once she had taken the meat, I sat down.

Adt, there is so much for you to learn. First you must be prepared. I only know that we are expected. And I must get you there. Somehow!

She had spoken no words. I felt that in my mind.

Must she invade my thoughts? I wondered.

"This mind thing…it can't work unless you want it to. Or when you are open, consciously or unconsciously. Like when I cried for help. You responded to that. We have a connection. You'd make a good student of Hanjahn."

I must have looked dumber than I felt.

"Hanjee...what's that?"

"Han*jah*n!" she corrected rather sharply.

"Oh, Hanjahn, so what?"

"We of the Hanjahn are learning through the Zygo. But unlike the Mutis who look into the future and—well, the Hanjahn scholars focus intently to understand and come to terms with those talents.

"A Master by the name of Han Jahn asked the simple question: *What do the Mutis actually do, and is it possible to learn how to assimilate the practice?*

"His logic was simply: this isn't magic but science. So others could learn it. And that's how the Powers of the Zygo came into practice.

"The Hanjahn Studies make use of our own natural abilities, based on the science of discovering some of the natural talents we all possess. Much of what the Mutis do, we can do. Hanjahn discipline is a highly developed practice of the Zygonian principles. After a while, you'll learn the Zygo through the exercises I will be teaching you. I won't have time to clarify details; you must trust me. I promise that fuller understanding comes once you are proficient as a Zygon."

She said more, but the words sounded like a lot of foolish religious gibberish. There are so many self-proclaimed gods on Noomas, every community having its own form to turn to in moments of need. She spoke like a blind devotee of a Holy Man who apparently possessed and taught the *Secrets of the Universe*.

So I let that pass through my brain like soft wind and merely listened to the music of her voice itself, soft, lilting, seductively hypnotic.

Sarleni seemed completely convinced by her own sense of right and wrong. She believed.

A frightening thought.

I managed to keep from laughing at her convictions. And I flatly rejected all of them.

She seemed to pick up on my attitude and patiently smiled: "We could use some water."

She held out the water bags. I took them, happy to be with my own thoughts for a few moments as I returned to the stream. By the time I'd returned to camp she had already cooked the meat, using sticks to hold the chunks over the fire, charring them black on the outside, still rare in the middle. I was impressed.

We had a quiet meal and afterwards decided to take turns doing guard duty, me first. Keeping the fire going was basic to keeping us reasonably warm. But primarily it was needed as a deterrent to protect our small camp from hunting beasts of prey. We were in an open area in front of the high cliffs. I watched the shadows flicker rhythmically against the ground and almost fell asleep. Maybe I did. Exhaustion had drained me. Time seemed to shift fast. Sarleni woke; I slept. Morning came and we gathered what little we had and started towards the distant ocean.

We were both locked into our own mental whirl. I felt a deep compulsion to return to duty and battle against the Diano. I wanted to be a part of it. So, to me, Bel-loniea was our only possible destination.

The sights and smells of the land filled my senses; the forest and the flowers beautifully scattered generously throughout the greenish-blue foliage. The landscape was a paradise of colors and scents. This morning was a pleasant journey, almost like some camping trip. We were actually relaxed after our rest.

The distance from our night camp to the ocean was further than we'd anticipated. Far off horizons can be so elusive and difficult to judge under the best circumstances. That evening it felt like we had made very little progress towards the open sea. Our long all day trek seemed endless.

We set up a small camp, and after a meal sat watching the sun setting towards the still too distant beach. I let my eyes savor the creamy grasses swaying gently before us.

The lofty forest branches murmured in the background as she said: "It is beautiful here, don't you think?"

"Yes, quite."

"Not like home, really."

"Oh?"

She looked out across the darkened ocean, lost in thought, entirely oblivious to my presence.

Then as a chilly breeze flushed across the beach, she turned, said: "I was sent here to your lands, and for good reasons. It is enough for you to know…well, not yet!

"Not yet what?"

She slowly sank to the sand.

"You aren't ready." And that was final.

I just sat there, stunned.

She lay down on the sand, curled into a tight ball, almost a fetal position. "Good night."

I studied her for a moment, about to protest at being so severely cut off, and then decided maybe she was right. We'd had an exhausting day. We both needed rest.

"Good night," was all I could manage myself.

It was a long time before I, too, eased closer to the fire.

Then I heard her voice softly half-whisper.

"Adt, I didn't mean it that way. We are tired, and we have a long way to go. And tomorrow…understand?"

I decided anything I might say would automatically rekindle my

own confusion. Why she should be so frustrating? Her vague remarks were as elusive as everything else about her.

"It's okay," she softly said. "I understand."

They were soft and gentle words. And strangely enough they
soothed me.

Why let it be so upsetting? We had other matters to contend
with.

A voice in my mind seemed to say:

*Just rest, relax, let your mind float in a clear dimensionless
place, freely release all the walls that surround you and let the universe absorb your full being.*

I tried to discern where those thoughts had come from, but it
was impossible to really think that deeply. It felt as if I were in some
kind of weird trance. Darkness caved in around me, causing
thoughts to quietly settle down through my mind.

At best, sleep comes in slow degrees. Even with exhaustion it
doesn't, generally, rise instantly. My mind was captured and suddenly rammed into a strange new place, where I had never been. It
was like a projection into my private depths. Vague thoughts formed
that were not mine. Did not belong to me. Then this shifted into
something else, images with an edge of frightening reality.

I was enveloped by a strangely dark blanket. Soft shadows rippled into harder ones. I tried to focus on a fuzzy picture that was reluctant to sharpen in my mind. Then suddenly it became starkly
clear!

* * * * * * *

*I was in strange room, the walls purple, much like the city
streets of Bel-loniea. But there was a very bright, soothing light
coming from somewhere, and yet nowhere, and distant voices were
chanting wordless sounds, more like moaning waves without meaning.*

I was not alone. Forms emerged, one at a time, then in groups.

*The room filled with other figures, all hooded like the Mutis,
and for a startling moment I had the illusion that I'd entered into
some secret chamber where they held their ultra secret meetings.*

I found myself shivering, my skin clammy, damp.

Nothing to fear, *Sarleni's soft voice whispered in my mind,*
you're here with me.

*I was jarred from one mood to another. Racing anger raged at
me. The images faded into a gloomy dark, and then struggled back.*

This is where I study the Zygo and learn my skills. This is

where they teach us. What you see is how we practice the art of "reaching out"—which is exactly what I'm doing right now with you. Nice, isn't it?

Somehow I would not have described this experience in the same way: Invasive or impolite and even rude would have been more accurate.

Laughter bubbled into my brain, and it wasn't coming from me.

"Well, get out of my mind!" I muttered.

You don't have to shout.

"I'm not!" I hissed back very softly, mockingly, in fact.

Speaking is shouting here. And I can feel your thoughts without you verbalizing them. Just think and I'll hear and respond.

Relax the tensions of your thoughts; don't think resistance. Just experience, just allow yourself to flow with my thoughts; just allow yourself to float and imagine and be an open channel for the images and ideas I want you to experience.

A calm peace filled my mind, smothering all other emotions. I was in a state of complete relaxation. It was actually pleasant. So much so that I didn't want to leave it. I simply wanted to embrace the feeling; to let it envelope me completely. The scene dimmed.

Stretching out in all directions was an endless forest covered white with the chill of winter. The three moons tipped over the horizon, just above distant mountains of pure pale blue. A cold breeze flushed across my face.

This is what it looks like outside. We seldom come here. Very cold. But beautiful. I've always loved being here.

A soundless murmur encompassed me and once again I surrendered to the gentle sensations filtering through my mind. I was surrounded by warmth; this was a lovely place rich in colors, softly shaded light and the chatter of children playing. In the background I could hear the voices of men and women in light conversation. A large table nearby was filled with bowls of food and vases of flowers of all kinds. The walls were draped with intricately woven tapestries of forested scenes and even strangely unsettling landscapes marked by odd shaped domes and towers that faded into the background horizon.

This is where we once lived according to the history records. This is my family's ancestral home. This is where I grew up. This is where I come from. These are my people. I wanted to share it with you, so you can understand…

The words broke off, as if suddenly disconnected.

The walls melted into a rainbow of jumbled textures and colors until they shimmered like new, strangely illusive flashes of odd shapes. Nebulous forms reached towards me from some far away dimension. I could not begin to describe them. And yet they felt real and then were lost.

I vainly tried to grip hold of this strange, vexing sequence of events that possessed my sleep as wakefulness brought me back to the real world.

* * * * * * *

I was shaken by the dream, which was more like memory of reality than a fading nightmare. Some dreams are illusive and instantly disappear. But others simply won't go away.

This one embedded itself into my mind at the very moment of waking. And it was impossible to make it fade.

The sun was up, bright, and almost blinding after the night darkness.

Sarleni was already awake and had brought some water from a fresh spring she'd found at the stream that ultimately rushed into the ocean.

"I see you're finally rested," she greeting me.

I started to say I'd had nightmares. Maybe the expression on my face showed a hint of that.

But her words were clearly directed to my thoughts: "Dreams can be difficult! They can be hard to understand. Sometimes. Other times, they are directly real, and only seem illusion. Sometimes they are honest communications."

There was the feeling that we were having a two-way conversation while in reality she was merely talking to me.

Annoyed, I said: "Let's drop the dream stuff."

Sarleni smiled warmly and leaned closer to the small fire we'd built, warming her hands, sitting cross-legged. The light cast a glowing frame against the darker shadows of her fine features. Breathtaking. I watched silently, just admiring her.

We ate without talking, then gathered our few belongings, along with the small sticks she'd fashioned into pointed, almost knife-like tools. We went to the stream and refilled our water bags and started out on our long journey.

Generally I led the way through the low grasses, but at times Sarleni was either at my side or a few steps ahead of me. It was impossible to ignore her. She moved with a lilting, even sensual stride.

I almost felt guilty about staring at her. If Sarleni had been a normal slavegirl, it would have been different.

We'd exchange few words.

Then at one point Sarleni said: "I sense that the passage north is open."

"North will get us back. We must go to Bel-loniea."

"That's not where we are supposed to be," she stated rather conclusively. "We are expected. And we can't have any foolishness about that. When one is expected, one appears. Of course you understand that. What else can we do? Orders are orders. We are expected. We obey that expectation. Simple as that!"

So much for logic!

"Expected by whom?" was my retort.

She slowly shook her head: "I don't know everything. Just that I'm supposed to be with you, and we are supposed to be somewhere...we'll be told. But we are a team."

The tone of her voice was certain, yet the words were vague and implied more than they revealed.

Again I couldn't help wondering if she was in some illusional state. The words made little sense.

She smiled, almost laughing. "Oh, Adt, you can be so silly. I mean, after all, just because something doesn't fit into your personal bias you think it can't be real. Believe me, there are things that will...you'll see. Like the Mutis, some of us can sense our future like distant shadows patterned against an almost invisible wall. It is there but simply difficult to read. But it is as real as I am right now."

I started to object but her finality was absolute.

"Adt, isn't it true that all your life others have considered you different?

"Don't we all think we're different?" I asked defensively and still trying to be reasonable.

"I'm talking about reality! And it has nothing to do with your amazing ability with the sword. That was a natural ability. But you have other talents. Your mother...."

"My mother?" For a moment I simply stared at her, startled.

"Yes. Your birth mother. Not the one who raised you."

"I didn't...."

"I know. She's a strange shadow in your mind. I have sensed that."

"What do you know about her?"

"Not any more than you know."

"I know nothing. My father spoke very little about her. In fact, next to nothing."

"Don't you think that rather strange?" Sarleni asked, almost mysteriously, as if knowing more than she was admitting.

"Not really. They met not too far from where you must have

grown up. My father was on a mission in the northern section of our continent. He has said very little about that. Never seemed to want to tell me much. But she was always highly spoken of. I mean, it was apparent they loved one another. And they had a very deep bond. But she…simply vanished. I think he was devastated by that loss, yet seemed to understand—I don't know. All quite secretive. I'd just get pieces of the story like:

"'She was a powerful woman in her society and had commitments. Your birth was important to her, and your safety. She felt I was best equipped to raise you.'

"It never made sense to me, but no matter how much I probed, it was a closed subject. He would at times simply say something nice and change the topic of conversation. But never gave me more than that."

"Mysterious."

"I don't know, to be truthful. He avoided details. Only that she had gone away. With the slight notion it was her duty to do just that. No other explanation."

"Don't you find that strange?"

"I suppose so," I admitted. Actually I'd always considered it merely a fact of life. One finally accepts what they are told by a loving parent.

Sarleni said: "It is natural to believe a caring father's explanation. Even if it's not logical or completely satisfying."

It was a strange statement. And she just let it hang there, without adding anything more.

I wanted to drop the topic.

The expression in her eyes softened as they continued to stare deeply into mine. It was as if we were physically connected. Then she looked away.

The trek towards the ocean was much like the previous day. We moved through open grasslands and listened to the background warbling birds and distant animals. We were never threatened from land or air. The ocean seemed to move closer by slow degrees.

It was well into the afternoon before we actually rounded the tall ragged cliffs and came to the end of the forest to our right. The slim narrow beach ran flat for a long expanse and finally lifted into rolling dunes where the cliffs had met the shoreline before disappearing into the sand.

We paused on top of the first sand dune, surveying the horizon where these desert-like dunes continued on to blend into the far coast. In the distance we could see where they disappeared into dark forest covered hills. A huge wilderness faced us.

45

I wanted to make it to the nearest forest, thinking that this might be a better place to spend the night. But the trek was further than we could manage in a single day. We both seemed to come to the same conclusion about setting up camp right there, near a valley between large dunes that faced the ocean.

It seemed to be safe enough with a roaring fire to keep us warm during the night, and the animals away.

"This will be fine," Sarleni noted, almost as if answering my thoughts.

We were both exhausted. Sleep was more desired than food, though we filled ourselves with some of what was left of our meager provisions. I wished for even a Mio-stick, that tasteless brown food that was the standard traveling provision of warriors. It would probably be necessary to hunt some more meat the next day.

But before even trying to sleep I looked up at the sky. A splendid array of stars stretched out in endless patterns. We were somewhere south of the median plane and the heavens were twisted enough to make me realize that we were truly lost.

Sarleni's suggestion that we go north seemed a reasonable idea, of course, and I also figured that was our only option. But how far were we off course? I had no idea.

This time when sleep came it was peaceful, without dreams; and thankfully so, for the next day brought disaster.

When morning came, I sat up, glad to be awake. I was relieved to see the world around us had not changed. For a few moments I was experiencing peace. All I could think of was the joy of returning home. We'd find some way. Lost or not!

As we finished breaking camp I found myself looking at Sarleni, who was facing the distant beach. Her hair floated slightly in gentle waves. What a lovely sight this woman was in the morning sun.

The slow, cool breeze from the ocean blended with the half-whispered song humming from her soft lips. She turned and smiled. For a moment our eyes met and I felt even more at ease.

Some of the things she had said the day before seemed less important. She had a right to believe anything she wanted. Once we could turn towards Bel-loniea, she would surely follow. I was convinced of that. But things worked out quite differently.

We had hiked most of the morning along the hard sands and dunes towards the far distant tree line; the sound of ocean waves growing stronger. The wind was sweeping down on us cooling the hot fire of the sun. It was a lovely day. I was actually beginning to enjoy these moments with Sarleni. What a strange adventure with an even stranger woman.

Then without warning everything changed.

The attack came down on us from the rising cliffs. There was no time to consider what was happening. Even Sarleni's apparent mental powers offered no warning.

First came the sound, then the shush of air.

I felt something hard grab my shoulders, yank me up from the ground and swing into the air with brutal strength. There was no way to resist. I was an instant captive of some huge flying monster that I couldn't even see. Whatever had grabbed me from behind was now lifting me into the sky. I heard Sarleni's startled scream of surprise. I felt such a pang of wild concern for her safety that I completely ignored the fact I was just as helplessly captive to…what?

I had no way of knowing. I couldn't turn. I couldn't even move under the powerful grip. Some unknown creature clawed at my shoulders.

Then a needlepoint slipped into my arm and darkness immediately followed.

A figure emerged, obscurely draped in shadows, almost formless.

* * * * * * *

"You are in great danger. We have only this window to communicate. You've been captured by the Haknords, ocean merchants, slavers. Events are moving too fast!"

The words stopped for a moment, hesitating.

"There is much about your history you don't know…."

The voice dwindled, the image flickered, then returned, more sharply, then continued, but breaking up.

"No time…Sarleni can't do it…accept the Zygo…truth is locked up in your mind…won't open to us…discover your totality."

The face contorted and became translucent again and for a moment seemed to almost evaporate completely away.

I felt dizzy, and the black started to return. A sudden surge of light fused into being and I once again could see this strange illusive figure, glaring at me.

"You have to stop fighting; stop resisting. You are like a wall shutting her out. Even fighting my power right now! It is exhausting. And this is new to Sarleni. She's your link. Remember: two are stronger than either of you alone. She must teach you the Zygo without fail. When the power of two unites it becomes a powerful force like the two ends of a long rod being jointed together. When that rod

fuses between the two of you...everything will be clear!"

The face grew more intense.

"What you must accept is that your ultimate destination is not Bel-loniea, nor the northern ice sheets, but across to the other side of world. That's all we know."

I struggled to look away from the lined, drawn features floating just a short distance from me. The eyes were kindly enough, crinkled at the corners, lids almost disappearing into the sockets. The lips were thin, like leather straps, yet held no sense of contempt, but rather spoke in a lilt that was almost caressing.

"Sarleni takes herself very seriously. Understand that. You were not supposed to meet so soon. But events have forced all of us. You must link."

The face distorted, warped; the features stretched oddly and then pinched together as if some invisible hand were closing around that gentle face.

"Listen...no time...you've been taken prisoners...I can't see into the future, I can only sense things...and report what I know. You must...believe me...."

There was a fuzzy shivering quality to his image. His voice in my brain was tense and frantically trying to communicate to me. "You will learn much...your heritage is with us...you're blood-line...your mother is the key.... Try to remember back...into your past...." The voice was getting weaker. "...It is important to remain connected to Sarleni, open to her...remember we are all a part of the same universal mind, the same...we all exist in a same state, made of the same essence and energy...some of us can easily blend together...for that is the key...blend...blend...."

The face melted into a cloudy vapor and the voice cracked to silence and I was surrounded by nothing, then light.

* * * * * * *

For some time I was left confused. I had difficulty remembering what had happened last, before that strange dream. Then it all rushed back into memory. Something had grabbed us, flying into the sky and then I'd passed out.

I was now aware of lying on my back against something hard. I wondered if maybe this was illusion, too.

My eyes opened.

I became conscious of a rocking sensation.

It wasn't that of a grav-disk. The gloomy surroundings were not a complete blackout, but nonetheless limited light.

I was in a strange, confined room. It was a dank and musty place, with hard lined wooden beams above me. I could hear the constant, steady sound of swishing through water at a rapid speed.

There was a bareness to my surroundings, and not far away was another form lying on a slightly raised area, a linked chain restraining it. I didn't need to guess who that might be. The profile was gently breathing. Sarleni. We were alone in a small, dark room. I decided we were in an ocean vessel of some kind; and apparently quite large.

We were prisoners, locked away in some deep hole in a kind of strange craft making its way across some unknown ocean to some questionable destination—and fate.

How did I know all that?

CHAPTER FOUR

CAPTIVES OF THE HAKNORDS

Savage rage took control of my body. Every muscle strained against the confining hold on my wrists. I could hardly move. Sanity returned, along with logic. We were captives. There was little that could be done, at that moment.

Conserve your energy, Adt.

It took a moment to realize that thought came from Sarleni.

The realization of what was happening sank in and I remembered.

The dreams; and now this!

Yes, we're in a boat. A huge one. I could sense it. And some very strange minds out there, too. Above us. A guard that isn't... doesn't seem quite human. Not a Muti, either. Not pure animal, but nasty, bestial.

Instantly I felt both invaded and relieved. She was conscious!

My body went rigid against that mental invasion.

Sarleni's voice whispered, "Do you have to shut me out like that? It is so nice when we're connected. We're captives of the Haknords. They were the ones that grabbed us up in what they call a Gatherer. I don't know much more than that."

"How long have you been conscious?" I asked in a reasonably polite voice.

"Just a little longer than you. Do you remember the dream?"

I automatically fought down a sudden fury. But that emotion tainted my thinking and mood. I tried to soothe my annoyance. I tried to be polite.

Then I attempted to sit up. But I'd been strapped to what seemed to be a table-like slab lying on the floor.

I was about to say something when suddenly we heard footsteps. A bolt slammed and a door swung open. It was enough to announce that somebody had entered the room.

We were surrounded by several ugly looking brutes. In the dim lighting creeping through the open doorway, all we could perceive was gnarled, shriveled and bony shadow-features. Only later did we see details: Their faces were distorted, almost human, yet somehow bird-like, with large hooked noses and thin lips hanging over jagged, yellow brown teeth. The skin was just off white, a pale gray, with a slight edge of blue. Their eyes were big bright orange circles, almost lidless, as they stared furiously at us.

Amid unintelligible grunts we were released from the slabs we'd been so brutally strapped to. They snapped leg-irons to rings in the floor. We were confined to the same area of the slabs, but at least we could now stand and stretch.

They shoved a bowl of food in front of each of us, and then backed out of the room, closing and bolting the door behind them.

We ate the slop that was in the bowls as if it were one of the most delicious foods ever offered. I realized how hungry we were.

Sarleni said: "What do you think they'll do with us?"

I didn't want to admit my first thought. I shrugged.

Then she said, "Probably sell us as slaves."

That was also my conclusion.

"Yes, I think that's what you believe." Her voice was resigned. "Well, I'm certainly dressed for the part!"

"Dressed?" I wondered, vocalizing my thought. "Is that just a costume?"

She looked nervous, and then made that annoying discounting action with her hand. "Like you *don't* say, we'll probably be sold as slaves or worse. You're a fine warrior. They'll want to make use of your killing skills, to amuse them in death duels."

Yes, I thought, *it was a very good possibility. It was not uncommon, even though it was illegal in my part of the world. Captured warriors were often forced to fight to the death at private parties for the amusement of bored guests. Drinks would flow as blood saturated the arena grounds. It was an ugly practice most civilized people considered brutal and immoral. A duel between equals by mutual agreement was a socially accepted part of life, when it could be justified. But forced combat to the death was contemptible.*

"Well I don't plan on submitting quietly to their desires. And I won't let them harm you."

"How do you plan on stopping them?" she inquired, face almost expressionless.

"Always expect the unexpected, I was taught by my father, and I expect to rely on just that. I won't go down without taking a lot of those dumb brutes with me."

51

That sounded insanely foolish, even to me. But she smiled gently. "I know. You are a brave swordsman, a gentleman and a warrior of great courage. And we will not be left to die here or rot. I'm sure of that."

"I promise it."

She smiled again. "We can make use of this time. Plan. And we aren't entirely alone."

"What does that mean?"

"Our friends won't let us die here. We have a mission!"

"Fine friends, fine mission. Great weapons! I suppose we'll just somehow walk off the ship, across the water and into some magical Orb to fly off...." I let that pass, unfinished. The contempt in my voice had said it all.

"No, Adt. It doesn't work that way. The Orb can't find us right now, for some reason. Don't ask me to explain. Some things don't need explaining; just accepting. But we are too important to too many people. You'll see! This will be fixed."

I almost felt like laughing at that. They were brave words, but foolish convictions under the circumstances. Yet I want to brutally reveal my utter contempt.

Still, I couldn't help asking: "How? And where are they now?"

She thought for a moment, and then turned away, her face in shadow. "I'm not sure. I haven't felt...where's Moyi when I need him? Oh, well, never mind. Things will get better."

Brave, hollow words.

"This is a depressing conversation!" she declared conclusively. "We can talk about other things!"

"Like?" I wanted to know. "Where are they taking us?"

That led down to a quick dead ended silence. We sat there for a very long time, just staring blankly. Silence can sometimes speak a thousand words of its own. Time is eternal when there is no reference point, no contact with the basic order of nature. No idea whether it is day or night or how many days would pass or what would be happening where or when. Silence was deader than dead. Even the previous noises from the deck were dead now.

Sarleni sounded much smaller when she finally spoke: "Maybe we can get to know one another better? I'll tell you more about my world, my home."

I nodded in agreement. It was just the right kind of diversion to get our minds off the negative doom of our captivity. "I'd like to know more."

And so she started: "In a land of ice we have vegetation, but nothing as lush as what I saw in these last days—not like in southern regions. In the summers we get some foliage, grasses. But Helandi is usually a land of freezing winds and hard glaciers. Sometime…well, you'll get a chance to see it all." She paused and gave me a mysterious sidelong glance.

"Assuming we get out of here!" I couldn't help interjecting.

She frowned, and then after a short silence continued: "My people are scattered along the glaciers of the north, in clans, or groups of families. You would call them tribes, I suppose. But they are more than that. We are extended families formed into close-networks. The important thing is that some of these tribes, which are clusters of around 200 people, are joined more loosely with other similar villages. Not exactly like the complex central community of your Bel-loniea or other such city states." She stared at me for a long moment, face quite serious. "But they aren't unsophisticated. They certainly aren't dumb brutish savages or uneducated people. Even if you may think of them…as primitive, for that's what they want the world to believe. Sometimes this kind of honest illusion is the best protection from outside conquest…it is all simple, really."

She hesitated, sensing my confusion. "No. The so-called primitives aren't us. They are quite visible, and we remain in the background, so to speak, not obvious. Once you see it, you'll probably think of my home village in Helandi as quaint. But don't underestimate us.

"My people feel it is best to have a low profile. We are not warlike; not aggressive in the normal sense. We aren't in open conflict with our neighbors. We submerge in obvious places, but not in a manner that is obvious. It is never smart to reveal all. A little at a time. Nothing more. Sometimes it is best to show one layer, like lifting a mask, but only enough to reveal the first of many masks. Does that make sense?"

She sounded like a Muti.

Sarleni smiled, almost amused, continuing without much pause: "Our families are wonderfully warm communities. And it can be beautiful when we gather together for the Seasonal Celebrations and…."

She made a quick move of her right hand. "I'm sure you don't want a history of my people."

Again that smile warmed the air between us. How lovely she looked and her eyes seemed to sparkle mischievously as they met mine.

"Then forget history and tell me about yourself," I suddenly wanting to know everything about her.

"I guess I'm a loner. Well, for the most part. My schooling over the past years has been demanding, rigorous and focused for a very long time. I don't need to tell you how long, since it...well, don't ask a lady her age! That's none of your business."

I almost laughed, realizing that truth. I started to agree, but her hand waved me to silence, chopping the words in my throat before they could be spoken.

"In any case, as I was saying, our work is hard pressed and demanding. We explore the unlimited realms of our minds. We sharpen and develop its natural skills! It takes years for most. I've advanced rather swiftly!"

She blushed with a glowing edge of pride and abruptly stopped talking, yet I heard her voice continue in my head.

I'm sorry, didn't mean to lecture. But you did ask me....

"...to tell you the story of my life—okay. As a child I enjoyed playing in the ice, coming out into the brilliant winter landscapes with my family for afternoon visits with our clan. We always had elaborate festivals to celebrate the changes from winter to summer in Helandi. We'd race after the herds and flocks making their annual migrations. We would take our sporting challenges seriously. The swiftest amongst us are highly honored for our stealth and speed and endurance. During the coldest and darkest winter cycles we'd retreat to our cellar homes deep down in the Helandian ice caverns; huge spacious apartments and meeting halls, clustered around central supply centers. These massive cut-a-ways have historical links dating back generations. Sleek sled rails tunnel through passageways connecting our settlements. My family home has all the comforts necessary to grow up healthy and happy and protected and most of all, I can't begin to tell you how much loving support we have from each other. My parents worship the local Helandian god, Nuja. After all, she is the only symbol of life written about in the ancient texts that have been handed down by historians. I was prepared to study these philosophies according to the tests all students must take. Our Masters have very rigid standards that guide us into the various trades and careers we follow in later years. But things changed when I became interested in the Hanjahn system, and the teachings of the Zygo. I had special perceptive abilities. I've been a serious Zygon student ever since. Early training was hard and required me to concentrate on my inner energies. I was obliged to remain isolated in my small personal shell."

She sighed, then quickly said: "We get out, we gather together, but mainly it is in the mind that a lot of connections can be made. We only truly connect with a person who thinks on the same wavelength. Master Moyi says:

"It is colorized thinking. Two minds blending together in the same color.

"All very strange, in the beginning. But you'll see! You and I must learn to blend into one mutual color."

That last was almost thinking out loud, I noticed. And it didn't make much sense.

She continued talking, but my mind drifted. Suddenly she realized I wasn't paying attention.

"You must listen to what I'm saying about our minds. We must blend. We must start lessons. Believe me, it is important!

"The Mutis knew you had special abilities. And it is obvious to any sensitively trained mind. That's why you were chosen."

"Chosen?" I spat out, really annoyed, now. I felt an unreasonable wave of anger needle up through me. What in the world was she talking about? I wanted to tell her to drop the subject. But she just wanted to continue the running monologue at the speed of a ravenous Korda grinding furiously at a juicy feast—freshly killed male warrior, perhaps?

"I don't devour men! I'm *not* that way. I'm trying to tell you something important. You have special talents. And must make them work. We have been chosen."

Some women I'd met might use such flattery as a seductive gambit.

"Oh, I'm not like any woman you've ever known!" she continued, angrily.

Suddenly the door to our room opened and several or our captors entered.

Two of the guards had swords out, dangerously ready. They released our leg-irons then motioned us to stand. I was glad to be free to move. I didn't argue with their commands to leave this dimly lit, gloomy room. Beyond the door was a hallway. We were led up a steep ladder to the deck, and the bright glare of the outside world.

Enormous masts reached high in the sky. Rigid, monstrously large metal sails curved upwards, arched to capture the wind.

We were taken across deck, through a clutter of creatures much like those who had escorted us up on deck.

This was a huge boat. The ocean stretched out across the horizon in every direction. Escape was hopeless. To where?

The watchful guards shoved us to the center of the ship's wide deck. We were brought before a man sitting on what appeared a tiered pedestal that was part of the ship itself.

The gnarled creature sat there glaring at us. The near humanness of its shape was more perverse than its distortion of the norm. He

55

was obviously a different species from the guards. His skin coloration was a slightly blue tint that was indicative of a mutation.

But from what to what?

His nose was bulbous; the purplish lips grossly thick and pouty like some kind of ugly fish mouth. The green tinted eyes were both large and narrow, as the ears were floppy fat. The tinted flesh of his convoluted skull swiveled around thick bone masses. He gathered together the rose and blue marbled cloak about his fat bulk. His eyes glared steadily at us, narrowing in open hate. Why such rage? I could not guess. I decided this might have been his nature; glaring wrathfully out from behind thickly lidded eyes.

"What are these?" it screeched in a high-pitched voice. Then softer, like a low growl, "How'd they get picked up?"

The half naked gnarled figure groveled next to him muttered: "Oh, Mighty Knals.... Accident, I'm sure."

"Get rid of them. Over the side! We don't need this...we're on a different kind of gathering!" The bulky mass dismissed us with a nasty smash of his huge fist on the arm of the chair.

I was searching the guards and warriors closest to us, hoping to find a weapon within easy reach that I could grab. But it was hopeless.

A series of protest came from the crowd gathered around us.

"We can sell them!" one voice screeched.

"Yes...," another muttered in a low moan.

"Silence!" the Mighty Knals screamed. His eyes raced over those gathered in the throng, filled with contempt. His words fired out hot and loud in rapid succession. "You are stupid! Greedy! Lazy! Beastly slavers!"

A muttering of fearful complaints arose. They bellowed in semi-monotone, broken only by screeches and moans.

The men-creatures closest to me. They looked half dead. Their gnarled skeleton structures caused their skin to stretch and strain grotesquely transparent over sinews, veins and bones. The faces were masses of wrinkled webs netting across pinched bones. Yet none of these alternations were so inhuman as to appear animal, nor alien in nature. More like meanly shaped humans.

Knals bellowed again, sounding more like rasping, dull blades grating against naked rock. "Why were they picked up?"

"Just happened.... The Gatherers saw them alone. Easy capture."

"Easy capture or not, we aren't on a slaver hunt."

"They didn't know that!"

"They are stupid, dumb, half beastlings!" His eyes lowered as if examining his own large feet incased in thigh high boots. "Mechanical gatherers."

"They serve their purpose, Mighty Knals!"

"Not today, Zorcols. Not now." He glared wickedly at his underlings.

"Program the Gatherers to stop gathering such scum in their claws." Then pointing angrily at us, added: "And toss those two over the side for fish food!"

Zorcols said in a soft growl: "They take no space. They could be profitable at the slave market. The girl is what they call pretty."

He had not stopped staring hungrily over Sarleni's body.

And his venomous lust had not escaped the mighty Knals' notice. A thin grin spread across its leathered lips. "I see that."

"The Bazaar markets would bring a grand prize for her."

"Toy bait!" Knals nodded, a little more thoughtful.

"Yes, yes. And the man. He looks strong and could be considered meat for games!"

Knals glared at me, but said nothing.

Zorcols continued, talking in an even softer growl: "We are almost finished with the mapping. A little extra profit would be shared by all. What harm? And...."

"Shut up!" His words spat at the assistant so savagely that the words choked to a stop: "Grand Advisor, you speak too much! As my first in command you are far too verbose!"

A heavy silence followed. Only the moan of the wind could be heard over the rush of waves cutting across the ship's hull.

The leader leaned forward; eyes narrowed, slowly moving from Sarleni to me, and back to her.

Then suddenly glaring at me, asked: "What kind of battle did...it...give?"

"None. He was caught from behind. The claws held him. Shot the drug into both him and the...female...before they could react."

Knals' gross head slowly nodded, as if in deep thought. "The ultimate grab attack. The Gatherers do function smartly at times."

"Science does wonders!" some voices chanted from the crowd of the half naked men on deck.

"Silence! I'm conferencing with my officers, and your commander." His voice spilling the raw sound like a blanket over the audience. "So...what kind of price can we expect from these two pathetic wonders?"

One of his assistants, standing next to him, snarled: "We'll get plenty. I promise you!"

"You make many promises. These are...what?"

"A woman of beauty and a man muscular enough to make a good slave."

A good slave down your throat! I thought, seething at their audacity. *Give me a sword and I'll make Korda meat of every last one of these and....*

Don't let them rile you! I was mentally warned.

"Get out of my mind!" my snarled response was far louder than it should have been.

"What did he say?" the mound of grotesque flesh demanded of his assistant and anybody else who might supply an answer.

"Made no sense," came a nasty jeer.

I felt an invisible hand touch my thoughts.

Don't react! Ignore their exchange. Be above it.

She wasn't about to back off. I was too focused on what was happening to shut down on her. Then suddenly it seemed a good idea to silently exchange thoughts.

That's better! We need to connect like this.

Knals turned, eyes scanning those around him.

"Where's Skurals?"

A cold, thin voice rose over the mob like a chilling vapor.

"Over here!"

The crew members and guards split a wide gap on the deck as a tall, icy man stepped forward.

He was handsome enough, but with the stance and attitude of a predator. His slow, almost fluid graceful walk said much.

I didn't have to see the hard eyes to know most of his story. He was tough, and made of solid bone and metal hard muscle; yet lean and wiry. I instantly recognized a masterful killing machine; a skilled swordsman in his cold manner of movement. He flowed. His moves were almost choreographed like a magnificent dancer. His eyes flashed towards me with contempt, then hesitated, just long enough to take in more details. In that moment he revealed just a flicker of recognition. We were, in many ways, very much alike: skilled warriors, fully confident in our ability to survive any battle.

"Skurals, you're close to the Kamina. Have any ideas? About these?" The gross creature pointed at us with disdainful scorn in its eyes.

Skurals slowly turned, facing us for a very long time. Now he examined me in some detail and then gazed at Sarleni with a swift intake of admiration, but then returned his attention to me. "The woman, fine. You'll make money with her. The man, well...I would like to kill him. It would be a pleasure. Of course, in a duel."

The man stepped forward. Suddenly his hand was holding a

sword. He moved, without any warning. I felt a blade flash in the air, the point tuck under my chin, barely touching flesh. It was all one swift movement, an instant show of stunning skill. I didn't react, my eyes fastened to his, locked there, unmoving.

"As I guessed," he sneered in mocked aloofness: "A warrior. May have some skill with the sword. He shows control and confidence. Either that or he's simple minded. I could kill him right now, for your pleasure! Give him a weapon. Make it amusing. Fun for all!"

"Give me a blade and I'll amuse your body with its point!" I muttered just loud enough for the man to hear.

He smiled slightly and turned away. He now faced Knals, who leaned forward, intense. "I'd give you a good show killing him, if you wish some entertainment."

The man's sword was already sheathed. His actions had been swift, very skilled and I recognized a deadly arrogance about him, more savage, cold and brutally dangerous than that of the honorable swordsman I had known. In a duel he would kill with great pleasure and joy, cut by cut. "Come, let's have some fun!"

Knals snarled, eyes narrowed, mouth almost turned up in a smile. "And I should toss profits? What are you willing to pay for the pleasure of killing him?"

"I'm not here to buy. I'm observing. Nothing more. But for a fee I would be willing to kill him. Or even for the pleasure and joy of doing so." He turned; his icy eyes flooded over me in one swift dismissive take.

Don't respond! was Sarleni's mental warning.

I don't plan to. Let them think I'm cowed and cowardly. I have better plans....

"Yes. I would do it for free. Why not?" He laughed in stiff amusement. "But I'd rather enjoy the pleasures of the slavegirl's body for the duration of this trip. For that, I'd be willing to make a wonderful show of cutting his body up in little bits and pieces. Let the blood gush over his flesh! Make agonized screams fill the air as I slice at his body, until life slowly departs. I could chop away flesh to the bone, chunk by chunk. Honor him with a long, lingering torture before death arrives. And all, of course, for the pure pleasure of possessing the slavegirl!"

"Then you figure her worthy and thus expensive? I won't toss such valuable prizes into your hands, my dear Skurals. Enough to know that you give such value to the slavegirl."

"Suit yourself."

"I could have him strung high and whipped to death, or savagely skinned alive by any one of my crew here…and for nothing!"

"Some other time, perhaps!" Skurals shrugged, as if of little importance. His manner shifted, turning ice cold. "I'm a busy man. And I have been charged with supervising the mapping, which we must finish. The Masters of Kamina will be pleased with what we've done! You'll be well paid."

"Yes, of course." Knals shrugged that off as if he didn't care and then, looking back at us, making annoying movements with his shoulders. "Take them away! Don't bother me with this! Feed them. Keep them healthy. We have more pressing matters to contend with. The Mutis have made demands we must fill. We all know how they employ their human slaves! And not much better are they to us traders!"

Skurals almost chanted: "The Mutis are Law. What they wish is our command. Expansion and growth is their rule."

"Yes, yes, I need not be reminded. The mapping almost completed over the new territory assigned us. So…we'll deal with these two when we get to markets at Kasiisi. We'll be there in a few days." There was contempt and fear in his tone of voice, even under the horrid rasp. "We'll dump them there. She can be sold as a toy delight. He can be bought by anybody who wants muscle!" The creature waved us away as if batting some insect out of existence.

CHAPTER FIVE

THE TRAINING BEGINS

Neither of us said anything until the door to our cell had been slammed shut. We were, by then, chained, and alone.

Sarleni quickly caught my attention: "We have little time."

"For what?"

"Training you!" she stated without hesitation, in a very determined voice.

"To be a good slave?"

"Hardly!" she actually laughed. "Hanjahn exercises and teaching you the Zygo...we have to get free of these creatures and on our way."

"Sounds like a great plan. But I don't think that'll be effective against these happy slavers. Nor meet with their approval!" I looked upwards, to indicate our captors. "It'll take more than some religious chants to escape the friendly Korda-baiters up there."

She ignored my retort, saying: "We can't just submit without trying."

"I agree with trying...but something tangible would be more useful. Like a basic plan of escape to avoid slavery in some strange land."

I didn't even consider the fact that we were in the middle of an ocean. Where would be go, even if we could escape?

She impudently asked: "And what would you suggest?"

"Zygo me a sword and I'll cut our way out of this place!"

"Through chains?" she mocked.

"Do you have a better plan?"

We went into silence, lost in the obvious reality that escape might be impossible.

"The slave markets in the city of Kasiisi," she said in a soft voice, as if thinking out loud. A shiver seemed to rush through her. "I believe they are not like what we think of as slaves markets."

I snapped, ignoring her implication: "What was that all about the Mutis?"

"Strange, wasn't it?"

I nodded. "To quote: *The Mutis have made demands we must fill. We all know how they employ their human slaves!*"

Her answer rebounded in my mind: *Totally against everything the Mutis stand for. The Mutis serve. They don't enslave others. It is basically against their breeding, their belief system....*

I instinctively clamped down hard on my thoughts. That should shut her out.

She giggled, but merely shrugged as if to say: *doesn't matter, so close down if you must. I'll get you when you're sleeping!*

I realized how silly I was being. But I needed to escape from my own thoughts. The day slipped away and for the most part we were locked in a mental depressive mood.

I was in a deep stupor, conscious, but oblivious of my immediate surroundings when the world closed in around me. It was as if a huge invisible hand had reached out and encased my skull, shadowed over my eyes. All of my thoughts were drawn to something that felt alien, distant, yet close, reaching into the very center of my awareness.

This is not a dream was the first intrusive thought that entered my mind. *It is time to reach you in a conscious state.*

I instantly recognized it as a new invasion of another mind into my own.

Again I wanted to avoid, reject, and the apparition flashed on and off, scattered and then with a bolt of stunning power reshaped itself.

"Relax. Don't resist!" the loud message came through with a *pulsing light flowing across my vision. "I but continue our talk."*

Invisible fingers probed my brain.

The man Sarleni called Master Moyi, who had previously haunted my dreams, now appeared. He sat there, ethereal in nothingness. In fact, I realized, we were both where there was no grounding, no space, and yet all space to infinity.

* * * * * * *

"Just listen. There is much to learn. Stop resistance. I disapprove of your contempt for things you know nothing about! Listen and learn. Now.

"It is imperative that you understand the depth of your own abilities before you can begin the joining process taught through the

Zygo. *You have great natural abilities. These are untrained sensory gifts that are vital to your nation and even more importantly crucial to the existence of Noomas itself. Listen and learn.*

"An unpolluted mind is able to see something of the future, as do the Mutis. Total Nexus would bring visions of all that is and ever has been and ever will be. None of us have reached that state. Few even understand the concept. We accept the logic.

"Don't block wisdom through ignorance. Learn to accept ideas difficult to understand. We will help. Open your powerful mind to new concepts.

"A two-dimensional world is flat. In a one-dimensional universe we have only a central point. Nothing else would seem to exist. Does that mean it does not exist? That the single point could not perceive anything beyond itself? And what if it moved backwards to a non-dimensional state; what then happens? A nothingness?

"As we progress from the flat two dimensions to three, we find our present existing status. In our three-dimensional realm, where you and I and Sarleni exist, and even the Mutis fashion their lives, there are many wonderful elements that normal people know nothing about.

"The fourth-dimensional stratum is where the insights and precepts of Prophets originate. They have gained greater wisdom at this echelon. Accept this fact.

"When one reaches a higher awareness and a greater understanding, then it is necessary to embrace new ways of communicating. Words spread false illusions. The mind is something few have learned to master.

"The Mutis know more than most humans on Noomas. But some of us have discovered transcendence to another pathway to true knowledge. We all have some ability to reach such a mental state, but some, like yourself, resist and cling to the standard systems, and rightly so. "Ju-bilee has perfected and developed her own strange methods. Her clan has explored the Nexus and mastered many elements of it. But not the Totality. They have expanded the Zygo in unexpected ways and have special abilities that, perhaps, reach beyond even those of the Mutis.

"She is one of the most advanced and has abilities beyond those common to her clan. Ju-bilee can look beyond today, though not quite as deeply as a Muti, but deep enough to grasp variables affecting alternative futures. She and others have prophesied nightmarish horrors...warnings we take seriously. Her abilities and visions make her somewhat frightening to many....

"Prophets often form power bases by establishing mass reli-

63

gious orders.

"Our seers have insights into parts of the Ultimate Truths. But it takes more than a swift peek or even a lifetime search. Nobody has all the answers. And sometimes new hope awakens when a birthing manifests special abilities within a newborn child. The Mutis know this very well. They watch; closely monitoring the progress of our Wise Ones.

"We all have some of these unexplored gifts. Those who choose to become a Prophet, using a small part of their natural abilities, see some truths and end up believing they have seen the face of God. Which is a false conclusion. They had seen a splinter of light, sensed just a finite part of the True Realities. None of us see more than a glimmer of that vast infinity of Truth! And, perhaps, it is beyond our present abilities."

He paused, taking a deep breath: "We know only that great changes are about to besiege Noomas. There is a Messenger on his way. You are to meet him. Ju-bilee and her Muti connections have picked you for this mission. It is dangerous and difficult. In visions, she has seen alternate futures that include you in confrontation. The originating point of this event lies on the far side of Noomas. She reports a future conflict of vast proportions. She only knows the Messenger will arrive and you must meet him before it is too late."

A frown squeezed his features, then he closed by saying: "I must go! You're needed! Quick!"

* * * * * * *

"Wait!" I heard myself cry out.

The vision flashed out, like a flame being doused with water.

"Stay…come back!"

I heard noises around me.

"Take her!" a rough voice spat.

I was confused, half way between sleep and reality.

Distantly I heard Sarleni screaming my name. *Adt…Adt….*

I felt, more than anything, a wrenching pang of danger. A door slammed, a bolt snapped into place.

I glanced over to Sarleni's pallet.

She wasn't there!

I sat straight up desperately searching the dim darkness of the cell. My head screamed her name, mind wide open now.

Sarleni! Sarleni….Sarleni!

My impulsive reaction stunned me. Heart was racing and a panic setting in that I had never experienced before.

Then her gentle thought came into my head: *I'm all right, Adt. They're taking me on deck. I can handle this. Stay calm. Just be ready if I need help. I'll call for you.*

I felt helpless.

My chains were firmly in place. There was no way to break them.

Then Moyi's words about *total Nexus* flashed into my mind..

Nexus was part mythos and legend; fairytale magic used to save heroes from fantasy monsters. Children accepted it all as a reality. Some people thought it a science from ancient times. As a child, I'd experimented with suggested chants, but when nothing resulted I'd lost interest.

But Sarleni's abilities were real. I moved into her favorite cross-legged position as much as my chains would allow and closing my eyes forcing myself to breathe deeply.

Sarleni, I'm here.

Adt! Just watch! Wait!

Darkness swirled around me, then light flickered and patterned itself into moving shapes.

The upper deck began to grow sharp in my mind. A dozen or more grizzly keepers and guards muttering among themselves were milling around Sarleni. It was late in the night, two moons hung on the horizon and lanterns blazed along the stanchions. She was standing in shackles. I could almost feel them around my own legs. I could see only what her eyes were seeing and what her mind was thinking. There was a singsong playing in her head that puzzled me.

Why was she singing a nursery rhyme at a time like this?

Ding dong dilly do,
Little boy has lost his shoe,
Lost his cap and mantle, too
Run to find them, we must do.

What was she doing?

Stay calm, Adt, I think this is working.

Her singsong grew louder, more rapid and desperately rigid in its pulsing rhythm.

Several men seemed to be wandering about lost, in a daze, as if looking for something that kept avoiding them. It looked very peculiar.

Ring ran shilly sham,
Ice and snow will freeze the land,
Wind blows strong, I cannot stand
Run to safety, I demand.

Some of the guards seemed to huddle, bewildered now. The

ones closest to her were now visibly shivering. Did she have some sort of a spell over them? All I could do now was to observe and wait.

She seemed to have them bewitched, in a strange way, almost helpless. Over and over she sang; verse after verse. How long could she continue to hold these creatures in such a state of confusion? Certainly not for long.

Then she seemed to falter as if confused, looking down for a brief moment and then weaving slightly, as if about to faint or fall.

My whole body strained in the effort to help her. But, of course, that was impossible.

She slumped, fell, and then up-righted herself. *I'm okay.*

Then the unmistakable screeching voice of Knals broke over the crowd.

"What is going on here? Why are you not keeping your watch?" His hulk came pounding on deck knocking over several stunned guards until he was facing Sarleni, with Zorcols close at his heels.

"So, you want to play?" he challenged. "And what insanity. She's for the slave market." The vengeful sneer on his face matched those savage words. "You think you'll get any price for her after you've violated her?" He moved in close to Sarleni. I could almost smell the stench of his half rotten teeth as his rough hand clawed at her black locks.

She let out a startled gasp.

Adt! Her voice was trembling in my mind now. *Adt, I need you—now! Stay open. Just that!*

Anything. I had no idea what I was doing. I only hoped that there was something to this HanJahnology to help her. But what?

At that point I felt suddenly drained, as if something had sucked all my strength away. If I had been standing I'd have fallen face down. A tunnel of dark raced around my vision, closing in, then widening as I sensed her voice change or was it even her?

Knlua yieh! Tapa!

This was a deep chanting, so similar to the Muti mantra.

It was not exactly Sarleni's voice but something coming from her mind, much deeper, more solemn.

The chant rumbled on and I saw both Knals and Zorcols step several paces back and stare at each other.

Knals screeched, "Get her back to the cell. Immediately! If I ever find any of you disobeying my orders, you'll enjoy the taste of my whip. Now move!"

I could no longer see what was going on. But I was feeling her resistance. She was being jostled around and was pulling at something; I'm not sure what was happening up there. Now I was getting only vague glimpses, swirling about me like dark shadows.

And that deep droning, almost commanding voice continued beating in my head. Or from my head, I wasn't sure if I was sending or receiving.

All at once the beating in my head stopped as the cell door was flung open and Sarleni came tumbling in, her leg irons were swiftly fastened again to the posts. The men left without a word and we were alone in perfect silence.

It was then that I realized how tense every muscle in my body was.

My thoughts tightened on our urgent need to find a way to escape. But how?

Sarleni shook her head. "Forget escape. We're safe for now. We can't do anything about that...yet. This is a time to learn."

"We should be thinking about escape."

"That will come," she countered, rather calmly. "First, we must continue your training. That experience proved we are capable of great power together, but it was not enough. Without the Zygo we cannot discover the totality, the Nexus, wherein lies the unlimited power of our mutual strength. If they had not yielded to my chanting, then I would have needed you to take stronger action."

"In what way?"

"I know, you are not ready yet. We must change that. Okay?"

That last word, asking permission, caused me to relax. I nodded, more patiently willing to cooperate.

"Learning is the art of growth," Sarleni began, as if quoting divine text. "Only in growth can we become masters of our own selves."

"That's standard in *The HanJahn Studies of the Zygonian arts,* which contains many such great truths. Like: Master the lesson and you discover the Process."

I literally cringed from that line.

She laughed in a delightful, bubbly way, and then winked playfully. "Don't you want to discover the Process?"

"To where?"

"To higher insight, and higher understanding, and higher...." She laughed again. "And you must learn fast! Don't struggle to find logic, be open to new, strange, ideas."

I decided to do as she suggested. It was less boring than looking at the walls.

"We can begin by exploring new possibilities, new awareness, new understanding within our own conscious being. All we have to

67

do is let our boundaries expand to new skills. It is like building muscle tissue, allowing our minds to discover in a new way…."

I was aware of a certain lilting musical quality to her words, which gradually faded into a background melody, a rhythm and beat, a throbbing halcyon of sensual sound, moving through me to relax the muscles, and send soothing balm to every nerve until I felt weightless to my core.

It was far more pleasant to relax into the melodic aura of her feelings enrapturing my every cell.

I didn't want to leave this joyfully relaxed state. It was like sleeping, but fully alert. It was like dreaming, but with control of my mental choices.

So right, was her almost beguiling message. *Isn't it wonderful?*

I felt as if even the blackness was lifting slightly.

Somebody is approaching. This is enough for now. We can practice again later. Quick. Awaken!

Fully conscious, I was sharply alerted to my immediate surroundings.

The door creaked open. A grizzly oaf plopped bowls of foul smelling slop by our pallets and then retreated as briskly as he'd come in. It took little imagination to stir out of our meditative studies with this rank aroma filling the room.

After dealing with that horrid meal we tried to refocus our mental connection.

What we'd experienced together was my first awareness of a new open sense of acceptance of her lessons. I was curious. I actually wanted to reconnect. I was beginning to believe new possibilities. Perhaps it was, also, a desperate need to embrace hope in a futile situation.

The days patterned themselves after that. They would take us on-deck some mornings for a short "airing" but that was not every day. To avoid boredom we practiced this strange thing called Zygo, which kept our minds occupied.

She taught me exercises that at first made little sense; they seemed to be merely word games.

"Think sleep, without sleeping!" Sure.

"Open your mind, slowly call me in." Easy trick.

"Consider a large X, focus on it."

She slipped smoothly into my mind, projecting thoughts there like seeds planted in virgin soil.

Relax your whole body. Let the tension out. Remember that a blank mind is not an empty one, but purely an open slate upon which new learning can be fused.

Think Molinaieasoinaiea.

Now that was a senseless word that I couldn't even pronounce! *Mol-in-aie-a-so-ina-i-e-a...just try it.*

I tried bits of it as she instructed.

She insisted that I keep repeating that series of sounds, over and over.

Breathe with them, Adt. Just breathe with them.

After a while it was relaxing, if nothing else. It killed time; it helped to soothe my seething mind.

Thought is rhythm, is depth, is open, is rich, is wide, she chanted. *It is narrow and shallow and it is full and thick. It is all things and all things are it.*

Obviously right from her *Book of Learning.* I had, by now, given up trying to understand such statements. I tried to merely keep open.

Life is a living, continual process, and an expanding horizon that can fill our inner selves. Just imagine it as a living being, deep within you.

She never explained; and I understood explanations didn't work.

The results, alone, count. Be open and you will discover amazing power.

Then she would burst out: *Open fully to me!*

And an invisible mental door did open, just ever so slightly. But then it slammed shut again.

I had learned how to shut my mind down. It brought back memories of my childhood mind exercises with the Mutis that I had forgotten about. They were vague shadowy recollections and without more than a sense of having happened.

At night, dreams came. Most of these faded. Soon it didn't matter. Few lasted more than the scant moments it took to gain wakefulness from sleep. But one pressed itself deep into my memory. It emerged from a deep darkness as I was floated in an endless sky.

* * * * * * *

The woman came out of the mist, arms reaching as if to embrace me. Her voice murmured like the soft sound of wings fluttering in the air.

We were now moving above a strange landscape. Far below were mountains and plains, and off towards the horizon yellowed desert territories blending down to the dim coastlines that cut land from ocean.

We were flying over the world at fantastic speeds. I could feel the wind roaring around my head.

"Isn't it exquisite?" a voice asked.

I tried to shake off the trance like feeling around me. But it only deepened further into a thick, dimly lit forest; a jungle of twisted vines and knitted huge monstrous tree trunks. But none of that was of importance, just background for the vision of this female figure before me. Her arms lowered to her sides.

"Is this better?" she acquiesced; taking one of her favored positions, cross-legged on the ground. It wasn't a graceful move, yet it made her all the more appealing in its simplicity. Stand. Sit.

Was this Sarleni? Or some other semblance? I couldn't really focus on her face.

"I needed to talk to you, needed to let you know more about me and—"

It was Sarleni. Now plaguing my nightmares!

Emotion flared up.

I felt a wild fury leap up within me; unreasonably. I wanted to shut her out. I tried to close my mind down, to hammer the door shut to any outside invasion.

A surge of power crushed in on my vision, on my body, like a hand squeezing hard.

Her image transformed, melted, the face narrowed, skin fading yellow then deep brown as the bones started to press up against the flesh.

I wanted to cover my eyes, or look away, but couldn't.

"Stop resisting. Let her find the natural links between you."

The face was lined, and strangely kind. The eyebrows heavy and arched. And those eyes, almost deep reddish orbs, glared into mine like lightning probes. I felt as if something were stripping my very thoughts, grinding away at the edges of my inner skull.

Then almost as an afterthought, he said: "Once you connect and have reached full Nexus I will never have need to return to haunt you. I say no more!"

He vanished!

CHAPTER SIX

COWARDLY CHALLENGES

And I was now looking at Sarleni. This was not a nightmare, but reality. She was sleeping quietly, breathing very lightly.

My mind remained half-haunted by the dream—or had it been some kind of projected message? The acute sharpness of those images ripped through me like the blade of a bluntly edged sword.

The visual presence of Sarleni took dominance, and I watched her; fascinated. My eyes were literally caressing all of her.

I felt a flush of guilt.

This was too much like sneaking into a woman's private bedchamber while she was unable to guard against such an invasion of her privacy.

Despite my resistant ego, I clung to her seductive beauty, in a desperate struggle to blot out the horror of the nightmare.

When my thoughts shifted and brought on an instinctive reaction to her obvious loveliness, my inner alarm went off.

How could I allow myself to be as invasive of her privacy as she had been with mine?

"Oh, it is all right," her voice invited, sleepily.

"After all, you're just human."

"What?" She was awake! I panicked, involuntarily.

"Don't be embarrassed."

She sat up, rubbing her eyes.

"It is important that we continue the training. The Master was right."

"*What* Master?" I bellowed, beyond restraining my surprise. I was profoundly disarmed by her statements and casual acceptance of my staring so long and hard—and how many of my thoughts had she been able to read?

"We both just had the same dream. Well, mutual counterparts of it, lets say," she continued matter-of-factly: "It was me at first, but

71

you broke it off and then Master Moyi interjected. Even I was surprised by his appearance. One never knows where he is or when he'll pop up like that. Can be somewhat annoying. But he's right. We must begin again. And this time try to let me all the way in."

If only it had been that easy.

And so, we once again entered into those frustrating lessons. She was determined to make our connection a deeper, fuller and richer experience. I still found it difficult to break down all the barriers blocking what she continued to call the total Nexus. Even though I actually tried.

But it began to get better. And as days passed I continued worrying whether we would ever escape and avoid being sold as slaves. We were lost on Noomas and captives of slavers who were determined to sell us for profit. Even if we managed to get free, where would we go?

There were the continual on-deck breathers. The sun usually was burning hot, brightly lighting the sky. But not always. Even on gloomy days the ocean's endless undulations felt amazingly overwhelming in quite a lovely way. I had never, previously, been exposed to such an experience and I found myself fascinated, staring out across the horizon. I could almost understand how people might fall in love with manning such a vessel, despite its rugged hardships. I had heard tales of seafarers devoting their entire lives to the oceans of Noomas. For short periods of time, for me, it was certainly breathtaking.

But the men who ran this ship were hardly the romantic types, and at best seemed to be of limited intelligence.

The crew was rather sullen and not too bright. They would glance our way, but seemed lazily disinterested, aside from their occasional drooling and breathy grunts towards Sarleni when the officers were not within hearing distance. The guards themselves continued to watch carefully, but became slowly more complacent as we showed no signs of resisting their commands. We observed every slight change, most of the time communicating silently.

I felt our best chance of ever escaping would be only if these creatures thought us to be non-threatening, cowardly, meek, submissive in every way. It was a difficult illusion to maintain. I avoided any eye contact, any sign of aggressiveness.

But it wasn't easy to hide my real intentions under a number of circumstances. My alertness had to remain covert. Connections with Sarleni had to stay vigilantly undetectable. Keeping my own private thoughts barred beneath those guises was yet another challenge. And conditions on deck created even more risks. Two of which were starkly dangerous encounters that I found next to impossible to ignore. Playing coward is not a simple game for any trained warrior.

One morning I managed to move closer to where the Gatherers were kept latched to the back of the ship. My guards had been lax by then, allowing us more freedom of movement. The Gatherers huge golden wings were folded up tightly; their talons bolted to the deck by large mental flanges. Upon closer examination it was apparent that they were not real living creatures so much as mechanical combinations of flesh and metal. Huge purple eyes remained open wide above large, sharp red beaks. They would look around as if watching, but showed no expression. One got the impression that living beasts were enslaved in artificial bodies. It was a horrendous mating of flesh and machine. I saw the bolted extensions of what would normally have been jointed claws, but in reality were blunt metal gripping clamps. Those were what had held us so helpless while being flown into captivity onto this ship.

I was fascinated and didn't notice the man who came up behind me until his hard, cold voice said:

"They have their virtue. We are, of course, quite proud of their development. An experimental scientific masterwork."

I turned, startled. Standing there within easy reach was Skurals. This was the man who had wanted to skin me alive with his sword, thinking he could do so even if I were equally armed. It would be a professional pleasure to challenge his skills with my own. The man was sleek and cold, standing there, fully armed, hands relaxed at his sides. His steel grey eyes glared cunningly into mine as he spoke again.

"They are living and yet dead. Not as sophisticated a combination as is now beginning to develop. But they are easily programmed into serving their masters. A living slave is better off than these poor creatures. Consider yourself lucky that this isn't soon to be your fate!"

I wanted to engage this man in any kind of combat. But under the present circumstances it was too balanced in his direction. If I had a sword in my hands it would be a pleasure to drive the point deep into his heart, or right between his icy eyes. It was not even unreasonable rage; only simple knowledge that he deserved killing. Not only had Skurals plagued me with his insults but also dared to ask for Sarleni as his mating toy. For that, alone, he deserved my fury and contempt.

Sarleni's warning thought was unneeded.

Don't let him bait you!

"I don't intend to," my response was silent without a flinch, in

order to conceal my split attention. I asked him, in as pleasant a voice as possible:

"What are they?"

He stared at me, the eyes narrowing to slits, and then he stepped closer.

"It would be a shame to turn you into one of those…at least not before I could have the pleasure of running a blade through your body a few times!"

His left hand lifted, index finger pointing, then stabbing out at me, hitting my chest to illustrate the targets he would enjoy thrusting into.

"Do you think," I countered, in as controlled a voice as possible, "that would be an easy task?"

"Why, of course!"

He laughed and without any warning let the back of his hand slap softly across my cheek, a controlled act, insultingly lending no pain. It was more a contemptible caress.

"As easily as that, my dear boy!"

His hand slipped backwards to strike me again, this time a bit more harshly. I was prepared and managed to move my head to one side, causing him to miss his target.

"Good play!" he exclaimed in disappointed surprise.

"I do suspect you'd be an amusing challenge—so few of those around any more. Makes the joy of killing less rewarding. Nothing like plunging the point of a blade into a man's guts, letting it cut through deep in a death-thrust spilling out entrails, dripping in rich, thick blood. Ah, the pleasure of seeing men's eyes shocked in realization their useless lives have been…so easily…terminated. The delight in seeing their surprise. Horror. Death is one fate they cannot avoid. For it is already a fact. I love delivering that kind of wisdom to such fools. They are all rather crude, brutal and unskilled fellows. Maybe someday I'll have the pleasure of killing you."

"I would hope to deny you that joy!"

I managed to say, controlling a far more direct comeback.

"Don't all of your kind plead for such mercy?" he chuckled.

"What type is that?"

"Cowards. Braggarts. Fools! Men who helplessly hide behind a woman's protection!"

The man's eyes flashed, head nodded slightly, indicating the direction where Sarleni was watching us. My anger must have revealed itself, for he laughed broadly, sneering as he said:

"Yes, I have not forgotten that lovely lady. Maybe I'll bid on her at the slave market. She might be a pleasure for a night or two.

Don't you think? Any man would pay much to fondle her to his pleasures. Right?"

He was mockingly being buddy-buddy, as if we were friends.

"Think." he continued, leaning even closer,

"To place your hands on her flesh, to enjoy the pleasure of such skin under your fingers tips. Ah, maybe she might be worth a Proctoress' ransom. Don't you think? Oh, I forgot. I would imagine you have already feasted on the pleasures of this slavegirl during the darkness of night or under the glow of our moons. Now tell me. Is she as enjoyable as she appears to be? I'm certain you could relate wondrous tales of all-night pleasures in her lovely arms. Please, share your discoveries with me, for I wish to be tempted beyond my control to buy her for my own personal nightly feasts!"

Sarleni's thought slashed furiously at me:

Don't react! Blend out. Flow. He's dangerous! Remember...let him think you a coward!

That jarred me almost as violently as the instant rage that had welled up at his words.

My heart raced violently against emotional upheaval, the heat of it all surely raising a noticeable flush to my face.

But I managed to shrug, mentally blocking my volcanic emotion, draining it down into a deep chasm inside my mind, locked coldly in place.

"She's but a slavegirl! What can you expect?"

I tossed off, as if it didn't matter at all.

He jerked back, clearly surprised.

I pointed to the Gatherers. "You were saying about them, I do believe. Tell me...and exactly what are you?"

He glared at me, controlled fury like hot ice in his narrowed eyes. When he spoke it was in a tightly constricted voice. "Something you need not know anything about."

Then, as almost an after-thought, added angrily:

"Go back where you belong!"

He jerked back his hand, thoroughly dismissing any further exchange and directed me to return to where Sarleni was standing midship.

She was relieved and actually smiled as I approached.

"You did wonderfully. For a moment I thought you'd leap at him. Did it really bother you that much?"

I knew what she was implying, but didn't, for sure, know why. She was, after all, like most women: vain and self-serving. Or was she?

Sarleni laughed in light amusement, and then did something unexpected. She reached out and touched my cheek, gently.

"You were a dear."

Then her hand fell swiftly away, as if aware of having reached beyond a socially acceptable line.

I'm sorry, was her directed thought. *But you were amazing. And I could sense your real anger. It was nice how you felt so protective of me, even under these circumstances. You were quite convincing. Thanks. I'm flattered.*

I wondered what she meant by that.

And you did play it smart avoiding real conflict with him.

Shortly after that episode, we were herded back down to our jail room.

Though on another day things almost got beyond my control. Meek and cowardly was not my natural state of mind, and when directly challenged it could be difficult to control my temper.

My attention primarily concentrated on examining our surroundings; counting paces between guard posts, the deck's width, thickness of the masts. I was calculating precise maneuvers, should any mode of escape prove valid.

But in the middle of the ocean it seemed near impossible

The mists gathered in around the ship at times, surrounding us in billowing whiteness. It was often impossible to see much beyond the ship's railing. Generally they avoided these gloomy places as if considering them a death trap. Then other times, when the sun was out, distant islands and even landmasses, showed on the horizon. The ocean was vast. Our situation seemed hopeless.

But it was the shouting of voices beyond the hull that caught our attention one morning and caused me to feel any hope of escape.

We moved to the railing, looking over the side, and saw that several of the raft-like power launches were out there, actively gathering fish from the ocean. We had noticed them latched securely to the deck, but never had seen them in use before. Now we could examine them more closely in action. These launches were handled by only one man, who directed everything, including the fishing nets.

So, this was how the food supplies were replenished.

Sarleni tapped my shoulder. I turned. The look in her eyes was pleading.

I felt the mental probe again attempting to reach into my mind. I opened to it.

Interesting! If we could get one of those, maybe we could escape....

But I had also wondered about that. I watched the man press the small wheel on the platform rising at the front of the craft, which instantly bolted through the water some distance from the ship, then turned. Stopped. The man went to the net, hanging from the back and gathered up the struggling fish caught in its knots.

I felt a rough, brutal hand grab my shoulder, spinning me around. It came unexpectedly.

"What are you two doin'?" the creature's face snarled. "Go... get back!"

My automatic reflexes caused me to lean threateningly towards the guard.

Adt, don't!

I glanced at Sarleni, whose eyes widened.

He's armed! Watch out! Behind you!

I twisted, ducking, just in time. The guard had swung the hilt of his sword at my head, in response to my apparent attack. I side-stepped as a second deck hand attempted to bash in my head. Then I straightened upright, under the blow. And instead of returning the attack I played it smart and in swift surrender raised my hands, keeping sharply alert to any further danger.

I let everybody see a pliable, submissive man.

The guard, who had attacked me in the first place, whipped around, snarled furiously and slapped the back of his hand at my face. I couldn't avoid the stinging blow. My vision blurred.

Adt, back up, away!

My body moved one step back.

Cold air flashed across my face as the guard's hand just missed me.

"Stop!" a growling command came from some distance from us.

I recognized Skural's voice.

"We'll have none of this!"

That surprised me. I would have expected this man giving approval to such savage treatment. Suddenly I saw him come into view. He had a sword in his hand and without warning the point discovered the throat of the man who had struck me.

"You will be more careful about whom you attack without permission. Do you understand?"

The fellow looked horrified and cringed. The blade twitched and I saw dark red appear under his chin.

"Next time, remember."

Then Skurals turned towards me, and again that sword point targeted another chin: mine.

"I see you are at your cowardly best. Quite a change from the other day, I might add. I wonder about that. If you were free to engage me, we could, perhaps, have some fun. Now, couldn't we?

Do you want a sword? I can arrange it. I'm sure a bit of amusement would be welcomed. Cut you up a bit, dice your flesh, bring the blood to your skin and allow your bones to breath more freely. Maybe even expose some raw meat to the sun. A slight cut across the cheek, or a couple back and forth on your chest to remind you of the encounter. I promise not to cripple you.

Our Haknords here would not want their property damaged. But a cut here and there, a fleshy wound to prove you are a real man, not just a sniveling coward, or one of those Gatherers' combos. For surely it would take one of them to be any real challenge to my blade!"

He laughed mockingly, eyes daring me to take up his gloating challenge.

Don't! We can't escape that way!

"I think not...at this time," I measured my words, rather softly.

"Yes. The timorous one, of course. One almost forgets when looking into your sullen eyes. You're only half a man, doomed for the slave markets with no hope left for freedom. Beautifully muscled and well proportioned. And certainly a handsome fact that some women would might find pleasing for their pleasure toy...if you were but half-man enough to make full use of your potential physical parts. Just shows, one can't tell by outward appearances. One can look strong and brave and be a bungling fool. Or seem quite the opposite and actually be hiding a fury and murderous intent that...well, one can never tell, now, can they? And I've been warned by our Commanding Officer here on board this Haknords ship. So... politics wins out. But one day, perhaps. Given a chance we may discover the real you!"

"If you say so," was all I could choke out. We stared each other down and recognized something raw and basic.

The man continued more conversationally:

"I imagine, under other circumstances, we could enjoy a lively few moments together, crossing blades."

"As you will,"

I mused, knowing full well it was something we both desired. I knew we were destined to meet, sword to sword. Someday. Then I'd kill him!

"So. Are these Kordas annoying you?"

The man laughed nastily.

"One of them tried to, oh, mighty Lord!" I spat out.

Skurals understood exactly what I was saying. His eyes narrowed, lips compressed as he stepped threateningly forward.

"I think your manners deserve a bit of taming!"

Something in my eyes seemed to radiate pure hatred, such challenging fury that he paused.

I said: "Ah, but sire, surely you wouldn't want to strike a helpless man?"

Skurals blinked hard; then forced a laugh:

"Okay. Right. I have to admire your fortitude. Just what were you so boldly attempting to do? Annoy my little friends here?"

I, in turn, had to admire his quick wit. He was playing right into the game, knowingly and swiftly. Actually delighting in it.

"We were looking out at the ocean towards those billowing clouds that hug the water."

"Something to keep away from, if that's what you were thinking," the man noted, softly. Suddenly his attitude was more relaxed.

"I would not suggest escaping in that direction, if I were you."

Those men who were near enough to hear gasped in surprise, obviously taking his line literally.

"And how would we do that?"

I wondered, mocking controlled surprise.

"You wish my advice?" he scoffed at me with a cruel laugh.

"Then, of course, ride one of the Gatherers. Those bundled up creatures over there. Jump on one of those and simply tell it where you want to go. I'm sure they would willingly follow your verbal directions."

"Is he mad?" somebody asked from the crowd.

Skurals laughed. "Quite mad! And not a fool, either!"

The man made a dramatic movement of his arms, hand almost slashing across my face, just missing it. A skillful action, and we both fully understood the blunt meaning.

"Those dumb mechanical creatures would not respond. They are programmed to do just want I tell them to do. Our scientists have developed them. Both human and machine! A masterful little invention by the Kamina."

I asked, unable to resist: "Who are the Kamina?"

Skurals whipped around, glaring at me.

"Something you don't want to know about. Or maybe you do...but you won't find it a pleasant discovery. For they will soon be expanding their empire in ways that will serve their purpose...and certainly not yours. And we will rule all who come under their command. Conquest is their..."

He broke off, and suddenly stepped back.

"Enough of this animal chattering. Your future is locked. We will never meet blade to blade. Sad to say. For I could enjoy cutting you up for Korda meat!"

Adt, don't! Sarleni's repeated warning was consistent.

Before I could have said anything, the man turned away, and commanded: "Take them below!"

CHAPTER SEVEN

ESCAPE FROM THE MONSTERS

I was hustled with strong hands, grabbing me on both sides, crudely dragging me away. There was no reason to resist. In fact, reason advised I remain quietly submissive, even appear fearful, crushed. And I did.

The next thing I knew, we were back in the cell, chained. The door slammed shut.

"Are you okay?" Sarleni inquired, concerned.

"Furious, to be truthful! You almost got me killed out there!" I accused, glaring at her through my blurred vision. She was standing too far away to reach.

I was fuming. It didn't matter that she had also saved my head from a brutalizing blow.

All my fury surfaced, aimed directly at this helpless slavegirl.

I completely exploded.

My hands shot up in fisted rage as if to strike out directly at her.

"You weren't *closed* to me, and it was important to warn you. You know that."

"No, I don't!"

I lied. How foolish we can be under unreasonable pressure. But I was a warrior, trained to defend and do battle, not become a submissive prisoner, tossing in a green leaf of surrender.

"Come on, we survived. And we have a plan."

"We have *what*?"

She smiled, but then shrugged.

"I think you know what I mean."

I didn't want to admit *anything*.

Her face grew intense for just a moment, and then I felt that insistent probing. My mind locked into a rigid mental fist, clamped down tight.

"I told you to *stop* mind reading!"

I nearly screamed in rage. Without even thinking, my sword arm shot up, menacingly holding nothing but air. But the implied threat stunned both of us.

She glared wide-eyed, face in shock.

"No more!" I commanded.

No more probing into my mind! I thought. But then said it.

"Now just stop that. It is distracting, rude and most of all, dangerous!"

My arm slowly lowered, I was shaken.

"Sorry. Just difficult...all that up there!"

"I understand."

How could she?

"But I do. I truly do. You were wonderful! I was so proud of you!"

That stopped me. I didn't know how to respond.

It was a long time before either of us spoke.

I'm sorry, was my thought. And then I verbalized it:

"I'm sorry. We seriously need to come to terms with this whole mind thing."

She seemed to consider that for a moment, then reluctantly spoke.

"I'll not intrude on you unless it is life and death," she promised. "Or you agree to it. Is that fair enough?"

I bleakly nodded; letting that action, rather than thoughts or words, communicate my reluctant agreement. I was still shaking and not quite ready to negotiate.

"We should continue your training!" she said softly.

I glared at her. "Give me a few moments."

She turned, sat cross-legged and was silent.

We all need time to be alone. Really alone. And we hadn't had that luxury since the night of my freedom from the Dianos. In fact, I had no alone time since I could hardly remember. Events had been blasting at me relentlessly without a break. We had been tossed together in a battle for survival against all odds, against the very elements. And now, here we were, trying to find a central bonding element. Something called a Nexus, which was no more than a mind warping theory, for all I knew. Except that the nightmares were real enough. And certainly this enigma of a slavegirl called Sarleni was real enough, although baffling in every conceivable way.

But all reason aside, her bravery spoke well and we were all we had at this point in time.

Much time passed. Our captors periodically hauled us onto the top deck. There was no longer any rhythm to this. One could only wonder about the logic of it all. Whether it was day or night, fair weather or foul seemed to make no difference. Sometimes many days passed without intrusion, except for that nasty gruel they shoved at us fairly regularly. It was almost if they wanted to poison us with its rotten, moldy condition. Guards seemed uncaring, indifferent, just following orders. They would come; unlock the door, and roughly haul us up the ladder, swords drawn, or one of those Kay-guns thrust at our backs supposedly to keep us from trying to escape. To where they thought we might run, I didn't know. Yet I kept alert to any possible route. We noticed that the launches had not been in the water again during any of these walks. All the other times that we were allowed on deck, they had all been secured to their moorings.

Our captors were brutal men. I hate equating them with normal people, but they were human enough, even if somewhat slow witted. The Haknords acted like a band of pirate-like businessmen. Ocean Traders, scooping up people and animals and anything else they could auction off at open markets. Spies for hire selling their services to any who wished to pay a healthy price. They were marauders loyal to the highest bidder.

It took little imagination to discover their devious intents from minor snips and snatches of conversation we overheard.

Some of the officers clearly were of a different race, and certainly had more sophisticated minds. They appeared more calculating and more dangerous; especially Skurals, who seemed to be of a special class all his own.

Sarleni guessed that most of the crew was, possibly, very distantly related to the more primitive natives that lived up north.

They were obviously not given much education.

This kind of hierarchy was, to some extent, common, but not to this extreme. In Bel-loniea a farmhand, for example, is respected and properly trained for his trade and is not burdened by the higher education expected for royalty. The middle classes become proficient in advanced schooling according to their avocations. All must learn to read and write, and are taught a basic concept of the world in general, if only from their local, rather primitive parochial schools.

What we were seeing on this ship was a reflection of a severely callous culture similar to ancient methods where overlords kept control over ignorant commoners. The masses learned little about the world, just enough to keep them content. Feed them, give them shelter and room to breed, and most creatures were happy to serve any master. Obey and survive; or die.

The secret was to keep the crew terrified of their betters who held life and death over every living creature on board the ship. And retain that fear on land and in their homes. The ignorant are always ruled with an iron hand through fear and lies. They might even believe in the promise of future rewards beyond death. It matters not if they embrace lies or truths; all that matters is that they remain subject to their masters.

While not a common practice throughout civilized nations, it was a standard method of savage dictatorships.

This, I reasoned, could work to our advantage in dealing with the crewmembers and guards. Once armed, I didn't doubt my skill to delete their lives, one by one in open combat. They had limited skills. The trick was to engage them in a narrow area where there was no room for possible attack from behind or the side. I merely needed to arm myself. And we needed a way off the ship.

My absolute attention outside the holding cell was to memorize everything, to absorb and sort possibilities. Any escape plan must not be an impulsive act, but a thoughtful strategy. We must act without obvious warning.

So I watched and divided reasonable ideas from mad fantasy.

During all this period, Sarleni was drilling me with lessons in her mind games, which only made half-sense to me.

I continually practiced shutting my mental doors. I had learned that the body must always respond willingly to the mind. And now I was learning things about my mind that were somewhat challenging and disturbing.

Sarleni would send me messages at moments when I was unexpectedly open.

Seek surrender to the Zygo, Total union and release, freedom and capture. Join such opposites into solidarity, to shift from half to whole.

It was thought-clutter to me. If I had challenged any of it, she would have come back with: *The Master's Teachings!*

So my mind was fully occupied, in and out of the cell, night and day, in an exhaustive series of continual exercises.

Think deep; think shallow; think expansion; think contraction.

Night dreams came, but thankfully the majority slipped away upon awaking. The Master apparently considered Sarleni's lessons enough for me to handle. That was slightly encouraging.

At least captivity under these complex circumstances was not boring.

To me it seemed one could spend a life-time trying to understand some of her quoted statements such as:

Learning is narrowing possibilities while opening up to all of them in one massive willingness to accept the impossible in order to make the possible an authentic living entity within your mind.

On deck, at times, I noticed in the distance, the peaks of mountains that indicated land, or at least islands. But they were always very far away. The other alternative to endless water was fog and low hanging clouds frequently shrouding the horizons. Our course seemed to consciously avoid clouded areas, hidden from view by these opaque blankets. They were white shadowy vaults. Mysterious places that hung there like a thick feathery jungle into which one could not see. These were natural hiding places inviting me to give serious consideration to their billows as an ideal target for any escape-plan.

Our best chance of escape was to utilize one of those launches that served as fishing boats. If we could ever catch them in the water, again. They were flat platforms with a lifted pedestal in front for the control wheel. We figured out that grabbing one of these and racing for a misty cloud cover might make escape possible. How to implement our plan was another issue. Still, hope fascinated my thinking when we were back in our locked jail-room. Hope is a twin-edged sword slicing mind and spirit in a number of divisive territories differing with one another. Escape? Death? Foolishness. Smart choice? Dumb move? Where to? Escape promised, at least, the chance of survival.

I slowly formulated ideas as to what we must do, and as soon as possible.

So, we waited. I played meek and cowardly, cringing, doing exactly as told. And as a result the guards became very lax and unconcerned.

Then our chance arrived, abruptly, surprisingly.

The guards came to take us on deck for a morning stroll. They were thoroughly accustomed to our submissiveness by this time. We shuffled after them to the deck, spending time in silence; being ignored as we breathed the ocean air. Below, over the side, I noticed that the fishing launches were docked, except one, which was apparently activated. And I finalized my plans.

It was time to act.

As they ushered us back to our cell, I knew what must be done.

They impatiently goaded us to enter the room, obviously more interested in getting back to their own interests or whatever it was their meager minds enjoyed for entertainment during the long, boring hours at sea.

I did not warn Sarleni about my plan. The guards were over-confident, and several were already engaged in quibbling over some gambling game going on above deck.

I pivoted just as we were crudely shoved into the room by our captors. My maneuver startled the guard behind me so that his bag of coins scattered all over the threshold.

Even Sarleni was surprised, but responded even before I projected to her: *Escape!*

My body automatically switched to swift attack mode.

The Haknord behind me quickly reacted, and the sword in his hand flashed downwards at my head.

I ducked in close, grabbing the strangely gnarled arm, twisting downwards with such force that I not only could feel but also hear the sharp snapping of bone and the crackling rip of tearing flesh.

The creature screamed as numbed fingers released the sword.

I caught up the weapon's hilt before it reached the floor. My fingers drove the sword, leaping point first, into the poor fellow who had tried to end my life.

There was no time to worry about anything. I let the blade swing swiftly past the fallen body to challenge the next threat.

The warrior rushed at me, but came to a swift stop as I lunged, blade slicing easily through his flesh and bone. The weapon was light and the hard edge so sharp that it cut through anything that got in its way as if flying into empty space.

Now I was between Sarleni and the guards. Furious hatred shone out from their bright orange eyes. Those bird-like faces were set hard as stone. For some reason, the warriors froze after seeing the swift death I'd inflicted on their first two members.

"Out!" I screamed, waving the blade in a wildly complex pattern designed to stun them into a frenzied fit of terror. "Away!"

They stupidly stood there blocking the passage like a scattered row of dumb boulders.

I didn't want to needlessly slaughter these helpless creatures.

"Go!" I threatened them with a short thrust and another wild series of chillingly complex motions with the blade. If I'd taken one step forward my sword would have cut right through the first row of these semi-naked guards.

They looked alarmed, but stayed their ground. I had to admire that. Well, for a moment only. It seemed possible they were just too stupid to understand my threat.

"Away, or I'll make diced meat of you!" That sounded threatening enough.

"Just kill them!" the commanding, cool voice of Sarleni sounded from behind me. A delicate, soft hand tapped at my lower back, as if to shove me into the guards. "Kill them, be quick! Kill kill!"

Who did she think she was? Pushy, to say the least. And savagely blood thirsty. But reasonably logical.

And that's exactly what I planned on doing. Only problem was that bulky dead bodies could be a major hazard, blocking the small, narrow passage and thusly, our intended escape route. If I could get them to retreat even a little, past the entrance to the room beyond, we'd have a better chance of escaping. Success required speed and surprise.

I lunged forward, the sword's razor tip butchering through the semi human jungle of dumb beasts, not even waiting for them to react. It was a brutal assault against an enemy that didn't have the ability to adjust.

My fingers directed the sword into a pattern of bloody cuts, carving deep into their bowels. It was like flying through empty air, their bodies yielding as livestock to the slaughter. The sword was magnificent. I saw hands, fingers, and arms flailing through the corridor as the blade eagerly sought targets. I tried to think of the creatures as mindless, inept animals. Yet they were living, breathing, thinking beings. Life of any kind has value.

My blade was dripping in bloody gore as I swung it skillfully through this stubborn wall of flesh.

In actual fact it took only moments. They fell like weeds, indeed, and we were soon stumbling over their crumpled remains.

I noticed in my only glance at Sarleni that she was wide-eyed with surprise.

Get a weapon. A Kay-gun! I instructed.

My attack had come on so unexpectedly that the guards had no chance to use hand weapons. All they could do was react to its fury.

Our only advantage couldn't last long.

Sarleni swiftly grasped the danger and followed my lead; she grabbed a small handgun and pressed close behind me.

We advanced, as a unit, as almost one mind. I understood what, in part, was happening: she was clearly reading my surface thoughts. Though, in fact, I wasn't even thinking, merely acting. And she got all the subtle silent messages.

Sarleni responded as if she were physically linked to a part of my muscle mass.

I witnessed her credible use of the Kay-gun, exploding its pellets into the bodies of the guards who were finally backing rapidly away. They parted before us, most falling dead, weapons flying out of their hands.

I noticed that we'd fought our way on deck. And for a moment I was almost blinded by the sun. The sky was glowing against the low-lying shroud of white clouds screening the ocean. The sun burned bright and hot above the shimmering vaporous blanket on the sea.

Shrieks of surprised commands filled the air, catching my immediate attention. We continued cutting fiercely through the churning workers who had been involved in their daily routine of running the ship. By this time I didn't consider it killing so much as clearing a path through unwanted obstructions. If any one was in our way, they went down under my blade. Few had a chance to draw weapons; some managed to back off to safety. But surprise had stunned their resistance to our deadly attack. They had not expected us to attempt an escape. I suppressed the urge to flaunt my ecstatic pleasure, yet an involuntary smirk escaped my lips. We were making quite a bloody team against the pitifully unprepared crew and guards.

We shot across deck as a single unit in full battle assault, and had won the moment. And only that.

We exchanged silent instructions.

There, over there! Sarleni warned and I turned, my blade finding an oncoming body, slicing into it and then racing for another.

I saw something for her to demolish ahead of us. *There, blow a hole into that group. Make for the railing.*

This was where the launches were latched when not in the water. The space was still empty. Chances were that one of these raft-like powerboats remained in the water. I had planned on that; our escape depended on it.

An explosion blew away the men near the railing, taking part of the hull. We rushed to where the opening now was, hardly looking down.

"Hurry!" I called out, never once checking to see if she was okay. I rushed forward, blade flying at any one that attempted to stop us.

A Kay-explosion burst to my left as Sarleni doomed an attack before it reached me. A man's body exploded into a bloody mess.

I saw, out of the corner of my eye, Sarleni take careful aim at one of the huge Gatherers strapped to the back of the ship. Its head shattered into oblivion. Then she aimed as swiftly across the bow at the second Gatherer, sending another fatal explosive pellet into its body.

That was a very smart strategic play on her part. At least those mechanical creatures wouldn't recapture us.

We continued, now finally free of any opposition.

Skurals had been standing on the aft deck, stiffly, quietly watching our progress; staring intently at us, not moving. I wondered what was going on in his mind. Was it too late for him to do anything to stop us? The loss of the Gatherers made it obvious that they were out of the equation.

Not far from the ship, billowy mists spanned from horizon to horizon providing a worthy destination. We could hide there.

We reached the railing when I heard a scream of rage. I turned towards the voice.

"Kill them!" Skurals was whipping out his sword.

He then leaped from the aft deck at a furious run towards the railing, sword waving in his hand. The man covered the distance at amazing speed. He was determined to stop us, more precisely, to kill me.

I could face him down or run. There were no other alternatives.

This was hardly the time for a duel. Escape was our only chance of survival.

Without checking to see more than hazy shapes below me, I grabbed at Sarleni and thought: *jump!*

CHAPTER EIGHT

SURVIVAL

We leaped over the side of the railing, without so much as a thought as to where we'd land. Well, to be honest, I had noticed the small launch. I'm sure that somehow she sensed things, too, without visibly seeing. The woman was a confusing mix. Insightful. Intelligent. Bossy. And quick to shift from dominating to submissive roles, without so much as a split-second to let a person adjust.

We landed on the hard surface of the launch, and I reached for the controls.

"Kill them!" a voice shouted from above us. The man operating the launch turned, with knife in hand, lunged at Sarleni, who aimed and fired into his chest, pulverizing him away. With a startling vengeance she attacked his crumbled body shoving him overboard. Her Kay-gun slipped from her fingers and before she could catch it in mid-flight, it had disappeared into the ocean.

"Kill them!" the shout echoed again from the ship above us as several darts clattered down on the launch deck dangerously near to us.

I hurriedly fumbled at the control plate whose speed dials and wheel pressed flush against the launch's cool, hard, syn-metal surface.

"Push it!" Sarleni demanded.

"Don't let them get away!" another voice screamed in fury, as several explosions splattered water across our bow.

"Hurry!" she shouted, annoyingly, as if I were a mindless Torki.

Everything was happening very fast and there was no time to even think.

The wheel was uncomplicated. I pushed on it and the launch leaped forward. Just in time.

Kay-bomb pellets blasted into the water where we'd just been. By now the craft was cluttered by arrow-darts that had managed to miss their intended targets.

I directed our craft right into those billowing clouds that hugged so close to the bubbling waters. And in no time we were encased in a dim glow that revealed little beyond the launch's outer frame. We were swallowed up in white semi-gloom.

It was easy to understand why the Haknords avoided such places, for one could not guess what might be within the milky shroud. We were hidden from them, but at the same time all else was mysteriously hidden from us. Anything might bubble up out of the ocean without warning.

I made a wide arc to the right with the wheel, then after awhile shifted left to let it straighten out. Hopefully this would place us in a position that discouraged successful pursuit.

Sarleni pressed up close to me, almost touching, as if attempting to seek protection. Yet there was an invisible wall between us. Instinctively I wanted to place a protective arm around her, and draw her closer. But, strangely enough, couldn't. I was treating her like some kind of untouchable Proctoress, rather than a commoner or the slavegirl she appeared to be. It didn't even make sense, but there it was.

"Where to from here?" she asked, as if I were required to know all the right answers. She looked up into my eyes, like a little child, searching for reassurance.

"Beyond getting as much distance as possible between us and the Haknords...I haven't the least idea."

Where were her super powers, now? I didn't have the heart to ask that question.

"We'll be okay," I mumbled protectively, actually feeling extraordinarily sorry for her. Male instinct confused my determination to treat her as royal blood. I wanted to do more than extend mere verbal comfort. She seemed so normal, helpless, just a young, lovely girl. Some men might have taken advantage of the situation. I was determined to keep a proper space between us.

She actually seemed lost.

"Things will be okay," I encouraged a bit more kindly. "We'll be fine. We're free. We have choices. And that's what counts! We'll find a safe place and, in time, discover a way home."

"Oh, I'm sure of that. In time. But...right now I'm hungry, thirsty and tired."

"Finally. She's human after all."

"Why do you say that?"

"You're the mind reader. You figure it out."

She frowned for a moment, shook her head slowly from side to side, and said: "You're not transmitting!"

I was about to reply, but decided to loosely shake that one off as an admission of her limited powers to reach into my mind and strip it bare of all its secrets.

We were destined to spend far less time directing ourselves through the thick mists than we might have expected. We had no idea where we were, how far to any land mass. More importantly, what any place might provide in hopes of ultimate safe rescue. Or which direction to go.

The ocean that now surrounded us so closely was far more threatening, and far less beautiful. We could reach into the cold water itself with a sense of pleasure, and yet there was the recognition that some monstrous creature could leap out and swallow the launch in one gulp, us included. We were standing on a very small raft-like structure, skimming along this liquid surface. A storm could easily drown us. We were, in fact, hardly safe, and actually in great danger from mere natural elements.

But we were free of our captors! And that counted for a lot. I only wished we had a far safer craft to continue our travels. To where?

They will tell us, came Sarleni's thought. *We are not alone!*

I resisted any response.

"Oh, Adt," she was most annoyed, "can't you have a little faith?"

"Great help your so-called friends have been, so far!"

"How do you know they didn't arrange all this to help us?"

"Rather subtle of them, wouldn't you say?"

She smiled. And obliquely remarked: "Even the Gods only put forth opportunity, and let us choose the path!"

I had, of course, no solid parry that would hit home. A true believer believed such concepts. Blindly. I seriously questioned their logic with a thrusting mind, attempting to shred the illusive with sound reasoning.

The foggy mists threatened to consume us, as moments slipped slowly by. The sky darkened before there was any change in the cloudy blanket in which we were submerged.

It was very cold, damp and I felt alarmingly helpless. It was one thing to be on a larger craft, manned by experienced seaman. But quite another to be thrust abruptly upon the surface of this soggy world, with no seamanship experience at all. We had to find land to give us safe footing, where we could more easily survive. It would be impossible to live very long on this small craft without food or fresh water.

Time passed slowly. We continued to drift. Then suddenly Sarleni became abruptly alert.

"We aren't far from landfall!" she murmured softly. "I can feel it. Out there! Land!"

She pointed through the condensed vapors enveloping the world before us.

Without a word, I decided to head in that direction. Land, no matter how small or large, would provide solid ground, food and fresh water.

The ocean was rough, but the launch held steady through the ever-thickening mist.

Listen, just listen, a silent directive forced itself into my mind.

Scenes, vague at first, then solidifying, started to reveal indistinct coasts. I struggled with the wheel to continually skim over the churning waves, keeping our course aimed at the shoreline that was now expanding through the waning haze.

During the last moments we were practically swallowed into the wild frothy foam, crashing louder against the shore. All at once, everything cleared as the launch raced maddeningly towards the yellow sands.

I don't know what hit first, our launch smashing into the beach or the huge breaker that smothered us in one last ravenous attempt to draw our bodies back into the depths of the ocean.

Something choked my lungs, like I'd been hit in the stomach. I doubled over as the launch skid to shore, yanked back and settled down on the grainy beach.

"We made it!" Sarleni sighed with relief. And it took some moments before my ears registered that she had actually verbalized those words.

Maybe she is human, after all, I figured with a sense of delight.

"You don't have to insult me!" she complained with an edge of indignation. "We have things to do."

There she went, ordering me around like I was the underling and she some high priestess or Proctoress.

We are as powerful and high as our minds let us be! What we think, is what we are. What we believe is absolute truth.

"Stop that!" I snapped, glaring at her.

"That wasn't from me!" she shot back, very alarmed. "It was Moyi! My teacher. The Master! He's watching us. He's there to help."

Well, why doesn't he help?

There isn't much he can do other than teach. The rest is up to us.

93

Great help that is! I groused, annoyed at such limited super-human abilities from specialized cult gods from the north!

Her oration continued, but verbally, and obviously quoting some specialized text:

"We can only learn, as students. And life is the school at which our minds feast and grow. The living experience itself is a series of events, which if understood, brings great joys, great moments and glories, but most of all, bestows on us lessons that encourage unlimited growth."

She was enjoying her role of channel and teacher, and spouting lines from Ancient Text her people considered Religious Law.

"Enough." I didn't want to be lectured.

My attention was now turned to investigating our surroundings. It was a comprehensive survey.

Bleak forests tangled with thick vines and even thicker underbrush lined the slim beach. Fitalos were flying wildly above, in wide circles as if observing us. I even saw in the distance, lifting now and then through the tangle of the jungle, what looked like deeply purpled huge Jjdah trees. If true, they'd be valuable to us. The bark was known for its healthy food-substance and was easily peeled off. We could gather some of its nutritious fibers for fast energy.

This was our first impression of our surroundings.

I hoped this would be a friendly place, where we could make some intelligent plans. Up until now we'd been reacting to situations beyond our control.

My mind worked over our options while we dragged the launch up to very dry sand and stones. I found a rope in the bow and managed to loop it around a slender tree trunk and knot it tight enough to hold.

Sarleni was humming happily as she started gathering notis and tamie berries, those nuts and fruits, for our morning feast. Better than nothing, I figured. Jjdah bark could be gathered later before we left the island.

For a while I stood there on the beach, examining the terrain, wondering just how large this land might be; what it could contain. The jungle-like forest that faced the ocean was certainly both promising and foreboding. This was a dense and mysteriously unrevealing place. The distant sounds of the wind and the soft rustle of leaves feigned stealth-like animal activity, unseen. We'd have to be careful.

Damned shame she lost that Kay-gun! I muttered to myself.

I didn't do it on purpose!

I nodded, sympathetically. "I know. Still a shame. We could

94

have made good use of it in hunting, and protection against dangerous animals. My sword has its limits."

"We should make bows and arrows. Spears would help!" she
proposed, softly, almost in a hesitant whisper.

"What do you know about them?" I immediately regretted making my snide retort. I don't know why I was being so irritable with
her.

"My people hunt. I told you that. I'm considered quite proficient with the bow."

"Incredible!" I wondered just how good that might be.

"I'm very good!" she stated rather firmly. "We should make
bows and trim arrows from some of those shoots, there." She
pointed to the edge of the forest. "Lias make good arrows if they are
trimmed! And the branches of those fulis trees are firm, flexing
wood—we can fashion bows. Find some lowlife creature like a
kdula and we have the necessary gut to string the bow. Down a tial
or daoi bird for feathers for the arrows, and your sword will do its
duty for the points and…well, I'll make quivers for carrying them
on our backs."

"You're a manufacturer of weapons!" I was impressed.

She actually laughed with delight. "And don't forget spears.
You can do that. I mean, after you've helped me with the bows and
arrows."

I chuckled as we started doing exactly as she had proposed.

After gathering the required shoots and branches for the bows, I
went and found some tough ruosh rods for spears. I then discovered
a wild orni vine, which would serve as a taut string, rather than the
gut from some helpless rodent. Once stripped it would stretch
tight—and thin like a strong wire. When I returned to the beach I
saw that Sarleni already had the funis branches stripped for bows
and was rapidly trimming the lias stocks into nicely straight arrows.

"You're a weapon's machine!" I laughed, joining her.

"I'm not so helpless as you think," she proclaimed proudly.
"And don't you dare say: nobody could be that dumb!" She laughed
at her own statement. "See, I even mock myself!"

She looked beautiful in the morning sun gazing across at me full
of pride and joy. Suddenly she leapt to her feet, bouncing up to her
tiptoes, reaching high into the sky itself, deliriously happy. She
raised her arms into the air and did a delightful spin, then faced me
with a wide grin. "I do think we're going to succeed!"

It was the first time she had actually admitted any doubt that we
couldn't succeed. That said more about Sarleni than anything else
I'd noticed so far. Regardless of her convictions she had the same

reasonable doubts all of us humans do. Of course. But she could be so annoyingly confident in supernatural powers and Masters of great quotable wisdoms.

We went about the serious business of finishing the job of creating some very crude hunting weapons. With my sword I quickly slashed the two branches into crude spears that might prove useful. The bows worked well with the vine I stretched tightly into place, giving them a nice bending arch.

By then Sarleni had finished two handfuls of rough arrows. Extending one bundle to me, she said thoughtfully, "Until they're feathered they won't sing well."

Without more conversation we stood, each armed with bow and arrows and a stout spear shaft.

Sarleni hefted her gear with such easy naturalness that it was quite obvious she was very comfortable with them.

Handling such weapons was one thing, using them another. I'd have my hands full teaching her some basic tricks with these crude hunting tools.

Without words, we started towards the thickly mounted forest searching for a place to penetrate the tangled woods. I found a small thinning area over a few vine-covered dead logs and through this directed my steps, eyes continually searching for the Jjdah trees, to pick its bark. It was a great energy-giving food. And a much desired change from our present tiresome diet. It didn't take long to find the unmistakable gnarled stalk sticking up from the ground like a giant root. I pointed, she swiftly snatched a small sliver of bark, broke it in half and tossed one piece to me.

We gratefully started chewing on the tangy fibers, whose tasty, almost biting spice was satisfactorily filling. I tucked a few slivers into my pocket as I saw her do the same thing.

We continued on, and I found strength revived as the ocean breeze soothed through the trees and underbrush. I was also thinking of Sarleni. Her lessons with me had certainly been interesting, once I'd stopped resisting the whole mind thing. Not that I was buying it all. Though now I saw definite advantages to such connections.

In a hunt such silent communication would be helpful.

Yes, she said. *Ideal for a hunt and battle and other times... you'll see.*

I tried to keep from being annoyed by her casual interjections into my thinking. I clamped down, shutting off projected thoughts. I had to keep my calm in order to teach her some proficient hunting skills. At least now I'd have a chance to glow in her eyes rather than continue to be the mere student.

Yes, I convinced myself, it would be rather nice being the instructor this time around. Now we were in an area of my personal expertise. Swords, fighting, hunting, fishing, these were men's dominions. At last I'd have the fine-line edge.

We came to a meadow, cut by a wide stream. The sight of animals flocking nearby caused Sarleni to take a crouching stance, moving back, close to me. We almost collided.

Let me, she pressed anxiously, without hesitating to feed an arrow into the bowstring and then pulling it slightly back. Stepping forward she strode with a surprising agility, covering the distance to the small flock of kuian hovering near the rushing stream.

There was little to do but watch, though I was vigil for any possible dangers that might come her way.

The first arrow sprang from her bow and flew towards its intended target, but slipped sideways at the last moment. The birds soared into the air, but not before she had already whipped another arrow onto the bow and sent it flying. Again it missed.

"Korda dung!" she screeched. "We need feathers!"

She rushed toward where the birds had been, bent over and raised up, jumping in the air, her right hand was holding something. "Got it!"

As I came to her side I saw that her hand held three gleaming purple and yellow feathers.

"This," she announced proudly, "will make my arrows sling right on target." She placed the feather into her side pouch, grinning from ear to ear. "Bet you thought I was a pretty bad aim."

I needed no time to think. What impressed me most was how swiftly she reloaded the bow. She had been clutching several arrows in her right palm when shooting.

"Oh, that's just a trick I learned, fast reload!" she shrugged, "Though without feathers it is difficult to fly the arrow right where I want it to land. All I could hope for was finding loose ones on the ground. But I tried to hit a target. Better to try and half-fail than not try at all!"

"Another one of your Master quotes?" I actually chuckled at the possibility.

"No. Just a common truth! We must keep trying! Kill, kill!"

"Are you honestly that blood thirsty?" I wondered out loud.

"I'm blood hungry!" she retorted, convincingly winking at me. "Come, let's get something to fill our bellies. I just love showing off to you!"

So much for the possibility of actually teaching her how to hunt! Again, she had made a mockery of me in her lightly bossy style. Yet, strangely enough, this didn't bother me. I felt a certain amount of relief knowing she might be a very good partner in battle. In fact, so far, she had proved to be just that.

Without another word we retreated into the surrounding forest and crouched, waiting. Things settled down around the flowing water and animals began to gather there once again.

How about a mliuen, Sarleni suggested silently to me, *or a nian, or one of those qulit?*

I nodded to a group of small inane, rodent-like furry animals. *If we both shot into that group—*

She nodded and was already stretching her bow, arrow in place, aiming. *I'm ready. Are you?*

She didn't even glance my way; her attention was on the brownish mass of nians clustered together almost as one continuous carpet at the edge of the creek.

I already had an arrow stretched on my bow and aimed carefully at that large target not too far away. We were sure to hit something, even without feathered arrows.

Now! Sarleni ordered. Her arrow raced from bow to target, just ahead of mine. Both arrows vanished in the group of nians who, for a moment, didn't react. Then they scattered. Slow-witted creatures.

Success! She screamed in my mind. "We got one!"

As we approached we discovered one of the nians balled up with an arrow right in its middle. The other arrow was flat on the ground. Sarleni picked it up and shrugged. "I think this is…well, perhaps mine. You hit the winner!"

I gathered the furry ball by the arrow shaft. "How do you know that one is yours?"

"Oh, I just know those things!" she vaguely remarked, shrugging it off. "Let's return to camp! I'll roast our dinner! Not too tender, but rich in flavor. Just enough meat for the both of us. Once the bones have been ripped away and the skin nicely trimmed I can make a small pocket bag."

Was there no end to her skills?

She started heading back the way we had come. Conversationally she thought: *We have berries and bark and…we can gather more water. Oh, I forgot!*

She turned, reached into her pocket and yanked out a small leather bag. "I still have this!"

It was one of the water bags she'd made that first day we'd camped together. I was stunned with surprise. She tossed it to me, nodding towards the stream.

CHAPTER NINE

A WORMY PIT

Sarleni's style confounded me. Her silent dictate that *I* gather water, felt degrading. More like that of a mistress commanding her slave. I obeyed, but under resistant objection. I was partially impressed by her and partially annoyed.

Of course, Sarleni was one frustrating young woman.

Did it really matter? I pondered silently, joining her on our return to the beach.

Should it matter? She asked me. "I mean…what difference does it make? We're a team. And we both bring our personal skills into the partnership. I'm genuinely honored to be here with you. There are many who consider you quite important. So…let me add my few talents to our oneness."

Oneness? That was a somewhat peculiar assumption. *We are a team and a team develops oneness. We blend. We flow together into an envelope of totality. Your talents and mine make one collective universe of personally shared skills. We are stronger paired together than separate. That's all!*

I was glad that she remained silent all the way back to where we'd left the launch.

I gathered wood and then made a fire the primitive way by rubbing sticks together. Skilled or not, it was tedious, but worked.

By then, Sarleni had skinned the nians and skewered them with small-sharpened sticks. "I'm ready to roast the feast!"

The meal was satisfying; the meat tough but chewable, and we were almost content enough to relax.

It was then that she grew very serious and said: "I have something to show you. We need to examine this."

Standing, she fished into the pocket at her hip. "I saved this."

She found a large flat stone on the sand and spread a sheet of parchment out onto its broad surface. "What do these markings mean?"

I was now standing over her, intrigued. It looked like some sort of a chart. This was a detailed map.

"Where'd you get that? On the launch?"

"No. Not the launch. I got it when I was being violated on the deck by those dreadful ogres. One of them dropped it when I did my singsong, so I grabbed it up just before they were ordered to take me back to the cell."

"And I thought you'd stumbled!"

"Yes. I didn't dare reveal what I'd done. Though they were dazed with my singsong…it has limits. So I just pocketed it and… well…here it is. Impressive, isn't it?" She sounded so delighted. "This could be pretty important, don't you think?"

"Why did you wait until now to tell me?"

"I forgot! Sorry. Noticed it when I grabbed for the water bag."

We both stared at the map. It showed a large seaway with several shorelines; detailed coves, water depth markings, land heights, a number of labeled areas, none of which were familiar to either of us.

The titles appeared to be archaic names. We had both studied historical writings similar to the ones we were now seeing. But one line, in a clearly alien dialect, caught our attention: *Illysæ ad Mördi Tăli Muti.*

I asked: "Do you know what that means?"

"Something to do with the Mutis?" she wondered. That was obvious.

But a chill fed its way down my spine for no logical reason. I wanted to shake it off, yet couldn't.

We focused on the markings around this remote island isolated from the other larger landmasses. The water depths signified mostly shoals and coral reefs completely surrounding the land. That would make it impossible to access by any sizable ship, except for a few deep soundings, apparently disconnected.

Sarleni was studying a different part of the chart, trying to decipher another land marking: *Distrie diu Kasiisi.* It was probably a seaport. It looked like the hub of a wheel with lots of winding spokes of roadways oddly heading right off into the ocean in most directions. We spent considerable time taking in the implications of this find.

I had seldom thought about the lands beyond the continental dominion and territories of the Proctor of Bel-loniea or other city-states with which we traded.

All the landmasses up to the ocean had been mapped, mainly from grav-flyers. We knew where most continental civilized centers were located on our side of Noomas. The ocean had nearby islands, many of which were settled. A few explorers have gone further. The majority of our population was more focused on family and clan and nation, not distant landmasses and unknown empires or civilizations.

Those who sought distant lands had almost always failed.

The Mutis had advised that what was beyond our continental borders need not be our concern. Though we had continually expanded normal trading routes and connections with other nations like the Dianos. All was restricted to the surrounding ocean and some nearby islands, and to some limited degree, the southern territories. And we knew very little concerning places like Helandi.

This map revealed how little we knew of our world.

Out there beyond the horizon was a different, alien landscape.

We were lost.

She rolled up the scroll and tucked it safely away.

Adt, isn't it peculiar how the Mutis have always restricted such explorations?

I was dismayed to discover again, that it was Sarleni in my mind.

Oh, come on, Adt, don't be a Korda! You must remember: acceptance is all! Non-resistance can be the strongest resistance when focused. Just accept.

I started to object, but she continued, verbally: "You know, Adt, it is puzzling me, how the Mutis mandated limits of our explorations. They always used gentle persuasive tact, so convincing that most of us accepted it as logical...almost...law."

"A few expeditions have explored beyond our settled territories," I pointed out.

"And what did they bring back?"

I nodded. Mad reports. A chill twisted down my spine. My eyes met Sarleni's and for a moment it felt as if we were both thinking the same thing. "They survived, some of them...mad or not!"

She laughed a little nervously and then shrugged. "Maybe we're strong enough to avoid madness. More than we already are! Perhaps that's why we've been chosen."

"I would hope so. Especially considering your super powers! And all that!" It was a nasty crack that Sarleni chose to ignore.

She said: "Well here we are, far beyond those weird taboos. And I feel just as sane as I always was!"

I couldn't avoid a mocking grin.

"So we're crazy." She laughed. Gazing off across the horizon, she hesitated, continuing more seriously: "What is out there? Just ocean? Or places the Mutis don't want us to explore! Until now.

Haven't you sometimes wondered about them?"

"In what way? Can you be more specific?"

She cut me short with: "Why create limits? My people have explored our inner depths. The mind has no measurable limits. We learn to navigate it all in our own way. But it is an internal process at first, not external.

"And the Mutis surely have created boundaries." Her right hand slashed the air, vehemently accenting an invisible wall. "Limits! Senseless! Unless they are hiding something from *us* or hiding *from* something…and I think it may be some of both."

Those words struck my mind like a boulder smashed against a muddy cliff. "What would they be hiding? What could they be hiding us from? This? Places like this? For what reason?"

"How would I know? We don't know what this land mass is. An island or…what dangers might be here. We barely made it here."

"But we have weapons now. Crude but effective. And a campfire. And food. Isn't that something?"

"Maybe if I trim the arrows with the feathers we can do better!" She was fixated on the tolls and weapons, suddenly all business.

I watched as she artfully trimmed the feathers, and then lashed them tightly onto the firm rods with the same kind fibers I'd used for the bows. Her fingers worked amazingly fast.

"Oh," she explained, noting my silent admiration, "we all learn these skills. Don't your women in Bel-loniea do the same?"

"Mostly huntsmen and warriors in the field but not usually women. You are quite skilled."

"Yes, I am." She wasn't smug; rather more matter-of-factly ending that exchange.

She could be most infuriatingly bossy and dismissive at times.

"Oh, Adt, do something useful. I'm not bossy. I'm just practical. Doing my best. Why don't you get some water? Or some more shafts for arrows? Some berries or nuts! Just stop judging me and being so angry!"

She gathered the arrows together next to the bows. "We need a quiver for them. Find something…a Jjdah leaf might work. They are big and strong. I could bind them together with the fiber. Until then, I'll rest!"

Without another word she curled up next to the fire, closing her eyes.

Bossy, demanding, dismissive!

I needed space to clear my thoughts and anger. I snapped about face and marched away from the beach.

It was some time before I noted my surroundings. I was already into the forest, which was quite different from those at home. I hadn't been paying much attention to where I was going and felt momentarily disorientated. Then I heard the breaking of waves, turned and saw the ocean a short distance down a trail.

An amazing tangle of foliage and shrubs formed an impenetrable wall on both sides of me. Stiff vines tangled together into an impressive barrier along an evident game trail that I'd unconsciously chosen to follow.

I was still paying more attention to the anger feeding into my mind than where I stepped. Without warning, my foot slipped. Then things happened so fast I didn't have time to react. Something grabbed at my chest, tugged at my loins, dragging me into a harsh pit, stripping the sunlight away. A slashing whip crossed my face, blinding vision. Vile rotting stench and fumes stung my eyes and choked into my lungs. I almost passed out as the world spun round me. Something slithered around my ankle, coiling up the calf of my leg, wrapping; gripping tight; pulling. Whatever it was felt dry, yet, slimy; hot, cold; smothering and sucking.

Both of my hands were on a thick vine, holding on tight. I should have had my sword ready to cut away at any kind of dangerous threat. But all I could do now was to hold on tight.

A spinning sensation whirled about my vision as a powerful snake-like band tightened about me. The huge leaf on the vine snapped in my face, stingingly so, causing me to loose my grip on the vine. I was yanked downwards, deeper into the tangling, twisted abyss.

A voice screamed out. It was mine.

I was pitched into absolute darkness.

And consciousness was slipping away as my head continually bashed against slippery tough tuberous vegetation.

I struggled to gain some kind of balance. Wrenching with all my might against this horrific tendril, my arms locked tight. My fingers grappled with the vine, desperate to yank myself free.

For a moment it yielded. I was about to adjust my hold but it seized its advantage; skidding along my leg, now twisting about the other, binding them together. I tried to release my sword, but it was too late.

I felt the horror of death bearing down upon me. I was trapped with no way out, no way to get help. Sweat went dry and my throat constricted. We all face death at any given moment; and this, I was convinced, was mine. The life long waiting to face a final end had come.

Oh, Sarleni, what have I done!

I wanted her near, just one last moment, before I died. There was so much to say and share. And I'd die willingly if but to hold her close. What an unnerving concept! But I desperately wanted to be comforted in the end of my living existence. To die is one thing; but alone is dreadful, I had now discovered. The prospect had never even occurred to me before.

My thoughts cried out, for the first time seeking help from any source. Panic surged through my veins like a drowning wave of unrestrained emotion, overwhelming me. I was willing to believe anything that might avoid death.

Sarleni! I screamed.

The world was clouding over; consciousness slipped down into a weird kind of hole all its own.

Sarleni...help!

A lightning bolt slashed into my skull, erupting through the very brain cells. It burst in with an intense welling of power from outside of me.

I'm here; use me! Open up. Let me explore! How'd you get into this tangled mess?

It attacked me!

I didn't even bother thinking now. Energizing power bolted throughout my body, blazing my inner mind with brilliant awareness. I saw that twining flat belt around my leg turn white, crackle, then shrivel to lifelessness.

In the dim light below I could barely see. Within the shaft leading to the bottom of this tunnel were things slithering in and out of skulls. White bones were scattered among obvious animal remains. Some looked human. I'd fallen into a wormy pit. A trap built by some horrid underground vegetative creature. My mind and body were again on automatic; sword in hand, slashing at the remaining winding mass of leathery coils still clinging to me.

The sword cut at the struggling tentacles furiously writhing in their escape from its razor edge.

Once free, I scrambled upwards through the gnarly shaft, which twisted towards the surface light. Only then did my mind attempt to reorder events, to flash through the memory pictures of those skeleton bones in the gruesome pit below me.

With one final exertion of strength I reached the surface and then dragged myself out of the pit. I was drenched in sweat and trembling. I looked around, expecting to find Sarleni there, but I was alone.

Fury raced through me.

Without so much as an afterthought I turned, insanely slashing

104

at the already lifeless vine.

The rage lessened and I turned to get away from this horrid place.

This time, as I trampled through the jungle foliage I was keenly alert. Though I was experiencing a kind of furious sense of relief.

Oh, the male ego. I'm as helpless to that as any man. I'd survived the nightmarish animal-plant. It had almost swallowed me up alive. I was reacting emotionally, not logically; deeply shaken.

Then I reached the beach within sight of Sarleni and I felt overwhelming joy.

She was sitting up, staring intently as I approached.

"You should be more careful!" she scolded like teacher reprimanding her student.

"Careful?" I blurted, defensively.

"I thought it would kill you!"

"Kill me?" I tried to laugh that off. I was determined not to admit fear of anything. "What're you talking about?"

"Your scream of terror!"

"Terror? No! Just surprise!" I felt it was a half-truth. I rejected that word: terror. "I was surprised!"

"Well, surprise," she condescended with a shrug. "If you must. But…. And I wanted to help!"

"Thanks!" I muttered, exhausted, still shaken from the stinging attack. I wasn't being reasonable.

"You're okay. I saw to that." Her voice was angry sounding. "I did what was necessary! I don't understand why you're so hostile. You'd be dead, right now, if we hadn't connected in that pit. You'd be food for that horrid, winding creature, you'd be on your way to joining those bones down there!"

She was right.

I felt slightly dizzy, exhausted, and weak. She just kept talking.

"There was no time to get permission. I reached out and there you were…we were linked. Weak as it all was, we managed to make quite a team, now didn't we?"

I wanted to deny it all. So I brushed all that aside. I felt too exhausted to argue with her. I felt lightheaded and just sat there trying to sort things out. Then my thoughts drifted. I wasn't aware of losing consciousness. But I did. Just like that!

A gentle hand touched my shoulder. "Rest time over!"

The touch was very soft and warm, almost sensual. In fact far more than I wanted to admit. My eyes opened to see Sarleni leaning over me, a frown on her face. She stepped away.

Had she been aware of the lovely spark of pleasure that ran

through me at her touch?

"You'll be okay, now," she managed, settling back.

"What...happened?" I became alert and surprised about spacing out like that.

"I let you rest. Washed off the nasty cuts that vine caused. I think they drugged or poisoned you a little. So I just let you rest for a while."

"Grand warrior I turned out to be!" I muttered, patting my leg where it had been bruised and cut by the flesh eating plant. I wanted to thank her for saving my life, but the words choked dead. I felt like a fool. Embarrassed? No. Just angry at myself. How foolish of me to get into such a situation.

"We must make plans, Adt!" she told me. "It is getting late. Night will bring danger from that jungle and we have to avoid being in the open."

I started to ask what she was talking about, but one look at her altered attire chopped any question down to the raw bone. Her shoulders were bare. I could hardly avoid staring. Sarleni looked almost breathtakingly seductive. She had ripped away the outer garment. The torn material was used to bundle some provisions together.

"Oh, I gathered these while you were resting." She almost laughed, then announced: "We should get off the beach...for the night!"

Sarleni dashed off and there was obviously nothing else to do but follow.

We approached the launch.

"We will be safer here." She tossed the bundled food onto the deck and then turned to extend her hand towards me.

I ignored the offer. After all, I was quite able to help myself onto this little raft-like craft. I was embarrassed. I didn't know how to respond to any physical contact with her.

We huddled in the craft for a moment saying nothing.

"Well," she asked, turning to face me: "What do you think we should do?"

"I thought you had all the answers." I rebuffed rather stiffly.

"Oh. I do have a good sense of direction. But don't know everything!" she almost laughed at me, but soundlessly. The mockery was in her eyes. "A trained student will see much more. Even the Mutis respect our Visions." She was speaking so softly that I could hardly hear the words, and sometimes wasn't even sure they weren't more in my mind than in my ears, "For the night we are safe enough on this platform. At least safer than on the sand. I don't know why.

106

Whatever might threaten us would find this craft an unknown puzzle. Of course we could consider leaving now." Her arm pointed across the ocean. "I sense that is our ultimate destination. The map will lead us."

But not in the direction of Bel-loniea.

"Nor is it the direction to Helandi," she answered my unstated thought.

Once again she was reading my mind. The connection had saved my life. As long as she didn't abuse that, why bother, why argue with the obvious?

She smiled and nodded, sitting in her usual relaxed double-cross-legged position, looking out across the rolling ocean. The sky was already revealing dimly twinkling stars.

I could almost feel slight tension feed into her body, then relax as if forcefully willed to do so.

"I think it is time for rest," she stated firmly.

A shiver rushed over her and I noticed she was cold from the chilled mist that fell over us after sunset and the loss of her vest. I removed my mantle and handed it to her. Without a word she took the wrap and then curled up on the wooden flooring.

I found myself looking at her for a very long time, wondering how things might be if she were truly a slavegirl. Rather erotic ideas teased my mind.

I felt a sense of odd guilt.

Angrily I wondered why I shouldn't imagine such thoughts about Sarleni. She was sleeping! What was wrong with embracing my own private fantasy?

And slavegirls enjoyed being with a man. Even a Royal lady could inspire wild fantasy and desire. What harm? Who could know what I might imagine? Our minds were private places.

Then it struck me.

By Korda skulls! She had me boxed and cornered and helplessly naked in my very thoughts. What an invasion, a virtual rape!

I had to hold down the anger festering in me.

Presumably, I was safe, as long as I kept a conscious wall up to shield any invasion into my thoughts. The connection only happened when I opened to her. That was different.

But her ability to read my thoughts was next to mental rape!

Damned!

I could not tolerate that kind of invasion. Our minds were private territories. Sarleni was a complete stranger. I wouldn't trust my best friend, Torlo, this far into my thoughts; let alone this young slavegirl. And yet she affected me in a way no other woman had ever done before. I couldn't escape that. I felt compelled to protect her. Of course. As I would any woman!

Suddenly I felt very cold, and told myself the chilled air had caused a shiver to race through me.

Well, at least my wrap warmed Sarleni.

I'd done what any gentleman might do.

I decided to hold that thought, that mood and just settle into the job of keeping night watch.

I took the regimental stance at formal alert as required of a guarding warrior on duty. I screened my mind to all else. I was relaxed. In a vigilant state where nothing could surprise me. So I thought.

CHAPTER TEN

JU-BILEE

The night was warm, the breeze coming from behind me, the jungle resting beneath looming shadows. The sky, oh, the lovely sky of Noomas, our remarkable world with its celestial expanse of endless jewels sparkling against the darkness. When one of the three moons makes an appearance the black brightens slightly and the stars grow dim. When all three shine at night they overpower all else with their splendor, dominating the twinkling masses behind them. Even the heavenly clouds vanish. Torlo had told me about these huge Galactic gatherings of dust with thousands of suns like our own, hidden in their misty depths.

This amazing view is always breathtaking.

I scanned the heavens and monitored the beach and jungle. Sometimes I let my gaze float to Sarleni, all curled up, sleeping. She was transformed. I nearly forgot the annoyingly bossy side of her. Now she was just a lovely woman resting quietly.

I remembered home and imagined how Sarleni would love such a beautiful and wonderful place.

Bel-loniea is so different from what she had shown me of her own home in Helandi. The northern territories were a cold and rather unfriendly, secretive land in comparison to the lush vibrancies of my country.

I decided: Sarleni would surely find in Bel-loniea a warm, welcoming gathering of openly charming people and comfortable homes. Our buildings face the sun in day and the star filled sky at night. How could she feel otherwise? We are the center of a great nation. The Proctor commands a powerful army that keeps the population safe in a world that can, at times, be hostile and frightening.

The city is incredible. Streets wind and circle and some just go like wild in straight lines. Homes scattered in sections, many roofless—for people are building upwards as their families grow in number. The homes of the Royalty are clustered near the central zones, surrounded by their servant's village-like quarters. Most charming of all are the outdoor markets. Shops boast colorful blankets, clothing, pottery, jewels and food for barter. Mid-day clamor competes for attention; everyone hawking loudly in cacophonic rhythms. These open bazaars are common throughout Noomas. The marketplace is near the military quarters and the Proctor's Palace designed in a grand circle where people can wander among the colorful stalls. Many dealers gather here. Even the Raiders come, especially frequenting the slave trade. But their fine collections of foreign artistry are among the most exotic that I had ever seen.

Our famous Bel-loniean Pleasure Palaces are renowned for their richly draped halls and finely furnished private rooms. Royalty and commoners alike, mingle in magical interludes.

Trained personnel cater to guests, expertly teaching and invitingly soothing anyone seeking companionship. I enjoyed many evenings there.

On hot days, people favor the Scented Pools, a garden not far from this trading Mecca. Fountains gush upwards into the sky, spilling watery cascades into huge puddles below so children can play and cool off.

Small parks slip in among trees carpeted in lovely gardened grasses, trimmed with borders ever blooming flowers.

Shaded pathways frequented by lovers sharing quiet solitary moments together.

I wondered if I'd ever see any of it again.

I had always loved strolling the streets in the afternoon or early morning, dreaming about my future.

This all charmed my mind as I stood guard over Sarleni, the ocean waves behind me beaconing to the secret mystery of the jungled forest beyond the narrow sandy beach.

I could almost smell the scent of Bel-loniea's spice markets; hear the soft, lilting songs of the street musicians. The wind around me was humming melodies in my ears.

It was hypnotic. And startling. Nearly believable. It seemed so real.

My eyes lowered to Sarleni, wanting to make sure she was there. I needed to know that this wasn't some kind of illusion. Her slumbering silhouette was a visual hook to current reality. I half expected she wouldn't be there.

But Sarleni remained sleeping, quietly. I could make out her breathing. For the illusion was strange. I had somehow entered a space very much closer to her. I could touch her. I was breathing

110

against her flesh, her face.

I was lost in her long tresses, so black that they appeared to vanish into the night.

The illusion was very strange and deeply startling; disturbing.

I shook my head, trying to rattle such thoughts away; clear them like marbles being rushed off a Kanoa game board. I wanted to clear the table of my mind of these strange images mocking at its core.

Dizziness raced in to fill the vacated space.

I felt light-headed. The night swelled around me.

"Got you!" a strong, feminine voice taunted me.

I turned and shrank backwards from the apparition looming in the translucent moonlight.

For a moment I didn't recognize her; only knew I'd seen her. Then I remembered, with shock.

I was looking at that woman I'd seen distantly during that first hunt for meat. Before the Gatherers had taken us into captivity. I had discarded her as an illusion.

"See, I was real!"

I had not thought of her since then. Too much had happened. The phantom had been deleted along with the fantasy.

But now here she stood, just offshore, almost within reach. If I stepped off the launch I could easy grab her, make sure of her reality or lack of it.

Yes, you can do that, Adt, if you must. But I'm not what you think I am.

Another mind-racking creature! I thought, heatedly.

She challenged me with a throaty laugh that rose to a screaming bellow. The sound shattered upon my ears like thunder slamming deep inside a cavern. It pierced the very center of my mind.

"I am more dangerous than you can imagine!" the woman warned. "I have powers beyond the Mutis and beyond those of your...Sarleni! But I would never use these powers against either of you! I perceive things...others cannot!"

Something whipped through my body as it went hard, rigid. The world faded then refocused a wild vortex of shimmering light pulsing around me.

* * * * * * *

"Oh, yes, Adt, absorb it all in and enjoy it while you can. For we have methods beyond...." The woman's arms spread outwards, embracing the eternalness of the universe itself.

"We are like the endless strands of my hair, each and every

hair linking into distant places, touching, trusting, charging, crushing, if necessary. They all find and wind and curl up into their own tangle. Long and so thin that you can't see them unless they are gathered, clustered together. Like this!"

She ran her hands through that long hair, stretching the tendrils outwards, beyond the horizon itself. And her fingers merged into them. The strands were shimmering, expanding and I realized that in but a moment they would crowd around me like a groping wave of strangling tentacles.

My sword whipped out with such complex ferocity, that the eye could never follow. I was commanding its infinitely fine edge to mow down the threatening arms of golden-red hair that wanted to lace over and around and even through me!

She slowly threw her head back as her full lips roared with thunderous, soundless, deafening laughter.

Coppery shards of red hair shot to the ground in terrible battle with one another.

* * * * * * *

The dimness returned, the darkness folded in around me, then shape and sound returned.

"You see the powers are me. And I have not harmed you."

The woman stood there where she had been, arms at her side, hair cascading smoothly almost to her feet.

A peculiar smile crossed her face. Not seductive, not evil, not even challenging. She was studying me quite seriously, pensively.

"Not at all bad, all things considered, Adt! You react well. I'm proud of you!" she decreed in a deliberate tone, each word quite thoughtful, almost as if she were talking to herself. Those lips spoke each word, sharp and determined.

She continued to consider me, "You have learned much. Your powers are extraordinary. You will be needed soon. Stay vigilant. Pay attention to details presented to you."

Then a sudden shrill laugh sprang from deep in her throat. She spun in a rapid waltz-like twirl, becoming a twisting torrential tornado, arms shooting upwards. Then the image whirled away.

Like that, she was gone.

The jungle night was quiet.

The wind coaxed my body alert, fully awake, standing almost at attention in its guarded stance so close to Sarleni.

I felt dizzy for a moment, and then took a deep breath.

What an odd kind of illusion. I knew it was real enough. It had felt like a mixture of both. And that simply couldn't be.

I glanced at Sarleni again, to simply make sure she was not gone.

She was there.

I almost relaxed, but not quite.

It was then that I felt the sword in my hand; knuckles white from my rock hard grip. I glanced down, half expecting to find wispy red hairs clinging to the edge of the blade. Of course it was clean. Even in the moonlight I could see that.

Slowly, somewhat puzzled, I sheathed the sword.

It was some time before Sarleni stirred.

I wasn't even aware of her having stood until her voice said: "Time you rested. My turn."

I didn't speak; I nodded. I was afraid to speak. I didn't even look directly at her. Silently, I curled up in the exact same space she had been resting. And it was remarkably nice, feeling the warmth still there where her body had rested.

I don't think it took much time for sleep to close down my awareness. I was confused. Maybe somewhat dazed and stunned, and certainly exhausted.

Sleep came. And no dreams.

I woke, startled. The sun was bright in my eyes. I felt the launch rocking slightly.

Then remembered.

I stood. The rope that I'd tied to a nearby tree was taut. High tide, I surmised. The water was not very deep and the rocking very gentle as waves washed upon the shore, lapping the sides of the small flat craft that had brought us to this island.

Sarleni was not far away on the beach, a small fire playing near her.

She saw me and waved and I simply lifted away from the launch, splashing ankle deep into the water and in moments was on wet sand.

As I approached she was cheerfully boasting about her new find: "Hi! Have some fruit and these...Lowio eggs!" she bragged. "I got them in the trees over there from a nest."

I was amazed. "You've been busy."

And you must be rested, now." She extended a flat plate-like stone filled with the hot food. "A morning feast for a mighty warrior and his feisty slavegirl!"

"Oh." I managed a sleepy smile. "So! Stealing babies from helpless birds. How brutal can you be?"

"Isn't that what they are for?"

"Well, to be truthful, I'm impressed!"

She looked admirably proud. "Well it can be nice to serve as well as to be served. We are all here to grow and learn and become our fully developed selves, don't you think?"

Amazing.

"Not so amazing," she admitted with a shrug. "But thanks! I found the eggs when I was looking for lltorn leaves to make quivers for our arrows. I've also fixed the spears with loops to hang over our shoulders!"

Sarleni sounded so happy and proud. I managed a smile, and for some reason felt foolish.

She explained: "No big deal. As for the rest...well, a fire, a flat rock.... I washed it off a bit, heated it up and...you have a cooking plate of sorts!"

She looked delighted with herself as we started to devour our small morning meal. It would not have tasted better even if smothered in freshly ground herbs and oils.

I glance at the sand around her feet near the fire, where a large flat, thin stone lay. Obviously she'd used that to cook on.

"Yes. You're right. I did."

I realized she was responding to my thoughts.

"Please, stop that."

"I'm sorry, Adt, but it just is...like breathing. I've never met anybody like you, I mean, with whom it was so easy. I can't do that with other people. You just talk inside my head! I can't help responding."

She again smiled quite innocently as her eyes lifted to meet mine.

Sarleni sighed, looked out across the ocean. "That's a long way. I wonder...if only we had something faster!"

"We're lucky to have this launch." I felt the same pang of uncertainty.

But where were we heading?

"We've been brought together for a purpose. I think you know that."

She sounded so serious, so desperate.

I frowned, puzzled.

She moved her hand, in that directing manner of hers, said: "No, don't start getting all knotted with anger. We don't have time for foolishness."

Her hand chopped the air again. "Adt. I mean it! Now just listen."

I felt every muscle go ridged in angry retort, my mouth hung

114

open.

She started talking rapidly: "I've been sent for you and... unexpectedly was told that even though you were not ready, I had to do my best. And you are...not nice all the time. I understand that. And...and it is so...." She broke off and I saw she was breathing hard and the look in her eyes was emotionally charged, strained. She took several deep breaths. "We've been through all this before!"

I started to say something. What, I don't know. But for some reason I felt the desire to comfort her, as a man might a dear friend, a father, a daughter, or....

I didn't get to finish that reasoning. She made that jerking hand motion again and before I could speak was on her way into another run of words:

"You have to listen. This is serious. The world is threatened. I just know so little...I don't understand it all. But we're destined! All I know is what Moyi reveals. We must work together. So stop resisting. We must *learn* together. You have to start using your natural talents. I know about the Mutis difficulty with you. They are a part of it, too."

She broke off. Gasped. The air sucked into her lungs as she froze. Snapped shut, saying nothing. Almost turned to icy stone.

Her eyes were glassy, in a daze. Then she suddenly twisted with such force that I hardly could follow that swift lifting of her body.

"You!" she screamed. "Ju-bilee!"

In the distance, beyond her, on the beach, coming towards us was a woman's figure, streaming with long red hair flying behind her.

It all struck me too fast to really absorb.

Where had that woman come from? Was the land inhabited? What was she doing there?

Sarleni's voice was in my head at that very moment. *It is her! Ju-bilee!*

"What?" I muttered. Then I recognized her: this was the woman from my nightmare dream. Was I still dreaming?

I know her. I've seen her many times over the years. Ju-bilee is one of the Special People, very learned and powerful."

"What are you talking about?"

Sarleni turned. Her face was a mix of emotions, fear and amazement, horror and pride, confusion. "I don't know what she's doing here. But she's very dangerous, private and highly respected. Few have seen her like this."

The image had stopped some distance from us.

It waved, beckoning us to come to her.

I grabbed Sarleni's wrist so fast that it startled both of us. The contact was softly pleasant; causing a heady sense of surging power to blend between us, fuse us. She moved quickly as I directed towards the launch.

I thought: *We have to get out of here!*

I don't know what drove me. It wasn't even reasonable. Perhaps instinct. I was reacting on the stunned disbelief that what appeared to be a nightmarish illusion had, instead, proven to be reality. This was too much to accept.

My hand grabbed the sword from its sheath on my side.

A scream shattered the morning. Quite loud and long, like an explosion. Violent ice rammed down my spine. I half turned to face this strange woman, still standing there so far away.

Ju-bilee in all her glory.

All at once, her arms extended in our direction, like spears thrust forward in attack.

Things happened too fast to do anything but record them mentally after the fact.

The rope that held the launch was stretched tight one moment and then the next I saw it fired bright.

From the woman's extended hands a lancing white line of energy fed into the rope. The fibers turned red and parted in a puff of smoke. The rope withered and snapped. My eyes followed as it whipped at the launch, jarring it outwards, pushing the small craft deeper into the ocean.

Time froze. I wasn't even breathing.

I watched, fascinated, not moving.

Then I heard Sarleni's voice in my mind: *Don't even try.*

I realized instantly what she meant, for I had thought to run after the launch, stop it. This was our only escape from this island.

I started forward, but Sarleni resisted and I realized she was holding my arm in remarkably strong fingers. It was possible to pull away from her hold, but even as I considered doing so I watched the invisible force drive the launch rapidly across the waters.

Sarleni's thought underscored the obvious: *It's gone!*

What's happening? I wondered.

She's powerful, I told you.

I turned, looked at where woman had been, only to see that the beach was empty.

"She wants us to follow," was Sarleni's reply to my non-spoken question.

"How do you know?"

"I know, Adt. Simply that. She has centered within our strength.

116

She's not just some teacher, like Moyi. In fact, she can do things that others can't do." A shiver rushed through her. "Maybe it is natural to fear unknown power."

"What are you talking about?"

"She's here and isn't here. She's illusion and projection and reality. All at the same time."

"That's nonsense!" I bellowed, angrily.

"Quiet, Adt. No sense in screaming. Waste of energy. And we need all of that and more. Conserve. Learn. Be open. We have to move. We have a mission."

"Oh, stop it!" I growled, self righteously. She was standing so close to me now. We had both been looking down at the empty beach. The waves were continuing to break on the shore, whispering morning moans. Splashing water. In the distance we could see a hill and other shapes too far away to define details. Jungle advanced up around those peaks.

At least we were on solid ground, I rationalized, trying hard not to accept the fact we could be stuck on this island for the rest of our lives. I understood this kind of environment. Food and water were at least plentiful. We had a fighting chance of surviving.

Without speaking we started gathering basic provisions. She had bundled the arrows into two packs with fibrous twine. I shook my head, thinking, somewhat discouraged: *for what purpose?*

We have our mission! She pointed out, gathering the bags now filled with fruit and nuts.

I resisted laughing at that, fought down the bitter retort. But she sensed my reaction, said: "We aren't defeated."

"No. We can survive here, at least. Getting off this island is another matter!"

"We will find a way."

"Are you mad?" I countered, my gloomy mood lingering heavily in those words.

"I know things."

"Mind sharing them?" I retorted, angrily.

"I sense it," was her reply.

I glared at her, wondering about the confused trace of hope that mixed with my anger. She was being so evasive.

I decided to shrug it all off, to focus on practical reality; survival. Turning, I silently started down the beach in the direction the elusive Ju-bilee had been waving us to take.

It was some time before I spoke. It looked so hopeless.

"Do you really know what you're doing?" I asked, foolishly.

"No. Do you have a better plan? We have to do what is obvious.

Ju-bilee isn't a fool. She's here for a reason. I trust her. She's from another clan, but she is also one of us. Scary or not! Take my word for that. "

Sarleni sighed, and then repeated: "Do you have a better idea?"

"Help we need, but this?" I tossed my hands in the air. "We didn't have much hope before, but at least some chance off this island."

"I thought you were glad to be on solid land!"

"Sure, but if you still believe in this…mission thing…and well, see what I mean? Now what?"

"Just believe in our mission. In Moyi. In Ju-bilee! My people. Their plans for us. This I believe very strongly about. They won't let us down!"

I'm a fighter, not a believer!

To me we were lost somewhere across a strange ocean, in a strange land without any obvious way off! These were hard facts.

Or so it figured. But since meeting Sarleni things had become half real, half illusion. It might be all illusion. Maybe just an imaginary place this Sarleni had invented in her thoughts and projected into mine.

Could I believe my own convictions? Could I believe anything?

Sarleni stopped, twisted around, faced me: "If you don't want to believe me…don't. I'm following Ju-bilee's directions. You do what you must!"

With that Sarleni stomped away, without another word.

I stood there stunned, listening to the waves breaking on the shore. The wind chilled the air and the sun baked hot.

Follow me, the thought entered my mind.

Follow her, the second thought teased my reason. It was all madness. *She can't manage alone, without you!*

I hardly realized that I was now running after Sarleni, determined not to leave her in danger.

CHAPTER ELEVEN

THE DUEL

Neither of us spoke as I came up beside her.

We just continued down the beach, heading towards the distant rocks and hills, where the sands disappeared against low cliffs.

What would happen there? What was the reason for that woman, Ju-bilee, to beckon us?

On we trekked down the beach until the rocky low cliffs blocked our way.

Soon we came upon a pathway matted out of the brown sand and dirt. It wound up the side of the cliff and ended where stone stairs began; evenly spaced, beautifully fitted together, blue in color, lifting upwards all the way to the top of the cliff.

This was blatant evidence of civilization; and from the markings on the stone steps, a curiously odd one.

"See?" Sarleni whispered, "You never know what wonders will come your way!"

I didn't even respond, but simply stepped in front of her, sword now drawn, fingers holding it lightly, at instant alert.

As we mounted the first step, Sarleni gasped in surprise. "Look!"

The woman called Ju-bilee appeared at the top of the cliff, waving us forward, then she turned and stepped out of sight.

Once we reached the top of the cliff the foliage was thickly matted to the very edge of the stone steps. We found ourselves on a gardened pathway leading to a not too distant wall of stone cut by an arched opening. For a moment I saw Ju-bilee beckoning again, before she slid out of sight. She appeared both real and illusion. Maybe more of the latter.

See, she wants *us here!* Sarleni's thoughts were almost as disbelieving as my own.

Then the unexpected happened.

119

My sword reacted even before my mind actually detected the three brutes who had stepped from the arch. Without hesitation they whipped out their weapons.

They were lean, powerfully built warriors girded with the weaponry of armed guards, leather tog, boots, harness, and sword.

Sarleni shrank back for an instant. I felt a shudder sear through my mind. I'd actually sensed her instinctive response as if it were mine.

"Where are your colors?" the larger of the three demanded, studying me. "Identify or die!"

"Let him die, we'll tame the slavegirl!" the other men laughed.

One man growled: "Let him watch while we ravish her, then kill him!"

They all laughed, advancing.

The first man once again asked: "You're colors! Identify yourself or die!"

I saw they all had a purple sash in their belts. It was probably a common sign used to identify one's rank and nation. Something we obviously didn't have.

Fight or flight? My instincts kicked into my nerves, bypassing all reason. Like a cornered Traztu-beast, my reflexes darted back and forth, but only for a moment.

I instantly pushed Sarleni back with my left hand, feeling her body shift at my touch.

We must kill them. Her mind told me this in no uncertain terms. Her energy focused with mine now. And not at all frightened. I felt a gentle push of Sarleni's hand against my back; her silent urging confirmed the issue.

Yes. Go, hurry!

I didn't even bother commenting when her satisfied thought invaded my mind: *Smart.*

Why bother? I cursed to myself. It was pointless to expect her to shut up.

Right. Don't listen. Be stubborn. Be a big man warrior with a closed—

My mind shut tight, like a banging door, loud and clear. I felt her tiny fist tap my back, not a hurtful blow, just an annoyed rapping as if to say: Oh, damn!

"Just kill!" she softly insisted behind me.

The men were already almost within reach, grinning grim faces furious with a wicked delight at the chance to cut me to a mound of blood and bone.

"Outsiders aren't welcomed!" the larger man barked.

"Surrender the woman…or die!" the man next to him advised.

"We are strangers, not enemies. We wish you no harm."

"She's a slavegirl all of us can divvy up!" One of them bellowed, his eyes fairly stripping Sarleni's body. "She will top off our party! Just what we've been looking for!"

They laughed scornfully. And the one behind lifted his left arm, hand holding a wine jug. They were probably drunk, carousing.

It was obvious what they had in mind.

"Step aside, warrior. Or die!" the first man demanded for the second time. "Surrender her and maybe we'll let *you* live."

They laughed in contempt, standing there grimacing.

One said: "Maybe we should kill him first…for the sport of it. Give everybody some entertainment before the—*look at her!*"

I had already felt Sarleni's mind swell with fiery rage and knew she was holding her bow stretched tight, an arrow in place.

No! I dissuaded her. *Let me!*

My sword leaped, the first warrior's smile was sliced into a scream of raging pain. I withdrew the blade from his chest and the others looked startled by the swift death of their companion.

I sense more men…hidden. Sarleni was noted.

"Find them!" I snapped.

One of the warriors in front of me snarled: "What did he say?"

The other shook his head. Both men had their swords aimed in our direction.

They were standing there, unmoving.

I laughed, taunting them. My sword weaved only a little, back and forth, hedging on one pivotal factor. Which man it would cut next? Sarleni's gentle musical chant kept time with my blade, but it was in the background, not interfering with what I was actually doing. She was finally showing restraint when I was in combat. I knew she had relaxed tension on the bowstring.

The man to my left screamed loudly towards the hills: "Help us!"

I had hoped to avoid more killing and perhaps may have done so, except for the four more warriors, who ran towards us, swords drawn.

I felt Sarleni's tension on the bow and advised: *Don't, unless necessary.*

Without mercy I struck with a swift twist of my wrist thrusting the sword point at the nearest man. The poor fool made a desperate attempt to parry my blade, which smoothly slipped around his and then in and out of his body, instantly shifting to his companion. I just pushed the man's extended sword aside, bashing the hilt of mine into his face. As he fell backwards I slashed his chest, cutting deep through flesh and bone. He joined his two dead companions without a sound.

My blade was already facing the onrushing new combatants. Four of them: now four blades to avoid. They came at me with a swift series of cutting thrusts.

There's yet another one, Sarleni warned silently. *I'll hold him back!*

"Give me a moment!" I requested, louder than I meant. Her now familiar chant swept past me briefly and then faded.

One of the men laughed, as if I'd spoken to him. "Already begging for your life?"

"Hardly," I countered, almost conversationally. "Want to join your companions?"

"Give it up. We outnumber you."

"Hardly!" I retorted.

The men spread out in front of me, and it was obvious what was about to happen.

Without even a hint at what I planned, my blade sent its flashing wicked point past one warrior, slipping in under another's guard, then out as he fell to the ground with an agonized scream. I cut aside another's blade, swirling left to engage his companion. I lunged. The man avoided my first cut. I thrust; instantly killing him. Twisting to face the third warrior; with a cruel slash of my sword, I knocked his weapon aside, cutting a gaping wound across his neck, almost severing head from shoulders.

My blade continued moving and pushed aside the deadly threat of the remaining sword attempting to end my life in one instant attack.

I had to give the man credit; he wasn't running, even after seeing his companions so easily being killed.

Instead of ending things right there I emphatically said: "Stop!"

He was startled enough to momentarily halt his attack.

Before anybody could do anything at all, a loud voice came from behind him. A tall, very lean man came into sight.

"Let me handle this!" The voice was frigidly commanding.

The warrior facing me lunged, automatically.

Without even thinking I parried his blade to one side, letting mine slip easily into his chest. He fell forward without a sound.

This new warrior shrugged somewhat coldly as he stepped forward, his gait was like that of a powerful animal. He was a cold killing machine. Each stride broadcast complete confidence and the competent style and grace of a skilled swordsman. He would be far more challenging. Maybe even dangerous.

There is a very basic sense of timing and control, almost a dancing elegance to any highly trained artist with the blade. And there's a swagger to a hardened killer who enjoys the pleasure of engaging in the brutal art of toying with a combatant. This man's icy eyes glared at me with sadistic joy.

His style was like a lovely gliding bird winging across the heavens, revealing all I needed to know. This was a professional swordsman. My father had similar techniques, and he had taught me all he knew about in the art of swordplay. Only a confident swordsman could flow with such brazen and instinctive conceit.

Killing commonplace warriors was hardly a challenge, nor joyful. Facing a skilled artist of death was another matter.

Back away, I told Sarleni. *This is serious!*

That dangerous? Her mind asked without hesitation. *Should I send an arrow into his chest?*

No! But this is serious enough to need room, so stay back, put down the bow, and leave me space to maneuver. Just make sure nobody joins us.

Her steadfast silence was unquestionable and I felt secure that she would remain so unless something unwarranted threatened me.

The man had passed the dead warriors, a slim smile of contempt on his thin lips. He spread his empty hands wide, presenting a temptingly exposed target of his unprotected body. "Now, my friend, would you like to live or die?"

When I didn't respond he continued: "Is she worth it? Give her up. I have nothing against you. Nor am I impressed by her apparent warrior-like archer mode!"

Sarleni didn't even blink in response.

"I'll tame her, easily enough, once you're dead!"

"You will die as foolishly as your friends did!"

"They are no friends of mine; just some of my men-at-arms. Kordas without competence. No intelligence. Other than admiring your woman there."

"Is this the way you treat guests?" I questioned.

"Every situation is different! These men were harmless fools, and drunk. They'd been partying and drinking wine. I'm not so stupid. And your slavegirl will make a nice addition to my collection of such lovely toys! Come; be smart. No need to join these suckers in death! I only want the woman!"

Those eyes were pure ice. "Give her over or die!"

Oh, the disgusting snide derision in his voice, the flash of complete confidence in those eyes as they stared directly into mine. He was an officer, in the habit of giving orders that were instantly acted upon. He actually expected me to comply.

"On the other hand. Perhaps you deserve to die, too. Considering how you murdered my men here! Bungling though they may have been." He laughed in contempt. Slowly he drew his sword, lifting its point towards me. "Yes, it will be a pleasure killing you, then ravishing your woman! She will be a divine feast of pleasure! I might even keep her afterwards, if she's good to me!"

I ignored these last comments, saying nothing, merely standing there, waiting for his next shot.

I was tempted to lunge at the man's chest, just to see how swiftly he would react, which evasions he would make, what defensive mode would he take in order to avoid my blade.

It was exactly what he wanted.

And I wasn't falling into that obvious trap.

He read my inaction correctly and just stood there, waiting.

For a long moment neither of us reacted, nor spoke. I heard the melodic song of a bird, then the answering twitter of a distant winged friend. The wind murmured softly through the surrounding trees, and the sun baked down on my body.

One more corpse would fall to the ground in a short time, and this fellow believed it would be *my* dead remains.

I half smiled.

He said, with an amused smirk on his face, "A condemned man deserves to know the name of his executioner! Call me Srrila! My blade is famous for killing hundreds of braggarts like you. I promise a lovely death, neatly carved with grace and care upon the canvas of your flesh."

"Well, thank you." I made a subtle salute with of my blade, as if snatching an insect off a wall. "I do hope you are a true artist!"

"Why, of course!" he chuckled. "A man of wit!"

He took a bow and as his head lifted, his body straightened, a flash of his arm whipped upwards, blade point extended just slightly, not quite touching mine.

I didn't flinch, nor reveal any reaction at all to this trivial attack. A less skilled swordsman might have been startled into a defensive position. To me, well, it was standard stuff.

My father had taught me early on: "Always expect the unexpected. Be relaxed and ready, but don't react to the standard feints."

The man revealed surprise at my lack of response.

Point one in my favor, I mused, secretly enjoying my advantage. *At least the fool was more challenging.*

He's no fool!

124

"Quiet!" I demanded.

The man flinched. Considering that he'd said nothing, and my statement was well beyond reason, under the circumstances. No wonder he was startled.

Point two for me.

Sarleni countered: *Be careful, he's dangerous!*

Quiet! You promised!

We could tame him with a little mental smash in the gut! Let's do it!

"What?" I asked, almost turning.

That was a bad mistake.

Srrila had attacked! I felt the air. And just in time, my fingers instinctively shifted. The man's blade was so close that if I hadn't deflected his assault without thought, my body might have landed on the ground, dead.

Point One for him!

He was impressed, and for a moment neither of us budged.

Srrila spoke first: "Nice trick!"

The man was far too talkative to be smart at this game.

Might have been nice to step back and croon a laugh of contempt. I had learned to avoid these easy temptations. It could give the edge to a desperate opponent.

I remained quiet, waiting, sword relaxed and pointed towards him.

In serious duels, long silences can rattle; and it takes more than thrusts and parries to win a match. Survival lives in judging the other's intensions, thoughts and predicting their next tactic before they make it.

My mind was absorbing Srrila's bearing, the way his feet were planted, the way he balanced his sword, even how he breathed. I watched the glint of the sun sweep along its blade in his hand. But I was especially aware of his eyes, face, mouth. Anything and everything that could strip bare his thinking.

I was watching an adept dancer flashing through a series of magnificent steps, complicated actions driving his body through rapid and graceful spasms of movement. It can be an artful dance of swordsmanship, the skilled ballet of death.

I soon surmised this man merely as profoundly capable, but not a master.

Duels can be swift, even between two equally matched fighters, or a prolonged battle of wits. The temptation was to enjoy this game and dance through an endless maze of glorious patterns.

But I had to protect Sarleni. That fact made things far more serious. The duel must swiftly end. Even a clown holding a sword can kill if underestimated. And this man was a trained killer, a nasty animal who enjoyed torturing a person.

This was not the time to enjoy chancy pleasures.

I decided.

With a quick feint I drove my blade point first towards his heart.

The man snapped my sword to one side with a sharp parry followed by a curling thrust bringing the blade of his sword up and under and around my own.

He was fast, smooth and masterfully accomplished.

I shrugged his weapon away as if it were an annoying pest.

"What a wonderful challenge!" he muttered, lips tight, eyes narrowed. There was little humor in his words.

Point three for me.

"Go away," I warned in contempt. "Before you die!"

A harsh smile half formed on his face, then froze. He started to say something, and then those lips tightened.

I attacked. My sword lunged, sliced, lifted, parried around his block and then dipped again close to his chest, point slipping across the skin, creating a red line from left to right. His blade had popped into place and extended his life for a moment longer.

The frown that squeezed his eyebrows together revealed much. He hadn't expected to be cut by this particular opponent.

"Korda! Your woman will scream in agony when I take her!"

It was a desperate snare trying to throw me off balance.

I sighed and repositioned my blade. This time I decided not to go for an instant kill.

He was now attacking wildly, frantically, and quite skillfully seeking to find an opening to cut through my defenses. Even a trapped animal will fight to their last breath.

I deftly avoided his parries and let a line be drawn diagonally to the first one across his chest.

He leaped back just a fraction, obviously startled by the second blood cut.

"Die, Korda!" he wretchedly screamed, with a startling explosion of attacks, lunges, parries, slicing blows trying to reach my body and bring a deathly end to the combat.

Each pattern triggered a second and third and fourth as he desperately sought access, a place to insert his blade through empty air and into my body.

Kill him kill him kill him! Sarleni all but chanted persistently. *Kill kill!*

Srrila's desperation made him fatally destructive. I was not about to be cute and playful under such an assault. He was now frantically aware that I was more dangerous than he'd bargained for. His confidence was crumbling with each attack I so easily parried.

At this point it was necessary to pay attention to every detail, to focus every muscle and thought to countering any pattern of attack and decoding serious thrusts from mere feints.

He was displaying the savage skill of a terrified man. He was doomed; he was angry, frightened, demoralized and desperate to avoid death

Life means everything when death is imminent.

And that made him very dangerous.

He could only hope for the chance to accidentally slip past my guard. An insect flying into your face can make the difference between life and death. Anything can be a distraction in such duels. Over confidence is the most treacherous trap.

By now I wanted to finalize things, fast.

When his feverishly weaving blade faltered in a split moment of time, I flung it aside and thrust.

His mouth opened, his eyes looked almost relieved for just an instant as death wiped all life out of existence. My blade disengaged from his falling carcass.

CHAPTER TWELVE

INTO THE CAVES

I sighed, saddened by this killing. I had not known these men; I felt nothing personal concerning them; other than contempt for the actions responsible for their death. I had been forced to kill.

As I was about to turn to face Sarleni, she darted in front of me, her face glowing, eyes gleaming bright like twin stars as they looked up into mine.

"You are so agile," she admired. But there was a much deeper edge of significance in her words. "And you didn't...move. Your feet didn't move!"

I allowed my arrogance to surface: "Why, of course not! He was more skilled at the art of swagger than at mastery of the sword!"

She frowned, smiled, frowned.

After wiping off my bloody blade on one of the dead warriors, I sheathed my sword and took in our surroundings, wondering what was going to happen next.

Sarleni picked up a knife; slipped it into her belt. "The bow is for distant killing. The spear is for closer range. And the knife, for in very close. I must be prepared."

Strange how matter-of-factly she rolled out those words; almost as if quoting from a training lecture.

I warned. "And fighting with a knife isn't quite the same as sending an arrow into a man's heart."

She shrugged that off. "A nice tool to have, in case, anyway!"

And I let it pass, saying: "These men were fools." I hoped there weren't many more such men around. They had been drinking. I picked up one of their purple sashes and tucked it into my belt. Perhaps that would be enough to make me look friendly or at least identify me as a friend, rather than an enemy.

She thought for a moment, frowned again, then looked through the dead warriors' hip pouches, taking a handful of coins and pocketed them. *We might need these!*

I almost laughed. "Are we going shopping?"

She waved that annoying way of hers, as if to say, who knows? But didn't send any messages my way.

A more commanding voice in my brain interrupted our discussion: *Come...you'll be safe. Just follow me through the ruins!*

"Ju-bilee!" Sarleni cried. "We must follow her."

I cast my eyes at the arch ahead, following the flighty woman flashing quickly out of sight.

Sarleni was already hurrying towards the arch.

I wasn't expected to even *think* an objection. I didn't bother.

I hustled past her.

I lead. You follow. My mandate was final, leaving her absolutely no access to argue against my authority.

My actions said it all.

I simply bolted ahead, cautiously watching for any more threatening thugs. She padded along behind me. I could feel her presence, in a literal way, not just a "feeling" we all have when we're not alone. With Sarleni, I now felt she was an actual extension of myself.

Upon reaching the high block wall beyond the arch, we headed down a smooth stone pathway, rather rough and uneven at times, winding through crumbling ruins with forest growth around them, through them, sometimes seeming a part of them.

A tangle of odd structures and looming dark shadows broke the sunlight from above.

The pathway led up along the decaying sides of ancient buildings, then it broke into a twisted jungle massed around broken walls, half hidden in the barricade of knotted undergrowth. It continued until we reached another archway now lined with crisp hedges opening only to the sky.

Still tense and wary, I picked up my pace, anxious to leave this dreadful place far behind. Then I heard Sarleni call out. "Adt! Wait!"

I turned; annoyed about her poking around back near that second arch. She poked into the lush, thick vines. I heard her cry out in surprise. "Take a look at this."

Trudging back, my curiosity got the best of me. She'd raised a clump of heavy vines concealing an opening in the rock. A narrow slit ran between the stones and a dark, dank passage opened to a huge cavern in the hillside. It was a tight squeeze between the rough stones, and we had to crouch down to get into the dingy grotto beyond the arch.

She rushed excitedly ahead. All thoughts of Ju-bilee were abandoned. Our attention turned to what was ahead of us.

A small alcove opened up; sunlight filtered down through the steep cliffs above.

The walls were lined with intricate ornate symbols and carvings. Sarleni stopped, said: "Look at them!"

She took out her map. The inscriptions were nearly identical to several of the landmarks on it. Just as we thought. The implication was obvious: the people who had built these caves were also of the same race that originated the symbols for this map. Whoever had drawn the map had been aware of the ancient people and their civilization.

Strange chills traced down my spine. The connection implied what? Maybe nothing.

We crept through this cave to the far side, which opened to a wide grotto expanding into a fairly large courtyard surrounded by other grottos, and possibly artificial tunnels cut into the mountain. Creative artisans had decorated them with deep carvings and symbols. This was almost like a central plaza, but carved out of solid rock.

And I was reminded of what I'd been shown and told about Helandi.

Yes, Sarleni agreed, *very much like how my people have carved their homes out of ice, and in some cases into solid rock. But this has a more primitive feel about it. Cold and raw.*

I threw a grim smile towards her, considering her descriptions of Helandi depicting a frozen part of the world quite different from these tropical zones.

You know what I mean! She murmured silently into my thoughts, but there was a hard edge of nervous laugher to her statement.

No warm tapestries, or paintings or....

Right. Just rock walls!

We both stood there for some moments taking it all in. Our exchange had been an awkward reaction to this strange and unexpected sight. The sky above was crisscrossed with narrow twisting bands of thick clouds surrounded by the canyon-like walls.

Below us, on the ground, was a fire still smoldering in the center. Half eaten meat-sticks and wine skins told us this was probably where the now dead warriors had been having a private party.

Sword in hand, I surveyed the many hiding places surrounding us. Sarleni did the same with an arrow-cocked ready to shoot at anything that moved. Slowly we approached one of the shallow dens where we discovered an arsenal of weaponry, chains, manacles and other tools and devices; mostly rusted and broken, not of much use. And even further we found skeletons bones shoved into crevices. In one of these boxlike rooms we discovered a number of skeletal remains shackled to the walls. In one case there seemed to be shreds of dried flesh draped between the bones.

"Who would do that?" Sarleni gasped indignantly outraged. "It can't have been ancient, but recent...."

I nodded. This place had been used recently. This fact, plus the still glowing coals in the mid-central plaza, indicated this place had been in continual use over the years.

Again a chill ran down my back. I glanced at Sarleni and saw a tear slip from the corner of her eye. We didn't say anything, but both of us noticed the tiny frames of several skeletons still in tact, curled up against the cold stone hollows. We felt like we'd disturbed some intimate ground and without speaking, we slipped back to the central courtyard area.

My eyes searched for any sign to indicate we weren't alone. But the place seemed deserted.

I felt something surging up throughout this horrid place. It felt alive, while at the same time had no life at all. Yet the sense of something alien welled up through the air itself enfolding around us.

The dark ebb leaching through my mind was strange; with a throbbing pulse much like the whir of some mechanical device. I had never experienced anything quite like it in dream or even with Sarleni's bizarre mind exercises. It was not illusion Nor was it any common occurrence.

Then all at once the area before us faded.

* * * * * * *

A new scene emerged: a huge plain of an almost empty uneven landscape stretched out to the distant horizon. A number of scattered arches throughout suggested distant ruins peaking up above the surface rocks.

Out of the heavens, a pillar of fiery white and red appeared, belching out of a huge metal cylinder slowly descending to the ground among pillars of ruins. It roared like a screaming Korda in agonized dying pain. Finally, it settled on a distant plain, surrounded by low hills. Then in rapid motion strange things began to happen. I could hardly follow the pace. People raced out of a hole in the metal cylinder and began constructing buildings as if by magic! Expanding and growing, overlaying over the surrounding ruins everything seemed to shimmer, as if wanting to disappear into an illusive dark space within my mind. Everything looked sharp and vibrant in color, yet seemed like some kind of dream illusion.

Then it began to fade slightly and all at once I was standing in a strange street of towering buildings, cluttered by masses of people roaming around, some in strange carts that drove around on their own power. This was a modern city unlike anything I had ever known.

Something must be reading my mind, digging deep into places I seldom consciously accessed. It was the only explanation I could make for what we were experiencing. It was all illusional, almost transparent. Sarleni was standing at my side, but almost frozen. Her eyes shimmered bright, glancing around at the amazing visages that surrounded us.

What's going on? She wondered in a stunned voice. *Where are we? What is this place?*

I didn't even get a chance to respond before the uncanny display vanished and we were once again in the large cavern of ruins.

Then it faded momentarily and before me was a beach stretching out to my left and to the right was a tall cliff, surrounded by low jungle growth. A pathway was cut along the cliff, moving up to a looming castle at its top.

I couldn't make out the details through a misty fog gathering around the scene, but it was enough to embed itself on my mind for the short moment it lingered before fading.

Again we were standing in the cave.

I didn't need to ask Sarleni if she had seen the same things, I knew she had.

I feel something evil and horrid here! She announced, reaching out for me. Our fingers intermingled; each of us needed the counterbalance of human connection. The mutually shared illusion was unnerving.

Nothing human, she whispered almost audibly. *Mechanical; like a recording device of some kind.*

She was right. It felt as if something automatic, without soul, without life, had simply projected itself into our minds.

We moved closer to a small structure, which had a doorway still intact. Inside something we saw there startled both of us.

A human skeleton was strapped to the far wall, shreds of flesh still hanging from its bones. Even as we gazed, the slightest disturbance of the air brought some of the leathery flecks crumbling to dust on the ground. Touching it would cause all of it to vaporize. This one was far older than those we'd seen in the other room. We just stood there, looking, wondering.

As I turned to leave I felt a presence course through me like a wind wafting across my flesh.

Disturbing sinews coiled into the depths of my mind with savage allusions to events and concepts totally alien.

A soft, whispering voice teased at me.

This is the result of something despicably vile. We can only imagine where it came from. We don't know. Things changed drastically in our world. We were violently infested by some kind of hideous sickness that killed many who resisted, and others were simply changed into monsters. It was only a short time before all our civilization had been crippled and wiped away.

The last of us had designed ways to neutralize the sickness, but too late. We leave this record during our last years of life, existing in the ruins of what had been such a beautiful world. We had built such a lovely homeland here, our colony...was...and...then....

* * * * * *

The voice faded and then went silent. I stood there in this small room unable to make much sense of it all. Surely this was an illusion of some kind, but from where?

Even Sarleni was silent in her stunned surprise.

Without warning the verbal explosion of Ju-bilee's mind literally grabbed at us, raging: *Get out of this place. It is ancient, and dangerous.*

We both tore away from the room and back into the main chamber.

This cavern was ugly and suddenly quite vague; like looking through a thick fog. I found myself leading the way out of this dark, gloomy place engulfed in a sense of confusion.

Get out of here! Came Ju-bilee's powerful commanding words again into my mind. *This is one of many Ancient Places we have been aware of...but we don't understand their purpose! Some kind of recording device imbeds alien ethos into our thoughts. Illusions and madness follows. It reflects an advanced science. Whoever these people were, they could not have been native to Noomas.*

Her image appeared in front of us, pointing behind her. "Come, this way, out...!" she spoke before vanishing, again.

We followed her instructions without even a comment, right into a narrow passage. When we were outside, on the pathway we'd deserted, neither of us said much. We were caught in deep confusion, even lingering depression over those hideous relics in the

133

caves. I wanted to ask Ju-bilee what else she might know about such places, but instinctively knew it would be a waste of time. I didn't trust the woman, regardless of what Sarleni said about her. Yet we followed like little children rushing after an impatient parent.

Ju-bilee would frequently glance over her shoulder as if to confirm we were still within sight. I doubted she needed to do so. I knew she could sense us behind her. Besides, neither Sarleni nor I were inclined to do any more exploring around these ruins. Ju-bilee had sufficiently convinced us to move forward. We'd seen enough in those ruins to feel something truly evil was brewing on Noomas.

A couple of times she disappeared. Other times she'd be standing, gazing back at us, wave, turn and then vanish. It was difficult to tell if she was flesh or some kind of lucid hallucination. In fact everything that had happened since we'd come in contact with Ju-bilee was almost dreamlike.

She's genuine, Sarleni assured me. *And so is all of this...it is happening. And I agree. It feels so strange...But Ju-bilee in on our side!*

The woman clearly sensed my hesitation, for she sent me a direct message:

Adt, trust me. I would never harm you. In Kasiisi you'll be accepted as just another visitor...you have the colors. Play tourist...this is where you'll find your way off this island. You have a mission to complete! That's vital. You've been chosen for very sound reasons. No time to explain. Just do as I say! Trust me.

Her mysterious messages were a bit calming but nothing more. As to trusting Ju-bilee, that was another matter.

I asked Sarleni: "Did you hear that?"

"What?" she looked puzzled.

"Ju-bilee?" Then I opened my mind to project the woman's message.

Sarleni responded emphatically: *She doesn't lie!*

The ruins alluded to a time when there had been a town or settlement on this island very long ago.

But somehow over the years they must have become some kind of torture chamber. What kind of history could they tell? Where was this alien civilization now?

Strange soft moans muttered through the trees and crippled buildings of the dead still lingering around the pathway we were following. Hollow sad whispers surrounded us, suggesting more than wind vexing stone. It all befit the uncertain substance of the woman called Ju-bilee.

I told you, she's real enough!

Silent communication also suited our surroundings.

Ju-bilee says there are many islands with ruins. But not on our side of Noomas. The map I found is....

My mind slammed tight. I don't know why. But angry fury raged through me. I stopped and Sarleni pressed into my back, moved away, then I felt the rapping of a small fist knocking gently on my shoulder.

Knock, knock. Let me in, she was insisting.

I muffled a small amused laugh, which actually came from nowhere.

...and let me in! Oh, there you are! Now, Adt, stop doing that. This is serious.

I winced, but remained open to her.

Ju-bilee considers the chart important for it covers areas we know nothing about.

We came to a sudden turn. She now stood there before us, in front of a wide expanse of ocean.

"Come this way," the woman audibly guided. "You'll find what you need down there!"

She turned towards the edge and slowly descended.

Follow her! Sarleni urged.

I felt frustration being bossed by both women.

I simply continued on, saying nothing.

Stop being a child! She chided me.

"I'm not!" But I was.

Well, then be an overbearing warrior who won't take intelligent guidance—

I didn't consciously shut the door on her thoughts. But it slammed shut.

"That won't do you any good!" Sarleni was brashly biting her words. "You can't shut down your ears!"

I was foolishly blocking her, for she was a pool of information.

We stepped to the edge of the cliff and looked down.

Below us was a huge bay with a wide sandy beach spread out between the sea and a large, modern settlement built right up to and into the cliffs. People were milling along the streets and in and out of buildings. We were stunned.

A series of docks stretched out into the water, and moored a number of ships of different sizes.

For a moment standing there in front of us was Ju-bilee. "That is Kasiisi. You'll find what you need."

"What?" I desperately wanted more information.

But her image faltered and before disappearing she said: "Always beware and all will be safe! Below is a connection to the future. Death and survival exist like two lovers embracing arms, intertwining. This is where you begin your true journey together."

We both stood there, now looking down at the seaport below.

I wondered what Ju-bilee meant.

CHAPTER THIRTEEN

KASIISI

Sarleni filled me in on what she knew about Ju-bilee: *We think she can only warn us when danger is near. Sometimes she says that she only has impressions from future variables. It is like looking at one's reflection in a pool of water that has been distorted by cross-waves. Details are lost. Only shadows are softly played against one another. All are distorted shadings looming across multiple patterns. Just enough to give warning of pending dangers. Not everything is revealed.*

She shifted to oral communication.

"Adt, I sense jeopardy down there, too. There is something about the very texture of it, a gloomy mixed mood, even in this friendly atmosphere."

"A city is a city. Nothing we can't handle."

"Maybe."

"I understand civilization!"

"This is different from the places. I feel it. I don't have the sensitivity Ju-bilee has. But I'm not blind. And the city...."

"Yes, the Haknords were heading for Kasiisi. The slave market. They were going to dump us here. Down there we now have at least a better chance than we did with them or even on that launch Ju-bilee lost for us."

"See, she isn't all bad!" Sarleni laughed, lightly.

Despite my lingering annoyance at Sarleni's twisted logic, I was beginning to feel hope. And though I found it difficult to accept what she had said about Ju-bilee's motives, I understood how critically important the woman's information could be. We all have premonitions about the future, mostly based on wishing or dreaming. But some people can turn possibilities into good guesses. The Mutis are certainly skilled in such visions. And apparently Ju-bilee was highly gifted, too.

A heavy mood held us in a stranglehold for a long time, then Sarleni broke the silence: "Isn't it beautiful! We were destined to be here. I swear that must be so."

My eyes searched the cove, studying a number of ships anchored there. A few were quite large, some distance from the harbor, and only a couple of them reached the size of the Haknord vessel.

"There are so many of them," Sarleni observed, pointing to the nearer, docked ships. "If we had one of those smaller ones...we could get safely away!"

I almost laughed. "You're ignoring all the people down there! Do you think they'll give us a gift?"

"Well, I suppose, we could borrow one!"

"How generous their owners must be!" A tinge of humor colored my words.

"Then we'll just have to steal one! That's final! With one of those we can continue our mission."

This time I laughed out loud, "A wild mad thought!"

She was right, of course! We could get off the island and start taking control of our destiny. Up to now we'd been pretty much shoved helplessly along, first the storm, then captured, escape and now this. We had been reacting, rather than initiating anything on our own.

"We're going to get a ship!" Sarleni insisted enthusiastically. "I know it."

"Okay, okay!" I reluctantly conceded with complacent surrender. "So it's an idea! Better than no plan at all. But stealing a ship is no small thing; it'll take more than pure luck. Your Ju-bilee is a mistress of wild notions. Maybe she'll come up with some workable ideas. We could use her rope burning act and any other tricks she may have up her sleeve. What do you think?"

"I don't know what she'll do. Nobody does. She's powerful; yes...a true force in our world. Don't be so flippant about her ways. She may never be understood. And nobody has authority over her. Her purposes are not controlled. I'm amazed at her appearance here and now. So it is *extremely* significant that she has chosen to guide us."

"But now we're on our own. Right?"

"Perhaps. On the surface...yes...so it appears. You can think whatever you like. The learning process demands expansion of on our ability to resolve problems on our own. Without outside help.

"Still, it is important to remain open to her at all times." Sarleni looked seriously up at me, almost frowning. "Even if you think you are alone, you must always be willing to connect to superior powers."

That sounded suspiciously like some grand Moyi motto.

"Yes, he teaches the way," she stated, defiantly.

"Words won't get us what we need!" I argued. "No matter how full they get with over-bloated wisdom."

"You're contempt is…distressing!" she snapped back. But there was a gentle hint of humor to her statement.

"Advice is useless, when quick mobilization is required."

"You are the action and the weapon, and I am destined to focus and channel the joint power of our Nexus," she continued to expound somewhat flippantly, paused, then impulsively added: "And when it manifests itself we will destroy all opposition to its potency!"

Bloodthirsty lady! I thought.

Your sword draws the blood, not mine! She refuted reasonably with just a touch of irony, since she had no sword.

I decided to avoid further debate: "Down there are civilized people, a port, a place to begin. We'll explore the city. See what is sensibly available. Then we'll make plans."

Logical actions are something I can positively work with.

After our little experience in the cave we needed a breather. We needed time to sort things out, but most of all to just have a momentary rest from these constant on-rushing events.

Lovely idea! Sarleni mused softly, almost like a gentle whisper. *Play tourist!* She giggled mischievously.

"And I have these…." Sarleni rattled the bag of coins taken from the dead warriors. "I think maybe we can find some decent food. And who knows what else. They'll have a bazaar down there near that slave market."

Regardless of our banter, I knew Sarleni was right about everything. Getting one of those boats would be our best chance of escape from the island. How we'd manage to pull it off was another matter that needed careful planning.

Silence followed as we both took in the spectacular view.

To our right the water reached out to the horizon. The liquid world blended into sky itself. The ocean breeze blew its salty air around us, whipping Sarleni's long black hair in rippling waves behind her.

Another long stone path cut down along the side of the cliff. We would have to be careful navigating this steep, uneven climb down into the city. Kasiisi spread out below us much larger than I had imagined. It was not some commonplace seaside fishing community, but a more complex municipality where people obviously came for trade and recreation. It had the signs of a popular vacation resort supporting a larger community. This was a well-developed township with a rich central hub surrounded by a starburst of busy streets. I detected the familiar gleaming dome of what looked like a Pleasure Palace.

Sarleni spontaneously burst out: "Always something for the men!"

"What?"

She pointed to the dome. "And something for the women, too, I might add."

She'd picked up on my thoughts. I lightly teased: "You're shocking me!"

"Well, those establishments are, after all, where men *and* women gather for unlimited enjoyment of life." She turned, leaned close to me, and teased in a mocked shy whisper: "So they say in polite society."

I was amused. "How delicately you put it."

"Why, Adt, I do believe you're blushing!"

"No, I'm not!"

"Well, in your thoughts you are! How cute. I don't mind. After all, you men do find us women something to brag about and to barter over and lavish with generous gifts to and…well, I'm not an innocent virginal maiden." Then winking, she nudged me, saying: "How do you think we learn ways to cow our lovers?" With anybody else I would have enjoyed bantering every line she had tossed me. But I was uncertain just how far to play into that kind of game. Thankfully, she stopped. I saw several facilities that appeared to be beach resorts, where families might go for vacations. The stairs came to a stop where they entered a main roadway leading towards the central district.

On our way down I'd continued studying the smaller boats docked in the cove. They were probably privately owned. Flat barges ferried among the larger ships anchored further out; probably supply vessels. I searched but had not spotted the Haknord's slaver among them.

By the time we reached the bottom of the stairway I was sufficiently satisfied with my surveillance. With the purple sash as my code of affiliation with some sort of brigade I decided to move boldly into the general crowds, as if we belonged.

People bustled along, quite busy with their own affairs. The variety of races and garments made it clear that Kasiisi was a town popular with tourists from many diverse lands. Yet in Bel-loniea we had never heard of this place.

Everybody ignored us, or, rather, accepted us as fellow vacationers. This was in stark contrast to the lethal greetings the now dead warriors had presented. That encounter didn't make much sense considering what we were now seeing.

This was a highly friendly resort where people felt safe to visit and enjoy themselves. Plus this town seemed a very lively port where international trade was a major attraction.

Why the hostilities we'd encountered with those drunken warriors?

Sarleni picked up my thoughts with an odd reply: *Maybe it was all an illusion!*

"You have to be kidding!"

She hesitated and then turned to look seriously at me: *You saw what Ju-bilee could do. The dream she created in your mind when you were on guard. Maybe the warriors never existed.*

"Illusion…I doubt that!" I glanced down at the sash in my belt. "Then where did that come from?"

She nodded, thoughtfully. "And the coins I took. I suppose you're right!"

Maybe we'll find some answers here in this town.

Sarleni declared: *Yes. This is where it all starts.*

I crushed my snide rebuke, but not soon enough. Her next thoughts revealed she had sensed my reaction.

It's true, Adt. We've been directed here. We were brought to this place. The storm and then the Haknords who wanted to bring us here. Even in escaping we came here. What other evidence do you need? Surely we've been guided by Moyi and by Ju-bilee.

I decided to ignore her skewed logic and pay attention to what was taking place around us.

Thick throngs of various peoples now crowded the passage as we approached the central districts. We soon began to observe subtle distinctions between travelers and locals from their attire, which seemed almost universal. Locals wore smocked tunics and various leggings generally worn by laborers denoting their many crafts in the shops and market place. Most travelers were on foot. Capes and cloaks and head wrappings defined the clans and villages from which they came; some bringing livestock and carts filled with their wares of the day. I quickly noted a blunt distinction of class. Tailored cuts obviously showed a pride in status. Even the shopkeepers displayed surprisingly intricate needlework on their collars and sleeves and any other portions that were not hidden beneath their apron coverings. The clothing defined the trade and station in life.

Yet it was all alien from the Noomas that was part of my culture. The implication was that we were very far away from home. How far, we still had no way of knowing. The night sky had given some hints that we'd been moving away from our homelands, for the arrangements of the stars was curiously offset.

It seemed possible to me that we could get some direction from the people here, maybe maps, or information from the local authorities. Surely they would have basic knowledge as to where this island was located in reference to other known landmasses.

I continued to lead the way through the curving street towards the city center.

The shops were cluttering both sides of the roadway, colorful places, much like those in some areas of Bel-loniea. Though, in this case, the focus was more on cheap, colorful trinkets. A large placard listed *Events, Taverns, Inns, Eateries, the Slave Market,* and at the bottom was, in ornate script, a small arrow with a final listing: *Kasiisi House of the World.*

"An authentic tourist attraction!" Sarleni nodded knowingly with a twinkle in her eyes. "I think we have a lot to see...quite an impressive street! What a mix of people and shops."

Families happily juggled colorful packages and tour guides with lively children tagging along under foot. Now and then we saw warriors and even some sailors like those who had been on the Haknord's vessel. The diversity was puzzling. A mixed crowding of tourists intermingling with brute warriors and traders, pirates and slavers. But one peculiar thing stood out as oddly different. We noticed no slavegirls wandering alone along the streets. The slavegirls seemed to always be escorted by at least a man, or a family.

Sarleni picked up on this and promptly fell right close behind me, as a dutiful servant, or slave-mistress, in mimicry of those around us. *Slavegirls don't seem to be the same here! Not unescorted!*

We walked along the cluttered street, not quite side by side, for Sarleni remained a step behind, as a proper slavegirl might do with a warrior companion. This complied with what we saw around us.

The streets displayed buildings one or two stories high, with colorfully draped awnings and terraced racks filled with products of all kinds for the purchase. Outdoor cafes were at every corner and the aroma of scented foods and warm drinks continued to invite us to stop.

I didn't know exactly what I was looking for, but in a short time we found it quite difficult to avoid the savory fragrances tempting our senses.

Finally I gave it up, glanced at Sarleni, who was smiling hungrily.

"Yes, let's stop here!" She sounded full of expectation, shaking her bag of coins and pleading with her eyes.

The corner cafe was small, and we found a nice table near the entrance. Across the street was a small tourist shop mainly catering to a female clientele.

We watched the people milling past us, Then food was automatically brought to our table without being ordered; it seemed to be the only meal they served. The plates were half filled with grilled Korda, sliced razor thin and smothered in rich brown Kianl sauce, a very spicy and pleasant seasoning. Yellow starchy roots steamed in this same sauce and lightly fried leafy orange vegetables looked pleasant enough, though were foreign to me.

I couldn't place the pungent fruit drink in tall, slender green glasses.

Sarleni murmured: "A jila."

"What?"

"Juice of the jila plant." *Oh, we aren't that isolated up north. We get exposed to a lot of your special...oh, you don't know about the jila. I forgot.*

I grumbled with my mouth full: "What are you talking about?"

We get some trade from the mid-territories. Between your lands and the primitives, as you call them. They do more trading in a number of places...that's how we know they even exist.

The meal was delicious and we hungrily gobbled it down like starved prisoners of war.

When we'd finished the server came to take our plates and I asked: "Where's the Slave Market?"

"You selling or buying?" he demanded, gruffly, glancing at Sarleni.

I must have looked startled, he laughed, saying: "Most people going there are selling or buying. I see your woman here carries weapons. Is she a companion or your private property? Servant or slavegirl? Are you buying a partner for her or selling her?" He was eyeing Sarleni as if he himself wanted to buy and devour her. His next words proved that to be the fact.

"She's lovely. Looks intelligent. Any man would want her! Now wouldn't they?"

"What business is it of yours?" I answered, quite annoyed.

"I was just interested. We could make good use of someone like her. Be an attraction. Is she trained? Outside of pleasing her master?"

I got the coarse meaning of his words and didn't like it. In fact,

143

his whole attitude was so mixed and twisted that it didn't make much sense. But the tone and implications were crudely insulting.

"She hunts and is capable enough with the bow, if that's what you mean!" I reported in a voice meant to sound threatening, yet keeping my cool. "She kills on command!"

"Well, if you want to sell her, I'll make a generous bargain. Save you the trouble of the slave-marketers robbing you!" He sounded impressed as if my comments had been a sales pitch, rather than a warning threat. "I could use her around here. Be quite an asset. We always profit from smart, sexy ladies like this...an attraction, you know. I would imagine she's quite pleasing in a...personal way." He winked and grinned, his eyes feasting on her like a wanton lover.

"She's not for sale, for one thing. And she doesn't please her master...."

"What he means," Sarleni quickly inserted, "I please...him, but by choice, of course."

The man glared severely at Sarleni, furious. He glanced at me. "You *let* her speak that way? A slavegirl, companion or woman! I can't believe it!"

I leaned way back in my chair stretching my arms wide, now taking up the mood Sarleni had initiated.

"Believe me, she's worth it." I winked as if sharing some kind of perverse, man-to-man secret with him.

"And," Sarleni snickered with wicked humor, "I'm a very cooperative...slavegirl. My master here is quite a man! Very few could match him. I'm honored to be his personal, worshipping slave. I don't think you'd be much of a substitute for him!" She shrugged that off, smiling coldly up into the man's shocked eyes.

I gloated: "She's some special, admiring woman, now isn't she? And quite outspoken, I might add!"

The man glared first at me, then Sarleni. He looked genuinely shocked.

"Slavegirls only speak when directed to!" the man muttered, stepping away.

Did I do something wrong? Sarleni joked in my mind.

Her humor touched me. But a more important element was obvious. *Apparently they have a strange idea concerning slavegirls.*

She nodded. *I think they believe we're supposed to be pleasure mates.*

Well, you're far from that, believe me!

Is that a compliment? She countered, a gleam sparking the corner of her eye. *Or an insult?*

144

Strangely enough I didn't have an answer to that. Not an honest one.

She merely smiled, flirtatiously.

I don't compliment or insult! I declared firmly.

She looked away, across the street.

I think maybe we should leave, don't you?

I considered that, glanced at where our server had vanished into the shop. *Give me some of those…things you stole!*

Her eyes lowering submissively. Then I felt the tokens in my hand. "That should be enough."

I walked into the shop finding the man who had insulted Sarleni so savagely. "How much?"

He glared at me. "Why do you put up with that from a paltry slavegirl?"

"How much?" I ignored his question, slamming the coins on the counter in front of him. The man had wanted to buy Sarleni as a pleasuring slavegirl. I felt the fury raging up.

"Let me see what you have there!" He looked, started to gather up all of coins. "That should be enough."

My hands snapped over his. "How much?"

I felt him struggle to be free of me, and the alarmed expression on his face said it all. I squeezed down a little harder.

"Maybe you wish to make this one on the house!" I charged, with a civil sneer edging on threat. "To redeem your insult!"

"What insult?" he whined, in obvious pain.

I persistently squeezed down harder.

"You Korda!" he groaned in pain. "Okay. Get out of my shop! You thief!"

"Stealing from you would be laughable!" I scoffed, and smugly turned, leaving the coins on the counter behind me. A thief, I wasn't. But I enjoyed the pleasure of making my point with the Korda slime! How dare he think of Sarleni as a cheap gutter slavegirl to be bought as a toy to fondle and caress and mate with in the dead of night! He was lucky I hadn't killed him.

145

CHAPTER FOURTEEN

THE SLAVE MARKET

I returned to our table, but Sarleni was already making her way across the street to the clothing shop.

I dashed after her, charging loudly for all to hear: "Woman, back!" sounding convincing enough to make my point. If somebody thought her action had been too brazen for a slavegirl, my reaction would certainly compensate.

Sarleni was swift at coming to a stop and looking demure.

I don't like being this kind of slavegirl! She looked down at the ground, dejectedly. "I am sorry, master! I just found it…so lovely. I wanted to see. Forgive me. Please. I beg you!"

Don't over do it, I chastised her in jest, controlling the urge to smile as I glanced around me. I shrugged, as if to appear a foolish but caring master of an outspoken, brazen slave. "She is new with me!" Then I gruffly lectured: "Ask permission. Politely!"

"Please, oh master!" Sarleni silently laughed at me: *Now don't you over do the masterly role*

"You wanted to shop? Is that it?" I spoke casually for any audience within earshot.

"Oh, yes…master!" she almost hissed too softly to go past my own ears.

As we came up to the shopkeeper I explained awkwardly: "We are…new here.…"

"Visiting? On vacation?" The woman smiled warmly at us.

I fumbled for words: "We just arrived in town. She wants to look."

"Looking costs nothing! Where're you from?" she asked conversationally.

I motioned clumsily in the direction in which we had been heading.

Sarleni informed her: "He has brought me to Kasiisi as a gift."

What are you saying?

Quiet, I know what I'm doing! I can read some of her thoughts. Weird. Fuzzy. But true. It sometimes happens.

The woman nodded. "You are a lucky woman. Many warriors are nasty creatures, drinking and fighting. Even killing. Many will steal lovely women at sword point from helpless masters. They are Kordas freshly off-duty, partying and seeking pretty toys to play with. These crude beasts favor the cheap taverns, cheap girls, and drinking themselves into a stupor…

"The friendly tourists and respectful, family people who come to our spas and entertainment centers are more like your master, here. I can see he is generous."

"He is *very* generous," Sarleni quickly affirmed. "And I obey his slightest command, directly!"

"Indeed!" the woman exclaimed knowingly. "I was a slavegirl once, too. And…I was lucky."

"Oh?" Sarleni asked, picking up a nicely folded scarf.

"Yes, he owns this shop and has made me a partner."

"Is that usual here?"

"Sometimes. Isn't it the same all over?"

"Different situations require different solutions."

"Ah, you read the *Words of the Eemel*! You are truly lucky."

"Every word…before I was his," she admitted lightly.

"Oh, you come from an educated family, then?"

"I did. I suppose."

"Very strange. The Eemel normally don't allow consorting, unless…well...never mind." The woman frowned, then shrugged. "But then, like you said, different situations let different rules be set into motion. And this is a place of free exchange."

"My people are from the southern islands. We have more freedom there."

"Yes, I've heard. I was wondering. Were you taken recently?"

"Very much so!" Sarleni softened her voice. "At sea. But it is a boring story. I am learning the proper ways of a slavegirl to her loving master."

"Yes, I noticed you coming across that street toward my store without permission."

"He is a kindly man," Sarleni conceded. She leaned closer and raised a gentle hand to stroke my cheek. It was a very intimate touch. She hesitated as if awaiting permission. I tried to look permissive.

At her touch I felt a startlingly unexpected rush of pleasure. A very un-gentlemanly desire was rising in me from that momentary

147

contact.

What are you doing?

Oh, are you bothered? Her quick retort was so innocent sounding: *Sorry. But we do have to look convincing.*

Just don't...overplay it!

I promise! I know what I'm doing.

I stood watching in amazement.

"He's a gentle, lovely man, I can assure you. Very special."

The woman said: "I know exactly what you mean! A caring lover, right?"

"Oh, so right. I was very lucky." Again she brushed my cheek, and ran her fingers down my arm. *Have to make it look sincere,* she continued a bit too playfully. "And he's very strong! As you can see!"

"Yes, he does look very hard and lean. Any woman would delight in knowing his touches, I'm sure!"

"And a wonderful fighter with the sword. No man can stand up against him."

"Don't brag, it could get you both in trouble. There are many warriors around who duel at the drop of an insult. It can be dangerous. Many women have been taken away by force."

"Nothing he couldn't handle. I promise you. He's very strong! And very dangerous to anybody who challenges him!"

What are you doing? I demanded, most uncomfortably as her fingers possessively squeezed my arm.

Only what's necessary! Sarleni assured me, while at the same time saying: "How much is the scarf?"

The woman raised an eyebrow: "Two."

Sarleni glancing at me, asked: "Can I?"

"Help yourself," I encouraged her, as was obviously expected. My voice was raw, husky. Her touch had sparked something very basic.

Sarleni took coins from her pouch and asked: "Is that enough?"

The woman's eyes widened. "More than enough. Here, pick another. I wouldn't want to rob your master."

Sarleni said: "No, one is enough, thanks."

I asked the woman, "Where is the slave market?"

Sarleni added: "My master wishes to see what is available. He is rich and likes to have many servants and slavegirls. I'm delighted and greatly honored to be one of them!"

Even I was impressed.

"Down to the center of the city, near the docks, actually. Be careful, warrior. Skilled or not, it can be dangerous if some bold drunk challenges you. Many dangerous people there if you aren't watchful!"

"I appreciate the warning," I said, hoping to sound casual about it. "We came across some warriors up there…"

She glanced in the direction I pointed, up on the cliff. "Oh, in the ruins? Yes. There's a new military base at the northern end of the island and they carouse around in the ruins…drinking and fighting and bringing women to satisfy their needs. Up there…it is…best avoided. It is a lawless territory where nothing is valued but raw power. No policing; no rules. Many people are killed and forgotten. You are lucky to have survived."

"Do the authorities know what's going on?"

"They basically turn a blind eye, but they are aware of the problem. In some ways, it keeps most trouble out of the town. Down here there are serious rules to protect families and paying customers. It is good business to not bother customers, as long as they stay out of dangerous places. This is an open city. You should know that. You must surely be foreigners."

"We are. Just drifting."

"Dangerous drifting. Best to know what you want and get on with it."

I considered what she was really wanting to know and decided on few words. "I think my blade will defeat any dangerous threats."

"You're probably right, here in town. But I strongly advise you to be alert. Our community is a bit wild beyond the tourist spas, less policed. Only the digs get thorough protection. But those are special projects."

I wanted to ask for more details about that last part, but Sarleni instantly sent me a warning: *Don't. Best to act like we know. She's talking about the ruins…archeological studies.*

The woman went on with: "Like I said, it can be dangerous up there. Be cautious."

"I will."

Sarleni broke in: "My master also wishes a place to stay for the night. Any recommendations?"

"You'll find some nice ones closer to the open bazaar. Those are inexpensive Inns. Go there, unless you can afford one of the tourist spas."

We both started down the street in the direction the woman had indicated.

Before I could ask, Sarleni was already sharing her thoughts: *I couldn't read much, just surface hints. There's something mysterious going on here. That military base she mentioned…I felt her fear* rise when she brought it up. Her warnings were cryptic, filled with far more emotion than the words implied. She is frightened. But I couldn't know why. That Eemel quote came out of nowhere. The "Words of Eemel" are important religious philosophies. She believed I should know all about it. No explanation.

It was impossible not to be impressed. How many other things had she picked up on since we'd met?

Not as much as you think, Adt. The more we accept the Zygo the more we discover. What Moyi teaches is very, very important. Once we've blended—okay, I'll shut up!

Since I'd been actually interested in what she was saying this time, her shut down was a surprise.

She merely smiled up at me, and then glanced at our surroundings. "We should find a place to spend the night."

"Why, of course!" I agreed, forcing a soft chuckle. I felt foolish for not having thought of that one myself.

Sarleni murmured softly in my mind: We'll be considered a normal master and slavegirl. They'll suspect we're lovers on vacation, so it won't be at all unusual!

I nodded and thought: Nothing like making a show of it for the common folk of Kasiisi.

Adt, you're right. Best we go elsewhere first!

"Oh you dear...master! You do say the nicest things. Now we must take you to the slave market! The women are supposed to be pleasing and seductive. Just like me. And you may want to add one more to your personal collection!"

What in Kordaland are you talking about? "Who could be more desirable than you!"

"Oh you'd be surprised. There are many such women. Even more charming, perhaps. But none as loving, I promise you!" We have to make it look good!

Wouldn't a slavegirl feel jealousy? I wondered.

Not this one! She hummed softly to herself as we continued down the street. After all, we have to recognize, at least publicly, that you are like other men.

Oh, now! Come on, Sarleni! Surprisingly, I felt slightly embarrassed.

Well, you men have needs. Us women are keenly aware of it. And needs must be fulfilled.

And you...women have no such needs? I shot back, feeling a little combative.

We have different kinds of needs, of course. Some more than others!

150

Don't you want to appear quite able to satisfy your…master?

People can think what they want. Thinking doesn't make it so. I'm not at all embarrassed by useless imaginings. Just so it stops there! But you must appear more like a lovely bull Korda mastering his own herd of females!

Where do you get your ideas?

Robust men are the same the world over. Kasiisi is for people of all tastes. Families and singles equally benefit from its many attractions. And you're a young warrior who would grab life with both paws. Why, you might even seek the Pleasure Palace…we must keep our public appearance conforming to the local customs so people won't notice we're not like them.

I almost laughed Sarleni was beginning to become quite an interesting companion, with a clever wit beyond her annoyingly challenging mind. I was actually enjoying her game playing.

As we approached the slave market, I noticed rougher men than the average tourist. No children were visible as we came closer to the auction arena.

The stalls were now larger as we entered this part of the market. Stands were in front of open warehouses. The first ones displayed men, totally exposed, stark naked. And around them eager, richly garbed middle aged women laughed and pointed and whispered in casual humor.

Sarleni puffed in self-mockery: "I'm shocked!"

But she wasn't.

She stood a little in front of me, leaning forward to get a good look at the men exhibited in a straight line, facing the crowd.

Haven't you ever seen a naked man? I thought to her.

No answer came back. Only silence.

With a sense of inspiration I tapped her shoulder with a lightly closed fist.

She whipped around with a bright smile. *It is annoying being ignored, isn't it? You aren't the only one who can shut off the communication at will, Adt.*

She turned, pressing through the throbbing crowd to get closer to the slave platform. I followed her, and again tapped her shoulder, annoyed by her sudden change in mood. Earlier she'd been so playful, even humorous, and now flip flopped to aloofness. *Come on, Sarleni! Stop it!*

You don't have to tap me; I'm open to you.

So, why are you angry with me!

I'm not. Then she laughed. "Oh master, they are such strong men! Just like you!"

Stop that!

This is horrid, isn't it? She flashed suddenly quite serious.

I nodded in response. The men stood there stripped bare, exposed to people crowded in front of the platforms. But it was more the general attitude of the whole scene: crudely carnal. People were comparing sizes, shapes in unrestrained vulgarity.

Sarleni continued. *They are selling human flesh as if this were a meat market! Those women over there are giggling and laughing in delight. Very wicked ladies!*

Sarleni turned, facing me. "Oh, Master, didn't you want to see the women?"

She spoke loudly for the benefit of those around us, forcing me to respond.

"Yes. Now you behave. Behind me!"

I turned and she followed. There were two other male stalls. Then we came to the ones with slavegirls. And on the first platform was a stunning array of six beautiful women facing a mass of male eyes wildly taking in every inch of their lovely bodies.

Sarleni observed: *They are just like those women back there, sucking it all up like starving Fitolas.*

And not giggling! I noted, defensively.

But staring their eyes out! She was decidedly less amused than before.

"Come and make these lovely pets your personal property. Specially selected from exotic lands, their unusual charms will add value to your collection of loving maidens and increase your social status among your comrades. All will envy you!" the man on the stage was proclaiming. "Come, grab them fast. They are hot bodies for your ecstatic desires!"

A gruff male voice in the crowd shouted: "I'll buy one of them juicy things!"

Another challenged: "If you can out bid me, you will!"

The room virtually exploded with rowdy laughter from the crowd of eager buyers gathered about the platform.

The man on stage cheered them on, pointed to one voluptuous young woman, asked: "What'll you give for this tasty? Look at her, so sweet, so lovely, with soft and yielding flesh, full velvet lips, a body to enjoy late into the nights. Imagine her in your arms, obediently submissive to all your hungers. Her body is a feast of joy. Imagine…just imagine…what am I offered for her?"

Voices started shouting rapid-fire bids one after another, laughing and crudely joking.

I had only heard wild rumors of places like this. Such stories were not taken seriously. Most people mocked them as wild exaggerations. Nothing more.

In Bel-loniea it would be impossible to market women under these conditions. This was selling flesh, not bonding servants, nor even your normal slavegirl. Back home our women were never abused. And if they were, the authorities crashed down on those responsible. A slavegirl had less rights than a commoner; but they had rights! They were owned, but had the same human privileges as a servant, who worked for wages. The slavegirl lived with the family, while the servants were free to go to their own homes at night. And sometimes a slavegirl was given her freedom of citizenship to find her own living quarters and work for whomever she might wish. Situations changed.

But this auction reeked of subhuman qualities—even livestock are not treated so abusively. Worse than sheer possession. These slaves were being sold like animals to be kept as household toys.

Sarleni forced another laugh: "Don't any of these exquisite ladies please you, master? Would you not bid for their charms and lovely treasures?"

Apparently the expression in my eyes said it all and she promptly dropped her voice and changed the subject: "We should find lodgings!"

I gratefully nodded.

Both of us fell silent as we turned and left the slave market. We stopped at the first clean appearing lodge. It was the typical two stories, with a small office. We were given a place on the second floor.

The room was small, the bed not as large as I'd have liked. We could lay in it without crowding, but it didn't allow for much privacy.

The window looking out over the street was small, but showed the rooftops of the buildings across from us. Nothing appeared much different from any other lodge or Inn I'd seen in the past. The normalcy itself felt unnatural and out of place.

With a proper slavegirl it might be ideal. I could not avoid my own impulsive thought.

Sarleni went about examining the room, noticing the furnishings beside the bed. It contained two chairs and a table. A washroom was outside at the end of the hallway.

"This will do fine," she ratified, obviously satisfied. "We can make ourselves comfortable and continue the training here. I think we should practice the Zygo now, and after a dinner, a few more sessions, maybe."

"And when do we make plans for tomorrow?"

"Oh, they'll take care of themselves. Explore the city more? Do a little shopping like the rest of the tourist?" She laughed at that.

"You must be joking!"

"Well, we do have to appear to be tourists. And we can't just magically make things happen. What would you like to do?"

"Find some maps. Learn more about this part of the world."

"We have this one!" She patted her hip pouch.

"I want more information, to be truthful. I have no idea where we might be."

"Why, on Noomas, in the middle of the ocean, on an obscure tourist island of some sort. Probably the vacation spot of the world for all we know! Well this part of Noomas, anyway. Obviously quite popular! "

"See? We need to know more."

She smiled warmly, and then shrugged. "Well, I plan on enjoying our stay here. No reason not to. We may never come back...and it is lovely, now isn't it?"

For a moment I couldn't tell if she were being serious or merely joking. There was an amused glint in her eyes as she let them wander around the room.

"Maybe tomorrow we can take a joy ride in the bay? I'm sure we can just go out there on one of the boats." She said. "If somebody won't take us, we could...just take one for ourselves, I'm sure of it!"

"What, steal from these nice people?" I mocked her. "What do you think I am? A thief?"

She laughed, then said: "The people visiting here are rich. They can afford the loss. And they aren't all just nice people, either, from what we've seen."

Once again her eyes met mine, lingering. For a moment she said nothing and I felt a sense of confusion under her gaze. What was she thinking?

"Don't you wonder about all the people who have come here and used this room?" She patted the bed. "Soft. I'd imagine many...well, never mind."

Her face grew serious, flushed slightly.

"Sarleni," I cried, in mocked alarm. "Now *I'm* shocked!"

"No you aren't," she laughed in delight. "You're a wicked young warrior and you probably wish I was one of those helpless slavegirls we saw down there."

She broke off, frowning. "How horrid! Those poor women!"

Tomorrow will open new doors to the both of you! Train hard. You must prepare yourselves!

We both looked in surprise at one another.

"Ju-bilee!" Sarleni exclaimed.

CHAPTER FIFTEEN

HOUSE OF THE WORLD

We waited for more, but silence was all we got from the strange Ju-bilee. The room had turned cold.

Sarleni frowned. "I opened wide for her."

Then she shrugged, as if putting all that aside. But she was deathly serious now. "Game's over! Down to business."

She sat cross-legged on the bed and facing one of the chairs motioned me into it. "Sit! Time to learn more. Time to center. Time to expand your amazing power and strength."

I hesitated for only a moment. She was right. I needed to know more. Right away.

I neglected the chair and assumed the same cross-legged position on the opposite end of the bed. She sighed and shifted around to face me.

"Time for the Zygo. You are very quickly becoming an excellent Zygon. Now some deep breathing and deep centering."

Back to the bossy Sarleni.

We closed our eyes and began.

I cleared away all mental activity letting my mind travel through a new maze of networks. I soon found it almost pleasant to open and close thoughts at will. Yet it still was a strange, alien place where time and space had few boundaries.

Trying to describe this experience is almost impossible.

Like being in some kind of illusive landscape with little shape; endless threads reached out, stretching themselves to the distant horizons extending in every direction. No matter where you looked. Left, right, up or down. It didn't matter. Words fail. All was vaguely frosted over in multicolored hues. Ill-defined shapes danced behind murky shadows. Everything swayed in multi dimensional rhythms, shifting and flowing, sometimes gracefully; other times splintering like shattered glass. I found it tricky to sort illusion from reality.

Our connection continued to be much like an asteroid drifting through stellar nebula, navigating its way among endless patterns of eternal pathways into unending nothingness. And the gap grew, expanding our mental boundaries.

Bazaar in its language with two different dialects, yet it was an intense experience of the true essence of Sarleni. Nearly physical. Disturbing. The intimacy of this was unnerving. Unnatural. And at the same time so seductive that I clung to the connection.

Sarleni carried me through an invisible tunnel into her mystical world. I was entering a different room, though with no free reign to wander around at will. A part of her was locked away, walled in and solidly shelled off.

We were both blocking very deep portions of what we were from one another. A fuzzy part of our shared space remained, at the core utterly blank, an empty nothingness. Dreamlike and relaxing; two people sharing communal space.

* * * * * * *

Details began to dissipate once the connection was cut and we awoke from the deep trance.

At first blinding color blared a deep red and slowly faded. I was aware of staring at Sarleni who sat there almost touching me. Neither of us actually moved, but as the room took shape her image appeared to glide back beyond reach. Then as one unit we both stretched our limbs, fully awakening to the plain surroundings of a dim room.

The sun had already set.

Ready to find some dinner? We both thought simultaneous. Without a word we left the room and then the Inn.

The warm glow of lanterns flickered along the cobble streets. Couples strolled arm in arm. Delicious savory smells wafted from the eateries. We made our way to an open market place where we silently supped, lost in our own thoughts.

Both of us were captivated by the pulsing moods of the awakening nightlife.

Wandering around, we soon discovered the section catering to rather raucous festivities. Here was a mixture of young people milling around as couples and singles, much like us, enjoying the taverns and gaming halls that surrounded the town's Pleasure Palace. And we saw signs that pointed towards luxurious spas, probably nearer to the waterfront.

People wandered arm in arm along the main street. In shaded alleys couples were clinging to one another, locked in obviously passionate embraces.

I think, Sarleni silently observed with light humor, *we're in Kasiisi's wild night zone!*

Is that what you call it back home?

Not exactly. In the icelands we call it the hot zone!

"You gotta be kidding!" I chuckled.

Not at all. Back home we aren't blending exactly like that...

Blending? I thought one saved that for private room exercises.

Hardly. Well, not the kind they are doing here. She nudged closer, her hands closed around my forearm like many of those around us were doing. *Now, don't you get alarmed. This is only for effect.*

I regarded her soft touch on my arm with a secret sense of pleasure.

She glanced up into my eyes, smiling. But her mind revealed nothing of what was going on in her head.

Then we approached a huge domed building. This was, according to the banner above the opening, *Kasiisi's Palace of Pleasure.* Beyond the large entrance was a brightly lighted room crowded with people. Couples and singles came here for intimate unions any time of night or day. These establishments freely provided private rooms, and when somebody was alone they had ample partners for an evening's companionship.

In a loud voice she asked: "Would you like to join them?"

Hardly! Then verbally: "Our own room is right down the street and you're all I wish to handle!"

"You do say such nice things." She merely hugged close, as one might to such a compliment. But her thought was more direct: *Nice play, they'll never guess we're not what we appear to be!*

"Ah, but a woman of your talents surely can be exhausting for any man!" I challenged loudly enough to carry to anybody within easy earshot.

"Really, now. Are you too tired to grant me an evening of pleasure?"

"I'm for it! If you're up to it!" I laughed, wondering how she'd handle that line.

Thanks, Adt, but no thanks! I do believe we've had enough for one day. I'm actually rather tired. I sense you are anxious to investigate the town. Find out all you can. I will be going back to the room, resting.

Protectively, I scanned the surrounding area, spying for any danger that might be in the immediate vicinity before I nodded my consent to her.

The grin on her face told me she knew exactly what I was worried about.

Oh, I'll be safe enough. The streets are crowded and I'm well armed. She tapped the knife tucked at her waist. *And this is the tourist section, regardless of the obvious wild romantic activities taking place right out in the open.*

I relaxed and grinned back. Silent communication can be very useful even for basic connections like this one.

She sauntered off back towards the Inn.

I was uncomfortable about Sarleni being alone. But the streets looked safe enough. I decided to explore on my own, figuring that Sarleni would take care of herself. I was actually glad to be free of Sarleni for a little while.

The general mood of the town and our walk through the block had been disturbing, forcing us to fake a relationship that didn't exist.

This town and island reeked of sensuality. And I became aware of many young women moving together in groups. Women were not so freely unattached in the area where we'd first entered the town. But the people there were also clustered into family groups and slaves and servants were consistently escorted along those streets.

Needless to say, this section of town was far, different from the part where we'd first entered Kasiisi. This was below the slave markets and near the docks, a more seedy section. And now looking more carefully I saw there were a number of entrances that opened to inns and taverns that apparently served a more erotic clientele. Every once in a while women with and without male companions would enter or leave such places, dressed quite skimpily.

"Hey lover," a soft, throaty voice called. I felt a hand clamp onto my arm. "Come over here!"

My body bristled all over. A lovely young woman was standing next to me, her body mostly exposed. She was wearing a wrap around her hips, baring most of her thighs and legs. And at top the blouse was so open as to be immodest.

"I'm not expensive. And I'll gratify you. Come up to my room." Her fingers caressed my arm. "You feel so nice. A strong warrior. Girl like me likes to be with a strong man like you."

"Not interested," I managed.

"I don't charge much, honest!" she pleaded, actually sounding quite alarmed.

"I'm not interested, thanks," I said politely.

"Don't like girls?" she accused. "We have some boys here that might—"

I laughed and disengaged myself from her, walking away as briskly as possible. I bumped into another woman, a bit more mature, and delightfully voluptuous.

"Mind your manners!" she snapped, angrily. As I turned facing her, she quickly brightened, said: "Oh, the pleasure is mine!"

For a moment I stood there, looking at a stunningly attractive woman with long, streaming hair that wrapped around her naked waist in braids. Her breasts were draped with a shear amber vest. She smiled with wild, full lips, sliding closer to me: "I don't charge at all. The pleasure would be all mine."

The liquor on her breath amplified the shiny gleam in her eyes. She pressed close and pushed her body against mine. "Wanna enjoy me?"

I noticed several other women nearby and a few men watching. They looked amused at my situation, being publicly assaulted by this drunken female.

"Thanks," I excused myself. "But on business."

"Business?"

"Yes. Need to find a place to buy a map!" I explained in a loud enough voice to carry to the spectators.

"A map? I have one right here! You are invited to study it all you want and discover all its secret places." She laughed coarsely and wiggled her full breasts making them dance enticingly. "Wouldn't you like to explore my most private territories?"

I grinned, shrugging at the bystanders. "Does anybody know where I can find a map?"

One man laughed boldly. "I think she has one right there! You could check out its details!"

"Yes," she murmured, "and go for every island and inlet. I'm a needy territory that loves to be mapped by…."

"Anybody?" I laughed.

One man took my request seriously and said: "Down the street!"

"Oh, come on," the woman invited rather crudely. "I'll let you see mine all you want. I'd just love having you examine the details."

I wasn't sure if she was some kind of joke, or putting on a show for the audience. Or serious. But when her hand reached down along my chest and started to slide lower, there was no doubt left as to what she was about to do.

I firmly pulled away.

Without a word I strode across the street, and down where the man had pointed, searching for the store where I could get some maps.

The two women had sparked something that was quite powerful in me. My natural longing for what they were selling was certainly evident. We men are pretty basic, with little resistance to lovely women willing to share an evening of pleasure. There were, obviously, a lot of women within easy reach who would either sell themselves or eagerly leap at the chance of a romantic adventure. Tourist towns were attractive magnets for people seeking casual connections. I had, many times, enjoyed such quick intimacies. We're all human.

Before I knew it, I found myself standing in front of an open doorway, looking into a spacious drawing room. Large cushions scattered around on the floor and lounges lined the walls where more than one person could stretch out in passionate embraces.

A number of men mingled with the beautifully adorned, elegant women.

This was a Pleasure House similar to the ones I was fond of in Bel-loniea. But this was a very flashy one. And would appeal to a wide range of men and women. I hadn't been aware of having walked up to its entrance.

"Can I help you?" a lovely, soft voice inquired.

I turned. A very pretty face was gazing up at me. Blonde hair flowed around it. She was dressed in a nicely arranged garment that tucked about her body in a very classy manner. She extended her hand, open, palm down.

"We specialize in ecumenical ecstasy for our varied clients from many realms. Your satisfaction is our bliss. Our competent staff has fused their diverse talents to provide unprecedented results. We delight in creating your greatest fantasies beyond all expectations. Please make yourself at home. Are you staying in town long?"

Her pitch was so eloquent, so sophisticated and fast that I found myself saying: "No. Just tonight, maybe tomorrow."

"Well, then. Perhaps I could encourage you to relax and enjoy some of our amenities. Our sensual professionals are the most famous in Kasiisi. Our House of the World is a famous establishment." Leaning closer she half whispered: "We'll take you swiftly around the world or for a full night of pleasure."

It was then that I realized what had caught my attention. There had been a sign above the entrance: "House of The World" carved over a map of Noomas.

Of course, I rationalized: I'd misunderstood it as a house of maps. Even I found that somewhat difficult to believe.

I felt foolish and wondered what I was doing there. The woman lightly touched my arm. "Would you like me to show you around? I can give you a private tour before you decide what you truly want. Your desire is my wish to fulfill."

I stupidly said: "I was looking for a shop where I could get maps and...."

"Of course. And you just saw our place and stumbled in!" She laughed lightly in amusement. "I've heard a lot of excuses, but that tops them all. Oh, come on, we can have a lovely time together! You don't have to be shy with a woman like me. Or like any of us here. We're all eager to please your wildest fantasy. Nothing is new to us. We've done it all, with all kinds of men...and women, to be frankly blunt about it. We're here to satisfy your more private whims to their fullest extent. This is truly a house where dreams come true!"

She ushered me into the large room and I followed without any resistance, and not exactly knowing why.

It was then that I saw him. I was stunned. For a moment I just froze.

The woman sensed my reaction, but didn't know why. Yet, instinctively she directed me into a shadowy corner.

"Is that better?" she inquired.

My eyes hadn't moved from the man. Every muscle tensed, rage churning through each one like a volcanic fire.

What was he doing here? He was like some kind of nightmare. But this time things were different. Here we could duel to the death and nobody would mind, in fact they'd probably consider it wildly enjoyable entertainment.

Skurals was engaged with a group of women, preening like a Korda Beast in heat. Two women were fawning over him. And he was laughing at something.

I had to control my impulse to rush across the room, sword drawn, and instantly cut him down.

But one curious thought nagged my attention: What was he doing here? Then I answered that. Of course. The Haknord slavers had apparently arrived at this island. It was where they had been heading.

"Come," the woman was imploring. "There's nothing to be worried about. Whatever it is, you're safe here. Come with me, we'll slip into a room...where nobody can find us. We'll be safe there."

I glanced at her, and felt her coaxing me back down the secluded hallway, nicely draped in expensive hangings.

A bit uncertain what to do, I let her draw me to a door and then lure me in with a gentle tug on my arm. "Come on...we'll have a lovely evening. I'll promise you an interlude you'll never forget."

162

For a man of action, a warrior trained to kill and do battle in the name of his Proctor, I was acting like a clumsy farm hand. And rage was not the smart function of a gentleman officer of the Bel-loniea forces.

I shook my head and without a word turned, went back down the hall to the front lounge where I'd seen Skurals. When I returned I saw that he was gone. That fast.

I rushed to the entrance, onto the street. Instantly I saw a tall figure half way down the block and started after him.

Pushing my way past people, I forced myself not to run. A part of me wanted to absolutely kill without warning. A saner part kept asking: What are you trying to do?

A soft hand tugged at my shoulder. I shook it off.

"Don't you like ladies?" came an insulting voice.

I glanced back at an attractive young woman glaring at me.

When I turned back to find Skurals he was nowhere to be seen. I rushed forward. I don't know how long I continued to search, but he had vanished.

It was close to midnight when I finally gave up and started back to the Inn to find Sarleni. She lay curled up in a small corner of the bed, deep in sleep. I was too tired to question ethics. After sliding my gear on the floor, I carefully lay down on the bed next to Sarleni and almost instantly drowned in dreamless sleep. Yet throughout the night I woke periodically. I was aware of her nearness and at times we touched. I did my best to ignore this, but found it most disturbing.

* * * * * * *

I was glad when the morning sun gave some light to our dingy room and I got up with a sense of relief. I had lain there in bed during waking moments trying to form some plan to get us off the island. There were the boats in the bay that could be easy for us to handle and would serve our purposes quite nicely. Assuming we could snatch one.

Sarleni was still sleeping when I looked out the window at the early morning traffic. Only a few people moved along the cobble stone roadway.

I saw a couple of young women of the night, giggling and rushing along in the shadows. Their wraps hung from their weary limbs in disarray. They were obviously retiring from their evening adventures.

I glanced at Sarleni, sleeping peacefully on the bed. Then

looked away. I wasn't blind to her physical charms, nor blinded to the fact that women I'd been with were bland in comparison.

Korda dump! I thought, furiously. The whole situation was crazy. Slavegirl, warrior and a shared room normally meant a romantic interlude. But this wasn't a normal situation. Nor was she a normal slavegirl.

"You're awake, I see." Sarleni murmured, sitting up. "What a wonderful night. Did you sleep well?"

Her eyes flashed mischievously.

"You know damn well!" I snapped, angrily.

"Well, I wouldn't do this with just any men. It is nice to know you are a grand gentleman."

"Oh, you've known the other kind?"

She grinned and shrugged. "We all have lived our lives. You've had yours; I've had mine. Enough said."

Sarleni stood, stretched, and then yawned: "I had a wonderful sleep. I feel rested and ready for our next session."

"Well, I'm not! I want something to eat."

"Yes. We should do that."

"I want to look around." I needed to search for Skurals again, but I was not ready to share that information with her just yet. Anyway, she was thinking other things, which avoided the more serious business. I played along with her trite game.

"Of course!" She was being a bit too agreeable. Maybe smug. "You wanted to get some maps or something. I would like to do some shopping, myself."

"Oh? We have that much…buying power…."

"I have only enough for some meals. I wouldn't think of buying anything. Might snip a thing here or there." She beamed wickedly.

"Steal? Oh, Goddess of Thieves have mercy on me! Don't drag us into trouble with Kasiisi authorities!"

"Not funny! We're on serious business, and we must be reasonable. What we need, we need. Our mission comes first. Time is a factor. We take what the local Gods deliver into our hands." She brushed the whole subject off with that little wave of her hand.

Of course she was right. Rationalization or not.

I divorced my thoughts as we left the room. A little later, while finishing off a short morning meal of hot Ka and freshly baked rolls, we watched the town waking. The streets, by then, were becoming crowded.

We had avoided any personal conversation and throughout the meal I managed to keep my eyes averted from her. We talked in generalities. Yet I felt myself more and more aware of the peculiar

164

nature our relationship had taken, after having been so close to her all night long.

My eyes automatically lingered on some of the women passing by. It is instinctive for men to look at beautiful females.

Sarleni noted the direction of my gaze and leaning closer whispered: "The women are busy making a fast trade!"

But there was a crudely obvious element to these ladies passing by on the street that was not so common elsewhere.

Sarleni projected: *This island has an uneasy feel to it.*

There's an openness that screams a culture far different from those I've known. And I don't think it is just me!

I glanced at her, thought: *Right. In Bel-loniea the standard fun palaces and taverns cater to the workers, warriors and servants, visitors and assorted loners. But it is not nearly as open as what I've seen here. Social politeness dictates a sheltered framework for these activities. We show more cultural dignity towards one another. More elegance.*

And, she thought in response, *fashionable men, of course, would never attend to such lowly places. I'm sure.*

There was brazen mockery in that thought and a slight twinkle in her eyes.

"Tell me," she asked, "do you find those women over there attractive, much to be desired?"

I felt as if she'd slapped me. She had spoken loud enough so people at the table next to us could easily hear. Was she doing it for show?

I decided to shrug that off. "Why should they? You're my delightful prize!"

That, I planted in a firm, convincing voice, winking at one of the men sitting within site of us. He nodded in amusement.

"Oh, Adt!" She nudged me with her elbow. It appeared far more forceful than she'd meant it to be. "You are embarrassing me!"

And thought to me: *I wouldn't blame you, really I wouldn't.*

For what?

Finding those young women...well...intriguing. Especially after last night.

I could hear her silent giggle.

"I'm sorry, Adt," she whispered softly. "I couldn't help myself. It is awkward! Forgive me?"

The waiter came at that moment and we paid for the meal and shortly were walking along the street.

Neither of us talked at first, then finally Sarleni said: "I think I'll just look around these shops. I'll be fine. Nothing to worry about. You do what you need to do...see you later. We can meet before midday and do more work together."

I didn't even have a chance to respond to her parting shot.

She was gone.

CHAPTER SIXTEEN

DANGER IN THE TAVERN

I decided to wander on my own, figuring that Sarleni would take care of herself. It was her neck. And we weren't in the forest or some dangerous jungle. Plus she'd shown hard evidence of being able to handle herself when the Haknords had her alone on deck. She was still armed with that small dagger. And this was, after all, a town for tourist and families. Regardless.

I'll be fine, Adt, her voice in my head assured me. *I'll keep out of trouble, and you do the same…if you can with all those wild ladies fluttering around.*

I paid her remark no attention and continued on down the street in a blind daze. Everybody needs space to keep themselves grounded. We'd been confined in a terrible situation for days. I kept a keen eye out for Skurals or any other men from the Haknord slaver ship, for that matter.

* * * * * * *

The sun rose high now and I wasn't having any success. I started to worry about Sarleni being spotted. I should have warned her. That jarred me with guilt.

I hurriedly made my way back to the local café where we were supposed to meet. There she was looking quite contented with herself, sipping her Ka. She had a small parcel, obviously having been successful in shopping.

By that time I'd opened mentally and projected my thoughts to her, keeping my suspicions about Skurals deeply buried. I permitted one obscure concern to be revealed her, only mentioning that I'd seen somebody who looked like him. No need to alarm her until I had made more concrete plans of my own about the slavers being in town. It was, of course, a large enough place for us all never to encounter one another. And even if they saw us, chances were high that they'd be too dim-witted to identify us.

I think Sarleni guessed or maybe read more than I consciously projected. She smiled sympathetically and said: "You look like you've been chasing wild Noaruls down an empty hole. A disappointing morning, then? No intrigue with the fashionable ladies of the streets? Ah, poor Adt. It sure must be frustrating."

And I hadn't gotten a map, either.

After lunch she insisted we go up to the room for some further studies. I was in a bad mood and reluctantly complied. By the time we were finished it was evening.

Without a word we left the room. The warm glow of lanterns flickered along the cobble streets where small groups of people strolled, enjoying the savory smells of food wafting from the eateries.

A short distance further down the street we found a rustic tavern. Its wide gardened entrance led us into a large enclosed pavilion, massed with a raucous crowd. An empty table under a vine-covered canopy looked inviting. Ale flowed freely. We could hardly hear ourselves think in the rowdy merriment blasting from the tavern. In such places there can be a marvelous sense of camaraderie filled with robust and often heated debates sometimes breaking into outright fights. But generally most encounters are quickly quenched by generous tankards of ale.

I like it! This is just great! Sarleni exclaimed with approval, plopping down into a chair. She relaxed comfortably into this setting. Nobody could have considered her anything other than a slavegirl; companion to the warrior. That's exactly what we wished others to see. Several men had been blatantly leering at her with hungry eyes. I found that quite annoying.

Ale was immediately brought to our table, without even being ordered. The waiter merely delivered and said; "Food is coming."

And he was gone.

"A friendly lot," Sarleni remarked, letting her eyes wash over the men in the room. There were a few other women, some wenches, but most were obviously personal companions, maybe even slavegirls, who draped themselves intimately over their male partners.

Perhaps, Sarleni's thought teased; *we should be interacting more, so we are not so conspicuously different from the rest of these couples.*

She leaned closer, and rolled her neck causing the long locks of jet-black hair to cascade away from her shoulders. A small action of her hand brushed past her wrist, finally settled on her other arm, now slightly bare.

I must play the part, don't you think? She leaned provocatively lower, exposing a generous view of her neckline. *There, I'm acting just like these other ladies. Now you do your duty, Adt! Act as if you're enjoying the view!*

She laughed loudly, saying: "You are a naughty man!"

Her knee nudged me under the table, and I felt electrified. What was she doing?

Play like you're my lover! Sarleni coaxed. *Otherwise you'll look...foolish! People see things...when they don't fit. Come on, Adt. Be a champ of disguise. Reveal your manly warrior flair as the seducer of a woman with whom you expect to spend the night. Come to think of it, that's exactly what you're doing...again! I mean, spending the night with me. Isn't that just delicious?*

She laughed again: "Oh, you are enticing me. And I'm just starved...for food, of course!"

Mentally she bluntly informed me: *Look to our left...we're being watched.*

A man was sitting at the next table, studying us very carefully. He had a hardened warrior's face, and appeared far more sober than might have been expected. Why was he staring?

Act like you can't wait to be alone with me!! Sarleni's coaching had turned grimly serious, yet her fingers were stroking my arm very, tenderly, convincingly flirtatious. *It can't be that difficult. I'm supposed to be your personal slavegirl and you act like I'm a cold old hag!*

She laughed even more boldly, and leaned nearer, her lips close to my ears, moving slightly, but saying nothing. For others it would appear she was whispering sweet intimacies.

I forced a laugh, my eyes skimmed by the warrior. "Well, just you wait until we're alone!"

"Why wait, luv?" she quipped innocently. For a moment our eyes met and the outside world faded for a split second.

"Not in public!" I gently drew Sarleni close, my hands on her the shoulders, holding her against me. Then I felt her pulse begin to race. Instantly I moved back at arm's distance. "Now behave!"

"You tease a woman to distraction!" she pouted most convincingly.

Stop it, I insisted angrily. The whole incident had unsettled me. Her coquettish act had almost crossed a dangerous line.

"Act like a lady!" I chided. *I'm sure you can fake it!*

"Of course, I wish only to please my master!" She nodded and leaned away. Then her hand defiantly stroked my arm and chest once more, very sensually; her eyes shooting daggers into mine, daring me to try to stop her. It was a blunt act of obvious intimacy. For show, of course.

I knew she was treading a dangerous course now, putting on a seriously engaging performance for the sullen warrior; wiping any suspicions that he might have had about her slavegirl training.

I think that'll convince any doubters, she noted, with a satisfied grin. *You look totally involved, now.*

She giggled, as if reacting to some secret message. Her body squirmed slightly. "Now, now, master. Not here! You said not in public, and that I must be a lady for all to see and admire. So if I must, I'll be a prim and proper woman from now on. I promise!"

That was loud enough for the warrior who had been watching us. He finally allowed a satisfied grin to crease his face and even winked at me and then looked away.

The waiter laid down two plates of rough bread cakes stuffed with some kind of shredded meat.

We thankfully ate in silence, relieved from the intense posturing act.

As we finished, Sarleni looked seriously at me.

I'm sorry, Adt. We must play lovers for the public.

I nodded. *You play the game far too joyfully.*

Oh. Is that a compliment? What a pleasant surprise. One would think you actually liked me!

An explosive yell from down the street killed any response from me. Then another yell, but it was more a scream of terror or fear. Everyone froze outside tavern; people turned, several stood.

A cloud of movement shuffled a man into our table. Shaky hands lifted up covering a gaunt, lined face of undetermined age. His eyes were wide with terror. Thin lips stretched over uneven bloodied teeth. We ducked in time to avoid a mug of ale that came hurling in his direction.

Another man rushed at him, holding his sword like a club. The brute was yelling obscenities waving the sword dangerously into the gaping diners who dodged and scattered a safe distance from the brawl

"Korda, shimali, okanoxs!" He jabbed the hilt down into the unarmed man's face. The poor creature ducked, and crumbled into our table, knocking it to one side. I leaped to my feet.

Sarleni was already standing, alarmed.

"Thief!" the armed man shouted, lifting his sword with an obvious intent to kill. His face was contorted in rage.

170

I hate bullies trying to harm helpless victims. Sword in hand, I extended its blade, circled the other's weapon, and whipped my wrist in a snapping fashion. The clatter of metal on stone confirmed the man's weapon had fallen to the ground. The point of my sword found an easy target beneath his chin.

"Just stop!" was my mild instruction.

He was enraged, but his eyes widened in open horror. Approval roared from the crowd around us, cheering me on.

"Kill him!" a woman's voice jeered, joined by others hollering at me.

The man's bearded sneer glared at me with open hate. "Why do you defend this slimy Tian?"

"Why do you attack an unarmed man?" My sword gently bit into his beard, careful not to draw blood.

As I lowered my blade he turned and rushed away from the tavern. By then Sarleni had managed to help the poor victim to his feet.

A murmur rippled through the remaining onlookers. Everybody turned away, pretending to ignore us and return to their previous business.

I wondered what evil had brought this man to this mangled misery. He was probably a thief or worse, a seedy-looking fellow. Maybe he lived on the streets and begged when that served his purpose. One sees people like this in all civilized centers. They could be very troublesome.

The man attempted to say something, but Sarleni shook her head, indicating silence. He submitted to her caring touch as she wiped the blood from his wounds with her new scarf, binding it around his broken head to ease the bleeding.

Sarleni warned seriously: *We need to get out of here before that bully brings back others. He's not likely to give up so easily. And this poor fellow here…may be helpful. I'm sure he knows his way around Kasiisi.*

I didn't question her. Obviously she'd managed to intuit something about the man and the situation.

I quickly settled our bill with the waiter adding extra for the cost of the broken table.

We exchanged no words as we nearly dragged him around the corner into a side street, then up an alleyway, cluttered in garbage and a few sleeping bums. We needed an isolated spot to sort this all out. By now he'd regained his breath and was thanking us profusely for saving his life.

"Shyiln owes you his life," the man almost hissed the words through broken teeth and the battered cuts on his lips. "He must pay you."

"Who's Shyiln?" I muttered, only half annoyed by his way of speaking.

"Why *this* is Shyiln!" he thumped his chest with pride. "A thief of talent and grace."

Sarleni laughed. "So I noticed!"

"The rogue had no business spyin' on Shyiln! Jumped him from behind. Caught Shyiln by surprise. No idea how he got Shyiln in the tavern. Strange.... Like magic. That cowardly Korda attacked Shyiln. The beast fights without honor.... And out to kill Shyiln! For what? For nothin'!"

Now he was brazen and bold in contrast to the terrified man he had been back there in the tavern. Frightened, for sure, or perhaps artfully performing for an audience in hopes of discovering a rescuer.

We left the alley, hurrying down another narrow street to a small gardened area with a tranquil pond surrounded with colorful flowers.

At a secluded bench, we stopped so that Sarleni could wash and tend his wounds. She applied a balm she pulled from her pouch.

"Tell us about yourself." I questioned, taking curious inventory of this odd man.

"What's there to say?" he moaned, grimacing in pain. "Truth is Shyiln don't know how he got there...in that place you found him." He shook his head from side to side. "One moment he was on the street, then the next...well, never mind. It happened!" Again he looked puzzled, dazed. Obviously he was mentally fogged; maybe half crazed. Perhaps hurt more than was apparent.

Suddenly he screamed: "Enough. Enough. Shyiln is no troublemaker. Just make a livin' gettin' what he needs when and where he needs it. That makes people angry."

"A thief makes people angry," I chuckled, though frowning somewhat seriously.

"Shyiln survives as best he can. You don't have to insult Shyiln. Robbery is a master's art. And, well, okay, he is just not a master at it. More a beggar and...a proud, skilled laborer! Yes! That's what Shyiln is. A valid way of makin' a livin' here. Take from the foolish tourist, when takin' is easy. Everybody's grabbin'. Even the law enforcers have their price. Believe Shyiln. He knows from *personal* experience."

I frowned, somewhat intrigued.

He responded: "Shyiln is a poor born. Never got schoolin' or trainin' like luckier people. We seldom get any breaks; no civil privileges. But we get by." He rubbed his thin arms and said, "Difficult makin' it. Shyiln is never a fighter. He does very well with what he has."

"Apparently you have survived up to now."

"Sure. Otherwise we couldn't be havin' this little talk, could we?" He chuckled. "Shyiln likes you. You are very clever and fast. That mighty sword-arm is powerful in action. Shyiln thanks you for keepin' that hairy monster from eatin' him alive. Well, not literally, mind you, but maybe fried in a hot pot. That shaggy Knoiaot and his beastly friends would kill me."

"Shyiln owes you!" He looked honestly worried. Then his smile widened across ragged teeth as he fumbled through his tattered pockets. "No coins here to repay you." Then looking up at me, his eyes growing bigger gleaming almost wickedly, he said, "Ah, but Shyiln has many methods, many connections. He is a proud man and pays his debts!"

"You seem to be quite knowledgeable and maybe you *can* help us." Sarleni proposed.

"Shyiln has his ways. He knows how to survive by hook and...." He faltered for an uncomfortable moment, gulped and mumbled, "But we all have to make a livin'." He chuckled, far more relaxed by this time. "Those men were nasty!"

"You should watch out," she advised.

"Shyiln does! Normally. Don't know why Shyiln picked at that pocket." He shook his head again, cocking it slightly, then gulping hard, continued: "And he got caught. Next thing Shyiln knew we were in that tavern...and...luckily you two were there. Thanks again."

Considering his rather confused connections I played a hunch by quickly asking: "Do you know how we might get transportation off this island?"

"Perhaps less than expensive?" His eyes narrowed and a twist of humor curled his lips. "Cheap as cheap can be cheap!"

"We need something to take us away from this island."

"Ah, you don't like our lovely resort?" he chuckled. "Or are there other more devious reasons for your quick exit?"

"What makes you say that?"

"Shyiln is a good judge of people. You're not from here. You are not a common visitor from your gear, though you wear the colors of the Kaminian regiment. Odd, though it is impossible to tell where you originate. And your general manner and accent must be from far places. We have many people from many lands. Shyiln has never heard a voice like yours." Then swiftly before I could react he added: "Oh, don't be concerned, most would not notice or make any sense out of it, nor care. But Shyiln lives by his guts, wits and smarts!"

"What do you think would resolve our needs?" I countered.

Sarleni interjected, "Something fast and private."

"Very costly. Privately owned craft can be rented, of course, with crew and all. Perhaps beyond your pocket change. Such luxuries are beyond the reach of our wildest dreams. Shyiln thinks you want somethin' *very* cheap as cheap as cheap can be cheap."

She nodded. "And we really don't care how we get it."

Careful, I warned.

Stop worrying. This is your basic thief without loyalty to the authorities. He feels a debt of honor must be paid. I'm feeding his needs. He's no fool. You're being too careful!

The man's eyes narrowed, and then flickered bright, almost twinkling. "Ah, of course you mean somethin' easily snatched for the takin'. Somethin' more suited for the great warrior and his lady. Somethin' those greedy tourists do not know how to handle. Yes. Shyiln can make it happen. Like pickin' the pocket of a blind man."

"If you can make it work," I agreed. "Without complications, of course."

Shyiln laughed. "Your servant, Shyiln can help. What're you seekin'? A fast ship and no hard cash to trade for it. No trouble!" The man grinned in pleasure. "Shyiln can...and *will*...help you! There are many such ships docked in a cove on the far side of this bay, mainly unattended, outside of a few off-duty warriors who camp on the beach. There is a lot of that goin' on here in Kasiisi since the military base was set up. Rough, crude people, these military types; no culture, just robbers and bullies and low grade thuds." He made a wave of his hand, then added: "Until recently it was off-limit to trainin' areas and installations. Strange that. Things keep happenin', changin'."

Sarleni asked: "What's so strange?"

"The military base? Well, don't know why they need to have one here. This has always been a tourist retreat. Well, in Shyiln's lifetime, anyway. But this island was an ancient place. Some claim very ancient. Has a long history."

"We saw the ruins," I noted.

"You came from the sunset region, then?" He pointed in the direction of our arrival to the island and Sarleni nodded.

"The misty jungles. People don't go there too often—can be dangerous. But the ruins," he continued. "There's a lot of exploration still goin' on here. Shyiln has many times been hired to do diggin' for them. Artifacts!" He winked wickedly, then added, "Grim ones, too. I've heard rumors that these ruins predate human civilization. More ancient stuff is under the surface. Scientists dig deep for them."

He shrugged all that off. "Anyway, there's a lot of activity here on Kasiisi—tourist trade has boomed! All expanded as a result of this scientific exploration. There are other islands like ours, too, scattered and…well, not of much importance to your needs."

Sarleni eagerly tried to keep him talking, obviously looking for more information: "Perhaps, but we're interested."

"Well, Shyiln doesn't know anymore about it. Sorry about that. Mere rumors. And you can't believe them. Whispers of alien creatures and strange civilizations. It matters little. They are all dead now anyway…them that built these ruins long ago. Just know that we have a lot of diggin' here and that brings trouble. Hard to sneak out a valued object. But small ones can be easy. And on the black market there's plenty of profit to be made. We survive."

I kept my words calm, asking rather evenly: "Then you'll help us find something that'll get us on our…way?"

"You sound desperate to leave our wonderful, popular resort spa. One would think otherwise of such a lovely couple. Why, she is a beautiful, desirable woman any man would give much to possess. And you, her magnificent warrior master. One would think you are here to only enjoy escape into…one another's arms." He stood and motioned us. "All can be illusions. We hide behind endless masks. A shame too, in a place like this. Mysterious things are happenin' that may drastically alter all our futures. Again rumors, of course. But they are always festerin' about the islands. You can't believe anything, any more. Noomas is a changin' world."

I think he's about to escort us out of the city! You need to retrieve our weapons. I'll stay with him. We'll be fine.

I started to object then decided she knew what she was doing. And we were in mentally connected.

"I'll be right back, stay here with her!" I instructed the man as I hurried down the street.

"You trust Shyiln?" He sounded surprised, and even a bit pleased.

"I trust *her*! She's a savage beast when crossed!"

It didn't take long to get back to the room, gather our weapons and then leave without being noticed.

When I returned to the park they were still sitting on the stone bench apparently deep in conversation. They looked up and we silently left the area.

He took us outside the city, to a ramp and a stairway much like the one where we had entered Kasiisi. We were on the other side of the city.

"Rain comin' soon," our guide sniffed. "Come, hurry on. Not much time."

The climb was tiresome, but the air refreshing, cool, and the sky clouding over. Finally, we were overlooking a small cove with a wide beach, and a pier occupied with small yachts, some large enough for a crew of twenty or more, though most of these vessels were designed for swift, safe travel with less passengers.

I looked down at the cove and small beach.

"I wonder where all these people come from."

"Everywhere, I suppose," Sarleni noted.

Further down the beach, a stone jetty reached out into the water to a larger heavily equipped watercraft.

A couple of men visibly carried some sort of gear along that jetty.

Our guide said: "Them? Come here diggin' 'round the ruins, ya know? Explorers or scientists—harmless 'cept for some over there. Troublemakers they are, the ones from the military division."

He shrugged as if it didn't matter, and pointed to a number of tents at the far end of the curving beach. "This cove's guarded. Hired hands—Korda dump! Swank duty, they call it. Big pay for makin' appearances. They drink and party with slavegirls. Rich tourists pay much for protection. They like havin' things safe and these guards are armed and skilled. Thieves themselves slaughterin' us honest types. So be careful. They enjoy killin'!"

I nodded, tapping my sword: "Know the types. Low-grade brutes. I don't kill for pleasure!"

"They do! They are dangerous." He had become quite serious as he spoke. And now he nodded, turning, to face us. "Shyiln leaves you here to decide what you wish. He wants to know nothin' more. Shyiln has a tongue that'll scream secrets if life depends on it. This repays your kindness. Just do what you must. We're even."

Without a word Shyiln raced off on thin legs, the cloak streaming behind him. He quickly disappeared.

176

CHAPTER SEVENTEEN

AT SEA

"Strange little man," Sarleni looked puzzled as she turned to face me.

"Maybe too strange."

We studied the cove, momentarily considering what this little thief had said.

"Lucky he came along, though," she said, looking down at the scene below us.

"Almost *too* lucky!"

Not luck! Came a familiar voice into my mind.

Sarleni whipped around, facing me. "Ju-bilee!"

She appeared before us like a faded ghost, flickering slightly.

I made use of him, and provoked his mind into picking that warrior's pocket. Then sent them into the tavern. He's a slimy one. But what he told you was true. New military bases mean expansion...we've held surveillances on this, too. Hints, vague messages have been intercepted. You must get nearer the center. Kamina is your ultimate destination. You've been advised.

"What's she doing? Monitoring us?" I fumed, almost losing my temper.

You are young fledglings in a very dangerous world. You have made some foolish choices and others are watching you. Be warned. No time to explain. Take that first craft. The one latched to the end of the pier. It is a fast boat, easily maneuvered. And well stocked with provisions that you will need. Stolen property currently used by thieves, Adt. Stop being so ethical! Shyiln will cover your expenses at the Inn as part of his debt to you." Ju-bilee's voice was strangely soothing, far less brittle than before. She smiled, winked and then was gone.

We stood there dazed.

"What'd she mean?" I wondered, scanning Sarleni's face for

some kind of explanation. The information was more detailed than some of her previous cryptic messages. I hoped that she was right about the boat's speed. We would need to make a very fast escape if we were to succeed in broad daylight down there. The harbor was exposed to the entire town and hillside.

Sarleni was saying: "Think we can slip down there without being seen?"

"I hope so. If not, we'll need to bluff our way. Or resort to this." I tapped the sword at my waist, pushing thoughts of Ju-bilee out of my mind and focusing on our immediate problem. Regardless of any ultimate destination, we could not leave this island without transportation.

My eyes were studying the cove, trying to decide the best way to access the pier without alerting the guards gathered up along the beach. Like our friend had said, this was swank duty for the regiments who would be letting down their guard, enjoying the beach. They'd be distracted by the lures of the tourist town. They most certainly believed their numbers alone would discourage any thieves.

A distant flash of lightning caught our attention, followed by a crackling snap of thunder. Cold hard gusts of wind suddenly shivered our spines. Dark clouds were rolling in fast over the harbor.

A light shower was already coming down. Below, the men hurried for shelter in the camps on shore.

"Let's go!" I pulled my cloak around me heading for the sloping path. "No reason to wait!"

I didn't want to delay.

It really wasn't far to the bottom.

We crossed the beach, the sand soft under our feet. A shout came from the camp. The rain had momentarily let up, but the wind was still strong.

Half a dozen guards were already rushing in our direction.

"Quick!" I yelled, reaching for Sarleni's hand.

But she amazed me, running with the agility of a Zionah, hardly making a mark on the sand with her tiny feet. "I can outrun them any day."

"To that nearest boat." I glanced behind us and saw the warriors beginning to gain on us, moving much faster than I'd expected.

Up ahead a huge man blocked the pier. He dropped the keg he'd been carrying.

He was a marvel of muscles and picked up a thick pipe gripping it tightly in large hands.

A voice far behind me roared against the wind: "Stop them!"

I rushed ahead of Sarleni, commanding: "Back!"

178

The giant stood his ground, planting his feet firmly at the edge of the dock.

"Stop!" he growled. "Or die."

I picked up my pace, rushing headlong at him. The giant grinned, muscles rippling as he launched a brutal blow at me.

My sword was already in hand as the pipe swung. He either intended to crush my head or smash my weapon into shattered bits of metal. Neither of his plans succeeded.

I simply slid the blade up under that huge swinging pipe. With one swift thrust, I sliced deep into his fleshy chest.

Blood spewed as I yanked the sword away from his body before it crumpled to the sand.

I turned, to find Sarleni poised with bow in hand, an arrow aimed at the warriors still racing towards us. One of them was already stumbling with an arrow lodged in his chest. I saw that Sarleni had sent a second arrow towards another man. There was no time to admire her skill.

My blade met the attack of two more thugs facing me, brushing aside their swords in mid-air, then it sliced across their bodies, as if they were one person.

Three others were coming quickly, but paused upon seeing their companions so easily killed.

Yelling behind them was a tall, magnificent warrior whom I instantly recognized. Skurals! This was not exactly how I'd expected to find him. My breath was hot with hate for the man. A number of warriors had already grouped directly behind him. Far too many for me to deal with in this open space.

I'd enjoy killing this man! But this wasn't a time for gentlemanly duels. One day, perhaps; not today!

Thunder roared loudly above me. The storm was beginning to reassert itself.

I turned to the docked sea-craft, beautifully large, with upper deck and a cabin below.

We leaped onto the boat, without checking whether it was occupied. It seemed reasonable to assume it was vacant.

Lightning flashed furiously across the sky.

"There!" Sarleni pointed aft to the wide console housing the controls of the ship.

The wheel was mounted under a short awning.

Men were now rushing at us, nearly reaching the pier. They seemed to have regained their courage under Skurals' shouting threats. And their numbers had already doubled. There were at least six or seven warriors waving swords and hastening to join us on the vessel.

Sarleni scrambled for the line attached to the bow and threw it onto the pier. As I rushed to the control panel a torrent of rain burst down on us.

At the very moment I touched the starter button, the craft leaped forward knocking a couple of warriors into the water and in a short time the island cove had swished away.

The power of this vessel was stunning; it literally skimmed over the ocean waves as if flying through air. We were tossed off balance, not having expected such speed.

Sarleni laughed with relief. "We've made it!"

"Yes, and just in time." I stared back towards the island fading in the distance and the mist. I saw no ships chasing after us, but the rain clouded all vision with its heavy downpour.

We were silently aware that Kasiisi was now far behind us. The storm darkened the sky.

Waves billowed up around us, but the powerful boat smoothly skimmed over them.

"A wonderful vessel we have here!" I exclaimed in delight. "Seems whoever stole this from its original owner must have revved it up quite a bit."

We huddled under the awning near the controls, protected from the thunderous rain. For a long while we just marveled at our sudden freedom and the very power of the craft we'd taken.

Suddenly the sky brightened. We had literally shot through the storm, which was now raging further behind us.

"Now we're really on our way!" Sarleni announced with grim determination.

She was so excited that her emotional impact reached right through me like a physical wave. I had learned to trust Sarleni.

Adt, this is our born, mutual destiny! Right from birth. I know that much.

That didn't even seem reasonable. She was doing it again. Drawing some kind of blanket conclusion from a totally unrelated event. Like she knew the script of our lives. This was totally absurd.

It makes perfect sense to me. There's a Divine presence in the universe that created all there is. I know it is true! This belief is just as real a part of me as is your physical skill with your weapons. Our very lives may depend on both.

I thought: *believing doesn't make it so. Personal convictions aren't fact.*

Sarleni looked directly into my eyes. *It is fact. That's what you must honor. We must accept one another with our private quirks.*

180

Truth is the pathway we use to travel from one place to another. If it works, then it has a reality. Do we need to understand more than that?

Then she added: *We're safe, at least.*

The ocean was now calm, the sun baking down bright, the horizon ahead was an endless unbroken line against the sky. She was right about that much. For the time being. We were safe enough, now, as long as the mythological creatures of the ocean kept their healthy distance. Great monsters were legendary. And several treacherous species were fact. But we were safer on this well built and speedy ship than when we were on the small Haknord raft. Now we had a sleek vessel that could shoot through the waters at such a speed that even a Kalorian could not keep up with us. They are hungry man-eaters; in fact they ate anything within reach.

I let my eyes race over the hold of the craft. It was a spacious cabin with a hatch leading below.

I gripped hold of the wheel. It was firmly latched in place, yet easy to turn. But when I released my hold it reset its own course, heading directly towards the distant horizon in the wake of the sinking sun.

I considered the dilemma, then surrendered to the fact I had no better destination. At least at this moment! We were basically in unknown waters. Lost.

I decided to explore below, and followed Sarleni who had already gone down the hatchway.

"We should check that map of yours. This boat seems to be programmed to follow a steady course. We're stuck with that. We need to see where we're headed."

Sarleni had already pulled down the small table hooked to the wall next to a cabinet. She lost no time unfolding the chart and spreading it out. The two of us traced a direct line drawn from the Kasiisi harbor straight to the small isolated island labeled *Illysæ ad Mördi Tăli.*

Our minds reacted instantly as our eyes met in serious acknowledgement. We'd recognized we were headed in that exact direction. Pre-programmed!

Was Ju-bilee behind that? She had directed us to this ship. She was continually monitoring.

We stared at one another for a long time hardly breathing.

A compelling physical fatigue overshadowed me. Wisdom dictated that we should take advantage of this time to refresh our bodies and mind.

Sarleni's gentle voice broke my tense mood. "I wonder!"

She'd pulled open the cabinet. There we found a nice display of fresh chilled food, apparently regulated from an inner cooling source. "How thoughtful."

"Just as if Ju-bilee set this all up for us."

"Who knows," Sarleni mused a little too lightly. "It might very well be possible. At least we have food."

Sarleni gave me a puzzled look, then said: "Why don't you go up on deck and check things while I…prepare something to eat!"

"Showing off your woman's arts in the galley?" I laughed.

"Limited!" she cautioned quite seriously. "But better than nothing."

I grabbed up the chart as she started plopping bundles of fruits and meats on the table. She looked outlandishly domestic even for her role as a slavegirl.

Back on deck, I was feeling the wind and the sun and the coolness all mixed together. The wheel was secured on in its predestined course.

We were speeding for an empty horizon. The chart's markings were unclear about a destination at a distance we could not even calibrate. By the height and angle of the sun, I guessed that this strange island would be our destination. But I had no idea how to estimate when we'd make landfall. That would remain a mystery yet to be exposed.

My hand swept over the power button, pressing it. The craft slipped into a slower mod. I pressed it once more and it came to a breaking stop. I was almost tossed off balance.

But down below, a startled scream leaped from the cabin and I sprang to the hatchway, finding Sarleni flat on her butt, against the left berth, food scattered around her. She muttered something unintelligible, turned and glared at me.

"Sorry." But my eyes betrayed amusement at her dilemma.

"Real funny. Here's a mess you might help me clean up!" Then she made that annoying jerk she always made with her hand. "Never mind. Just…oh, never mind!"

She was clumsily scooping the food off the floor.

I couldn't resist a snicker as I started to lift myself back onto the deck. Something rattled past me, hitting the steps.

I let out a roar of laughter.

She answered with a long string of curses and snide remarks until she abruptly collapsed in a heap on the floor, laughing at the silliness of it all. It was catching and I found myself joining her. Such laughter can be almost painful, even bring tears into your eyes. Finally we could stop, breathe again. She looked up at me quite exhausted and relieved: "Oh, just do what you do best!"

Maybe all this pent up tension finally found its release in good humor for both of us. I sure felt a lot better.

Fresh open sea air filled my lungs and I turned my attention to the compartments around the control panel. Perhaps there might be charts or some information concerning where we were. But I found nothing.

I started up the engines again. Sarleni called: "Adt, it's ready!"

* * * * * * *

The weather continually shifted from calm to stormy. Days and nights passed. But none of it seemed to challenge the craft, which simply swept over the waves, oblivious to their worst churning fury. When the winds became violent, as rain stormed down, we disappeared into the warmth of the cabin leaving the helm to follow its mysterious guide.

Sarleni grew pensively solemn. Much of the time she sat cross-legged on her chosen resting pad to one side of the cabin. She slept there at night.

This routine lasted for a few days.

Sarleni fanatically dedicated most of our waking time exposing me to the Zygo. I found myself beginning to look forward to the lessons, despite my resistance to her belief systems. Remarkably they felt powerfully energizing. Under these relaxed conditions it was possible to gain an amazing amount of profound insight in a very short time. Far more interesting was that our ability to connect mentally grew deeper in its intensity.

Unsettling though all this felt, it was, ultimately, a way to keep the days from being bland and boring. Plus it became more and more obvious that in some situations these newly developed abilities could be quite advantageous.

"Now," she said at one point, "we will stretch our physical horizons and prepare for real dangers! Like when you were trapped in the worm-hole I merged with you...."

She was now literally teaching me to move things with our joined minds, using this combined energy to manipulate objects; lifting, tossing, reshaping, even to changing their temperatures.

Such experiments were bizarre. We would sit opposite one another, both cross-legged and staring into empty space. At first we would just try to relax, center our attention at some mutual point within our shared mental bubble. Then as a sense of energy formed in the air between us we would lower our mental focus to the floor, where we'd place we wanted to affect. Sometimes it was merely a matter of thinking warm or cold, and watching a piece of paper crumble in response, or flare up into a red ball of flame. That was somewhat startling the first time around.

More frequently, though, we'd move objects around on the floor between us; a kind of game where we tried to increase our speed and accuracy at positioning it exactly where we wanted it. This kind of skill developed rapidly and swiftly felt familiar. Too familiar. Almost like a long lost memory returning. And in a way that's exactly what it was. I began remembering having played such games as a child; it was something I'd forgotten. Vague memories surfaced and faded. The hazy image of a Muti sitting opposite me, much like Sarleni was doing, teased through my thoughts. I tried to capture such memories into sharper focus, but they simply slipped away, as if not wanting to be fully revealed.

Sarleni was pleased at these discoveries.

"See," she noted at one point, "you were born with these talents."

"Yes, but I forgot all about them."

"And put aside. Why?"

"I don't remember. Seems like it was far more important to concentrate on my studies with my father. He was thoroughly demanding and serious about my education. Mastering the art of the blade, to learn how to successfully defend oneself in battle overshadowed all else." I thought for a moment, then stated: "I get a sense of being told...by a Muti, I think...yes. I was told it was time to progress...strange that I should have forgotten all of that. It seems as if I simply stopped playing catch and began playing warrior instead. Then I was intent on learning how to outwit my father. And that took many years of hard work with the sword."

"Like we are doing now?" she asked with a gentle smile.

"Well, this is easier," I admitted, silently adding: *and a bit more enjoyable.*

That last thought surprised me, for the sword had been such a vital part of my life. It had dominated everything. What Sarleni was exposing me to was a totally different set of skills. But it wasn't this that made these prolonged lessons so inviting. Watching during these exercises was a charmingly delightful added pleasure. I avoided the implications of that thought.

Sarleni merely continued to gaze intently into my eyes, though there seemed to be a slight softening in their glint, almost as if she knew exactly everything I was thinking.

I tired to shut down on her, the connection blurred, then retargeted deep inside my brain, almost painfully.

"Pay attention!" she instructed. "This is serious business. You must learn everything! Perfect your skills. Our lives may depend on it. The mission's success may balance on our mutual ability to reach the ultimate union in a total Nexus. Without that all else may be lost!"

She was so seriously intent at that point that I didn't even bother to question this pronouncement.

Most of our exercises seemed like children's games. I realized, though, that she was gradually increasing the energy flow as we gained our accuracy at moving these objects.

"It is like we did in the worm hole!" She would always go back to that example. I wondered why? But there was a light, playful tone to her voice, and the pleased smile was open, wide, her eyes twinkling. "See how much fun it can be?"

Then later she explained: "I have a strong ability to channel. I believe you are a major source of power."

"Back to belief systems?" I joked, a bit too lightly.

"No!" she snapped back. "I'm serious. You are the power and I am the channel that directs it to a target. I have special skills; you have un-tapped powerful abilities. We must discover how to open them up."

It sounded quite delusional. Yet I found myself fascinated and half convinced that part of what she said was true.

Then Sarleni underscored the power of what we were doing by an effective demonstration. She lifted a small dish, spinning it red hot and then flung it across the room as it flared into flame, cindering to dust.

This was no longer child's play.

The energy to burn a metal dish like that one was intense. In the forger's flames it would take a long time to simply melt the plate down—turning it to ash was another matter! But she used our combined energy to accomplish this instantaneously! That was startlingly effective in illustrating the power of these mind tricks.

What we did next was strange.

Up on deck, we sat in our usual position near the bow, as the ship skimmed over the waves. She had us focus out into the sea. After a few moments, she lifted a huge water spout into the air, but instead of keeping it vertical, like water spouts usually go, she spun it up sideways, twisting it into loops and arches and finally tossing it high into the sky letting it rain back down into the sea.

Much of what we did resembled party tricks. Carnivals are filled with people doing amazing acts. And when I mentioned this

185

she teased me with a bright, bubbly laugh.

"Perhaps some. Some are truly powerful, and not faked. But nothing like the two of us will be able to do."

Time passed and I also learned more about Sarleni and her curious world. She often described scenic places: "My childhood was filled with dreams and wonder about the world around me. I did not feel isolated. I'd walk in the icy fields with my family and I'd play with other children now and then, but I never really connected. There was always this missing part. Moyi teaches that our minds are a part of a whole; not completely finalized, even in maturity. Empty spots open channels within us to seek further growth. Our minds are hungry to be fed. Minds such as ours need to be awakened to greater growth. Once we come in contact with one in harmony with our own a new strength reveals itself. He said: *We mature and meet our uniting force. This is the Nature of our lives and our ultimate goal, our ultimate link in life.* Don't ask me to explain. I don't completely understand. I simply accept."

I didn't try to debate the issue. Yet there were memories in my past life where emptiness had been a part of my own experience. Many casual friendships had developed. Much of my life was focused on mastering the sword. Then came the selective mental exercises with Mutis, which had always jarred and annoyed me. One would take me into a room and ask permission to touch my forehead. It would then reach into my mind. Later I'd remember very little. It was more like a distant dream that refused to stay in memory.

What I experienced with Sarleni stayed solidly fused in my mind. Yet it was so alien to me—another level of extensive consciousness far from anything I had ever experienced.

Our exchange of ideas would frequently advance into serious debates. One that I found most interesting was to challenge her blind belief in an ultimate personal creator.

"They all claim to have the answers. Each and every local and national cult and religious order has their own total authority, one top deity. How many gods are there here on Noomas? And which one is the most powerful? Is it the god that rules over the largest empire or the god who rules over smaller domains? Surely the conquering powers will claim their god to be the one and only super god, the know-it-all god. But is it? Many small nations expand to become huge empires at one time or another during our histories. And they bring their gods along and elevate them to the top of the list. But tell me, which god would you claim to be the major one that created the whole universe? Perhaps it is a combination of many gods uniting into one magnificent gestalt! Do they collaborate? Do they fight like we do as humans? How do you know that they are real? How do you know which are true major gods and which are lesser ones? How do they divide power? Or is there even a difference?"

"Must we know all the answers?" she replied softly, without trying to answer any of my questions.

"I doubt we can know any of them!" was my frustrated dispute.

"Not understand Ultimate Truths."

"Believe, understand, know?" she countered with a soft smile. "Isn't it enough to just accept?"

Hot and cold, the debates would rise and fall during our undisturbed time together. Sharing ideas and concepts became more like an exercise, trying to understand one another, and coming to a closer joining with the least amount of resistance.

"How can these local gods claim that the Universe and all that exists revolves around Noomas? A rather fantastic assumption."

And it was on this point that we found agreement.

She smiled knowingly: "The mind is a wonderful place filled with many chambers, a machinery that perhaps reaches into a different kind of dimension. We breathe in air: why does that give us life? Explain the mechanics that make this work? You can't! The greatest minds of our world openly admit their limited understanding as to what makes their existence possible. What is consciousness? Where does the brain link to mind and mind link to consciousness and awareness? Are they all one and the same thing, or things within one another, or simply an unexplained reality making use of the physical machine that is our body? It goes on forever. All the unanswered questions are there to plague our attempts to understand. So...why should we expect answers?"

Ideas like that were stunning and confusing and ultimately unanswerable. Then she said a thing that startled me:

"This Torlo claims to be from another world. Our *Han Jahn* was also from another world according to the Masters. He brought the Zygo study from a far away place, they say—the basic concept, teachings. But it has been expanded far beyond what he'd begun so many centuries ago."

She explained, patiently, silently: *How wonderful! How exciting! A whole universe of intelligent life seeking answers, discoveries about what caused it all. Wonderful mysteries none of us can truly understand. How can one not believe in the unknown, the supernatural, if you must label it that way?*

I thought: *And what about your gods. Aren't they contrived at-*

187

tempts to cause people to blindly believe what is unknown and unknowable? Perhaps they are only mere illusions for ignorant minds to feast on?

She looked serenely pensive, caring, warmly responding, like a dear friend soothing over an obvious truth that wasn't being accepted.

"They are still there, under the endless names and endless images, and endless flowering brilliance of these many unlimited variations. Even an ultimate God communicating with its creations would need to speak in their own words or thoughts. And their symbols would vary from creature to creature. A Korda would need different words to convey the message of Creation. Assuming it could think like humans. And, of course, it can't. Now can it? So there."

Beyond these moments of linkage, this short period was oddly very peaceful and pleasant. Even the weather was calmly giving us a period of quiet.

Then one night things suddenly changed.

CHAPTER EIGHTEEN

THE KALORIAN

We had turned down the engines to a less frenetic pace and let the boat skim smoothly across the surface of the calm night ocean. The heavens were bright from the billions of stars flickering to infinity, for the moons were not in the skies.

Sarleni sighed: *Beautiful, isn't it? I wonder what they are, all those blinking eyes, so much like twinkling jewels.*

This sky had very few of the familiar patterns of my homeland. My primary references were the positions of the moons and the great southern star. I estimated that we were far into the southern part of the world, an area that, to my knowledge, had not been charted by our explorers.

"Those stars are beyond reach. Andon Janis teaches they are very far away and that nothing can travel faster than the speed of light."

Thoughts are not restricted in the way material things are, such as your speed of light.

Then she began speaking: "There are no limits! Moyi teaches we are what we believe and the universe compliments that belief." Her emphatic words bolted at me with unwavering conviction.

I replied objectively. "Even Torlo didn't have an answer to speed limits...."

I explained a bit more about him and about the famous Andon Janis who had been a leading scientist in Bel-loniea ever since he'd been accepted into the courts so many years before, after his arrival on Noomas.

"His stories of life have been widely published. As an influential member of royalty through marriage, he's greatly respected. His daughter is Proctoress of Bel-loniea. It was at the time of her capture by the Diano that all of the officers-in-training were immediately commissioned and activated. What had been a prolonged conflict

189

with the Diano now elevated into a major all out war. And I should be returning to that struggle."

"Bluntly stated, dear Adt, even your mighty sword would not affect the outcome of such a conflict. Please take no offense...Bel-loniea is one of many such orderly territories ruled by their personal Proctors. What I understand is that the entire world order is now being threatened. We are a critical part of a new international controversy.

"Moyi sent me to find you *by name*: Adt Dorta of Bel-loniea. He was definite about this." Then she added: "Your sword is not vital in creating a resolution to your minor conflict with the Diano. That will happen on its own. Very soon all people must stand shoulder to shoulder for the coming challenge which faces us all!"

None of that made much sense to me. The nations I knew shared commercial barter, but remained strictly segregated, never mixing among the tribes. The wisdom of the Mutis taught us to remain pure. There is legend of times when some mixed, but they had never banded together for very long. The local Raiders created trade connections with many more people than did any other nation state. We of Bel-loniea were one of many territorial city-states. We knew about other nations through contact or even just gossip and rumor. Most of the time they respected one another's borders. I had, myself, toured a few nations, such as the Kulaina and the Walinal in the far east of Bel-loniea. South of Diano were the Tantioan and the Mulainao territories, both at continual political conflict, but seldom at aggressive war. And these were only the major states, with many that were not much more than family-owned estates. Tribes existed in the Rianls forest and in the mountains of Kalfor. The thought of containing all these in some kind of unified order, some cooperative league, was almost beyond imagination. And I told Sarleni about this and much more. To which she listened silently and then shrugged it all away with a gentle smile.

"Things change. Nothing stays the same. Who knows?"

Then a hardened thought shoved into my mind:

Remember what Moyi teaches: Ultimate power comes when we allow ultimate linkage.

"That wasn't me!" Sarleni sat upright in shocked defense.

Ju-bilee had abruptly inserted herself into our private conversation.

Soothe your anger, Adt. National quibbles will have to be rested and relationships united. Right now none of that is at issue. First you must embrace the connection. It is in the fusing of two cores that perfect power is gained. You will be tested! If you fail...all fails.

190

I started to respond, but Sarleni's thought doused it out: *She's gone!*

Sarleni explained: "She confuses everybody, and few of us know much about her."

I felt stripped when she popped into our thoughts like that. It was access without permission; something I'd always disliked. I wouldn't want her as an enemy.

Sarleni laughed. *I don't think you need be concerned about that!*

Then sighing, she added: "I believe we should rest well tonight."

No words could have been further from the truth. I glanced at Sarleni as we both settled into our bunks.

I lay back, and decided to relax my mind as Sarleni had been teaching me to do. Focusing on an X, breathing very slowly. I drew in the darkness of sleep around my consciousness, like a lovely, comforting blanket.

I was drifting in an empty space; shadowy scenes engulfed me. It was more like sound waves revealing themselves in the background of my vision.

He still needs much training. But his very strength is resisting.

He's strong, I agree.

Open him. Widen the doors of his mind. Illuminate the flow and the message. Make him see what is necessary to—

Abruptly the voices broke off, as the speakers became aware of my presence.

He's here! Visualize!

I saw Moyi and Ju-bilee materialize, but only their heads floating in a golden cloud.

They stared at me. Their faces were drawn in tense, serious lines.

I felt a spinning black web weave in about my mind, and the voices fade away for a dreamlike eternity.

Then I heard:

Adt, this is Ju-bilee. There is much you must accept. And now. Without question!

I've discovered things from the past that leap forward into the near future. But they are not conclusive. Even the Mutis have limited vision. I can't see far enough into the ebbing flow of future variables. All we can ever know are possibilities. Similar to an exacting equation; add one elemental factor and all bets are squashed. The best one can do is to allow instinct to direct our power as the future develops.

I am aware of dangerous elements ahead of us all.

191

You will soon be tested beyond your conscious limits.
You have been chosen for reasons of your heritage.
Sarleni is yours to use. The two of you will meet a man who has
vital information we need! Take it to the authorities in Bel-loniea.
You have been destined for this mission since birth.
I'll say no more at this time. You need all your thoughts and en-
ergies centered on the vortex now heading your way. You will face
an overpowering storm that could easily swallow you up like a
starving Korda. With Sarleni you have a chance, if you listen and
perfect the Zygo. Only in the ultimate Nexus can you succeed. Dis-
cover your power and learn control!
Be always prepared for the worst!

Suddenly all was silent.

The universe faded to a gray nothingness hovering in a tangled
net of dreams; worlds away mingled with today and the past, lending no sense of time, into a misty limbo. I was floating, gently rocking like a baby in a cradle. I don't know how long I enjoyed this
blissful eternity in a peaceful embrace.

Then without warning the rocking changed to a violent shake,
yanking me to full wakefulness.

I was sitting up, sword already in hand, and wondering what
kind of new nightmare this was.

Sarleni's thought slashed at me: *Kalorian!*

Without a word I lifted myself from the cabin then my head was
out of the opening to the deck, looking around when the craft was
once again smashed violently to one side. The Kalorian had to be to
our right. I turned to face a huge wave of water gush over the ship
and the flash of a huge finned tail disappear in its mists.

These creatures can be as small as a man, or four times that size.
They are known to be furiously aggressive, especially during the
mating season. Many of the stories were more legend than fact.

But this one was incredibly enormous.

The Kalorian have a reputation of creating havoc and mass destruction. Their long sleek lines curve and snake from tail to neck
until tapering off into a huge head. Razor sharp teeth line greedy
muscular jaws that are savagely hungry for any kind of living flesh.

I saw its grotesque head, gaping mouth, and those almost orange eyes ferociously glaring in my direction.

Hunting small fish with a sword is one thing. Doing combat
with a head big enough to swallow a man down in two gulps was
another matter. Its evil eyes raged. The foul gnashing teeth dripped
green slime.

If I could reach the controls, and animate our craft to full speed, we'd outrun this not-so-friendly killer.

The button was above me to the left, as I rose and twisted to my right, facing the panel, my back exposed to attack.

I spun, sword point making a healthy arc at any possible target. The Kalorian had disappeared, but I could feel it rubbing against the bottom of the boat. Then just as swiftly that green-gold head lashed out from my left, having flashed from one side of the boat to the other in an underwater surge of power. Its reactions were wickedly fast.

Mine were faster.

I just thought my sword to its target and felt the point cut tissue. My attention was focused on pressing the boat's engine button.

I heard a startled cry from the cabin, and knew Sarleni had been thrown off balance as the craft suddenly raced across the ocean.

I signed in relief: *So much for monster fish assaults.*

There wasn't even time to digest that comforting thought before it was crushed out of existence. Two almost hand-like claws clutched to the railing of the now racing craft.

Again there was no time to digest any of this, only react.

We were flying just above the water, and this creature was hanging on as if we were taking him for the joy ride. Its gaping jaws snapped at me. My sword whipped back with a double slice, the first cut flesh, and the second slashed empty air.

This exchange had taken but a few heartbeats.

Sarleni's mind had now merged with mine, like a unified shield. Our thoughts were solidly melding with one another.

I'm here.

What now?

Think kill! Focus!

The power of Sarleni's thoughts and amazing energy bulged through my every muscle. She had combined her resources with mine, becoming a part of my body—plugged me into an energizing circuit. A black shadow fell over my mind, turning to white-hot fire, almost agonizing in its strength.

Kill. Kill!

More than a thought, I became the words, centered like a beam on the monstrous fish.

Kill. Kill!

It was like a light spear of energy, glowing into white fire.

That Kalorian head snapped back like a firecracker blown away. A green slimy slit cut beneath its yellow eyes, above those huge raging jaws. It was only a surface wound. But the creature acted surprised by this unexpected counter-attack. Not half as surprised I was at that moment. Those eyes had been studying me with violent red hate brimming beneath their opened lids. Its monster jaws gaped wide, ready to devour my body. The gleaming teeth were the size of a man's head. But now there was a subtle change, an angry understanding that I had struck a physical blow at its head.

Had it reasoned how we'd wounded it? I doubted that.

Still the Kalorian responded as if it understood the implications. One could almost imagine its thinking processes. Nobody knows how intelligent these huge swimming monsters are. Like I said, little is known about them. But those eyes studied me as if the giant fish wanted to read my mind before devouring me.

Was it wondering: what this human creature was doing, attacking like that? How dare it resist my demands for a meal!

Kill, kill, kill! raged the thought from Sarleni.

I felt heated energy rip through me. Snapping jaws reached out to eat me alive.

Sarleni was safely below deck. Yet I felt as if we were both under direct attack. The merging of our minds made me dizzy with uncontrollable power. I had to tone it back so I could focus.

It was at best, a touching of "mental hands" not fully locked together, nor intertwined. But its power coursed through my veins like a firestorm. A shell of energy invisibly billowed up around us.

Sarleni caused a protective shield to envelop us, and the fishy assault fell short of success. So did my sword. His jaws continued to snap at empty air, almost, but not quite reaching my sword as it plunged out to meet the creature's attack.

The fish weaved back, still clinging to the side of our speeding ship. The three moons were creating triple shadows in undulating waves. Our craft bounced to the forward momentum and the extra weight of the fish gripping its hull.

Sarleni commanded: *Embrace me with your mind.*

I didn't know what she was expecting. Nor did I have time to figure it out.

The huge watery monster recovered fast enough to make another attack. This time his snaking tail lashed over the bow of our speeding boat with such force that we could feel the explosion of power ram the craft off its determined destination. The autopilot counter-corrected, whipping us bodily off balance again.

Water gulped at us, spun the craft around. For a moment I was almost torn off my feet. My hand held the panel in a frantic grip. Then the rushing waters subsided and we were upright.

I felt Sarleni's grip on my mind slipping.

The Kalorian's head and jaws breathed close about my head.

At least Sarleni would survive that trap of jagged teeth.

My sword finally met that canyon throat about to swallow my body alive.

All I had to do was "think kill" and the blade would respond. The weapon spiraled into mad configurations of thrashing cuts that even I couldn't follow.

The fish, of course, was oblivious to all this. The jaws continued to close.

Sarleni's power welled up in me like an angry flame. Those jaws were closing tighter, fighting the invisible energy protecting us.

I don't know what happened, but I kept thrusting. One moment the fish was being hacked by my blade, then all at once a foamy breaking wave washed over us and then the Kalorian was gone!

Everything wavered almost phantom-like in that last moment and I had to refocus my eyes in order to see.

Now the moons burst into visibility, which had previously been hidden by the fish. The world appeared normal. Our boat was quietly racing across the ocean.

I waited anxiously for a resurgence of the attack.

Then a voice entered my mind like a wild demon from the pits of an underworld I never believed existed. It came out of nowhere, like an explosion.

Well done, but not good enough!

I shot at Sarleni: *Stop that!!*

Not me.

Ju-bilee pulsed into being, lingering in a half elusive haze, floating slightly, as her eyes glared grimly at me.

I used the Kalorian to test you. A good thing, too. You are not ready. A Muti would have ripped the two of you apart!

A test? Rage seethed within me at her audacity to place us in such a life threatening position. Inexcusable! How dare she!

I warned that you'd be tested!

My anger burned like red-hot coals at her casual coolness.

Ju-bilee had impudently intruded with deliberate seriousness: *You two failed. You need discipline. You haven't discovered the capacity of the Zygo. Nor understand how to focus energy. You play awkwardly with ancient tools. You wave power around like a dangerous sword in a baby's hands. You are without any sense of technique. All will be lost. The Nexus power can, under a master's focus, be so strong that it would have blown that fish to charred atoms in one instant.*

I objected sullenly: "Then find some grand master to do your fishing!"

Her eyes flashed with such fury that it felt like a physical blow across my face. I leaned forward, partly lifting my sword, letting natural rage power my anger.

She stood tall, measuring her words calmly: *You don't impress me!*

Back off! I felt like a helpless child before a scolding parent. My fingers gripped the sword tighter. *You can push a man just so far!*

A man? Ju-bilee scoffed, almost with contempt. *You're a child! Pride and male ego are dangerous illusions that can get you killed. You defend yourself like a silly Virgin Goddess! And they don't exist! Stop hiding. This isn't a game to be played out on grand gentlemanly swordsman rules or military manners ...we are beyond petty civilized ethics and concepts. This is a struggle for primal existence! Before the balance of Noomas will be shattered. It will take a master to defeat the barriers that stand between you and the connection, not a child.*

"Then send your masters to deal with it! Why us?" I fumed through clenched teeth, barely containing my wrath.

For reasons involved in your birthing. Her emotion softened as she continued.

Sarleni is a natural match and trained. You're the connection. No time for historical details. You must focus on your hidden skills to hone them into active weapons. And nothing more!

Right now you are stumbling, ignorant and untrained. Perfect the Zygo quickly and completely now. Or the both of you die.

Like the snapping of a tightly stretched string, the connection to Ju-bilee broke. She was gone.

I felt Sarleni fade from my mind, then drift back a few moments later as she slowly came on deck.

She said: *Ju-bilee's right.*

Where do we begin? I was still deeply shaken and uncertain about everything.

By opening.

What happens then?

Even I don't know for sure, only that this is the way. It won't be easy. We must fathom our energies through all mental walls to our very core.

We had come a long way over the last days learning tremendous truths at an amazing speed

We used every opportunity to exercise our new disciplines and teamwork, like when hunting some animal or bird to fill out our diet. It was a matter of being able to see with two sets of eyes rather than merely one pair. We shared visualizations as well as thoughts. At first confusing, then it just fit together, like alternating pictures scanned in a book. We took turns directing objects in each other's hands, though with some humorous accidents, that proved there were limits as to what we could and couldn't do. A few times our waterspouts would break up over our boat giving us an unexpected cold shower. However, our ingenuity was increasing. She was forming water bows and I would form the arrows and shoot them through the waves with astounding accuracy and speed.

Endless lessons filled our time slowly improving our ability to meld together. Yet we still held back a central core element. It was difficult to pry open interior doors into my very core. Sometimes Sarleni's impatience would get the best of her.

Eventually, she argued: "We need to reach deeper union. We *must* become one; not two separate beings locked in separate rooms, but one combined housing for both of us."

My thoughts shut down the mental exchange.

"I sense your fear, Adt."

"I just need private space."

She nodded, "We will learn how to open doors and shut down access to our inner selves. Yes we all have secrets and need to be safe from needless exposure."

It was obvious that we must join into a unified oneness, but how far into our private inner core?

Only later did Sarleni present her next argument. *When the time comes, we must implode and then embrace one another without resistance. In such a state it is believed we can be aware of all there is of the other.*

"And no privacy?" I blurted.

She smiled. "Afraid?"

"Aren't you?"

"I suppose. It is thought to work like our conscious awareness. We don't remember everything at any given moment. Focus is all. We join without restrictions, masks or walls." *Yet do not flow aimlessly through the corridors of each other's minds. Moyi believes that mental focus limits awareness.*

"Believes?" *Don't they know?*

She considered that, and then sighed. "Nobody has achieved Total Nexus. A few came close. Moyi has studied the most advanced theories. He says that Totality makes two into one conscious awareness; but not all memories are actively broadcasting information. We draw on only what is needed at any given moment. It is all documented in very advanced concepts…and nobody knows from actual experience. Moyi believes we are a unit that might achieve

Totality. That is why we have been chosen…or so he says."

I didn't even bother to follow that thought any further and Sarleni dropped the subject.

We continued on with our experiments and exercises. Despite our more dedicated attempts to reach deeper into one another, we continued to mask off that inner core.

I was relieved when we could back off and enjoy moments of quiet companionship. And both of us continued to reexamine the map that showed markings of *Illysæ Ad Mördi Tăli*.

We inspected the horizon often for signs of the island; then one morning we thought we spotted it in the distance. And it was exactly where it was supposed to be. The night sky now provided familiar constellations of the northern hemisphere of Noomas.

The distant hazy line on the horizon began to take shape, forming a jagged range of mountains upon the rolling sea. This was not a small land mass, but quite large.

The island had a lovely beauty about it; a flow and grace even at this distance.

Sarleni stood next to me, the morning breeze flowing through her hair, whipping it around her face. She looked delicately fresh, her cheeks softly flushed pink in the morning light.

She turned, smiled, and then swiftly looked away when our eyes met. She pointed, "Look!"

We could see a shoreline and even the trees beyond. And a pier extending towards us like a long, inviting wooden arm.

As if we were expected.

CHAPTER NINETEEN

THE SANCTUARY OF ILLSÆ AD MÖRDI TĂŁI

We watched as the island came closer to us, mountains lifting beyond thick forests that grew right up to the beach. Or was the forest reaching out towards us? We were both uncertain yet this land beckoned to us; inviting and haunting and vibrant. When we reached the dock, I tied the craft to a metal ring on the piling. We climbed onto the pier and started towards the shore. The ocean waves continuously rumbled against the murmur of the morning wind through the jungle. At the end of the dock a pathway tapered off into the undergrowth beyond a small building.

We made our way down the path, the morning breeze cool to our flesh. I was aware of Sarleni directly behind me, our minds touching, like fingers intertwining.

I wondered where it led, when Sarleni silently responded:

In through the jungle and buildings.

I see only one.

I sense more beyond.

The structure facing us had a small flat front, deeply carved with complex symbols.

Sarleni inspected them closely. *I've never seen any writing like this. But look there, under that larger part. My* eyes focused under the markings.

Somebody had written: *Welcome to Illysæ Ad Mördi Tăłi*

"A translation?" Sarleni murmured very softly.

"No doubt!"

We started past the brick and plaster structure. Small huts clustered on either side of the path, shadowed and dark, and empty. A quiet neatness told us that these huts were continually managed and maintained.

Neither of us speculated.

This whole place surrendered itself to safe, peacefulness, as if protected by some unseen power. No danger from night hunters. Human or animal would not dare to invade this tranquility.

The jungle climbed higher and higher. Eventually the tangle of vines and trees and brush thinned out. The huts became scarce and scattered, sometimes not even seen.

We stopped at a group of tionoi trees, and picked the juicy blue fruits, glad to find something common on this side of Noomas.

After a while, the forest cleared revealing a grassy hilltop. And just over the ridge stood a huge structure, surrounded by a formidable wall.

We watched from a distance. After a while we noticed activity at the gateway.

A fat obelisk, rose to a point, like a needle probing the clouded sky. A strange illusion swept through me, as if its tip had opened up and swallowed the heavens. Blinking hard, I turned to Sarleni. She was shaking her head from side to side. We had shared that momentary vision.

The stone pathway led straight from the forest to the oval opening in the wall around the obelisk. This was not a door, but an entrance without restriction to whatever lay beyond. People strolled down pathways passing what appeared low gardened areas bordered by lightly purpled hedges.

Sarleni stared at the setting, *Have you seen anything like that in…Bel-loniea?*

"Not exactly," I said, softly, just above a whisper.

"And on an island," she replied just loud enough to be heard.

The place compelled total respect and quiet.

What struck me was the size of the building with its pinnacle lifting up towards the sky like some element of special worship.

"That's it!" I exclaimed, full-voiced. *Almost a monumental tribute kind of thing…right here in a nowhere land.*

Sarleni grinned, nodded. *You're right. Like some holy temple or religious order or…I feel a…sadness, or foreboding or…*

"Death!" I muttered, agreeing instantly with what she was attempting to express.

We had come some distance from the shore where our boat had been docked. The sun was dimmed behind the clouds.

Without another word we started moving, down the long pathway that led to the obelisk nestled within the embrace of the low hanging hills beyond.

Overwhelming curiosity baited both of us. We were eager to discover whatever was within this structure; and we both guessed that much was about to be revealed. Why that should be, I had no idea. It was as if somebody had whispered a secret into my brain. We had been led here.

It wasn't long before we were standing in front of the wide entrance. Beyond that was a neatly trimmed garden between pillars that reached up into the sky several levels, supporting what was, apparently, a glass ceiling.

A person on the other side of a hedgerow momentarily peered at us and then scampered away as we approached.

Heady perfumes infused the air from the multicolored flowers on both sides of the walkway inlaid with tiles decorated with curling symbols.

"What a lovely place," Sarleni remarked, almost reverently. "Yet oddly foreboding."

I turned my attention to a man hurrying our way.

Spry in his step, his hunched body was slightly frail of frame, with a bouncy strength. As he drew closer it was obvious the man was quite old, his face wrinkled in a mass of lines. Then he was upon us, smiling broadly.

"Greetings." His voice held emotional generosity that disarmed both of us. "Welcome to the Universal Gathering of the Dead."

His face was pale and narrow. He was old, but not ancient. Wrinkled lines around bright gray eyes were warm with deep wisdom.

I tried to probe into his thoughts, but found nothing open.

Not unusual. Sarleni silently whispered. *I don't think he is doing it on purpose. Some minds automatically have a more solid wall of protection, a shell encasing all thought from the outside. You were almost like that...most difficult to reach when you wanted to close down. I don't think he's aware.*

The man had extended his hand, palm upwards in the universal ancient greeting. We showed our hands open to him, in expected response. This formality was seldom used any more.

"Welcome to our pleasures. Is there something we can offer? You must be most tired after such long travels."

I was alarmed. How could he know?

Maybe the startled expression on my face had communicated something to him.

"Oh, but of course. We are an isolated island and not many outsiders visit here, except those who expect to stay...but aren't of our race, of course. You are, quite obviously, foreigners from a distant land. Our island is far from the continental territories of the Kamina. And only those of Kamina come here to stay."

His statements, which he made with blatant confidence, were

puzzling to us.

Our host rambled in disconnected phrases. We listened intently to learn everything we could from what he told us about this place. He assumed we knew far more than we did.

"Come," he invited, "I am always happy to see new guests visit our Sanctuary. Not too many come here. I mean people like yourselves."

We hesitated, just standing there kind of dazed from the surroundings and his openly friendly manner.

He waved his hand for us to follow him

"Come, come, hurry up! I don't want to waste your time. Nor mine, come to think of it. This is a large complex and you could get lost."

As we entered the building, he led us down a winding corridor. "I would like to tell you all about our people. Stop me if I repeat myself. We are proud of our unique privilege to serve this sanctuary. Do you mind if I ramble on?" He jerked to a halt, frozen in place, staring straight at us, waiting for our reply.

Sarleni and I tried to maintain a serious expression, but we were both so amused inside and about to burst into laughter at this funny little man. We had no idea what to say! After a short pause, we nodded in unison. I guess he took that as our consent. A wide smile spread over his happy face as he made a little hop and plowed right into his story.

"Let me introduce myself. Most rude of me. My name is Kinelian, Manager of this establishment, at your service." He spoke with the smooth style of a long experienced story teller.

"We are organized with a small but very well trained staff. No need for a lot of people working here. Dedicated men and women, all. Many are involved in recording historical accounts for our members before they continue their journey. We keep things up to date. I sometimes spend many hours scanning over some of that text. This primarily develops a lot of my own insight into worldly matters. Luckily so. I don't get out much. A live-in. This is my world.

"Anyway, the staff is reluctant to meet visitors. Dedicated to their work here. It is our way of life. Those who come to stay, our clients, you might say, have no further need for worldly possessions. What little they bring gets distributed among our people for use.

Our staff rotates with the seasons. Our people specialize in harvest time and planting time, at least most of them. And our chefs are among the finest to be found anywhere. Some were born here, of course. Mainlanders will stay for six seasons, then return to their villages on Kamina. They are all equally as dedicated. Our native

202

islanders are more comfortable with isolation and quiet."

Our host took us through many departments showing us the crafts of their expert staff. Intricate weaving and cloth making. Paintings, pottery, metal workings, paper milling, libraries. And through the windows we saw people harvesting fruits, vegetables, flowers, herbs. He went on and on enthusiastically detailing with pride, the works of each specialty.

"Any worldly news comes from our customers and, naturally, from the mainland. So we aren't all that isolated. What we need is supplied. We're a dedicated lot.

"Come, come, this way."

He motioned us down another hall, and then to a large double doorway, which opened at our approach.

"Here we'll have something to refresh ourselves. You arrived just in time for the mid-meal," he said leading us into a comfortable room, whose walls were lined with yellow drapes patterned in lovely flowery designs. A window on the far wall revealed another room beyond.

"Here...be comfortable. You are my guests!" Then almost as a nervous afterthought, said: "Nothing fancy, we islanders are basic. The mainland staffers complain. They claim there are so many varieties of international cuisine that it is a shame to be so limited. But we are set in our ways. Far less sophisticated in seasoning and design. Of course, for our long-term clients, well, they are entitled to whatever they favor during their final stay on our world. Many demand hot-spiced dishes that would burn the insides of a normal gut. Or they request the watery concoct of Dialnaian delights, even the nine-legged crawling insects found in the deep jungles of Knokna. We'll provide them all as desired. Our cooks are master artisans, a necessary prerequisite to please any possible demands of our paying guests. Business is business. But for ourselves it is mainly simple fare."

He set us down at the small table in the middle of the room, and a male servant came with a tray of food. Steaming lianão buds and warmed ilkan ribs dipped in rich red sauce. The fruits were customarily enjoyed after the main course.

This was quite a feast even under normal conditions.

Nobody spoke while we ate. It was apparently a ritual of silence. He remained quiet and we followed his example.

When the servant returned and took the empty plates, our host said:

"Well now. You can see what a job it is for me to manage this place." A broad sweep of his arms encompassed everything around us. "Quite a responsibility, too, I might add. I have been doing this for many years. Most of my adult life, come to think of it. Been wed here and even raised our children after my wife's early death. All rather tragic at the time, but...we all have our tragic moments, our gains and losses. I'm a dedicated servant of *them*."

I frowned; he frowned back, and then gave one of his generous smiles.

"Oh, yes. Of course. I suppose explanations might be in order. I drift. I tend to get lost in my own thinking. A habit of being somewhat isolated much of the time. I think out loud, too.

"'Life is surrendered far too quickly. Devour the most of every moment. A life lived like a rich wine will not miss its container.'

"I read that somewhere. Confusing thought, I'll admit, but certainly impressive enough. Where did I read it?

"The mind gets staggered with too many facts.

"There's another quote that pops out of my brain: 'Never forget to spend your energies on feats that can be redesigned. Don't attempt re-hammering what is permanently finished.'

"A peculiar statement, too, come to think of it. I can get lost in quotables. They are all fashioned to confuse the normal mind down new channels of thinking. Sometimes quite rewarding, other times... well, 'A fool dances to music that runs backwards'."

He shrugged and laughed loudly: the first very loud sound we'd experienced in this tranquil place.

"I have allowed myself to become distracted. Please forgive me. I may not be an old man, but I've been told I act the role. Fancy that? Too much time spent in building habits of tender caring for those who have come to benefit from our Sanctuary...it has twisted my demeanor. All who arrive here are anxious to embrace their final rewards. This is the *House of Eternity* and beyond the hills behind us are the orderly beds for those who stay forever in our gardened *Pathway to the Afterlife*."

I had heard of special places dedicated by some cults and religious orders that housed the bodies of the dead. It was a common practice for many people to allow themselves to find a unique place to keep their remains.

I nodded, respectfully: "Not all people seek permanently marked remembrances of their existence. It is common for some to allow their ashes to be returned to the seas from which they had originated."

Sarleni solemnly added: "We did not know. You must belong to the *Ancient League of the Dead*."

"Ah, yes," Kinelian confirmed, grandly. "But you must truly be from far away *not* to know. Where do you come from?"

Sarleni spoke up with authority: "From the South."

"Oh?" He looked honestly puzzled.

"Very much South," she said quickly and without hesitation, but I felt a slender thread of hesitance from her: *Hope I guessed right....*

"The southern lands or islands?" he inquired quite intensely, leaning forward.

"Some islands are huge, some lands are small," she practically sounded like she was lecturing a profoundly grounded fact. "And all consider themselves the center of the Universe!"

Kinelian nodded. "Yes. I know. I have heard. Few of you come this far north. What brings you here?"

"Just exploring," I added without thought. I wanted to change the subject.

"What is it you explore?"

"Well...we're...." I looked down, as if embarrassed, but I was, in fact, uncertain, and desperately trying to buy time.

Sarleni quickly responded: "Newly joined. And on a voyage of discovery."

"Ah. A marriage creating its new journey of self-discovery. Our island is hardly an ideal destination for a young couple like your-selves...unless, of course, you wish to see what we all must come to terms with. Yes. What an unusual place to land."

I answered almost truthfully: "We landed here merely by chance!"

"I can believe that. Few strangers come by choice. I'm quite proud of what we've designed for our patrons. And we're so legen-dary I just figure everybody knows about us."

There was a lingering silence. "Come, let me show you."

We all stood and left the room.

As we started down the hallway he continued with: "This is the *Illysœ Ad Mördi Tăli*. A loose translation would be: *Sanctuary of the Mutis*. Don't ask for a literal translation, it won't make sense."

From the expression on our faces, he quickly saw our surprise. "But of course...I mean, considering you come from the South, and I take that it means more western than directly South, you may not know much about islands like this one, where some Mutis come to find everlasting peace beyond their momentary existence here and now."

He again picked up on our puzzled reaction.

"Yes, yes, of course, I talk in riddles, I suppose. Comes from conversing with our customers. They consider us just a little less evolved.

"There are vast ruins over all the lands that pre-date human arrival, and maybe even that of the Mutis. I suspect they may have come here on some kind of mission themselves, but long before us.

"That's the mystery of it all. We don't know. They don't know. I understand very little, to be sure, just bits from conversations overheard."

Sarleni asked: "You're saying that none of us are native to Noomas? How interesting."

Silently to me: *It is much as our teachings imply.*

"Not exactly...*interesting*. There are many worlds up there...." His eyes lifted towards the ceiling to indicate the heavens, then returned to us without a pause in his statement. "And I suspect we all came from them, humans as well as the Mutis. All come from different origins but follow the same evolutional processes.

"But the ruins here on Noomas...ah, such interesting places. So little is known. In fact, most of it is myth and mystery. Some ancient mounds with structures here and there survive in crumbled states.

"One conjecture supports the theory that whatever life-forms originally evolved on this planet may have been wiped out by some plague or war or who knows what.

"One can get confused by too much learning. Every authority has the Ultimate Answer and backed by amazingly impressive credits with endless titles and degrees of learning that would impress even the Mutis. And the common people don't have the ability to sort out clever evidence from fantasy. Perhaps it is best to remain uneducated. Certainly less confusing. Many Proctors depend on ignorance to control their populations. The masses blindly nod to authority. All you or I need to do is honor their wise council."

He abruptly broke off, as if having spoken more than he had meant to. "I prattle. My mind flies across wild speculation. Too much in here!"

He tapped his head. "And too little space there to contain all those voices screaming to be heard above all others."

The man chuckled in self-amusement and escorted us into an open roofless area. The sky was almost clear of clouds, the sun bright overhead.

"Here, follow me. I talk too much and know too little."

"No," Sarleni almost pleaded, "I would love to hear more. It is fascinating."

"Really. You don't say!"

It was my turn to encourage him to continue. "Very much so. We know little about this territory...."

206

He grinned widely.

We followed our host down a wide stone pathway.

The air was fresh and cool, even in the afternoon sunlight.

"Come, come, this way, you'll be amazed at what you'll see. I'm quite proud of what we've managed to create for our customers. They arrive under tragic circumstances. Sometimes they stay for a prolonged period of time before continuing on in their final journey."

CHAPTER TWENTY

BewarE

Kinelian led the way down a brick and stone path gradually turning from stone to dirt as it wound through a gardened landscape, leading upwards into the surrounding hills.

When we finally reached the top we saw the ocean stretched out below lush terraces spread in a series of flat runways, going all the way into the distance from left to right.

"This," he said, "is our Final Sanctuary. The resting place of the Lost Mutis, where they make their pilgrimage towards their eternal afterlife. They are lost in a place that is unfit for their true natures. Here their souls find peace, assuming they have them, and assuming they ascend rather than descend...well who knows? Right? We live and exist here on the belief that something happens after our life here in the now. But there are so many authorities on the subject of life and afterlife and some depressive thoughts about death being the end, and all sounding so convincing...one can never know. And the more we know, the less convinced we can become about any one concept. They are all so logical or just down right desirable...and even the more fantastic ideas sound appealing and well formed that...." He shrugged, almost helplessly. "I would rather subscribe to an afterlife as being more pleasant than...well, I certainly find it far more sellable. It is a popular target for life everlasting. Though, for me, not with these creatures dominating the next step into eternal life. Yet those that come here, of course, are of the gentle nature, giving, serving, wanting to...well, never mind. They are contradictory to those who run Kamina. And that's what brings them here, as you surely can understand."

I wanted details concerning what he had said. Perplexing, confusing and mystifying. Sarleni's silence quietly agreed.

Kinelian motioned us to another pathway gliding down to the beach below. It was a very steep incline.

We hesitated for a moment as he spoke in a very serious tone: "These sad creatures say little...just enough to reveal they come from a civilization where Mutis rule...hard to believe...and they were haunted creatures.

"Well...never mind."

He took a deep breath, then with a sweep of his arm over the distant horizon said: "Out there is the Kamina Empire. Little is known about it. The mainlanders who work here are from coastal towns. They are somewhat more sophisticated than the tribal people living inland. Rumors about the Kamina civilization are filtered through these primitives.

"I get mixed messages. Mutis that come here are haunted. It is puzzling. Some customers from other lands occasionally take a place down there with their fellows.

"It is rather mysterious.

"Mutis keep to their private quarters, back there." He made a vague wave of his arm, towards the building we had left. "They are shy of visitors and swiftly fade out of sight."

The man shrugged again with his narrow shoulders gathering together for but a moment.

"They hide beneath hoods and behind the mask of their shriveled eye-sockets. And they reveal only what they want you to know. Still, what I learned from a number of sources is revealing horrors...if true.

"But, of course, nothing, nothing at all I'd want to repeat."

"Why not?" I asked, now quite curious. He had become grim, hard and serious. "You can't leave it at that!"

"Ah, but I can. It is not my habit to spread rumors."

Sarleni almost whispered, leaning closer to him. "Spread them, please. At least for our ears alone."

He smiled for a moment, shaking his head: "Enough to say these creatures down here are resting safe from any real or imagined demons. I'm proud of what we've given them."

He took us down the cliff side, step by step. The stones were set in uneven rows, none exactly the same. Here we discovered rocks of different sizes in row after row, evenly spaced, some with markings, possibly symbols or artful décor.

"Many of these stones steps are from the ruins." He said, as we made our way down. Then later as we reached our destination, added: "This is where the Mutis of Kamina are placed. They come here to die. None of them lived very long. Not even one revolution around our sun. The size of the capstone depends on their status.

"While I've been isolated, I'm not ignorant concerning things

209

Noomasian. People do visit from time to time. Even Mutis from distant lands. I have many maps of all parts of Noomas, though mostly outdated. Kamina is more currently detailed. We get more information about that place. Hard information that is sketchy as best, but more timely than from other places. A lot of wild rumors. Nothing gets out without permission. But we never know who gives the permission, other than it comes from the Mutis. Anyway, enough of that."

He stopped, a visible shiver rushed over his frame.

"What's wrong?" Sarleni asked.

He hesitated for a moment, lowering his voice to a hushed whisper: "Nothing…just rumors about Kamina…if they are right…I hate to imagine."

I asked: "What can you tell us?"

He shuffled out among the stones, then back to us again as if to appear less serious: "Nasty business. Bad thoughts. Supposedly we are considered little more than semi-intelligent beasts to keep the machinery of their Empire functioning. Or as entertainers. Imagine such madness. Just rumor, mind you."

The man just stood there, staring blindly out across the ocean, until Sarleni asked: "Can you tell us more?"

His eyes snapped to hers. "Not much from personal experience. I've seen only one human who was raised under their system and it wasn't pleasant. He was crazed, had come here by raft, claiming to have escaped from deep within the mainland. He talked of revolution and a secret society trying to overthrow a Muti dominated Kamina Empire. This man was feverish and delusional. The scars on his body were deep and horrid. He died in a few days, leaving many questions unanswered.

"But he told of a mad place where human rights were non-existent.

Again he took a few steps, brushing over the tops of several grave markers in a casual acceptance to what he was saying, then continued:

"Things are happening in Kamina. That is the blunt rumor that keeps welling up time and again; and even stronger in recent times. For it appears that the Kamina Empire seeks expansion. And yet…."

He nodded towards the endless array of headstones. "All of these Mutis spoke little about their lives there, yet I heard a few bizarre tales of an upside-down culture which even they found distasteful."

He paused long enough to guide us down the last uneven step and onto solid ground. Before us lay massive rows of stones. "This is where we were instructed to place them facing away from the distant horizon. It was a commanding issue. 'So we can not see this evil place in our eternal dreams'."

He paused, a rather serious grin lifting his lips. Sweeping his arm over the horizon, he turned and said, "Out there is the continent upon which their empire exists. A place to avoid." His eyes shifted between mine and Sarleni's. "You don't want to go there."

Sarleni asked: "Is it so ugly?"

"Ugly isn't the right word. But this sad dying man rendered an extraordinary picture of a place with open cities, not walled up. For they all are part of a vastly joined federation of interlinked civilized centers. And all the farmlands stretch out between cities. He told of mountain resorts, of crystal clear lakes and giant forests lifting high into the heavens. Vacation inns nested within their roots.

They cater to a continual feed of customers who enjoy happy relaxing days of pampering pleasure."

She said: "It sounds lovely."

"It is a world of finesse, so he claimed. And—well, just one of many luxurious spots available to those who live in the lowlands. Plus you have the desert oases with exotic fragrant flowers where many come to bathe in the seas of salt, to float in those waters, basking under the constant sun. It truly is a world of wonder. Tall buildings of the cities leap into the sky. Huge pyramids throughout the land, apparently long considered Holy Ground."

"In the center of the capital of Kamina they have the Pyramid of the Prophet. He is the First Voice to Speak the New Truth as inspired by their concept of the True Creator."

Sarleni looked impressed, almost truly taken in by his words.

"This is, young lady, the land of the Mutis and not the land of our people. All of it, the very vastness of it is spread out for the sole purpose of catering to *them*. Not humans. Their resorts in mountain places and desert springs, are run with human slaves, and designed to fill the needs and desires of their Muti masters."

For a moment the man looked almost frightened as if he had spoken too much. Then he added almost in a whisper: "I don't know what caused me to say that. I don't ever say such things. Something compelled me!"

I thought to Sarleni: *What are you doing to the poor man.*

Wasn't me. I didn't do a thing.

He was silent for a long time before saying: "Well, crazy words or not. That's what the man said to me. Out of his head, of course. And some was reinforced from random stories sometimes told by our clients. I listen…and learn more than I should."

He was again silent, looking puzzled, shaking his head from side to side. When he spoke again it was in an even softer voice. "The Mutis who come here to rest, to sleep their eternity, are disturbed souls. And they come here to be free to die."

"Strange," I replied. "I thought Mutis were, by their very nature, here to serve."

"No group of intelligent minds will always agree on everything." He swept his right arm out over the rows of stones in the graveyard. Something was churning in his mind.

Now he spoke with more authority. "I suppose telling you will prepare you. I've been to speak more freely. These are the remains of those who rebelled and escaped. They were doomed to be executed or crushed because they had dared to challenge those in authority. Mind blocking has been forbidden. I'm not certain what that means."

I simply said to him: "Go ahead. You don't need to explain about that. We understand."

"Well, then, you understand more than I do." With a shrug of his narrow shoulders, he added: "I just know these stones represent the remains of heroes who refused to submit to anti-human dictates. They came here to die."

He looked sadly up at us: "Very strange and unsettling. If you want to take a closer look, then here you have it."

Looking was depressing. But the sun continued to bake down on us and finally I decided we'd seen enough.

Our guide motioned us back up the steps, saying nothing, remaining silent for some time. Finally as we were about to reach the top he turned, a sober expression on his lips, a narrowing of his eyes, as he said: "There are those above who now wish to visit with you. They wish to speak directly to you, rather than through me."

I glanced at Sarleni for some clarification but she could give no clues, either: *I feel nothing!*

"Come, come," Kinelian, commanded, sounding annoyed. His previous friendly personality had sliced out of existence. Now he was all business. "You are wanted!"

He turned and went the rest of the way up to the top of the hill, then he was out of sight, as we stood there uncertain about what to expect next.

Sarleni was gazing off into space beyond me, her eyes unseeing. Then she slowly shook her head. "Nothing."

"What?"

I called for Moyi. He has remained beyond reach for a very long time. I tried for Ju-bilee. Nothing.

The look on Sarleni's face was more startling than anything else. She appeared uncentered, frightened.

Then she spoke in a soft whisper: "There is something wrong."

"There's nothing to do but go up and find out what this is all about," I was hoping to relieve her obvious confusion. "My sword is swift enough to deal with any possible threat."

My hand was holding the hilt of my sword, ready for instant combat.

She nodded. *Silly of me. What would be here to threaten us?*

Yet we both had felt the cold shift of his commanding words.

Without waiting, we climbed the last steps to the top of the hill. We were greeted by the unexpected.

Standing there before this mass of cloaked Mutis, our host was as grim as a statue, leaving no doubt about the seriousness of this moment.

There were at least twenty Mutis looming behind him, their deep purple faces shadowed in the folds of their hoods, most of them revealing only one sunken eye-socket to stare blindly at us.

It was then that we both felt Ju-bilee enter our minds:

Beware!

There are times in everybody's life when events climb down so fast that all one can do is observe; watching without reacting. Standing there before this mass of cloaked Mutis, our host so grim as a statue, left no doubt about the seriousness of this moment. He had said the Mutis withdraw from outsiders; that they avoided all guests on the island. They had come here to die. They were supposedly timid, frightened, defeated creatures, crumbling slowly away within their foreboding skulls.

These Mutis did not concur with his description. They were actually more frightening than I wanted to imagine. I'd seldom been this close to more than a few at any one time, except in nightmarish dreams. Reality was far more daunting. They wandered throughout society on Noomas more like ministers of the faith, priests for some local religious cult. Their power was unknown, a matter of implied force in mysterious areas of the mind. Their ability to read into the future and project events yet to come had always made them an element of concern and even fear. They served as ministers of our marriages, and many times judges in legal and moral matters and for the most part they held control over elements in our lives that were beyond our own ability to handle. They filled in many voids in the power structure of human society. They were needed; they were respected and by many feared.

I stood there, stunned. Sarleni whispered in my brain: *Be care-*

ful.

A single Muti could be intimidating. No human could stand up against such strength or speed. They could cripple, maim, kill with little more effort than the projecting of one thought.

What did they gain from us?

I had questioned their ultimate authority in the same way I resisted bowing to the gods of Noomas. As if my life was defined in some universal conflict with these portentous creatures. Yet I always appeared respectful of their power.

Like I said, one Muti was enough to intimidate even a Proctor. More than three was overwhelming. Seldom were they seen in larger groups.

Twenty or more were next to terrifying. A chill rushed down my spine.

Sarleni tried to rationalize my fears: *If they wanted to harm us we'd feel that. I feel nothing.*

Somehow that wasn't reassuring.

"Come, come," Kinelian beckoned, serious but not in any way threatening. "They must escort you."

As we stepped forward, Sarleni's hand reached for mine. Our fingers interlocked and I felt her thought: *Whatever it is...we're not in any immediate danger; Ju-bilee has only warned us to beware.*

Mutis gathered around us like a large blanket of hooded giants. I felt stifled. Their very presence had always tended to invade my inner being.

Kinelian was saying: "I'm as amazed as you must be. These Mutis avoid strangers. This is the first time they have done this. But they requested both of you by name."

It was only a short walk to the entrance of a very small unmarked structure that opened down to a wide staircase.

Kinelian explained: "This is where they reside. They seldom leave this building until ready for their final resting bed out...where I showed you."

We were escorted down steep gloomy steps for some time.

The Mutis flanked us on all sides. They avoided any physical contact or communication, herding us in a singular direction.

Is Ju-bilee around? I asked Sarleni, who answered:

She faded once we entered this structure. We were communicating. She told me that this was a new circumstance, an unexpected one. She said: Things are far more complex. The Mutis of Kamina are very strong and have a deeply guarded area around their kingdom. Very little leaks out. Nothing comes in, nothing goes out. It is filtered in some way. Her mind was blocked from entering here.

214

SLAVEGIRL OF NOOMAS, BY CHARLES NUETZEL & HEIDI GARRETT

Just at that moment the Mutis in front of us parted, exposing a very large chamber with a high, arched ceiling. Small glowing orbs floating above us to light the room.

We were in a huge cavern, neatly cut out of stone, deep into a mountainside. There was a hallowed aura to the room dark and mysterious, the walls in rich brown tones, blank of any design. I was taking in our surroundings when suddenly the escorting Mutis drew back, submerging into the shadows along the walls. For all I could tell they might have disappeared.

In the middle of the room was a large, low throne upon which sat a magnificently morose young Muti, his hood tossed back, exposing its knotty bald head. There is not a hair to be found on their bodies. The structure of a normal Muti's face has harsh, unrelenting angles that catch the light with dark shadows outlining its rugged foundation. There is nothing of beauty about a Muti's face; ears twisted into tiny holes. Their spartan hoods shield humans from exposure to that distorted alien horror so it doesn't cause as much alarm.

But this Muti was far from the norm.

Its glaring purple features were expressionless, the thin mouth half open, as if about to speak.

Its bald head was adorned with detailed colorful symbols that wound down around the sockets where he eyes should have been. Hanging about its neck was a generous supply of ring upon ring of sparkling threaded jewels. The cloak had delicately embroidered flowers and fantasy trees woven together into an array of gaudy richness, totally unnatural for a Muti.

"Come forward. Closer, so I can read you. Adt Dorta and Sarleni enter. Now!"

CHAPTER TWENTY-ONE

THE KAMINA

Most people seldom looked directly at Mutis.

I glared back, holding down my feelings, although its face shone of pure, cold power. I wanted to challenge, not meekly submit. I had never avoided staring right into their faces, no matter how revolted I felt.

Those purple sinkholes glared blankly right into my eyes, grim but without real emotion. The membrane that covered whatever served as visual organs allowed no hint as to what might be going on in the Muti's mind.

The slit mouth tightened to a thin drawn line below flat nostrils. The bony face had that ageless look of something ancient or rotting, even though this Muti appeared to be quite young.

Beyond the outlandish makeup, elaborate gown and jewelry, it was hardly much different from any I had seen before. Muti's characteristically have features resembling twisted parchment crumpled aimlessly together.

Normally a Muti will touch your forehead to mentally communicate with you. This one made no such move. That puzzled me.

But I knew it was silently attempting to read our minds. I could even feel invisible probes trying to enter my mental space.

I blacked out all thoughts.

I imagined there was a solid wall between us. I visualized my skull as a metal plate through which its mind could not penetrate. I imagined that as a reality.

Sarleni detected its confusion: *This one can't read you. You've mastered a shielding...I can sense its surprise and concern. We've blocked its probes.*

I tried to relax in that comforting thought.

Those eyeless sockets revealed no emotions; with Mutis you received nothing but a stone face that could not be read. With humans, the eyes reflect so much.

"Your minds are a fog, but I know you, Adt Dorta!" This was not a question. It was declaring my identity, nothing more. "And Sarleni, we have never met, but you are highly spoken of in many circles as a gifted student. I welcome both of you and hope you have not been too alarmed. It was necessary to speak to you…this is the only place where it may be safe. None can know of this meeting. I come in secret. I need not identify myself. We may meet in the future; I sense this possibility. But a fog surrounds the two of you. We must await events. And we prepare for all alternatives. What happens next will depend on your own abilities and actions. Once you reach the mainland things will be dangerous unless you act carefully. I will help you get there…that's all. All links are separate, isolated from one another. Safety derives through ignorance. We are not given more information than we need to know. We must not let the Masters of Kamina get any hint as to what is actually happening. If they capture one of us they will learn only one tiny part of the whole design. That's all they'll get. The Messenger you have been brought to meet is waiting. To find him *go to the mountain and enter the castle*. Once on Kamina you will understand that instruction. For the moment, he has remained undetected. Serious attempts were made to kill him. Receive his message and take it to your Proctor."

I just stood there, listening, but not sure exactly how to react.

"All I can do, beyond making sure you get there, is to warn you: Beware."

That one word was far more startling than anything else it could have said. Was this some kind of code, or standard warning? It was the same message Ju-bilee had given. Perhaps this whole scene was another one of her fantasy events?

No, Sarleni assured me. *Like I said, she can't get in here. This is real. And the warning is just good council.*

The Muti continued: "I can advise only this: You face a challenge that involves a future of undetermined variables."

As it glared at me I felt its mental fingers surrounding my skull and then contracting, as if attempting to squeeze through soft tissue, hard bone and into my very mind. I remained hostile to any invasion, letting the emotion well up inside me in a raw wave of fury. Instantly it withdrew.

"Yes. You are strong. I see why Moyi was so impressed. To survive you'll need all of that strength. Stop resisting the final Nexus. Only in the core will you find your totality. Even it might not be enough in conflict. Revolution looms in all future linkage. Climax is but a beginning. Too much is at stake to play by rules. Winning is but a step forward. Beware of Skurals."

He waved his right hand and without warning a Muti came out of the surrounding shadows and placed a tray before us, upon which were two pink goblets. It hung in mid-air, floating slightly. Then the server disappeared.

"Drink to the success of your mission!" The Muti leaned forward from the throne, appearing to grow even larger. "Drink deep to your future. For everything depends on your success. Now drink!"

It was a command. And like two children before parental authority we each took one goblet and downed the pink liquid.

As I placed mine back on the tray, it shimmered, and then faded. The room swayed; darkened. I was aware of Sarleni's fingers slipping away, and then I realized that she had continued to cling tight to my hand until that moment.

Blackness throbbed. I was surrounded by a deep void without end. I saw images, but they were formless, faceless. I heard voices that were without words or even real meaning. Then it all became nothing.

* * * * * * *

And just as suddenly, the darkness itself stopped existing. Light popped back into focus. But the room had disappeared. I wasn't where I expected to be.

First I was aware of a slight rocking sensation, then the stunning fact that I was in the boat that had brought us to the island.

For a dazed moment I found myself sitting up, on the deck. Sarleni was sitting up within reach. All around us the ocean stretched to the empty horizon.

Had I been dreaming? That fit reality better than accepting such events as having actually taken place.

Then I heard Sarleni say: "We're okay. Ju-bilee's here, too. We are approaching Kamina. The drink was drugged. They brought us to the boat."

She pointed in the direction the craft was heading. "Out there, towards the horizon. I woke before you. Ju-bilee prodded me awake."

Behind her appeared an almost transparent Ju-bilee. She looked sternly at me, as her image seemed to solidify. "You have been drifting for a day. And I have been preparing for the immediate events. I can't stay. But I'll return. Moyi has been lost in a trance for a very long time, deep into a special meditation, in an attempt to glean more information about events soon to take place. But he has discovered nothing but that same black that Sarleni said the Muti told you about. Variables are shielded. Central Kamina is a filtered region. We only know what we've always known: It is the same as it has been for many years. The future, which is our now, has focused on the two of you. But we have never been able to see beyond that with much clarity."

"What are you talking about?" I demanded, feeling the frustration ball up hard inside me.

"Calm, Adt. Keep your anger for the proper targets. You are standing at a fork with many branches in all directions. The focus, the power generates the path down which our Noomas will flow—or at least the one that you will experience. And into which all of us will be drawn."

I started to object, but she waved that aside: "The universe is designed of many dimensional elements, like endless rooms containing an infinity of alternative variables. We make endless decisions and those decisions pick which rooms we may or may not enter and down which paths we may or may not go. Sometimes our choices close the network behind us; sometimes it is merely a matter of picking one of many very real alternatives that co-exist on different dimensional angles. Don't even try to understand. No human mind has learned enough to come even close to that wisdom. Those like you and I see further than some. Accept that much.

"I knew your father before you were born. His mastery of the sword has honed your skills to such a refined level that this, mixed with your genetic gifts, will serve you well in events about to take place.

"There are things I haven't been able to reveal...and can't. Only Moyi will grant permission...only from him can you obtain the necessary key to revelations. Only after you have reached a full Nexus with Sarleni will it be possible to disclose any more.

"If you succeed, the Orb will find you. And your return home will be swift.

"I must go."

She just vanished.

I looked at Sarleni in a dazed shock.

She nodded. "Yes, I heard it all. And it means no more to me than it does to you."

At that point the two of us merely sat there on the deck looking out across the horizon towards which the vessel was rapidly moving. Almost immediately we saw a dim peak lifting up over the water line. Slowly the whole horizon was an uneven dark shadow that continued to rise higher as we raced towards it.

What would we find there on this looming land? I wondered, as our destination became obvious. This was the continent of Kamina.

After all the time in training, preparation, the prolonged period of discovering so much about one another, we were about to enter into a different phase. Neither of us spoke, but moved in a unified fashion. We arranged the two spears, one bow and five arrows between us to add to her small knife and my sword. These were our basic physical killing tools added to any Zygo powers or Nexus linkage. She took possession of the bow and arrows and one spear. Thus we were armed against unknown forces that would be gathered to defeat our mission.

We were ready.

Our destination, at first, was only a peak in front of us, standing above the landmass. Then as we approached, we saw a huge structure that stood on a hill overlooking the coastline of sand and cliffs stretching out from horizon to horizon.

It was immense and breathtaking. Only vague rumors had ever come to our people about this side of the world. It was more like fairy tales told to children to terrify them into being good. Whispered nightmares related in taverns where liquid bloated the mind to invent terrifying tales. These were spellbinding fictions sung by aged crooners to wide-eyed children. No person of sane mind believed such stories.

Yet here we were!

This is what the Muti had spoken of, where he had sent us. I now remembered, with blunt understanding, the directions it had given: *The Messenger you have been brought to meet is waiting. To find him go to the mountain and enter the castle. Once on Kamina you will understand that instruction.*

And soon we would be entering a place that might swallow us up in one huge gulp and spit our bodies across the land in bits and pieces with no sign to indicate that we had ever existed.

"There," she told me as we left the craft and walked up onto the beach. "Up there is where we're expected to meet the Messenger." A visible shiver raced down her frame. *Something vile radiates from that place.* "Can you feel it?"

The stone fortress lifted up into the sky above the cliff, overlooking the ocean like some kind of monstrous sentinel. Huge hollows in the rocky cliff appeared like eyes revealing nothing but black openings into the harsh side of the building. The stones were shadowed dark, even under the bright daylight. But I felt the sun baking down on my back and a sense of relief at being on solid land once more, even if alien, even if dangerous.

Sarleni sensed my concerns: "The Muti's instructions were solid. This is where he sent us. When I look up there I feel a chill. Dark evil looms over this place. I can read nothing beyond those stark walls."

At this moment, on the shore of the Kamina continent, standing there on the lovely, lonely beach, Sarleni seemed to be only a gentle woman surrendering her fears, seeking protection from somebody she trusted.

Suddenly a flash of light blinded me. I felt more than saw an overwhelming vice-like power brace tightly around us.

"Take her, go back. She will be your completeness in a universe beautiful beyond all of those standing now before you!"

Sarleni leaned closer for a moment and I pulled her into the shelter of my protective arms. She felt frail and desperately hungry for safe haven.

"She is yours to take. Make a simple decision. Look into her eyes and see the longing there—forget lofty plans that lead to exhaustive and futile death. Save her from the influence of those that would use both of you for their own evil designs. We will grant you the real Ultimate Nexus framed in the flames of passion so complete that it will fuse your very souls in a universal embrace."

Sarleni clutched me. I felt her hands grip my arms, her fingers clawing, nails cutting deep into the muscles. The look in her eyes was wild with passion, surging lust now so deeply overwhelming that I was almost sucked into their depths in an unbelievable need to become one with her.

Then I saw another image and that was the cave in which we'd seen those rotting bones and the warnings from the distant past focused in my mind as a cruel reminder of what we were truly facing.

Fight it! Save us! Real terror flooded from Sarleni as I felt a hard shadow tear at my mind like terrified ripping claws.

Some invisible force attempted to drive me into places I had never dared to explore, into past memories, into spaces ceiled away. My whole life flashed forward and back, scattering memories rushing by too fast to jar them into any recognizable form. I was deep within a texture of my centering core and it was numbing.

That alien voice screamed at me: *Take her in your arms. This is what she wants, pleads for. Let your hands discover the soft silk of her flesh, let your lips cover the flowing, supple texture of her...*

I suddenly fought the raging fury of real desire throbbing through me. I attempted to blur those vivid images being bolted into my mind. My heart raced feverishly, sweat pouring from my brow as I strained against this crushing power.

She is yours to enjoy. Look at her. Feel her. Listen to her pleading. This is a woman who has been yours from the very beginning. All you need to do is leave and find your island of ecstasy.

Sarleni was clinging to me with such intense need that I found myself flowing downwards into a kind of swirling wild pit, unable to resist the longing desire in her eyes. This was a totally different Sarleni than I'd ever known; a passionate female, a desperately desiring woman of soft, yielding flesh, burning to surrender to her lover, her chosen man.

Take me away from this hideous place, Adt. I want none of this horror...let's leave...be together...I only want to be with you, to surrender in love, in passion as a woman with her man. It is what I've wanted from the beginning. We were designed for one another, and this path before us will deny our ultimate surrender to love's embrace. Please go back, leave...accept their wisdom before it is too late.

I wanted to fulfill her every wish, her every desire, to wrap my arms about her lovely form and melt into her body as a lover might, as our minds had come so close to blending together. These were words that I had secretly longed to hear from the moment I saw her. I wanted her in my arms; I needed to be captured within the warmth of her embrace for all eternity.

And she leaned into me, her eyes were now wildly passionate as they feed into my own hungers, her lips were almost touching mine. I could feel the warm breath of her against my flesh like a raging fire.

For a moment I surrendered, then instantly fought back.

This was not the Sarleni I knew. This was not the dedicated, fanatic true believer in a cause so important that she was willing to toss her life into a danger zone destined to crush our lives away, defeated in a final climatic battle. This was not the woman who had strung a bow and fitted an arrow in place in order to kill any thing that might be a threat. This was not the Sarleni who was mentally mated to me in the strange power of Zygo!

There was a shift in the emotional tone that slashed so deep into my mind.

"She is your haven, you are her protector. Escape into one another's arms and discover the loving ecstasy of union so complete that you will never need to seek another. She is more than a mere slavegirl, for she is fashioned to be your mate and mother of your flock. Bear your children in a safe place for future generations. Step through that open dimension behind you and avoid the destructive universe ahead if you continue on in this doomed mission."

I was struck with the fact that our lives faced an invisible fork into the future. We could now turn away and escape this ordeal; spend a lifetime somewhere on Noomas, safe, as lovers. And who would really know?

Leave, before you die! Came the bold warning like hot fire into my mind. *Go back. Claim your rightful retreat where all is love and peace. Take the path to ecstasy in the arms of the woman you love. No one will know. You will only remember meeting and falling in love and seeking union together in your special paradise...this is your birthright. This is your place in the universe! Choose life; not death!*

The sensible logic of that thought tempted me, coming from nowhere, so powerfully blossoming within my mind.

The chanting voice continued with a frighteningly hypnotic beat, reaching deep into my imagination. I couldn't resist its seductive music. And the message distorted all reality that I had ever known.

Yes, you have been deceived. You are foolishly following a path to personal doom. There is nothing here but death. You cannot escape it unless you now turn back. Go with Sarleni to the craft that brought you. Turn to the South. There you will find peace, and can experience ultimate happiness. Your True Nexus is there. For here lie only mad illusions and instant death.

My thoughts tried to resist. The words were driving hope of dreams fulfilled, of a reality that could be ours simply by reaching out, grabbing hold of this one and only promise of survival, life, love, utopia.

Take this road to personal happiness and have a world in which there are no nightmarish horrors, no Kamina to tempt you away from your natural human destiny with your lovely Sarleni.

I had longed to hold her, to know her as a true lover, and only resisted such seductive temptations for fear of being rejected. And now I knew she could be mine; was mine; this I believed, knew, without any doubt.

The choice is yours....

Do not delude yourself...the alternative is death.

CHAPTER TWENTY-TWO

CASTLE OF DOOM

At that moment truth eluded me. Reality was without actual form. Everything drifted distantly and dreamlike. I knew that the next step would take us into a future existence, closing all other choices forever non-realized.

Somewhere in that maze Ju-bilee's smooth flowing vibrations touch me: *The illusion is contained within the empty promise of those words. They tempt you away from the truth. They fear your power. Close down your mind!*

Instantly my vision cleared. The illusion vanished. Sarleni revived her own strength, pulling away from me. Then she stiffened, stepping completely free of my encircling arm, said:

"I felt that, too. Something terrible is up there. But we can't let it win. We must survive. There we will find final Nexus with our real future. I feel it."

"How do you know all that?" I wondered, as we started towards the distant hill and the castle. I felt right from the instant I saw it looming up there on the edge of the cliffs that I'd seen it before. Just a vague memory lingering from that dream in the caves of Kasiisi. I'd seen a vision of this place. How could that be? That wasn't even logical. It had to be illusion.

Sarleni offered: "Maybe a very real projection from the future."

"What are you talking about?"

"The Mutis aren't the only ones who can perceive the future. I have a limited ability as well. Who knows what Ju-bilee sees and knows of events yet to come. And you have mental abilities that have not even been tapped...yet. Don't underestimate your gifts. What we saw in those caves was real."

I merely ignored that, finding it difficult to believe, and not wanting to deal with it under these conditions. We had to remain firmly focused on the task at hand. The powerful suggestions we'd just experienced were still looming somewhere out there. I could not afford to play around with vague futuristic conjectures right now. Our very existence depended on sharp rational thinking without flaw. We were facing a very real danger and nothing but solid reality would serve the purpose of surviving whatever might be up there waiting for us. I could not let myself believe something that was, perhaps, mere illusional invention.

"I know things...Adt. Don't discount what I just said."

"I deal with reality. That's our only chance of survival."

"You know, too, Adt. Your mind is too cynical to believe. You still don't trust this blending."

"I don't know what I trust," I spat out. "That cave illusion...was just that!"

"No, Adt, it wasn't."

I shook my head, defiantly: "And whatever that thing was...just now...pulling me into...what? That dark temptation...."

"Some of its words were frighteningly true." She shifted, now standing firmly in place, not touching me. "I know things only because I am fully open."

I wanted to argue; I even wanted to feel the fury that had burst into me when I first met Sarleni, a bossy woman masquerading as a slavegirl. Her invention had been designed to confound anybody who happened to see her and it had worked on me. Despite its good cover and a safe illusion, I had not wanted to trust her candor right now. The slavegirl guise was a solid block into her true self: an impenetrable one. And I knew, now, that it was a mask that few could see beyond.

That charade simply proved that we are all far more complicated than first impressions or visual images might imply.

Sarleni stated: *We must generate Total Nexus.* "Be ready for... the unexpected. We may need more than your sword!"

I resisted comment.

She turned away and we continued on down the soft sandy beach in silence.

The breeze was both warm and cool, as if there were two beastie gods blowing at us. I wanted to look at Sarleni; I wanted to reach out to her, to once again connect.

She faced me, nervously smiled.

"We'll survive, Adt," she said. "We must and will connect in our totality...it must happen!" *At the moment of ultimate stress all resistance must melt or we fail.*

A shiver rushed through me. I experienced a powerful urge to protect her from any possible harm.

Save your energy, focus on what's ahead. That's all the protection we need.

Her thought jolted me.

My mind refocused and I was startled to discover we had left the beach and now were walking through a thickly matted forest of vine dripping trees. The ground under us was still soft, but more solidly packed than the sand.

We were following a path that curved along the side of the hill and then rose above the forest, overlooking the ocean. It was a breathtaking view instantly capturing us. The horizon was like a knife cutting across a clear sky.

"Isn't it beautiful?" she marveled stopping to take it all in. Her lovely face half-turned toward me. "Our world is there, beyond the curve of the world. Our homelands."

Here we were, on a strange hostile continent. We just stood there for a few moments taking it all in, deeply impressed at being in a place never visited by our people. It was impossible to avoid the thought that we may never see the lands of our birth again.

A moment later, she turned and started along the dirt pathway that circled upwards like a curling snake. At the top was a large arched stone entrance with a dark opening inviting nobody to enter. The huge structure beyond was ancient stone piled upon stone, lifting towards the sky. This was a fortress, marked with deep jagged scars of age. There was no doubt about this being a part of some long lost civilization, much like the ruins we had seen on the island of Kasiisi. And much like the vision I'd experienced in the caves. This was our destination, where we had been brought to fulfill an unnamed mission.

Be prepared when facing the unexpected, and there is a slim chance of survival, was my father law of combat and life.

Sarleni was listening to my thought and answered: "He was right. It is the only road we have left. Our minds are the final key that will discover victory—if that's even possible!"

We approached the huge entrance looming in front of us. It was a monstrous dark wall of wooden planks latched together with huge metal bands. It seemed to surge backwards as if eagerly withdrawing in horror from our touch. And without hesitation we stepped into the mouth of this ancient stronghold. Directly before us was a wide stairway of evenly placed stones that lifted up into the very guts of this forebodingly silent place.

All was darkly ominous as we made our way up the ruggedly smoothed stone steps. Odd corridors and passageways opened now and then into larger spaces, other corridors. We had no guide. Only our joint intent to meet whatever we were meant to find somewhere within these walls. And so we continued upward.

Everything seemed empty and uncannily silent. Little light seeped into these darkened spaces. One could imagine all sorts of foul predators lurking there in hungry wait for some innocent prey to ambush. One gulp and we would be food for monsters.

But, all was quiet. Only the soft moaning of air breathing through some hidden crevice offered a chilled breeze from the outside world.

"Up," she kept saying to me.

But now a very real sense of danger seemed to ooze down the steps towards us, a silent thing that had range and power and was invisibly searching for anything that might be invading its territory. It had no solidity, no shape. This *thing* was forming undetectable patterns. It was shifting, seething through the stones and through our pores like a poisonous vapor.

A mind, a consciousness, was up there, just waiting.

And if I knew this, Sarleni surely knew more.

Without warning something very real and pulsing entered the universe in which we were now encased. The air itself seemed to buckle around us like a living force of malevolent rage. Hot waves of invisible hate bore through my skin, penetrating the deeper layers of flesh and muscle like acid bubbling raw tissue. Something tried to merge into my very cells and atoms.

Powerful tendrils tangled around our minds coiling ever tighter, attempting to yank us into a swirling pit, dragging at our inner roots, choking at the very core of our awareness.

It fanned out like a wall physically restraining us.

A shrill ringing pierced my ears; a blinding darkness voided my mind and blotted vision. I was disoriented; thrown off balance.

I felt myself closing down as Sarleni's connection blurred, splintered, and then flashed hot around me. I squeezed tight around that slim connection, clinging in desperation.

The alien resistance faded. The entity slithered away, withdrawing like some invisible phantom slinking back into its own vile domain.

We had both stopped moving up that staircase.

"What was that?" I stared intensely into the dark gloom above us, still feeling that savage presence which had invaded my mind.

The illusion of being carefully watched hovered over us. Whatever it was dared us to continue.

We had not stopped our forward movement for more than a space between breaths.

Sarleni was noticeably shivering: *It is up there regrouping a nasty trap. Careful.*

Above us, the stairs leveled off to the right.

Ju-bilee abruptly hung in the air above the steps. She glared at us and her message shot fiercely into our minds.

Foolish children! You aren't strong enough to confront this monster! I'll deal with it. Adt, into the room directly above.... Skurals is there! And the Messenger...!

I was forcefully propelled upwards, not sure it was under my own direction.

Ju-bilee commanded: *Sarleni, come with me!*

Invisible hands lifted Sarleni away.

I started to object.

Ju-bilee began to fade. *You kill Skurals!*

Then she was gone. And so was Sarleni.

Just like that.

My mind was seeing through Sarleni's eyes as she projected images into the visual cortex of my brain. I was aware of her and a shadowy Ju-bilee who sent sharp instructions: *Let me focus through you. Be my lens and aim my energy. Fuse into me. Let me absorb you! Our lives...depend on it!*

I was joined to the two of them. But it was different from any other bond. I could only observe, not interact.

Then my own world swirled back into existence as I reached the top step, facing a corridor with open doors on either side. I was propelled to the nearest one on my right.

There was really no time to consider anything other than entering the huge cavernous room. Bleak walls were lit only from the sun filtering through long narrow windows. At the far end were two men.

I instantly recognized Skurals, who stood over a very small, old man, crumpled on the floor at his feet.

His attention shot towards me as he turned. The time for our duel had arrived.

Skurals stood there, sword in hand. Every muscle was ready; every part of him connected to the slender, gleaming weapon as if nerves ran from fingertips to the very needlepoint of the blade.

The man's icy voice echoed off the stones that made up the walls of this huge chamber.

"Well, we meet again, at last!"

I focused a mind probe around his skull and then dug deeper beyond skin and bone to reach his mental core. But I fell into a dark abyss and discovered a complete void. There was nothing inside,

228

nothing there to read. Not even a block. It was as if penetrating through empty space.

A grim smile formed on Skurals' lips, and he seemed to be mocking, laughing.

It was then that I realized he hadn't been aware of my search. Strange. The whole thing was impossible.

The two of us were now circling one another like two calculating killer beasts.

There was no prologue.

His blade leaped like a sliver of lightning, straight at my heart. Nothing else moved in his eyes or body. It was all one action of the whole creature called Skurals.

I reacted. His blade slid to one side, missing its intended target, passing in the air, almost touching my arm.

He barely nodded. It was a reluctant salute to an equal.

Now I took a very guarded stance, sword blade before me, ready to parry all possible assaults.

That one clash of blades said it all.

No joy here. Kill business.

In that split instant time seemed to compress, and I was again seeing through Sarleni's eyes.

* * * * * *

She was in a huge room, the walls set in blocks of stone. A massive desk stood on the far side of the chamber and sitting behind it in a large cushioned chair was a huge cloaked figured. I could not, at first, see its face, only the hooded shape, shadowed in darkness. This was an exceptionally large Muti and like the one we'd met on the island it was draped in a picturesque cloak. It looked up at Ju-bilee, glaring. Metal rings gleamed on its clawed fingers and bracelets flashed gold, green and even deep red, as it lifted its arms in greetings. Or threat.

The Muti's hood suddenly fell away and the wrinkled, angular purple face was starkly revealed. Its features were circled in curling, bright yellowish lines that underscored the dim glow from its deep dark eye-sockets. It slowly rose, a mammoth figure, standing at least twice my size.

The creature dwarfed Ju-bilee's image. Although she was somewhere on the other side of the planet her physical presence here was quite tiny as it stood between Sarleni and the gigantic Muti.

Size, though, meant nothing. It was the power of their minds *that mattered. Nothing more.*

I could actually feel the electrifying heat radiating from her mind.

The Muti stood there like a regal Korda, arms outstretched. The snarl on its thin, purpled lips breathed contempt and devastating aggression. I had never before seen this kind of emotion on a Muti's face. Some would show anger or annoyance at a human failing, but never this total degree of hatred and inner ferocity.

Sarleni blindly reached out for me, as if standing within reach. And at that moment I actually felt her hand finding my arm. Fingers glided down until our hands gripped one another. It was as if she were attempting to absorb strength from that desperate contact. I felt her abrupt fear of impending disaster. It was illusion; but quite real.

We were separated in space and yet touching.

The silence was deep, penetrating, like a thunderous explosion that possessed everything within its reach. Pulsating power flowed outwards from this cloaked creature with such force that I could even feel it race through Ju-bilee and then Sarleni.

The Muti slowly billowed larger, and the desk itself suddenly shattered in one powerful invisible sweep of dust.

This was the guardian Muti we were expected to annihilate. Ju-bilee had been right. We weren't ready to deal with this kind of out-right resistance, this massive mountain of mental strength. This was beyond anything we could have imagined.

The image faded....

* * * * * * *

Both Skurals and myself were like two statues, waiting to en-gage.

Suddenly he leaped and the grinding clash of blades resounded against the walls of the room. Metal on metal, snapped and slid, whip-like.

Fencing is like a wild, savage dance without music and Skurals' moves were amazingly fast. I'd never come across anything nearly as powerful. It was unexpected. I could feel the spectacular power all the way up my own arm. The experience was stunning, even frightening. I stepped back in order to keep space between the point of his sword and my flesh.

He lunged forward with a magnificent series of thrusts. My mind shifted, as if watching some screened images from another place and time.

230

Everything seemed to freeze in the room. Time seemed to narrow to a standstill. Sarleni's mind frantically slid into my own, presenting alarming images of her own struggle to survive.

* * * * * * *

Ju-bilee was standing in front of Sarleni. The huge Muti's form was like some gigantic mountain arched dangerously forward.

Raging fire sprang out from her fingers like lancing spears and crackled across the room in an instant flash of red energy. The Muti simply blocked them with a wave of his arm, allowing it all to fall away onto the floor in a splattering of dead sparks.

A hiss exploded from its throat as a beam of thick white fog leaped across the room at Ju-bilee. It was like a flood of lightning, encasing her within its cracking grip.

She merely swirled, arms raising, and in that instant bodily lifted away from the gripping hands reaching out behind her like raking claws.

In that instant she flew forward, across the room, hands locked together, arms extended. Her whole body stretched into a narrow lancing arrow aimed directly at the Muti's chest. It all happened so fast that it seemed she would not only hit, but literally penetrate the distorted shape of this monstrous figure.

The creature screamed another roar of raging fog, and when connected to her it turned deep red. But Ju-bilee's forward momentum was not stopped. She continued on, and suddenly her outstretched hands slammed into the Muti's stomach, literally passing through the cloak and outer flesh.

The Muti screamed and buckled, falling backwards as Ju-bilee was smashed to the far wall by the rebounding energy of its counter scream.

It was almost impossible to follow the details. A sudden gathering implosion burst into being and the image shattered away.

* * * * * * *

I was wrenched back to full awareness of the duel as I felt a cruel sting cut into my flesh. It was like fire. A bloody red line sliced across my left arm, above the elbow. I totally shut down on Sarleni.

Life depended on no distractions. That first drawing of blood was enough warning. Our blades were flashing wildly in complex patterns.

I could feel the sweat being squeezed from my own body, the thrilling surge of muscle and flesh reasoning out each move and counter move.

Then suddenly my own blade found his chest, ever so slightly, cutting across it, just breaking into the skin.

His blade didn't hesitate, ignoring any possible pain to what was a bloodless wound.

Then he thrust, bodily leaping across the space between us as I parried. My blade instantly glided around his. The point whipped into his side. The counter attack was designed to shatter through flesh in a splash of red. But no blood was exposed. Instead a rigid line of metal gleamed where flesh was ripped off in a slicing cut.

That stunning revelation announced one hard fact:

Skurals was not a normal man.

My mind instantly shifted, pieced together the obvious. What ever Skurals might be, he was something beyond the norm. Maybe part human, but also part machine.

I was instantly reminded of those flying monsters that had picked us up from the beach and brought us to the Haknord slaver ship now so long ago. Those creatures had been called Gatherers; Sarleni had destroyed them.

Skurals was, apparently, a more advanced model, a skilled, sophisticated human machine!

CHAPTER TWENTY-THREE

THE MESSENGER

It can be dangerous enough to face a master swordsman, but discovering one is engaged in a battle of wits and skill with a creature that was somehow altered from pure human flesh is unnerving.

An instantaneous pause exposed a technical flaw in Skurals' character. He was also totally unaware the non-human parts of his body.

Those cold hard eyes never move from me as his left hand explored the wound. Fingers discovered red blood on the slit where skin had been ripped away. His human part was slower in reacting to this discovery.

Whatever he was, whatever combination of animal and machine, to me he remained human; and the fury in his eyes asserted this fact. I believe he was as shocked as I was at what he'd discovered.

The slim smile formed on his lips.

We froze for only a momentary heartbeat. Then he moved. Blades touched. Rapid assaults followed parry after parry so swift that all my energies were focused on avoiding a death thrust. His style was unequaled to anything I had ever faced. His sword had terrific speed, like some kind of multi-bladed machine spinning so fast in front of me that its movement was only a blur.

Then the pain slashed at me. Unexpectedly. I don't know what caused the error, the blind mistake, be it accident or flaw; but the hard sting was undeniable.

It is said that a fatally wounded man may not even know he has been hurt. Recognition and pain may come slowly to a dying mind

I didn't die, nor even falter. But it was a serious warning. A second deep scratch for sure. Enough to say I had escaped death.

Double annoying to me was that this killing machine didn't seem at all impressed by this slight gain. Nor could I be sure of its humanity. Was this some kind of non-human alien mixture, or merely an extension of human flesh? Whatever Skurals was merely pressed on as if nothing had happened.

We continued to exchange brutally skilled attacks, barely parrying death aside.

Every nerve was keyed to the ultimate limits, all awareness centered on nothing less than finding that one moment, that instant opening, the flawed pulse between beats, the flutter where it was possible to slip beyond the engines of defensive metal.

There is a strange, subtle, almost imagined resistance when even the sharpest of blades enters territory other than empty air. No change in speed or movement, just a shift.

I felt my blade cut flesh.

Then all at once the dance stopped. Mutually, I believe. Instinctively, we paused, admiring one another in a strangely mannered way.

I remained silent, waiting, watching, listening. He was breathing hard, like me. And thus, quite human, again. I noted that there were several cuts on his arms and body, some of which revealed substantial bloodletting, flesh torn open exposing normal human muscle.

A number of cuts were imposed on my body, as well. We had done minor but nasty damage to one another.

"Again?" he tested me, just a bit overly confident.

He had revealed another flaw: an anxious tension on his part. My edge.

I lunged, determined to take advantage of what I hoped would end the duel right then. And I dropped into the hole skillfully designed by his devious mind.

My blade was allowed to approach his exposed chest, but a jarring rip hit my hip. Luck, more than anything else, helped dull the crippling pain. I felt a blunted stab that drew blood but more dully than might have been expected.

I'd slipped into his deliberate trap. He had exposed a target that was easily protected. Luckily, my over-confidence caused me to leap in too close. Thus I missed the full impact of his blade. My forward movement threw me beyond his attack. My body shifted, turned, once again facing him.

Both of us circled.

My blade had drawn blood, but by his design, not mine.

It was a mistake I had to avoid.

I was now keenly focused on the ringing sound of our blades clashing out their own musical ecstasy against one another. There was no room for further mistakes; the next one could be the fatal moment of death for one of us.

It all depended on who wore out first.

He baited me again in his measurably cocky way: "You but play. Come. Can you do no better?"

Each line was calculated; carefully placed between attack and counter attack, instant pauses.

"What are you? Human or automaton?" I snapped back, as my blade sliced lightly across his chest.

"More human than you'd imagine." He countered. "And more man than you will ever be!"

I said nothing.

We continued circling, touching, cutting, testing; wearing at one another's strength.

We were both slowing down.

"Come now. Kill me if you can!" he mocked. "Or is that possible...for I am more than human! And you are mere flesh."

He laughed in contempt as my blade cut another quick line across his gut.

"Is that your best?" he sneered. "You toy with me like a child. You can do nothing. I've never been defeated. And never will be!"

It was then that I realized I'd won, and he was desperate to cause me to flaw my defense, or miss an opening accidentally made by him.

The duel was draining both of us; human muscle, mind, and nerves can extend just so far without waning in strength. We were both feeling the effects of our mutual death challenge.

Silence says much. Conversation reveals more. He was aware of my skills and his own flagging limits, regardless of any mechanical skills. And now he hoped to create a finite moment when I'd be baited to careless superiority. Appealing to my ego. He was probing for even the slightest doubt in my character where I might question my own ability. The least fault could be fatal for either of us and he knew it. This was his last chance at life.

I noted it all. I watched. I listened to the prolonged sound of our swords converging in timeless patterns that grew swifter and more complex, steady and determined. This was our last, finalizing attempt to escape death.

I saw it, once, and then again. An opening. I ignored it at first, letting it pass. A pattern was flowing, again and again, and it wasn't a feint nor a tease or simply a clever trap.

I waited in order to avoid any mishap through over-confidence. I simply let my whole body shift into a relaxed totally alert system of action and reaction, while at the same time taking in the final details that would lead to a kill.

Skurals also took on a more relaxed stance, conserving energy to avoid instant death.

He didn't go into a spasm of mad attacks; his moves were now outwardly steady, unusually calm for one about to die. He methodically continued to masterfully defend and counter attack. I admired his noble bravery for what it was.

But he was beaten. We both knew this as absolute fact.

And with one swift thrust I ended it, slipping my blade through one pause, one counter-beat. The point simply went in like a whip, snapping at the center of his heart, withdrawing as he slumped face down to the ground.

I took no pride in my victory over his lifeless body. Only a mild sadness stirred within me, recognizing that death had been the only possible choice, right from the beginning. A singular living universe had been ended. And all that he was and could have been were lost forever. Man or machine.

Almost instantly I heard a familiar gasp and turned to see Sarleni behind me. Beyond her I could see the Muti crumbled up against the far side of the chamber. The scene behind her shifted, contorted and clarified. She was actually walking down the hallway through which she and Ju-bilee had previously disappeared.

"Are you okay?" I cried, and rushed to where she stood.

I almost reached out to embrace her, then held back, watching a sullen recognition glaze over her eyes: "I see you've killed Skurals."

"Where's Ju-bilee?"

"I don't know. She vanished. I lost connection. I'm frightened. I think that monster damaged her. They both seemed to have demolished one another."

She glanced over my shoulder at the Messenger lying on the floor.

I nodded to her: *He's wounded, badly.*

Yes. I know. But most of the damage is internal, was her response. *He's dying.*

The old fellow lay there, gasping, hand was holding his side where a deep wound ripped terribly into the flesh. For some reason it wasn't bleeding much, at least not outwardly.

The man's eyes moved back and forth, taking both of us in as he weakly announced: "I must speak."

"Don't...." I started to object.

"I must...to tell...before it is too late. I'm called Talni, and a member of the only movement dedicated to the overthrow of the

236

Muti overlords of Kamina. A lot has been invested in getting me here to meet you. They have watched and followed and…almost won. As you can see…I'm dead. That killer blade did damage that will not heal. They beat me brutally. But they didn't get what I came to give you. Here. In my arm. I have only moments. Just listen. Then act on my words!"

He placed a finger against his wrist, right next to a small scar. "I've recorded much…list to it. This image of me will respond to you…but we don't have much time. Listen…just listen…."

His fingers tapped the scar and a sudden glow surged from it, spreading rapidly throughout his body, bursting forth into a pulsing image of him that was almost transparent. I could see through it to the actual slumped form of his dying body on the floor. This image seemed strong and alert, now standing there, the eyes bright and intense. His voice was firm and low.

The story that this shimmering Talni told was alarming and hard to believe.

He looked at us, eyes deathly serious. "Chances are that I am now dead. This message was designed for Adt and Sarleni.

"The Muti Empire of Kamina is expanding its control and soon will reach out across the oceans. It has taken over most of this continent. They have absorbed all the human societies under their tyranny. They have enslaved all. And their appalling cruelties are beyond anything we've ever seen. We don't know what triggered this change. A vast number of Mutis are not yet converted; but they have no power against the Cult of the Kamina."

I wanted to object. Muti domination? It was alien to their nature. In fact, it wasn't necessary. We all followed their guidance without questioning. Yet the Muti that Ju-bilee and Sarleni had just faced in battle was hard support to this man's claim.

"As you know, no Muti can be mortally wounded by any weaponry designed purely by human hands…you must listen. Pay close attention.

"Do as I say without question…or Noomas will be doomed."

We had been taught the historical facts of many nations and knew the dangers of ultimate rule. Those in power would hold supremacy over a majority who groveled unquestioningly to irrational dogma. They would, if necessary, make idle promises of fame, fortune, even eternal life. They beguiled neighboring leaders into aligning with their schemes who would then bend to their seductive concepts. Such disciples gave new converts small information packets to mentally digest. This method appealed especially to the less intelligent, and even to some of the very wise and insightful; and certainly to all the power hungry. They were often sucked in, one convincing argument at a time, never told the full truth, or conclusive concepts. It was like reading an endless series of rules, each one blindly leading to the next.

This form of propaganda and proselytizing among territorial leaders was long ago banned. For many generations now, the Mutis have remained peacefully sovereign sages throughout Noomas, using their benevolent power to protect our many nation states from destroying one another's worship centers or power structures. Their wisdom and gentle vigilance has safeguarded our regions from such infringements for many generations. Religious and political freedoms have long since been a vital part of our birth right.

Beneath the shimmering animation I saw the slumped form of the messenger's broken body take a deep breath as his replication continued to speak in a firm, strong voice. Yet it was obvious that the man was weakening.

"Call them what you will...these organizations control the masses. The Mutis of the Kamina rule with a clenched fist. They have banded together into a powerful force, unlike a Muti cluster. They have expanded among themselves into immense gatherings of power centers. The peoples are helpless before them, bowing down in terrified homage to the Kamina. But it goes beyond any religious concepts. And further than class rule. Not even racial.

"We're not only talking about human submission, but complex Mutis! For they willingly embrace false promises wrapped in a dazzling array of convoluted rationalizations, apparent laws and idealistic belief-systems. These ideas are mixed with mythological memories all gathered together into a rainbow of blinding arguments. Their minds are unable to sort any of this out into different colors to inspect one by one. Such dazzle becomes the White-Light that blinds all reason, all doubt and leaves total submission!"

As we listened and thought about the overwhelming impact of what he had said, the man's body behind the shimmering image lay there, now breathing more shallowly. The projected recording flickered, and faded. The man's eyes looked tired and drained, but then lit up with renewed energy. The replica shimmered once again becoming opaque as it continued to speak.

"Step by step they accept further rationalizations and false conclusions. And in the commitment to each of these ideas they are skillfully prepared to accept the next one. Now they are so vested into the dogma, structure and mind-bending concepts that they cannot retreat if they wanted to.

"Somebody told me that if you can't boil it down to one line it isn't worth listening to or believing." A thin smile formed on his lips.

"Perhaps that is a bit callous, but certainly a subtle suggestion to keep in mind. The more complex a belief-system is to understand in principle the more dangerous it may be in its totality. In fact, the complexities hide the actual lie, the false conclusions, clouded over by convoluted rationalizations designed to discolor reality. They sweep you in bit by bit until you are consumed and are mindlessly devouring whole all that is fed into your now restructured psyche. They slice out bits and pieces at each step until you are an empty shell into which they pour their perverted sense of reality. And it is the green lock and key they use, one by one persuading others to submit and join their vile dominance."

"They have been converted to a new concept. They have been seduced into a belief system that coldly states they must not only lead and protect, but also control. No. More than control. They have reduced humans to raw energy that must be violently reformed, re-shaped into unspeakable subservience. They believe they are supe-rior, and humans are just part of the animal kingdom on Noomas. Nothing more. This fanatic element has taken over like a viral sick-ness spreading into their Muti minds and thinking. It is something so powerful that those who oppose are simply crushed away, either to submission or death...yes, Muti against Muti. They are not only dangerous to the human society, but also even to themselves. Zeal-ous conscripts become perverted monsters without any real ground-ing beyond the need for survival.

"And there are those in our underground movement just as fa-natically dedicated to survival at all cost. Yes, we *are* organ-ized...but very real dangers lay ready to explode into our lives. Dedicated members would willingly give up their own lives in a desperate attempt to dismantle the Muti dominance. Some radicals speak about all kinds of powerful counter-measures, even suicide missions to wipe out everything around them in one moment of glo-rious death and destruction. Taking the innocent as well as the hate-ful overlords. These obsessed crusaders point out, reasonably enough, that we're all doomed in any case. They are frightened and desperate to save what is left of our world at any cost.

"There are the religious elements, too, which promise all kinds of after-life rewards for all concerned in such mass killings.

"It is getting dangerous and we don't know how to oppose their arguments, for the alternative is dismal. We cannot tolerate being crushed into endless slavery. But we have not found any way to stop the on rushing events threatening to consume all in its mass, blind destruction. And it is ever expanding. Reasoned thinking suggests we should all take up arms and fight—no-holds-barred. This is an irrational debate. Humans on Kamina have no equal power to match the Muti forces and all our wisdom leads to the same fatal conclusions that take all to the grave: guilty as well as innocent. We've been warned by a very wise man that such a move would never bring peace and never win any kind of conflict, but merely devour all concerned in an endless, continual battle through generation after generation, to no end."

Without warning the image snapped out of existence and the real man, crumpled on the floor just lay there looking up at us.

He seemed even older than before. The lines in his face deepened then grew tight and pale. "I don't have much life left. You must believe me. You must go and tell the people of your nations the threat that is building on this side of Noomas. You must gather the Mutis there and warn them before it is too late. You must...take this!" The man extended his arm, "cut it open after I've died. There, at this scar, cut deep, remove the chip you'll find deeply hidden. It contains far more than what you have just heard in the introductory statement I made before leaving on this journey to you. Take the chip to your scientists, they'll know what—"

He broke off, startled. His eyes widened and it was obvious that he was looking beyond us.

We could feel what he apparently saw.

Another presence reached into our universe. Something vile flooded the room with so much rage and hatred that I could feel instant terror rush in at us like squeezing fingers. For a moment the air itself turned red, then blue, then a violent dark shadow flowed over us in an almost overwhelming force.

Sarleni and I turned as one being. Instantly our minds reached out towards one another in a desperate attempt to interlink.

There stood the Muti that we'd thought Ju-bilee had killed in her final explosive combat. It loomed there in the very entrance to this room. A huge mountain of death.

I felt an invisible open hand ram into my body. What kept it from crushing my every bone could only have been the shield we were creating through our binding mental connection. Yet I was propelled like a Kay-shell and slammed against the far wall.

It took what seemed forever to recover, but couldn't have been more than an instant.

Move, the command thundered into my head. I wanted to ask which way, but found myself automatically shifting left as something hard force splattered at the wall where I'd just been.

My hand gripped the sword. And without thought I was surging towards the Muti that was now leaning against the doorframe, using it for support. Its mangled body was arched; the outer shell was a mass of crippled bone and flesh where it had been brutally wounded by Ju-bilee's attack. It was obviously in a bad state. Fortunately for us. We could not survive the full powered assault of an uninjured Muti. Even in its present state it could not be subdued on my strength alone.

Sarleni was already bonding deep within me.

I opened all my resources within that shattered moment in time. All I could think of was absorbing Sarleni into myself, into the very center of my being, surrounding her, becoming a part of her, blending so fully that nothing could reach that deep without killing me, too. A flashing light blasted through my consciousness, then narrowed down, focusing to a white-hot whirling point.

We shot forward like arrows at the Muti as it ballooned up to gigantic size in front of us.

My sword extended, the point weaving fast patterns. The Muti's eye sockets riveted on the pointed tip, gleaming like a flashing bright star spinning in the dim light. Fire burned its purple hallows bright red, echoing the colors radiating from my sword.

All at once I was upon the creature.

It is difficult to know what happened next. I mean the sequence. My attack was thwarted time and again by a tremendous forceful counter surge of fiery heat. I was aware of a rising temperature of the hilt under my fingers. But then I thrust, a full-body lunge, driving the blade directly towards the right eye of the Muti. I felt flesh give, but just at that moment the sword was deflected by something invisible, bending it and drawing the point across the mere surface creature's eye membrane.

A blood-curdling scream deafened the room. Such rage, force. Such utter contempt and hatred. I could not only hear it, but also feel the waves vibrate through every cell of our now combined bodies. And it was two bodies in one, for Sarleni was truly encased within me, alive, as I was absorbed by her. We were a focused furious volcano pummeling through our mutually bound thoughts. We were in a total unity of one being embracing two personalities.

I thrust, but the sword was violently bent, and this time flung to one side. Again I felt that invisible hand slam into me, a backward move that shot my body right against the wall to my left. For a moment I was dazed, unable to focus. Darkness shattered my awareness with violent shards of malicious evil choking my mind down into a blind pit of total submission.

CHAPTER TWENTY-FOUR

THE NEXUS

Focus!

The word came at us out of a distant pall that now continued choking us. The force of that killing power was determined to exterminate all that we were, had been and could be.

Focus!

The word thundered through with crushing suffocation, engulfing our entire universe, sucking us deeper into its devastating hold.

Focus!

I recognized Moyi.

Deep.

Then Sarleni welled up stronger, permeating my inner consciousness, dragging me weakly upwards.

Focus!

Every nerve constricted into a finite point, fixing itself into one focal certainty.

My vision instantly gathered together scattered bits of light, bringing them back into jagged shape, blurred but slowly forcing them to take form.

Then our universe all snapped back into place.

I was looking at the Muti, standing some distance from me. Or so it seemed. Distance had no meaning. A world away or just right there within arm's reach would make no difference.

Until now the Muti had regarded us as separate human beings. Now it knew the truth.

I felt the intense hate surge up from the arching body of this horrid creature looming in and around us like an uncontrolled firestorm.

I needed every cell of power Sarleni had within her.

Spears! I demanded.

I switched the sword to my left hand and grabbed the spear. We both flung the weapons in unison. They sped precisely on target, one for each eyeless socket.

But the Muti whipped them to one side with a sweep of its arm. Then its horrid face contracted, inflating to a full seething wrath of violent loathing.

"Dare you!" it screamed, bearing down on us with claws spiraling out like twisted snake-like fangs. Those hands were groping menacingly, fingers pointing and parting, weaving like spiked tentacles on a crazed sea serpent. This was more than a physical attack, radiating way beyond the material and into the scope of incredulous dimensions. There were no walls against this kind of threat. No mental blockage possible.

Defend!

An internal voice commanded. It took a moment to recognized Moyi.

Expand, defend, or you die! Swordsman, fight!

I felt Sarleni move. She had strung the bow with an arrow and released it, aimed directly at the Muti's face. The shaft reached its target, but merely bounced off the hard-shelled layer of bony tissue near its right cheek.

My fingers clenched, my arm lifted, my whole body bulleted forward on automatic, slicing a sharp pattern parallel with those attacking tendril-like finger tips, suddenly so large that any one of them would have gored us apart.

Another arrow flew at the monstrous face. This one shot past its snarling lips, penetrating beyond the jagged teeth, lodging into its throat.

A bitter screech answered that attack. Nothing more.

My sword slashed the first finger. Light exploded into a bright yellow, then red, fiery starburst of flames.

This time, though, the Muti parried but not soon enough. I nicked the spiked nail right off, and its hand, arm and body shriveled to its previous size.

Sarleni's bow had propelled an arrow directly into its dark eye-socket, the point and shaft successfully penetrating deep.

A mortifying scream of pain tore through the room.

There was no time to consider options. I leaped forward.

What are you doing? Sarleni demanded, surprised.

Shut up. Quiet! I was talking to both of us for we had to be unified into one super Nexus. Mental energy billowed around my whole awareness. I knew her inside me and knew myself inside her. It was confusing, being bonded, more organized and all expansive. Our internal exchange had unified into a single channel. One mind and one thought. Yet separate. We were both one and two separate entities who existed in the same life bubble.

It had never happened like this before.

The Muti sent a powerfully charged wave. My body felt the impact and I experienced Sarleni's stunned reaction.

"Slaves. Humans! Creatures!" the thoughts hammered at me.

"Flow with me!"

The emotional change was so unexpected that I found myself non-resistant. I felt overwhelmed. Yielding. Releasing all thought, all sense of self into the arms of that mental voice.

Scorching flames blazed over my skin, licking flesh in churning waves of pain. My fingers went numb and the sword slipped away, and then fell with a loud clatter to the ground.

"Flow with me!"

The Muti continued to say, slowly stepping back towards a dark endless tunnel now forming behind its bulk. A wounded, crippled frame of the mighty Muti was now collecting itself together into something utterly different. This gulping chiasmic mouth greedily wanted to close around us. Its form began pulsing and opening wide. Bigger and bigger until it enveloped all things that had ever existed in my personal universe.

"Flow with me."

The words drummed over and over in my ears as darkness swelled, then swirled to blinding yellows and twisted twirling reds.

"Flow with me!"

And they began to close in around my mind so powerfully that I could actually visualize the words as claw-like, bloodied, and bony, gnarled appendages. They were the tunnels; the fingers were the flues, the shafts to the infinite. These were the channels into a void beyond description, devouring everything down into the black hole of its throat. And I was like some kind of energy ball onto which this monstrous thing was closing tighter and tighter.

"Glow with me. Become me!"

I had thought a final Nexus with Sarleni was complete, but now realized it was not enough. We had hardly penetrated the perimeter of our inner cores. We were intensely close. Bonded fully with joined energy. But without total penetration we would fail to escape the venomous snare of the Muti.

Yet we could not break through at this level. The insistent strain of the Muti's toxic trap pressed hard against an inner barrier that hung between her and me, so transparent, so lithe, and resilient that we had not previously been aware of it.

I now had to submit completely through this final block with

244

Sarleni.

We would die without the final unity.

The Nexus was still on the other side. And I must yield to it. Yet no one had ever been there before. How did I know it would happen? And if I lowered my shields, would not the Muti also absorb my yielding? Which bond would survive? How would I know?

I was trapped. I had only my own convictions. I had to believe that my yielding would join us invincibly. I had to embrace Sarleni's truth. And it had to be without resistance: one leap of faith into an unknown place. I became aware of Sarleni's own fears slipping into my own uncertainty. We were each reaching into this middle place, probing with millions of fragmented thoughts.

The Muti tightened its grip, persistently kneading hard into our hesitant union, wedging its venomous power right through my awareness and into Sarleni's.

A joining fire blasted out, engulfing all that was our total existence. This was surely the Nexus! I felt her surrounding me ever closer, even to my inner consciousness. I could literally experience her thoughts being formed. I had reached a depth inside Sarleni that interlocked all our conscious thoughts and immediate awareness.

Had we truly accomplished a final act of surrender soon enough? Before this evil killer could swallow us down its Muti hatch? Black once more smothered us into an isolating void of endless space.

The impenetrable energy that had been throbbing outwards now suddenly imploded.

Flow with me....

Then came an added: *Surrender!*

I thought that was part of the Muti's seductive command, then recognized Sarleni's strong essence in that word:

Surrender! she repeated.

We were still two separately sheathed energies. I could feel Sarleni struggle to reach into me. She was touching my inner core, seeking to become an ultimate part of it. I told myself to surrender, open, to widen a welcoming doorway into my inner self. I needed to expose my inner core that the gods of Noomas called the vital soul or central being of our existence. I choked on that concept. But now I must forego such petty resistance. Unity was survival.

Dark and light; color and nothingness marbled together, then burst into explosions of blinding images, all flipping past our mutual awareness. Now it was two as one. We were both aware of the same flood merging like two vast oceans raging into one another.

We were a tangled white massive cosmos of churning, embracing elements. We clung to one another. We were falling deeper, into an unrelenting seductive metamorphosis of limitless love. I dared no resistance despite what was happening. This was a vortex over which we had no control. We would either birth a total Nexus or succumbed to the Muti and die.

And I held fast to Sarleni. We absorbed one another into our personal centers.

A new dimensional universe was suddenly released. It was neither explosion nor implosion, but purely a burst of raw energy. This was a fundamental shift from one elemental truth to a new dimensional awareness of each other. I now knew all there was to know or could ever know about her and about me and about our place in the universe.

We had opened a book of infinite mutual knowledge, embraced intimately close, yet not read. Our histories were accessible, but not accessed. Our inner selves were naked. It was that simple

Fear nothing, for you are one and the same. Resist nothing, for you are totality itself.

Moyi's wizened counsel remained steady, penetrating our consciousness.

Merge beyond your minds, into your minds, through your minds.

Then another pulsing white lyrical sonnet descended and fused within us.

Love, oh, love, take us as one...as we are meant to be.

The two of us blended into an expanding infinity. Overlaid with a caustic shift, a harsh demand.

Kill kill!

A single beam of energy, braided together without any space between the atoms of our thoughts. Her mandate was now mine in this unified single entity.

Kill kill!

Another rigid force overwhelmed us. The Muti's mind whipped itself around ours like metal netting, linking tightly through our conscious existence. We felt its power squeeze in on our newly formed unity.

I felt unabashed resilience bursting us in a full spectrum of colors beyond the chaos, as two lovers embracing in the final moments of ecstasy. Or death. It was impossible to tell. For our union was too new, and the powerful force of the Muti's assault so overwhelming, crushing at us, that it felt we would soon implode into a finite point, then cease to exist.

Expand, embrace, conquer.

We were one. We thought as one. We reacted as one being and suddenly our bonded energies expanded around the Muti, absorbing it. Its intense hate, its raging mad need to survive amplified against our combined will.

That's when we began shutting down the channels to that Muti chasm, squeezing tight like an ever condensing vice.

I imagined a brutally rigid sword, infinitely large, and infinitely sharp; light and heavy in my fingers. And I brought it down into the Muti's life force.

I thrust. Then thrust again as it clashed with futility against my unrelenting assault. The gleaming blade sank deep into a whirl of sputtering stars, cutting, ripping, and tearing them with savage force. It lasted but an infinite moment. Something wailed like a terrible whistle. The horrid dying scream became all there was until a sudden explosive flash imploded between our crushing mental fingers.

Silence.

We found ourselves retreating from the inner core connection that we'd created.

Nexus flickered, and then faded.

The room returned. We were standing over the crumbled mass of a hooded form, splotches of living matter splattered all around it on the stone floor.

No longer linked, we could now think and act as separate beings.

We crossed the room, passing the remains of Skurals. A peculiar peaceful look rested on his face. Almost as if relieved to be free from his ordeal.

The effects of what had happened could not be fathomed. For something dramatically vital had revealed itself. No time to explore; no time to think.

We turned our attention towards the Messenger, only to find his eyes staring blankly, his body limp on the floor. Death had captured him at last, during our battle with the Muti. I leaned over and closed his eyes to a world to which he no longer belonged. He was twisted awkwardly into a strange position, right hand rigidly grasping his upturned left wrist. I gently pried it open. The scar was unusually shaped as a wide pyramid. Sarleni handed me the knife, and I cut deep along the wide base of the triangle. It was a bloody act, but instantly exposed a tiny flat sliver of metal.

Now I knew that what he had told was true. We had experienced the awful Muti power. We had witnessed that ultimate consuming abyss of darkness. And the Messenger had warned us that these creatures were quickly spreading. There existed a Muti Empire designed to dominate Noomas under a cruel and savage absolute rule.

I silently faced Sarleni. She let me know that she'd sent a message to the Orb.

I connected; they are near! "It'll be here shortly."

I had endless questions concerning the Orb, wondering where it was, why it had not come to us previously. How it would find us. Where it would take us.

I glanced at the Messenger's body, where it lay in stillness.

"We should do something about him," I said solemnly.

"No, my dear Adt. We must leave no evidence of having survived. All of this will be simply...cleaned up."

I was puzzled. But I now knew enough to trust Sarleni's people and their purposes. We both stood, looking around the chamber, flooded with dusty sunlight streaming in from the side. A large ornate archway opened out onto a terrace. We had not noticed the beauty of this place before. Rich tapestries adorned the walls. Large casements held glittering goblets and place settings. Obviously this was meant to be a royal banquet hall for celebration and feasting. Somehow that all felt very sad and out of place after what we had just undergone. The fresh breeze from the sea below felt so new and innocent. We purged our lungs from the stale stench of our near death.

I was aware of the irony of having spilled blood for the sake of life. Death was the nature of life, removing the old to make room for the new.

We were standing there, as we had always done. The Nexus and all that it had revealed was background.

And I had so many questions toppling through my head, along with Sarleni's thoughts now quietly present in the background of my own mind.

How smooth it had felt to have her within my head, even now, though we were not connected, I felt a warm comfort of her lingering presence within me. I knew a part of me was lingering openly in her even as we stood, silent, motionless, peacefully renewing our inner strengths together.

And yet there were other matters clouding my thoughts; like discovering what had happened to Ju-bilee. She had taken a brutal beating by the Muti. Had she survived?

I am well!

From nowhere, Ju-bilee's thought burst into both our minds at once. It was weak, but gained strength as she continued.

There is much for you to know, Adt. Perhaps you can feel the

248

truth. Your birth was a major happening. Critical events were, even then, moving rapidly towards what is now soon to take place. The very future of Noomas is in your hands now that the Messenger has completed his mission.

All this was destined. We knew you were born for a very special purpose.

This event and those yet to come were sensed at your birth. The coming conflict will decide who rules this wonderful world of ours. The united powers of the Zygo will be strongly required, as will that of the Mutis of our lands. And most of all, we must combined the forces of all nations that we can gather together in a grand Armada against the Empire of Kamina.

Go to your friend, Torlo Hannis, for he is destined to lead the way. The future conflict is set; only the results are unknowable.

Understand that events have evolved into actions that have roots in the past. They will decide the uncertain future.

It is time for you to know that your mother has been aware of you from the very beginning, watching and making sure that her son was well cared for and prepared for his future position in our world.

I'm proud of you, of everything you have done, and my blessings to you and Sarleni's future. Forgive me son, for having denied you my presence in your life. I was torn and yet knew that your safety and education were far too vital for all of our futures.

What kept me away all these years involved things that you may only guess at this point.

Abruptly, without warning, her image vanished.

Neither of us spoke for a long moment.

"The Orb is already circling the castle," Sarleni said. "Ju-bilee is...."

Ju-bilee burst into both our minds once again.

"I will be with you soon to explain many things. Sarleni will take you to the Orb. The Message must be delivered without delay. You must hurry now."

She was gone.

The full implication of her statement sank in; but not understanding.

Sarleni took my hand in hers. "Ju-bilee told me much. Over time I can tell you more. You will learn all there is to know about her dedication to you, as we return together.

"But now we must meet the Orb."

A broad sweeping staircase looped down from the terrace to an open lawn of an inner courtyard. As we approached, an Orb, settled down before us, its outer wall melting into an entrance. It was very

249

much like the one that had carried us away from the storm so long ago, only much larger and more sophisticated.

Sarleni dropped my hand and ran up to a tunic-clad lad who was standing within the Orb waving happily.

"Mahzit!" She cried as she wrapped her arms around him, both leaping up and down shouting and squealing in a wild dance. They had the energy of a herd of wild Zionahs.

"Well." said Sarleni, brushing her hair back in a futile attempt to look dignified. "I suppose I should introduce the two of you. Adt, I would like you to meet my young brother, Mahzit." To which, Mahzit snapped a comical bow in my direction.

"Adt Dorta." his broad smile was as welcoming as the large warm hand he'd placed upon my shoulder. He invited us into the Orb, then swiftly disappeared.

Now we were alone once more and she was saying: "The Orb will take us to Bel-loniea and to the northern territories. Helandi. Home."

The Nexus had revealed much. I was decidedly changed within my core.

It had also sealed my love for Sarleni and hers for me. This much was undeniably certain. We had experienced a reality never before realized by human or Muti alike.

And the feel of her fingers clutching mine silently sealed our mutual need and desire.

We both knew the Muti Marriage Ceremony by heart; it was a part of both our cultures. And we now shared the vows contained in its ritual questions:

The two of you will answer each question. The honesty of your words will reveal themselves to me—if they be true, your marriage will be filled with years of happiness—if you lie, there will be no marriage.

Do you love the other?

Do you both desire a lifetime of fully sharing yourselves totally with the other?"

Will you both be devoted and loyal to one another for as long as you live?

You are now joined, bound by powers greater than any of those upon the world, greater than any force within the universe. I have seen your past and your present thoughts and have looked into the future and know the great binding power of the love, which possesses both of you. Go happily upon your life paths together and know that not my words bind you, but only the greatness of the love you share. Remember there is no law in the Universe which can hold two people together stronger than their own lasting desires and love for one another.

This sealed our union and without a word we embraced totally as our forms sculpted together to let our lips touch. Time seemed to stand at bay. It was an intense Nexus and lasted for an instant, and for eternity.

We never really knew when the Orb left the continent of Kamina and started on its return journey, for we were joyfully involved in a mutual discovery that was, of course, our final Nexus.

EPILOGUE

Those were Adt Dorta's final words. From then on Torlo Hannis spoke directly to us.

"Time has past since their return to Bel-loniea. Events that followed were complex and far reaching over many lands. First came the direct report to the Proctor and then many private meetings with comrades and myself before Adt and Sarleni went to Helandi, where they settled in the northern estates of her family.

This was his original birthplace that he now adopted as his home. Here neither royalty nor slavery held any special value; only earned status counted. Their studies of the Zygo continued as he began to create a relationship with his mother, Ju-bilee. Here he has begun organizing matters for the coming conflict.

"We have begun diplomatic moves to gather together a massive Armada from this side of the planet.

"The micro-sliver they had removed from the Messenger contained highly detailed with information. Andon and our scientists are still retrieving valuable data from its vast storage banks. It contains the alarming accounts concerning what is happening in the Kamina Empire.

"Desperate rebellion has created terrorist organizations determined to destroy the Muti Empire at all cost. We can only hope to stop this fanatical movement before they have begun a universal annihilation that will involve the entire planet in a self-destructive mode.

"This may be my last communication with you. We are now ready to launch a massive Armada against the Kamina Empire. Failure will end civilization as we know it on Noomas. If you do not hear from me again, you'll know that we have failed."

Thus, Torlo Hannis' remarks ended.

We can only guess at the adventures he must have had.

We all hope. We all wait. The long silence is terrifying.

* * * * * * *

[Editor's closing notes:]

Since finalizing the above communication from Torlo Hannis some time ago, and having prepared this book for publication, we recently received the following from him:

> The landscape of Noomas has dramatically altered. I believe you'll be interested in discovering what happened since our last communication.
>
> My friend, Adt, had truly served his mission well. His great service for our people sparked events that changed everything on Noomas.

That was all we heard for several months, then the communication opened again, then closed, then reopened. Torlo Hannis was involved in events that demanded most of his time. But finally we received bits and pieces of his story. They are currently being carefully compiled, documented and translated into a readable form to be released by the Borgo Press Imprint of Wildside Press.

Conquest of Noomas tells the rest of Torlo Hannis' story.

ABOUT THE AUTHORS

CHARLES NUETZEL was born in San Francisco in 1934, and writes:

"As long as I can remember I wanted to be a writer. It was a dream I never thought would materialize. But with the help of Forrest J Ackerman, who became my agent, I managed to finally make it into print.

"I was lucky enough not only in selling my work to publishers but also ending up packaging books for some of them, and finally becoming a 'publisher' much like those who had bought my first novels. From there it as a simple leap to editing not only a science-fiction anthology, but also a line of SF books for Powell Sci-Fi back in the 1960s. Throughout these active professional years I had the chance to design some covers and do graphic cover layouts for pocket books & magazines."

Much of his work in covers and graphics are a result of having had a father who was a professional commercial artist, and who did a number of covers for sci-fi magazines in the 1950s and later for pocket books—even for some of Mr. Nuetzel's books.

In retirement he has become involved in swing dancing, a long time lover of Big Band jazz. But more interestingly world travels have taken him (and his wife Brigitte) across the world, to Hawaii, Caribbean, Mexico, Kenya, Egypt, Peru, having a lifelong interest in ancient civilizations. His website is full of thousands of pictures taken during these trips.

"Discovering these wonderful places actually exist, and getting a chance to even touch those ancient stones and structures, climbing some of the Mesoamerican pyramids to their very top, has been a life-inspiring adventure! It is fantastic to realize that our modern world is built upon such fascinating places, like the 2,000-year-old Petra, which was simply amazing to see. Almost as stunning as the pyramids of Egypt! All of which, I keep telling myself, are the remains of colonies developed by the Haldolen Empire some 30,000 years ago (related in *Swordmen of Vistar*)."

HEIDI GARRETT lives in Maryland where she has spent most of her adult life. She has two grown sons and a grandson.

She writes: "I have been engaged in reenactment activities from pirate feasts to courtly concerts, making music and merriment at various local festivals."

Her interest in sci-fi and fantasy brought her to a catchy roll-playing website called *The Gathering*. Here, as Damsel, she met a strange character named Thoris and "we played scenarios with knights in less-than-shining armor, rambled among the parapets and socialized in the imaginary halls—imbibing ale at the hearth and sharing tall tales until—at last—the damsel discovered her prolific counter-sparring partner was, indeed, a pro writer."

To learn more about him, she started searching out some of his out-of-print books, after having read the *Epic Dialogs of Mhyo* which is now published by Wildside Press. Since then, over the years, they've become great friends, and even met once when she came out west, to California, for a couple of days, spending time with him and his wife Brigitte.

They had always talked about doing some writing together and when Wildside Press suggested that Charles do some original books for them, he said: "Only with Heidi!" She had been working with him via the internet—email—on helping proof the revisions of his books when being prepared for their new updated re-printed editions. The results of all this is the present book and its coming sequel *Conquest of Noomas*, which is at this very moment being worked on by this dedicated writing team.

The authors want to thank Fred Blonder for some special help in a number of areas, far and beyond that of taking the picture of the young lady, Val Litt, used on the cover. His keen scientific knowledge helped to sharpen up some details that would have otherwise been missed.

www.ingramcontent.com/pod-product-compliance
Lightning Source LLC
Chambersburg PA
CBHW032034240626
47154CB00003B/900